MW00931826

FOR THOSE WHO ARE AFRAID TO BLOOM.

To
Bleed a
Crystal
Bloom

GLOSSARY

Stony Stem — *Orlaith's tower.*

Bitten Bay — *The bay at the bottom of the cliff below Castle Noir.*

Safety Line — *The line Orlaith hasn't stepped over since she came to Castle Noir when she was a child. It surrounds the estate—running the forest boundary and cutting through the bay.*

The Tangle — *The unutilized labyrinth of corridors in the center of the castle that Orlaith uses to travel around in a more efficient manner. These corridors are typically without windows.*

Sprouts — *The greenhouse.*

Dark zones — *Places Orlaith has yet to explore.*

The Den — *Rhordyn's personal chambers.*

The Keep — *The big polished doors guarded by Jasken. One of Orlaith's dark zones.*

The Plank — *The tree that has fallen across the selkie pond and is often used for Orlaith's training.*

Spines — *The giant library.*

The Safe — *The small door where Orlaith places her offering every night.*

Whispers — *The dark, abandoned passageway Orlaith has turned into a mural.*

The Grave — *The storage room where Orlaith discovered Te Bruk o' Avalanste.*

Puddles — *The communal bathing chambers/thermal springs.*
Hell Hole — *The room where Baze often trains Orlaith.*
Caspun — *A rare bulb Orlaith relies on to calm her attacks brought on by her nightmares and sharp sounds.*
Exothryl/exo — *The contraband drug Orlaith takes in the morning to counteract the effects of overdosing on caspun every night to ensure a good sleep.*
Conclave — *A meeting that consists of all the Masters and Mistresses from across the continent.*
Tribunal — *The monthly gathering where citizens get to voice their woes with their High/Low Master.*
Fryst — *Northern Territory.*
Rouste — *Eastern Territory.*
Bahari — *Southern Territory.*
Ocruth — *Western Territory.*

PROLOGUE

RHORDYN

The full-bellied moon casts a silver sheen across Vateshram Forest, the shadows stark against their illuminated backdrop.

My horse gallops around the deeper pockets of black, weaving a path between ancient trees, breaths labored, ears pinned back. Every now and again, he tosses his head in defiance.

I steal a look behind, making sure I'm not being followed.

Seven years ago. That's the last time I dared to make this trip.

I held off for as long as I could.

Wind whistles through the trees, an icy, Northern-borne breeze that carries a sharp scent and makes my hands tighten around the reins. Everything from the North comes with a taint these days: the wind, the food pulled off trade ships that have traveled down the River Norse, even the water that spills off its mountain border and fills our streams.

Eyzar slows, then stops of his own accord, snorting and pawing the ground.

"Steady, boy," I soothe, running my hand along his thick, muscled neck.

A deathly hush blankets the forest, and I cast my gaze around, listening, watching ...

A gust of wind breaks the silence, wailing like an agonized beast, teasing an acrid stench past my nose.

My brow buckles, breath catching.

Death. *Burning* death—coming from the direction of the safe house.

Aravyn.

"*Ya!*" I growl, digging my heels in.

Eyzar squeals, then charges forward, and every galloping thud lands with a dire echo in my head.

Too late.

Too late.

Too late.

"*Faster!*"

The trees finally thin, revealing two jagged slopes framing the smoldering remains of a once-grand home.

Eyzar rears to a stop, turning on his haunches. It's all I can do to keep him from bolting back the way he came as I stare at the devastating scene while ash rains from the sky.

Not fast enough ...

A roaring inferno engulfs the house that's lost all its shape, now nothing but crumbled stone walls, piles of charred rocks, and flaming wooden beams scattered across the ground like matchsticks. Shaded creatures are collecting in pockets of shadow, maneuvering toward lumps of fried flesh strewn throughout the clearing.

Too many bodies for a fucking safe house.

Someone screwed up. For their sake, I hope they're already dead.

Rabid howls preface a strange, sickening sound not unlike

the squeal of metal on metal, and a low rumble scours the back of my throat.

I leap off Eyzar, speaking to him in hushed tones as I tie him to a tree that's lit by firelight. Approaching the ruin in slow strides, I grip the pommel poking over my shoulder, tugging my weapon free; a virulent black blade that blends with the gloom.

The advancing shadows rear back.

I step over a severed hand missing three fingers, the nub dribbling bold, red blood that shouldn't bring me a sense of relief ... but does.

It's not part of *her.*

Them.

I keep going, passing limb after limb, head after head—the bubbled, blistering skin distorting features, but failing to hide the upside down v's carved into some of their foreheads.

What are the fucking Shulák doing here?

The thought is discarded when my eye catches on a charred leg heaped against a boulder ...

Blood roars in my ears, and a wild, thrashing anger threatens to shred the carefully laid fibers of my constraints.

Not only is the torn flesh seeping an opalescent liquid I'm too familiar with, but the limb is small.

Too small.

I sit on my heels, close my eyes, bite down on my fist ...

Too fucking small.

That anger builds and builds and—

The ground trembles, followed by another strident screech, the commotion spawning from behind the collapsed and burning dwelling.

Murderous mutts.

They're still here. Still *feasting.*

Again, that keen, scraping sound dissects the air, followed by a feral howl that carves up the length of my spine like a blade.

My upper lip peels back, and I shove to my feet, cracking my neck from side to side. I set off in the direction of the noise, but a gurgling whimper has my gaze darting to a willow tree; to the figure slumped at its base, her long, pale hair pooled beneath her head ...

Aravyn.

I rush to her side, landing on my knees, sword discarded on the ground. Carefully, I roll her toward me, heart dropping when my hands connect with the warm wetness of her half-spilled entrails.

"Fuck."

She releases an agonized moan while I inspect the damage.

The edges of her wounds have already begun to gray and fester, emitting a rancid, throat-clogging stench ...

Too. Fucking. Late.

Her frail hand settles atop the clear, heavy jewel she's always worn around her neck. "T-take it," she begs, looking at me with eyes wide and luminous, like crystals caught in the sunlight. So different from the others staring blankly from the ground out there.

I swallow thickly, tuck her hair behind her thorny ear, and loosen the latch, catching the jewel. The silver chain falls into my palm, almost blending with the color of her treasured blood on my hands.

"For h-her," she whispers, folding my fingers over the gift.

Folding my fucking heart just as much.

Last time I came, her belly was round and full, and I don't

have it in me to tell her there's a small, severed leg lying in the dirt nearby.

A fatal injury.

That Col—her partner—is probably out there, too.

In pieces.

A wet hack spills more of her onto the soil, and her hand lands on the hilt of my blade. "*Please ...*"

"I have liquid bane in my saddle pac—"

"*No,*" she gasps. "W-with your sword. *Please.*"

I pause, feeling her request stack upon my shoulders like a brick.

Giving her a terse nod that carves me up on the inside, I pocket the necklace and take the weight of the weapon, lowering its tip to the left side of her chest.

I hold her stare, a million words trapped behind the clamp of my lips.

Words won't ease her pain or stop her flesh from rotting—won't restart the night and bring her family back—so I hold them in, letting them scour my insides and fuel that pit of venomous rage waiting to unleash.

"*Prom-m-mise.* S-save her, Rhordyn. *P-please.*"

She's already gone.

"I promise," I say, holding her gaze.

The lie does its job, relieving the tightness from around her eyes, but the cost is a phantom skewer through my chest.

I promised her a safe house, too ... and now her family's dead.

She offers a sad smile, and an iridescent tear paves a path through the filth and blistering flesh on her cheek. "D-do it."

"I'm sorry ..."

For everything.

She opens her mouth to speak, but I don't give her a

chance to feed me the lie I can see brewing in her eyes. I plant lethal pressure down the sword and draw a gasp from her split lips.

Wide, glassy eyes darken with the shadow of death, taking on a depthless serenity I can't look away from fast enough.

She would have dished me placating words—told me it's okay.

It's not okay.

I hang my head and pretend the stars aren't staring holes through my back.

But they are.

They always are. And they always fucking will.

Letting my rage bubble to the surface, I pull the sword free and push to a stand.

Smooth. Cold.

Detached.

Without a backward glance, I charge toward a billowy flame devouring the fallen remnants of the thatched roof, then round a mound of blackened bricks and pause in a slab of shadow ...

Vruks. Three of them—eyes black bulbs, bodies much larger than my stallion and heaped with bulging pockets of muscle that shift beneath slick, gray fur.

Neither canine nor feline, but somewhere trapped in the middle.

Huge.

Mighty.

Merciless.

A heinous fucking plague.

Their stubby snouts are splashed red, an arsenal of fangs dripping their plunder. They're prowling in a tight, snarling circle around a muddy dome—a perfect half-sphere dumped in the rubble.

I tilt my head to the side, nostrils flaring.

One of them rears up, long, lethal talons punching from his paws before he shifts his weight and slashes at the dome. Sparks burst and that shrill etching makes me want to gouge my ears.

More ferocious snarls and howls score the air. The largest of the three dips his head, stamps his nose to the surface of the peculiar object, and *roars.*

Chaotic, feral frustration ...

And well distracted targets.

I untether the remaining threads of my wrath and stalk forward on feet that barely seem to touch the ground, whipping my blade through the smoke. The first head slides off bulky shoulders, but I don't wait for the beast to fall. I've already dropped and spun—the second Vruk yowling as I drag my sword through his stomach, releasing a spill of innards that steam the icy air.

Quick, clean deaths.

If only they'd given Aravyn the same consideration.

I seize the alpha's attention, his savage gaze charging into me. The air between us stiffens, and I lift my chin slightly.

The mutt leaps forward, teeth bared and talons spread, a fetid roar staining the air. His head rolls before he has the chance to blink again; the thick, muscular neck yielding to the same metallic kiss that took his fated brethren.

He drops like a boulder, liquid death squirting in rhythm with his failing heart as I release a sharp breath ...

"Shit."

Killing has a taint, and I *reek* of it. Doubt I'll ever be able to wash off the stench. But this world is not merciful, and neither am I.

Not anymore.

Weapon swiped on my coat, I resheathe it down my spine and shift my attention to the dome now greased in a layer of steaming Vruk gore. I crouch to study the strange object, sweeping a hand through the mess, revealing a crystal-like veneer that seems to shimmer with its own light source.

But that's not what turns my lungs to stone.

Through the reflection of writhing flames and my pinched expression, I can see a child no older than two, clothed in mud and ash and scraps of burnt linen. Her eyes are squeezed shut, hands bracketing her ears as she rocks, face twisted in a silent scream.

I spot her ear poking out through that mess of filthy, soot-stained curls, my eyes widening at the streak of fine, incandescent thorns lining the shell ...

Aravyn had a second child.

The weight in my pocket grows heavy, forcing my knees to the dirt.

S-save her. P-please.

I drag my hand down my face.

Those words are just as hungry as my curiosity. This tiny *Aeshlian* ... she's fossilizing her light, using it as a defense mechanism.

An impossibility.

Is she a crossbreed? Did Aravyn seek warmth in someone else's bed?

I scour the clearing of wide-eyed corpses for any witnesses. Only the shadows watch, collecting along the tree line that circles the devastation like a noose.

Irilak. *Hundreds* of them. Some bigger than the Vruk I just slayed, others less than half that size.

The scent of spilled blood must have drawn them in. It's been a while since I've seen so many gather in one spot.

I scan each writhing lump of black. Though I can't see their faces, their combined attention bores into me, no doubt waiting for the flames to ease so they can dart forward and feast.

They can't have her.

I sit on my heels, prepared to wait forever for her to drop the impenetrable barrier. I may not know this child, but it took *years* for her mother to agree to move into this safe house, and now she's dead.

This child deserves better.

Her *mother* deserved better.

I swallow my guilt and wait.

Hours pass, and I avoid looking at the willow tree, hating that it's the only tombstone Aravyn will have. That her body will be a feast for the wreath of hungry shadows just as soon as they get the opportunity to pounce.

The sky is burnt from the rising sun by the time the child's face smooths out, and her lashes sweep up.

I go very, very still.

Her wide eyes are aglitter with thousands of facets, as if she's staring out from a sky full of stars that hatched in her soul.

Her chin wobbles.

Patches of that crystal dome begin to melt, dripping to the ground as the overwhelming scent of her anguish strikes the back of my throat like a blade.

She doesn't move—just continues to sit there, tucked in a ball, looking at me with destitute eyes.

Studying me.

The wind howls and her teeth chatter.

I grind my molars.

She's going to fucking freeze if I don't get her wrapped up soon, but I refuse to snatch her from the soil. I need her trust.

Her *permission.*

"I promise I won't hurt you," I say, keeping my bold voice low, fearful of scaring her back into that shell where I can't help her.

She blinks once ... twice ... then finally unravels, bits of mud and ash falling off her as she pushes to her feet and takes an unsteady step toward me, then buckles.

I catch her before she hits the ground, and even through layers of leather and wool, I can feel how cold and fragile she is.

I pull her close and stand. "I'll keep you safe. Everything's going to be okay."

Charging toward Eyzar, I sweep my cloak around her back to shield her from the wind and the sight of so much death; the motion clearing a patch of thick mud from her right shoulder.

My arm stills. Stride stills.

The blood in my fucking *veins* stills.

Strange markings tarnish her exposed skin, like vines crept across it and left an inky stamp ...

Something inside me blackens and curls as words canter through my thoughts—words that were chipped into stone by a vile, grisly hand years ago.

Words that settle in my stomach like a rock.

Light will bloom from sky and soil,
Skin tarnished by the brand of death ...

I almost touch the birthmark cresting the blade of her trembling shoulder, then snatch my hand back and curse.

I promised I wouldn't hurt her.

I lied.

None of this made sense before, and now it makes *too* much fucking sense.

No wonder Aravyn kept her hidden. No wonder the fucking Shulák were here. No wonder this necklace is so heavy in my pocket ...

But she was wrong to pull such a pledge from me. Her hope was blind, set on the shoulders of the wrong person.

The child tips her head and tries to speak, but all that comes out is a rasp.

Nausea spikes up my throat.

She saved herself from three ferocious Vruks who tore her life to shreds, only to crawl into the arms of a fiercer threat.

There will be no glory in this death. No shade of honor. Only the blood of a frightened child on my hands.

Smother her while she sleeps or catch the lethal grace.

She looks up at me, trying to speak through a throat that's been scraped raw.

"It's okay," I lie, cupping the back of her head and easing her close. Her cheek settles on my chest again; a comfort that can only be temporary.

Make it quick.

I press my fingertips between her ribs, feeling the beat of her galloping target. That noose of shadows thickens, like the Irilak are anticipating the warm meal to garnish their banquet.

Fuck.

My neck buckles, face dropping into her soot-stained hair. Floral spice whips up and snatches me, dragging my nose deeper until my mouth is pressed against a fresh wound sliced into her scalp.

Liquid warms my lips, and I jerk back, but carnal instinct has my tongue darting out ...

The taste of her blood is a bolt to my brain.

My heart.

My fucking *soul.*

My legs give way, and I fall to my knees, pulling sharp slices of air through a constricting throat. Every muscle in my body hardens, veins pushing to the surface, my very matter trying to take up more space in the world that suddenly seems too small. Too cruel.

Too fucking dangerous.

I tip my head, seeking the fading stars through twisted ropes of smoke, teeth bared as if I could leap up and chew the prickles of light until their luster no longer sits in the sky. "*You bastards ...*"

I snarl, grip tightening.

No.

Pushing to my feet, I make for my horse in long, determined strides. I climb atop the saddle, bundle the child in my lap, and kick the beast forward—scattering the noose of shadows and my dwindling self-respect in the same ugly motion.

"Go fuck yourselves," I mutter, severing my sight of the stars by charging beneath the ancient canopy of trees.

The child will not die tonight, but not for the right reasons ...

This act is purely *selfish.*

CHAPTER 1

ORLAITH

19 YEARS LATER

The needle's sharp tip turns red from the lick of the candle flame, blazing with a fiery heartbeat. I whip it away and shake it out.

Vicious little thing.

Waiting for it to cool, I sit cross-legged on my bed and flit my gaze around the room, sweeping over the curved, obsidian walls pierced with large, domed windows every few feet. Between them, paintings big and small decorate the stone, pressed on with a homemade glue.

The gentle bend is only kind to things that yield, and I refuse to wake every morning to sullen walls that have no color splashed across them. I see enough of *that* walking around the castle every day.

All my furniture has been made to fit the space—a curved dresser, my four-poster bed with a headboard that arcs, even my bath molds against the stone cylinder of the central stairwell. Against the outer wall, a narrow table sweeps around a quarter of the circumference, its surface littered with bunches of dried flowers, numerous mortar and pestles, little jars of bits and bobs ... and rocks. Lots of sable rocks in various shapes and sizes, many dressed or half-dressed in colorful brushstrokes.

Turning my back on a smooth rock is always a challenge. Nine times out of ten, they end up stashed in my bag, carted up my tower, and assaulted with a paintbrush.

The exterior of my central stairwell has a fireplace and a wooden door pressed into it—the only way in or out of my chamber, unless you count the dramatic drop over the edge of the balcony's balustrade.

A few years ago, I painted that door black, then spent nine months embellishing it with a littering of luminous stars that perfectly depict the night sky. There's even a moon half steeped in shadow.

Something I can look at when the clouds are dense and angry.

I press the needle's tip against the pad of my middle finger until I feel a painful pinch, and a bulb of bright red blood races to the surface of the tiny wound.

My lips curl.

It shouldn't give me so much satisfaction, watching myself bleed like this. But it does. Because this blood, this little act of self-harm, it's not for me.

It's for *him*.

Rhordyn.

I place the needle on a clay plate atop my bedside table, then dip my finger in the belly of a crystal goblet half-full of water.

The liquid blushes pink—the color of a healthy, mid-spring bloom.

I sigh, wondering if he'll like it. If he'll think it too pink or too red? He never complains, never says *anything* about it, and that's just the issue.

Not knowing.

Swirling the flush contents, I pad toward the exit and

drop to a kneel, now eye level with the smaller door cut into the thick, aged wood speckled with hand-painted stars.

The Safe.

That's the name Cook gave it when I was too small to do my offering on my own. It stuck with me.

I've measured my life by this wee door—by my need to first stretch onto tippy toes, then stand flat-footed, then bend at the hip to access it.

Pulling it open, I reveal an empty cavity not much larger than my crystal goblet. Its walls are rough and grooved, as though hacked into existence by an irate hand.

I set my offering on the base; a pretty parallel to its cell of unrefined wood.

As always, I envy the stupid goblet for the way it's about to be gripped and cradled and drunk from ... *presumably.*

It gets so close to everything I shouldn't want, and has therefore earned itself my unrequited hate.

I shut The Safe, drop onto my bum, and slide back across the floor, arms knotted around my knees while I study the two doors—so very different from each other.

One, I often choose to keep closed, using it as a barrier to block out the world whenever I feel the need to stow away. The smaller of the two, I wish I could keep open at this time of night so I could look Rhordyn in the eye while he takes my offering.

I tried it once ... a year ago. Sat here barely blinking until well after midnight. He only came once I slammed The Safe shut and severed the bridge.

That's when it dawned on me just how much trouble I'm in.

Heavy footsteps echo up my tower, mixing with the tune of my hammering heart.

I close my eyes and count his steps, picturing him scaling the spiral staircase that winds up the inside of my stairwell, getting all the way to one hundred and forty-eight before his footfalls finally slow; as they always do right before he crests upon the upper landing.

I imagine him standing by my door, digging through his pocket, fitting the key into the lock—his lips a hard line cut across his face. I imagine a flicker of pleasure igniting those galvanized eyes when he reveals the crystal goblet laden with my boastful offering.

It's a pretty lie I like to paint; a fabled reality where he needs me just as much as I need him. Something that helps tame this unwanted *feeling* sprouting in my chest.

The door closes with a hollow thud, and I dart forward, pressing my ear against the wood, listening to the rhythmic beat of his descent.

When I check The Safe in the morning, the goblet will be sitting there, empty of liquid but brimming with questions that slosh onto me every time I remove it.

Why does he need it? What does he use it for? Does he like this ... thing between us?

Because I do.

I look forward to it; deflate when the moment passes. Lose myself to fantasies about it far too often—ones where I watch him drink me from that crystal goblet, holding his stare the entire time.

Ones where it's not shuttered away as if we have something to be ashamed of.

I pluck my brush off the bed and make for the twin balcony doors beside my bedside table, stepping out into the brisk, twilight air before I begin the tedious task of combing a day's worth of knots from my long, tawny hair.

I like to pretend I come out here to watch the evening mature, even as I tilt onto tippy toes and peer over the balustrade, searching the grounds for any hint of movement —my brush merely a prop to keep my hands busy.

Though I'm tucked in a tower that sometimes nests amongst the clouds, I still choke on my heart when Rhordyn emerges from the grand castle doors, stalking in long, determined strides across the field toward the forest that fringes the estate.

He never looks up. Never seeks me out.

He simply walks the border, then disappears into the smudge of sage, moss, and seaweed green that stretches as far as the eye can see in every direction but south.

Always the same monotonous routine I can't tear away from.

The sun drops below the horizon, cauterizing its spill of light, and a blow of cold, briny air plays with the hem of my shirt, prickling my flesh and making my teeth chatter.

I part my hair into three long sections and work it into a braid. By the time I've plaited the entire length, any remaining light has bled off the land and my fingers are numb from the chill.

He hasn't returned.

My footfalls back inside always feel heavier.

Stifling a yawn, I reach my bedside table and rifle through the many corked bottles stashed on a tray. I lift one and tip it from side to side, frowning at the tide of thin, indigo liquid sloshing around ...

I swear there was more.

With a huff, I jam the thing back on the tray, blow out the candle, and crawl into bed.

My bottom lip cops a beating from the nervous chew of

my teeth, and I curse, tugging the dense quilt around my neck and turning toward the northern windows.

The sky is a velvet blanket littered with stars that wink at me for the first time in a week. Light is spilling off the moon, pouring through the windows, highlighting the many glass bottles kept within arm's reach.

Highlighting the fact that all but *one* are empty.

I bite down on a shiver—one not born of the early spring chill but of the storm lashing my insides with pulse-scattering bolts ...

For the first time in *months,* I'm sleeping sober.

Their eyes are wide and unblinking, mouths hanging open as if their bodies fell apart halfway through the breath still caught between their lips. They all lost bits of themselves, and the pieces that remain are too still.

Too silent.

Only the monsters are left.

I'm missing something. Something important. I can feel it in my chest; an emptiness that seems to weigh me down.

I squeeze my eyes shut—block out the burning, crumbling world, and try to fit the pieces together.

A shrill sound akin to nails dragging down a plate almost splits me apart. Again and again it sings its spiteful tune, fraying my insides.

I bloody my throat with a scream.

Wetness dribbles from my nose, and I bash my ears with balled fists that threaten to cave my skull.

The warring vista falls away, eroding on a brisk wind until I'm standing on a cliff, peering down into a gloomy chasm. There's a peaceful silence that's no less terrifying than the shrill sounds that tore at me, and liquid is no longer dripping from my nose ...

It's gushing.

I stumble away from the jagged edge—

Lugged upright like a floppy doll, a sharp breath slices through my throat as my eyes pop open, a metallic taste heavy on my tongue. Steady hands hook around my upper arms but do nothing to quell the tremors.

My clammy skin is the only thing stopping my bones from scattering all over the bed.

A disheveled flop of auburn hair half shutters the frantic perusal of familiar brown eyes glazed by a flickering candle flame. Baze's lips are moving in sync with the ball in his throat, yet I hear nothing over the roaring sound inside my skull.

I realize I'm clawing at his bare shoulders and pry my hands away, drag them down my face, and *scream.* That scream turns to a sob, then bleeds into a raspy plea while Baze's lips keep shaping words.

You're okay. You're okay. You're okay.

I'm not.

My brain is a ball of sizzling, molten lava that's going to explode.

I can't escape.

Bracketing my temples, I squeeze my eyes shut, blocking out the world, rocking back and forth ...

A sulfuric odor smacks the air, and my eyes pop open.

Caspun.

I lean forward, lips parted, seeking that cooling balm for my insides.

Baze frowns and grips my chin, tilting my head. A splash of liquid hits my tongue, and I swallow.

Gag.

No matter how many times I punish myself with this bottle-bile, the taste never seems to grow on me. Yet I still reach for it, night after night, like it's the only thing keeping me tethered to the world.

Numbness rushes down my throat, stemming the calamity in my head and easing my swollen brain. I moan, then open my mouth for more despite the fact that Baze no longer has my chin in a vice.

"Orlaith ..."

I snatch the vial, wetting my tongue with another healthy glug. It's hard to ignore Baze's icy tenor as I swallow the slur of blessed, quag-tasting crap with a wince.

He seizes the caspun, eyes slitted.

"What?" I croak, falling back to the bed. I roll sideways and curl into myself while I wait for the last of the pressure to abate.

"You know what," Baze gripes before dragging a sniff from the bottle's neck. His face screws up, and he makes a vexing sound that almost makes me smile. "What the *hell* have you mixed in here? It never used to smell like this."

I swipe damp hair from my face and tick off my fingers as I speak. "Gingerwelt, lispin, rileweed, and dogwarth—that's what makes it smell like sulfur."

His head kicks back, eyes widening. "Doesn't dogwarth grow on horse shit?"

Unfortunately.

"It helps ease the m-migraines," I say through chattering teeth, bunching my pillow so I can nuzzle into it just the way I like.

"Wish I hadn't asked," he mutters, pulling the thick quilt up around my shoulders. "I thought you were moving past the nightmares? You haven't had an episode like this in months."

I shake my head.

I've just learned to cram my body full of things that sedate me enough to mask the pain; mixing everything under the sun with caspun to enhance its effect, then drawing deep glugs of the bottle pre-sleep rather than the recommended sip when I wake already ruined.

Not that I'm going to tell *him* that.

Caspun's not intended to be used as a preventative, but daily hangover aside, it works.

Baze stoppers the bottle and stabs it back into its spot, hand still pinching the top. Heavy seconds pass filled with only the sound of my chattering teeth, my sweaty nightgown now a burden to my plummeting core temperature.

"Wanna talk about it?"

"Nope."

There's not a single part of me that wants to tell him my stores are almost depleted. Or that I'm queasy about the inevitable conversation with Rhordyn—one where I'll tell him I need more caspun imported, and he'll say he gave me a three-year supply four months ago, and then things will get awkward.

Baze clears his throat, rubbing sleep from his eyes. "Okay, well ... now that I know you're not *dying*, I should lea—"

My hand lashes out, snatching his arm, making his well-defined brow arch as he peers down at my unyielding grip.

"Stay," I plead, and his dumbfounded gaze lifts to my face.

"Laith ..."

"I'm not too proud to beg." I make my eyes go all big, playing on the fact that he probably still sees me as a child, not a woman who shouldn't need someone to scare away the monsters that circle when she sleeps. *"Please."*

He looks to the bed like it's going to swallow him alive.

Resolve seems to settle on his face, and with a heavy sigh, he strides toward the open-mouthed fireplace, black sleep pants hanging off his hips as he crouches before the hearth like a panther.

Baze is liquid when he moves, even when he's blowing life into dormant embers. He just looks so comfortable in his skin ...

I wish I knew how that felt.

The fire roars to life, and he stacks it with wood, then makes his way around the other side of the bed. Climbing in next to me, he stuffs a few pillows behind his back and leans against the headboard, pulling a silver flask from his pocket.

"What's in there?"

"Whiskey. Home brewed." He unscrews the lid. "Tastes like horse piss."

Can't be worse than the shit I just ingested.

"Can I t-try some?"

He lifts a brow, studies me for a long moment, then shoves the flask in my direction. "Only a sip, and only because it'll warm you up."

I peel up and take the offering. "So many caveats. You think I'm going to take a liking to it and start distilling my own?"

He gives me a look that suggests I'm not far off the mark.

I roll my eyes and take a glug, choking the moment I swallow.

"That's disgusting," I rasp as the cool liquid burns a trail all the way to my belly where it swirls around, adding weight to my already burdened lids. I hand it back and bunker down, drawing comfort from his awkward angles and stiff demeanor. "But effective."

He sighs and drapes an arm around me. "I'm going to get castrated for this."

"Don't be so dramatic," I slur, dragging myself full of his rich scent—blooming nightshade with a hint of woodsy undertones.

"I'm not being dramatic." He takes a large gulp, hissing from between clenched teeth when he swallows.

"Tanith won't tell."

He smirks, studying the dancing flames that are gently warming the room. "To be fair, I doubt your handmaid will have it in her to make it up those stairs in the morning. Not after the state I left her in."

I jerk upright and glare at him, taking in his naked torso, bed-swept hair, the lazy smile ...

He waggles his brows.

My face twists along with my guts.

"I *specifically* told you Tanith was off limits!" I stab him in the chest with my pointy finger. "She's young, and she wants things you can't give her."

"She's older than you, and I gave her plenty, thank you very much."

Walked right into that one.

"What would Halena think if she knew you were messing around with my handmaid?"

He lifts a shoulder. "She was there, too."

My mouth falls open, closes, opens again ...

He chuckles, making the dimple on his right cheek pucker, and I consider tossing him off the balcony.

"We tried this thing where we used a ca—"

I stamp my hand over his mouth. "*Just* ... stop talking," I grumble, flopping down and nuzzling in.

He tucks me closer, retrieving *Gypsy and the Night King* off my side table. "Your loss."

"That's open to interpretation."

I listen to him flick through a few pages. "Well, I was going to read you a bedtime story, but some of this content makes me wildly uncomfortable."

"It's *romance*. Of course it grates you the wrong way."

"If I had to choose what to do with my last breath, I'd spend it kissing you until I slipped away ..." He scoffs, flipping another page. "Hate to break it to you, but no man talks like that."

"He talks to *her* like that." I snatch the book, close the damn thing, and stuff it under my pillow. "She's the exception because she's his *mate*."

Baze makes a choking sound and draws another swig from his flask, this one much deeper than the last. "That book is toxic," he bites out through a wince. "You should use it to stoke the fire."

"Can't. Tanith lent it to me."

He curses low and swallows another glug while I stifle a smile, watching dark shapes twist on my walls—dodging the burnt light my blazing hearth is throwing at them.

Moments drag, pulled taut like the anxious band around my chest.

"Baze?"

"Hmm ..."

"Will you stay until morning?"

I hold my breath, waiting for him to answer, pushing down the image of wide, unseeing eyes. Trying to ignore the pull of that chasm—the silence that seemed to reach for me.

"Sure," he mumbles, leaning over me and blowing out the candle. "My balls aren't that important, anyway."

CHAPTER 2

ORLAITH

The morning comes hard and brutal, with phantom chisels chipping at my temples.

I groan, the sharp thud a painful reminder that caspun is far from the perfect antidote. Effective, yes ... but not without some truly heinous side effects that worsen with every amassed dose.

Peeling my eyes open, I reach out and pat the other side of the bed, finding it cold and empty.

Seems Baze values his balls more than he was letting on.

Blades of gold shaft through the southern window, and despite my abrasive mood, I kick off the blankets and slide out of bed.

The jarring movement rattles my tender brain, but I drag my feet toward the window and place myself in a column of light that douses me with a cloak of warmth. I roll my sleeves, offering more skin to the early morning sunshine that's so very rare these days.

Pushing the doors open, I step onto my balcony, gripping the balustrade and looking out across the ocean often heaving beneath a slate sky. Today, it's a blue haze reaching for a dazzling horizon.

I take in the glassy stretch of Bitten Bay, gilded in the

morning light. I've always imagined some giant creature leapt out of the sea and took a bite from the obsidian cliff, leaving the black, sandy scoop littered with sharp rocks.

The name felt fitting to a five-year-old me.

One end boasts a rarely used jetty, an empty sea-perch pointing west.

My attention drifts to the heavily forested North, and movement draws my eye to where unbridled trees meet the vast field of manicured grass.

Rhordyn emerges from the dense, ancient woods that howl at night and whisper in the day, and my heart stills, all the breath escaping my lungs.

He's not alone—if you call the stag draped across his broad shoulders a companion.

Its slit throat drips blood down Rhordyn's front as he stalks in long strides across the grassy halo ...

My grip on the banister tightens.

His chin tilts, gaze darting up, and I feel like I've just been shot with two icy arrows.

I gasp and pull back, severing the contact, hand pressed against my chest.

The distant thud of feet echoing up my stairwell has my head whipping around, attention snapping to the door.

"Shit."

I dash inside, groaning as the movement makes my tender brain bounce.

One hundred and forty steps ... *ish.* That's all I've got left to dress and gather the loose strands of my composure before Baze lures me downstairs for an ass whipping I'm currently in no shape to contend with.

After draining half my pitcher, I peel off my clothes and toss them in the direction of the laundry bin. I pull on some fresh undergarments and wrap my breasts using a stretchy length of material to flatten them with practiced dexterity.

Those steps draw closer, and my heart sits heavy in my throat.

I snatch a black button-down and leather pants—my favorite ones that are well worn and easy to move in. I'm just fiddling the buttons into place when Baze yells out, "Twenty step marker. You better be decent!"

I race toward my bed and drop low, roll the rug, then delve my nails into the grooves and lift the slab of stone, revealing my cache.

Twelve jars *filled* with bitter white nodes that look like harmless sweets to the untrained eye. But they're certainly not harmless, and right now, they're my *salvation.*

Placing one under my tongue, I replace the jar, slide the stone back into place, and unroll the rug.

The door swings open.

I jolt, smacking the back of my head on the underside of the bed frame. "Ouch."

"What the hell are you doing under there?" Baze bristles, his feet rounding the bed.

The Exothryl melts into a creamy liquid I swallow back, snatching an old paintbrush off the ground before wiggling out. By the time I'm free, my heart is squeezing blood through me in fierce, urgent beats.

I peer up at Baze, waving the brush at him. "Would you look at that! I wondered where this had gotten to."

He frowns, scanning the room, studying my jar full of brushes a touch too long before scanning *me*—mainly my messy hair.

"I'm surprised you're even awake," he says, eyes

narrowing as I clamber up and dust myself off. "I thought you'd be out all morning."

Ignoring his comment, I concentrate on unraveling the braid that falls to my hip, then sweep my hair into a ponytail, the silence stretching between us.

Unsaid words piling up.

He breaks first with a weighted sigh, thrusting my wooden sword at me. "Here. I had the nicks smoothed out so it's less likely to split. Obviously I've got nothing better to do than to run around after you all day."

"Ohh, you're handy," I say with a wink, trying not to bounce all over the place from my sudden surge of migraine-melting, artificially induced adrenaline. "And Rhordyn pays you to be my friend, so quit sulking."

Muttering something beneath his breath, he spins and stalks toward the door. I follow, snatching my knapsack off its hook, a small smile tipping my lips. At least until he slams to a stop.

Colliding with his back, I let out a dense *oomph*.

"Wha—" My gaze drops to the discarded undergarment at his feet.

Oops.

"From now on, you meet me in the training hall." He shudders, pushing forward again. "And no more sleepovers."

I take a step and spin, leashed to Baze's prowling essence circling me like a shark; feeling his keen stare on my face, my hands, my feet.

The hairs on my arms are at attention, tasting the salty air for movement, the bare soles of my feet cushioned by thick, wild grass.

Every muscle is knotted, poised to pounce. Every shift that doesn't topple me over the edge of this cliff is a miracle in itself.

A blow of chill, briny air teases past my nose, attempting to tame my internal unrest ...

Failing.

"I hate wearing this stupid thing," I mutter, insinuating the blindfold knotted around my head. "What's it supposed to achieve except to scare me into thinking I'm about to step off the precipice and plunge to certain death?"

Another shift of my foot—another quarter spin.

Still alive ...

"By eliminating your sight," Baze proclaims on a sigh, "we sharpen your other senses. Touch, smell ..."

I scrunch my nose. "On *that* note, I wish you'd have washed my handmaiden off y—"

"Hearing," he interrupts. The air shifts, and so do my hands and the sword I'm wielding, intercepting his strike before it can land a hit to my right shoulder.

There's a splintering *twang,* the blow shooting up my arms. But it's not the force of the hit that makes me feel like my skull has been cleaved down the middle and wrenched open.

It's the sound our weapons make when they clash.

Our swords aren't made from a soft wood like the one I started training with five years ago—the one that struck with a dull *thud* and split after two months. We've since upgraded, again and again.

These are made from a petrified wood that's hard and sharp and brutal.

Jarring.

I block a blow swinging for my abdomen, splitting the air with another sharp sound that strikes its own sort of match. It takes me three deep breaths to temper the hot surge threatening to flood my brain, and by the time I get there, my patience is nothing but a brittle twig ready to snap.

"I *hate* these new swords." I remove my blindfold, squinting when the morning light takes a dig at me. "They're loud and heav—"

A blow lands to the back of my knee, sending bolts of pain lancing up my leg.

I wail, buckling.

My hands plunge into the fluffy grass, absorbing the full brunt of my weight as my palm clips on a stone, bloodying the air.

I gulp breath, spine curled, body refusing to move. "That wa—*wow* ..." I inspect the fresh graze. "That was just *mean.*"

Baze lurks around me in tight, taunting circles, passing by the precipice, seemingly unperturbed that one wrong step could send him plummeting all the way to the bay. "You're too easily distracted first thing in the morning." He casts me a sideways glower that chafes my skin. "Up!"

I scramble to my feet, careful not to edge too close to the drop. Straight ahead, the castle sits atop the ridge—a robust, gothic cathedral drinking every drop of light that falls its way. My tower shoots up from the northern wing like a stalk reaching for the sun.

Stony Stem.

It's partially decorated in dangling pops of purple from my wisteria vine, its long shadow cast left across Vateshram Forest.

"I'm not *distracted.*"

Just tempted to toss this stupid sword into the bay.

I grip the pommel with both hands, ignoring my stinging palm, bouncing foot to foot to alleviate the little balls of energy bursting through my veins. "Come at me. Right now. I'll prove just how *not* distracted I am."

He leers at me through the gaps of his wind-tousled hair. "No, Laith. I told you we're slowing it down this morning; forcing you to focus. Now, put the blindfold back on before I make you haul rocks."

I roll my eyes and groan.

Slowing it down when all I want to do is the opposite.

Sometimes Exothryl wears off quickly, other times not. This morning, the effects are lingering—churning me into a storm of bridled chaos—and I'm stuck doing *this.*

Slowing it down.

I pull the damn blindfold on, severing my sight of his menacing posture and bruising eyes. "I want my old sword back. I feel like I've been forced back to basics."

"It's only been a few months. Give yourself time to get used to the Petrified Pine. I actually prefer it."

The hairs on my right arm prickle ...

Wood whistles through the air, and I bend to the left, dropping to a crouch and lashing my sword in a wide arc. In my mind's eye, I picture him leaping back so I don't slash his kneecaps.

"I'm happy for you," I bite out through clenched teeth. "But I still want my old one back."

It might have taken me a while to warm up to it at the start, but I grew fond of that thing—even went to the effort of painting vines around the pommel.

"No can do. Mine split, remember? That old sword of

yours is too soft. My new one would shatter it in a single blow."

Such folly.

"Can't you just ... make another?"

"No," he says from behind, and I whirl, body bracing for impact. "That Snow Oak was imported from the Deep North years ago when there were still regular trading ships trekking down the River Norse. I know the new ones sound a little sharper, but you'll just have to make do."

My eyes narrow on his presumed whereabouts. "I'm sure you used a similar excuse three years ago when we changed from Inglewood to White Maple ..."

His sword whistles toward me again, and I intercept, our blades dragging as he pulls away. The sharp sound scrapes into me, *infects* me, raking a shiver through my entire body.

Mind emptying, I scurry backward.

"Stop!"

A burst of wind skims up my spine, flicking my ponytail, lifting the hairs on the back of my neck.

"The cliff is just behind you ..."

My heart lurches and I leap forward, squealing.

Baze releases a deep chuckle that has me snatching off the blindfold and tossing it over the edge of the cliff that was, in fact, *right behind me.*

All humor melts off his face as he strides forward and watches the thing flutter away on a whip of wind. "Well, that was immature."

"Good riddance," I snip, keeled over from my near-death experience.

That is *not* the type of exhilaration I was chasing.

Baze sighs so loud I can hear it over another gust of wind driving up the cliff. "Fine, have it your way." He turns from the drop and widens his feet, lowering himself into a fighting stance, flashing me a lupine smile. "*Fast* it is."

I loosen my shoulders and shake off the last of my blood-chilling fear, spurred on by the sadistic challenge forging in his sharp eyes. "*Finally*—"

"But you complain about that sword *one more time,*" he interrupts, "and I trade it in for something much, much worse."

I open my mouth, close it again.

He made the same threat two years ago, and I didn't take him seriously. Later that day, I watched in wide-eyed horror as he flung that sword over my Safety Line, knowing full well I wouldn't step across and retrieve the damn thing.

The next day, he handed me one twice as loud, almost twice as heavy, and it took me six months to adjust ...

I faux button my lips.

CHAPTER 3

ORLAITH

"These honey buns are the *best.*" I lick buttery filling from my fingers, the creamy explosion making the muscles under my tongue tingle.

Baze lifts a brow, drawing a sip of water and placing his glass back on the table next to a plate of scrambled eggs. "Cook is far too fond of you. After this morning's workout, you should be fueling yourself with protein. Not"—he scrunches his face, nostrils flaring—"*that* crap."

Ignoring the rest of the colorful spread, I reach for the pile of buns near the base of a silver candelabra, stuff two in my mouth, and throw him a winning smile.

Baze shakes his head and sighs. "Rhordyn doesn't pay me enough."

The big doors swing open, spewing light and a tall, robust male now stalking toward the long, obsidian table we're dining at.

I have to squint to battle the morning glare, but I don't need to see his features to know who it is. I know by the way he walks—like a fearless beast tracking through his den, reinstating his dominance. I know by the way all the hairs on the back of my neck stand on end from air now charged with a chilling tension I hate to love.

Twin thuds echo through the spacious room, and the doors ricochet closed again, barricading the sun.

I swallow my mouthful, watch every smooth, powerful stride, feel the blood drain from my cheeks when I realize he's headed toward the setting at the table's head.

An empty silver plate set to accept his presence. His meal.

Always.

Not that he ever dines with us. Which makes it all the more shocking when he lowers into the seat and drops his face into my line of sight ...

I'm too stunned to do anything but stare.

He's all hard lines and chilling resolve—square jawline dusted with two-day-old growth almost hiding his chin dimple.

The dimple I'm trying so very hard to focus on rather than ... *anything* else. Certainly not those broad shoulders. Nor the strong line of his neck or the peek of light olive skin visible through his unbuttoned collar.

He clears his throat, the sound a crush of his deep vocals, and my gaze darts to his beckoning finger.

A silent request for me to look him in the eye.

My chest feels too crowded to contain my lungs and fluttering heart, but I draw a tight breath and abide.

Sable, silver-licked curls that have nothing to do with age are currently pushed forward, half-shielding me from pewter eyes framed with thick, black lashes. Eyes that search my face before cutting across every other part of me like a shaving blade, leaving me utterly boneless.

"You're hurt." His words are nails hammered into the too still air.

"Just a graze." I wave my injured hand at him. "Nothing major."

"And the one on your leg? Is that *also* nothing major?"

Crap.

"I—"

His eyes narrow as I flounder for words, feeling Baze's attention bore into the side of my too-hot face.

Yes, I nicked my leg during training, then chose not to disclose it since I was so jacked on exo that to stop would have been *torture.*

Problem is, Rhordyn doesn't know we train, and I prefer to keep it that way. The only reason I agreed to it in the first place was because Baze let it slip that Rhordyn wouldn't approve of me learning to fight like one of his warriors. I'd be lying if I said I don't get some sick satisfaction from going against his coarse grain.

But that slice on my thigh? I have no doubt that if he were to inspect it, he'd know *exactly* where it came from.

"You were saying?" Rhordyn asks, challenging me with a hardness that practically begs me to lie.

So I do what I do best. Because lies are pretty little masks we place on our words to tint the truth into something palatable.

I straighten my shoulders, finding my spine. "No, nothing major. I got them both tripping on my stairs."

The words slip out like silk, but I can tell by the way his midnight brow jacks up that he knows my tongue is tainted.

I take a sip of my juice, smacking my lips against the sharp tang. "Clumsy feet."

"Clumsy, you say?"

"Mmm-hmm."

He reclines in his chair, ankle resting on his knee. His boots are covered in dirt and soot and ...

Blood.

I glance away, the honey buns becoming little lumps of lead in my stomach.

At least he changed his shirt.

"Well, you'll have to be more careful," he chides, waving off the servant trying to pour him some juice from a large, sweating jug. She's garbed in the traditional threads of our territory: black pants, black coat, black boots. A silver pin clings to her lapel with Rhordyn's sigil pressed into it—a crescent moon pierced through the middle by a lone sword. "Tanith will tend to it after breakfast."

I steal a peek at my quizzical handmaiden backed against the wall at the edge of the bare-bones dining hall, her auburn brow raised.

Tanith is all too used to the cuts and bruises and blisters I get from training.

To split the awkward tension, I set two more buns on my plate as if my appetite didn't entirely dissolve the moment Rhordyn entered the room.

He knots his arms over his chest and spears that chilling gaze down the table. "Baze."

The word lands like a boulder.

I repress a flinch, looking left, watching Baze's throat work.

"She had a nightmare."

Silence stretches between them, tension crackling. I sip my orange juice, marinating in the flow of soundless words that seem to have their own ill-tempered heartbeat.

"We'll talk about this later," Rhordyn rumbles, his voice a dark promise of something unpleasant.

A shiver scuttles up my spine.

"Of course," Baze grates out before pushing his plate of eggs to the side.

Rhordyn has the power to do that—to pluck you out of your pleasant atmosphere and stuff you into his unforgiving aura.

I peel a mandarin I don't intend to eat and pretend I don't exist.

"Why were you out so late?" Baze watches Rhordyn with a steady gaze while rolling his sleeves.

"Received an urgent sprite. Scouting ship returned earlier than expected. I went to meet with them."

Baze's hands still. "And?"

Rhordyn offers Baze a small shake of his head.

Looking down at my fruit, I battle the stubborn rind, wearing a frown that feels like it's going to leave a permanent indent between my brows.

Their silent conversations always grate me the wrong way.

"Orlaith?" I glance up, Baze's voice cutting through my inner musings. "What are your plans today?"

"You're paid to keep track of me. You probably know my routine better than I do ..."

He shrugs. "Your tasks don't always fall in the same order. What's up first?"

He's right. My routine does hinge on the weather, how badly he's whipped my ass during training, and whether or not people are visiting the estate.

But still ...

He's making small talk, something he *never* does, and that makes me uncomfortable. He's either trying to divert my attention or he has other intentions.

"Well, I'll probably visit Cook first ... check my nabber ... Oh!" I almost shout, bouncing a little. "I just remembered. I finished painting Kai's gift yesterday. Hopefully it's dry so I can gift it to him during my visit this afternoon."

The room chills.

Baze takes a swig of his breakfast juice before dishing me a cloying smile. "Sorry I asked."

Sorry he—

My attention pulls to Rhordyn, only to be assaulted by his stony glower.

Oh.

"You don't like Kai?"

Drumming fingers against his bicep, his lips form a thin line. "I never said that."

"Your face is wearing your opinion."

He arches a brow, and I swear the sterling pools of his eyes swirl. "You've never introduced me to him. How could I not like him?"

I open my mouth, close it, suffocating under the weight of his perusal.

I hate it when he does this; challenges me to step outside my comfort zone. Pecks at me like I'm something that needs *fixing.*

My solitary existence, my routines, my weekly escape to the bay ... they keep me in control, and I won't dare risk tarnishing the friendship I have with Kai simply to satisfy Rhordyn's dominant dispositions. Kai's the only thing I have that's truly my own.

Dropping my gaze, I stare at the small pile of mandarin skin that's zesting the air.

"That's what I thought," Rhordyn rumbles, and I bunch my hands so hard I punch little crescents into my palms.

Bastard.

Right now, I prefer it when he leaves that seat empty. Because *this* ...

This is not enjoyable.

A normal, relaxed conversation is obviously too much to expect. If I had known he was coming here to wield an attack on the borders of my personal limitations, I'd have walked out the moment he entered.

Instead, I let my fluttering heart get me caught in his snare.

"I'm done," I say, standing. "Places to be, things to see. I'm a very important person, you know."

"Sit down, Orlaith."

The command in Rhordyn's tone is a strike to the back of my knees. My bum lands on the chair, and my fists tighten further, face aflame.

He must know the effect he has on me. And based on the way his lips are hooked at the corner, I'm sure he uses it to his advantage.

Arms unknotting, he runs his thumb back and forth across his lower lip while I suffer a sharp examination. "I'm hosting a ball on the same weekend as the next Tribunal."

The words are a blow to my chest. "A ... a *ball?*"

"Yes. As well as a Conclave for the Masters and Mistresses —high and low. I've already sent sprites. There will be many new faces around over the course of a few days."

There's a certain lilt to his tone that has my spine stiffening. Has me listening to all the words he's *not* saying.

A challenge.

"I don't get it. You've never held a ball before. Or a Conclave."

My tone is steady, somehow hiding the fact that my heart is waging war against my ribs.

"Not since you've been here, no. But things are changing. I need to solidify bonds and ease curious minds."

"Okay ... well, thanks for letting me know. I'll stay out of everyone's way," I say, more question than statement.

Testing.

He's not done with me yet, I can feel it. He walked in here with a chip on his shoulder, and he's using it to slice up my shell.

His eyes darken to a deep, stormy gray. "No, Orlaith. You'll be attending the ball."

I suck a sharp breath, as if I've just been struck.

Attending? What's the use? Nobody needs to see me. And I certainly don't need to see them.

"*Why?*" I lash the word, but he doesn't flinch. Doesn't even blink.

"Because you're an *enigma.* The girl who survived a Vruk raid at the tender age of two."

"What's that got to do wi—"

"You keep to yourself when newcomers enter the castle grounds, and refuse to be involved with the monthly Tribunal."

Here we go.

"That's not true. I used to attend." *Sort of.*

"*Twice.* And if I'm not mistaken, you spent most of the time sticking to the shadows."

The shadows were more friendly than the stares.

The *whispers.*

My knuckles protest from the bunch of my hands. "I have no troubles to publicly voice, no interest in what everyone has to say, and therefore no reason to attend the Tribunal. Simple as that. I certainly shouldn't be *punished* for it."

His brows kick up, eyes narrow. "No interest, you say?"

"*Zero.*" I practically snarl the word, watching the muscle in his jaw feather the moment it leaves my lips.

"Well," he bites out. "So you don't choke on that lie, I'll offer you a chaser of truth. You're almost twenty-one. I've not seen any effort to overcome your fears, and my string of patience is thinning. Fast. You don't want to find out what happens when it snaps."

A vision of me being hurtled over my Safety Line springs to life, and my blood chills, becoming so cold even the fire crackling at my back struggles to thaw my icy composure.

Definitely should have walked out the moment he entered the room.

"As I said, you're an enigma. And people *fear* enigmas, Orlaith. They start twisting things to make sense of it all. The last thing I need is further discord in my Territory." He leans forward and plants his elbows on the table, clasping his hands together. "I need them to see you're *just* you. Nothing more."

A weight lands in my stomach; almost has me vomiting honey buns all over the table.

Just me.

Right.

Gaze falling to my plate, I swallow the smear of bile coating the back of my tongue. "I hate crowds."

Though the words come out a murmur, they're clipped—aimed to fend off the circling predator.

The statement isn't entirely true. I like crowds, so long as I'm watching from a distance.

But he's asking that I be *involved.*

"I'm giving you plenty of notice. You don't have to stay at the ball for long, but you will be there."

He might as well be hurtling me into the forest to fend for

myself, letting the ancient foliage chew me alive. Something he also has the power to do.

At the end of the day, I'm his ward.

I'm the one imposing on *his* life, not the other way around, so I should really make an effort to be more pliable. Attending a ball isn't going to kill me, but getting tossed over my Safety Line might.

"Anything else?" I bite out, peeling my nails from the flesh of my palms.

Rhordyn's nostrils flare. Only delicately, but I notice.

"I've instructed the tailor to fashion you a ..." he clears his throat, "a *gown.*"

I stare at him, wide eyed.

Baze chuckles low, and I find myself wishing this table were decorated with those knives and forks like I've seen in picture books—utensils Rhordyn banned from the castle. Apparently the sound of them scraping across the dishware left me curled beneath the table with blood gushing from my nose when I was young, but they'd be mighty handy to stab these two assholes for their obvious amusement at my expense.

"His assistant will be ready to take your measurements and shape the pattern at midday."

Lovely. My gown fitting will double as a torture session.

"Dolcie always pricks me. Can't Hovard do it?" He's never once drawn blood while making sure my pants were cut just the right way. He has gentle hands. But Dolcie ...

I'm certain she has it in for me.

"*Dolcie* will be expecting you in the tailors' wing at noon."

I open my mouth to speak, but with a simple cant of his head that looks almost feline, the words get caught behind my lips.

Releasing a sharp breath, I look to the closed doors, feet bouncing under the table.

I need to get the hell out of this room.

"That it?" I ask, and I know he nods by the way the tension between us snaps, like someone took a blade and severed the connection.

I swipe my bag off the ground and stand, then beeline to find some air to draw into my fossilized lungs, plucking an apple from Baze's plate as I stalk past.

"Hey!" he blurts.

"Hey, yourself," I mutter, the heavy whip of my hair swaying with every frustrated flick of my hips.

"I thought you hated apples?"

Two stoic servants pull the doors open, dousing me in a spill of sunlight, and I toss a smirk at Baze from over my shoulder.

"Kai doesn't," I say with a wink, hearing Rhordyn grunt as I exit the room.

CHAPTER 4

ORLAITH

You can always tell what time of the day it is by the varying smells in the kitchen.

Midday belongs to the hearty aroma of slow-roasted game. Evening's filled with fire-charred root vegetables and rich botanical seasonings. At night, the air is either pinched with the acidity of pickling liquids or sweetened by sugared berries being reduced into a jelly preserve. And in the mornings, like right now, there's the yeasty aroma of freshly baked bread ...

My favorite time of day.

Tentatively, I edge into the bustling kitchen that's pregnant with cheery chatter. Strangers from forest communities and tribes often stop by to deliver fruit, vegetables, and game, and the years have taught me to proceed with caution.

Always.

It saves me from the unfamiliar stares and whispers that were never quiet enough.

Lex, the sous-chef, is up to her elbows in dough, wrestling it into submission. She offers a friendly smile that lights up her sea-green eyes. "All clear."

I smile back.

Everyone *else* seems to understand that I don't want to

step a single foot outside my safe, ordinary existence.

My bubble of protection.

Drawing a lungful of goodness, I move deeper into the room that holds the heart of the castle; a woman with a barreling laugh and the ability to brighten your day with her wholesome recipes.

I reach for the steaming roll set on a small plate beside the hearth, splitting the soft, spongy dough in two. There's a glob of cinnamon-nut butter piled on the plate that I sweep my finger through and smear across the bread, taking a large bite.

"Morning, girly!" Cook hollers, and I spin, cheeks bulging as I offer her a wave.

Her rosy, silver-streaked hair is pulled into a tight bun, auburn eyes twinkling, full figure swaying. She sets a large, copper pot on the cooker, making water slosh over the sides.

I skirt around the edge of the kitchen, plate in hand, dashing into the cellar stacked full of grain sacks, rounds of aging cheese, and big barrels of wine. Knees kissing the cold stone, I set the plate on the ground and thread my arm down a circular air vent cut into the wall, extracting my nabber—a mousetrap made from a hollowed-out tree branch, some coiled metal, and a bunch of ingenuity.

I lift it, peering down the spyhole only large enough for a rodent nose to fit through.

Curled at the end is a small, frightened mouse who obviously has the same appetency for cinnamon-nut butter as I do.

"This is not your lucky day," I murmur, releasing the latch, lifting the lid, and digging my hand in to hook the squirming rodent out by its tail.

"Is it a fat one today?" Cook asks from behind, her warm,

robust voice basting me with an immediate sense of ease. "There's been something mighty big chewing holes in one of my grain sacks, so I'm hoping you've caught the vermin."

"Normal size," I answer, watching the poor thing swing back and forth, trying to twist up and bite me.

Cook hums her disappointment while I root around inside my bag, locating the jar with air holes. I unscrew it one-handed, drop the mouse in, and secure the lid. Spreading what's left of my butter on the nabber's internal wall, I reset the latch and slide it back in the hole.

"Any special requests?" Cook asks, and I smile, glancing over my shoulder. "Best get them in early. The kitchen will be busy over the coming weeks. We haven't had a ball here in *years.*"

I clear my throat and stand, stashing the mouse in my bag, ignoring the heaviness that settles on my shoulders. "What about some of those apple and pastry rolls you used to make when I was little?"

Her brows draw together. "The ones with lemon-toffee drizzle?"

I nod, wiping buttery fingers on my top.

"You only ever asked for them when you were feeling blue ..."

"I'm fine," I lie, forcing another smile. "Just an abundance of ripe lemons on my tree. I'll bring some down later."

"Mmm-hmm."

Time to change the subject.

"How's your granddaughter? Did you make it to Cardell to see her yesterday?"

That makes her cheeks swell. Her daughter and son-in-law are truffle farmers in a neighboring village, and recently welcomed their first, long-awaited child.

"I did. And she's a tubby one, unlike *you.*" She looks me up and down, clicking her tongue and shaking her head. "One of these days, I'll find a way to put some meat on those bones. Mark my word!"

We both say the last three words in unison, and I laugh, hooking my bag over my shoulder.

"Now, off you go," she says, shooing me. "The soup ain't gonna prepare itself. Bring those lemons down later and we can have a cuppa. I'll tell you all about my wee babe."

"Looking forward to it." I lift onto my tippy toes and plant a kiss on her freckle-dusted cheek, then pick up the plate and dart off, setting it in the sink before I head out the door.

The mouse squeaks his displeasure at being jostled about as I sprint down the cold, barren hallway lit by flaming wall sconces. I come to a T and bank left, slowing my steps when I reach a cobbled archway on my right—one that looks like every other archway in this giant castle.

But it's not.

It's one of the thirty-seven entrances to The Tangle—the unutilized labyrinth of corridors lumped in the center of the palace that twists and turns and splits and crosses and feeds into areas otherwise difficult to access.

My secret weapon.

These corridors lead anywhere and everywhere, if you know how to use them. Some pop out in doors that are invisible to the untrained eye, others lead to sensible places regardless of the insensible track it takes to get there.

Take the trapdoor entrance on the fifth floor for example; a tunnel that spits you out in an underground storage room despite not seeming to rise or fall a smidge.

In short, they're easy to get lost in if you don't have a

clear grasp on things, something I learned the hard way too many times.

I'm surprised I'm not a dehydrated corpse decorating a tunnel somewhere.

These days, Castle Noir is my own personal city, just like the ones I've read about in the many books stacked in Spines —the giant library.

The passageways are streets; the kitchen, a bakery that exchanges the best buns and cinnamon-nut butter for my mouse-ridding services; and the bedrooms are houses rich with people's lingering scents.

Like The Den—Rhordyn's personal suite.

The thought that these halls may soon be swarming with strangers over the course of an entire *weekend* sits like a rock in my gut.

Coming to a fork in the tunnel, I veer left, spotting a young girl bunched on the ground at the base of the wall.

My feet root in place.

Something bitter clogs my throat as I peer over my shoulder, then back again.

She's perhaps no older than seven or eight, shivering, her inky hair a messy shroud around her shoulders.

I don't think she's seen or heard me yet, likely because I move through the castle like a wraith, my bare footfalls softer than a gentle pull of breath.

Always.

Over the years, I've taught myself to move with the air and blend against walls. To meld with shadows despite the brassy veneer of my long, golden hair doing everything in its power to make me stand out.

I clear my throat and the girl jolts—her wild, fearful eyes darting to me.

Suspending my hands between us, I try to show I'm no threat regardless of the impromptu squeak that emanates from my knapsack.

"Are you lost?" I ask, crouching.

She nods, her heart-shaped face pale like the moon. "Wh-what's wrong with your voice?"

My hand flies to my throat like a pitiful shield.

"I hurt it when I was little," I whisper. "So, I sound ... *different.*"

Raspy. Perpetually broken and harsh, like I haven't had a drink all day. Not the smooth, honeyed voice some of the servants have. Never the lilting chime of my handmaid.

"Oh ..." she replies, still wound in a lump on the ground.

Watching me.

I'm thankful she doesn't ask more, unsure of what I'd say if she did. The only memories I have of the night that broke my throat are the fragmented ones that come to me in my sleep.

The screams, the smoldering flames, the strident scratching that scored so deep it left irreparable scars on my soul. Damage that prevents me from living a normal life lest a sharp sound trigger an impromptu attack.

I forge a smile and drop to a kneel. "Let's go find your parents, shall we?"

"I don't have any ..."

My smile falters, heart sinks.

I can suddenly see the darkness hiding in those emerald eyes; a haunting darkness I recognize.

"Well," I answer, trying to sound bright and cheery. "Where did you come from?"

She sniffs, wiping her cheeks with the back of puffed sleeves that cinch her wrists. "From the big shiny doors."

The Keep.

Doors I've never been allowed through. One of the dark zones I've yet to explore.

I think of the skeleton I once found resting against a wall not too far from here ...

Fair to say, I'm obliged to return this child to her rightful place.

"Lucky for you, I know *exactly* where that is."

I bridge the space between us with an outstretched hand.

She studies it, gaze dropping to my bag. "Do you have any treats in there? Or just the mouse?"

I lift a brow.

She gives me a shy smile. "I heard it squeak."

"Clever girl," I say, digging around for my jar of toffees. I unscrew the lid and offer the sweets. "One for each hand. For guessing the contents of my bag."

Her eyes light up, and she pops two straight in her mouth, then lets me pull her up.

We walk in silence, hand in hand, her grip tightening as we journey down crooked stairwells and silent stretches of tunnel. By the time I help her through a trapdoor that spits us out in a lofty, fourth-floor corridor, my fingers feel bruised.

I roll the rug back into place and brush the cobwebs off her dress, then turn to The Keep looming over us like an entrance to the underworld.

There are no windows in this corridor that seems unnaturally long. Certainly no other entrances nearly half as interesting as *this*.

Large sconces light the twin, handleless doors from either side, casting them in a golden sheen, the polished stone offering perfect reflections of ourselves. I ignore mine, stepping forward to knock four times, each echoing back at me.

A taunting heartbeat.

The child shuffles behind me as the mechanics grind into gear, and the door cracks open like the mouth of a monster, though just enough to spit out a burly beast of a man I recognize all too well.

Jasken. The keeper of The Keep. Or at least that's what I call him.

He's dressed in the classic garb of a Western guard—black pants, knee-high boots, and a swarthy coat that kicks out at the shoulders. Armor reminiscent of flowing ink protects the left side of his chest and spills down one arm, but leaves the other bare.

If I were to crawl inside the man, it would require three of me to fill him up. Even then, there would be space for each of us to shift around and get more comfortable.

He looks down at me with small, wary eyes, and I offer him a dazzling smile.

"Orlaith," he rumbles, voice surprisingly warm. From that sound alone, you'd think the man's a pushover.

Wrong.

"Jasken," I say, tipping my head in greeting. "Lovely day for a stroll."

One bushy brow reaches for his ruddy hairline. "I'm sure. Back so soon?"

Rude.

"I don't appreciate your judgemental tone. It's been two whole days since I was last here." I shrug. "Anyway, I have"—a ticket—"*someone*. I found her in The Tangle."

I swear the corner of his mouth kicks up. Difficult to tell

with all that rust-colored scruff covering half his face. "The what?"

I roll my eyes, reach behind, and nudge the child forward. She's staring at the ground, twining her fingers together.

Jasken's honey eyes drop before his head dips behind the door. "*Vestele!*"

I cringe.

He has quite the pair of lungs.

A woman with wiry hair and a wiggly spine hobbles through the opening—face pinched, cheeks red, hair pulled into such a tight upsweep that it almost smooths the years etched around her pale blue eyes.

"*Anika!* Kvath be damned, where the *hell* have you been?"

Her voice boxes my ears, but it's her stare that really stings—two icy pins stabbing at me and the child.

She yanks Anika through the doors, and the poor thing barely has a chance to peep over her shoulder at me before she disappears.

When I try to follow, Jasken slides sideways, blocking my line of sight—a mammoth, impenetrable wall. By the way his cheeks have rounded out, I can tell he's smiling somewhere beneath all those wiry bristles.

I'd smack that smirk right off his gruff face if he weren't so damn tall.

I frown, stamping my fists on my hips. "You take your job far too seriously."

"So you keep telling me," he says, tipping his head. "*Orlaith.*"

I sigh, mimicking the action, hands falling heavy at my sides. "Jasken."

Thus ensues the walk of shame.

Not my first, and I doubt it will be my last.

CHAPTER 5

ORLAITH

Castle Noir is brimming with secrets, but most of them are not my own. They're Rhordyn's or his ancient predecessors who are never talked about.

This one, however, belongs to me.

The door is old, the worn wood and rusted lock a testament to its age. A lock that was a terrible match for my hairpin and teeth-gritting determination when I first stumbled upon this place ten years ago.

I lift a flaming torch from one of the sconces and pry the door open. The darkness that pours out seems to howl at me, making my flame flicker as I peer into the throat of a gloomy passageway.

Whispers.

Though this entire castle is ancient, this place somehow feels *more* so. Like the floor felt the wear of decades of feet before the door was locked, the passage forgotten.

At least until I came along.

I step into the hallway and use the flaming beacon to light the first sconce, illuminating a section of my masterpiece.

This place curls into the moody guts of the castle, but I'm not sure how far down. The further you go, the more oppressive the darkness gets.

The *colder* it gets.

I've yet to make it to the end.

I walk fifteen steps into the sweeping hallway that digs into the earth before igniting the second sconce, illuminating the wall to my left and giving lustrous life to another section of my mosaic.

It's taken me the better part of ten years to paint this mural, stone by stone, each a separate work of art. Small, whispered stories I've brushed on the rocks that piece together and form bigger, overriding pictures I often try to ignore.

I keep going, igniting more sconces, the air temperature dropping so much the fifth barely gifts me enough glow to work with. I walk until I'm standing on the precipice between shadow and light, staring into an ocean of black that looks like it could swallow me whole.

Dropping to my knees, I lay the torch next to me and open my bag, digging past the squeaking mouse to a stone wrapped in cheesecloth to protect the whisper from getting damaged during transport.

I unwrap the layers and trace the delicate brushstrokes that make up a young boy sitting cross-legged on the ground, surrounded by a bed of black blooms. White sparkles decorate his eyes, and his hair is a twisted mess.

He's reaching, fingers forever stretched, and though I have no idea what he's extending toward, he looks happy. Like a bubble of laughter waiting to pop.

A sad sort of smile flirts with the corner of my lips.

I retrieve my jar of homemade mortar, untwist the lid, and bore a pallet knife into the muck. The gap in the wall is right in front of me, and I sweep the substance around the hole before pressing the whisper into place.

Leaning back, I study what I can see of the whole picture from down here at the edge of the light.

That's the thing about this place: no matter where you're positioned, you'll never see the full story at once. Just segments of it you have to piece together in your mind.

Given the bigger, overriding images I've immortalized on the wall, I've always thought that more a blessing than a curse.

Nodding, I rummage through my bag and retrieve my little diamond pickaxe, eyeing up my next target half-sheathed in shadow ...

The only rock not entirely eaten up by the hungry darkness.

Whatever I paint on it will only ever be half visible, and although there's something poetic about that, it also signifies the end of an era. Unless I somehow manage to light the next sconce, I'll have to start on the opposite wall or give up altogether, and I'm not sure how I feel about any of those options.

I rise onto my knees and start tapping at the mortar, cleaving the rock from its shell. It loosens a little, and one more knock sends it falling into my awaiting hand like a lump of shadow.

The entire castle is made from the same ebony stone; some rooms hewn straight from the side of the mountain. Other areas, like this passageway, have been built with bits of it—none larger than two of my fists pressed together.

I bag the rock and stand, spearing my gaze into the gloom ...

Maybe it's time to try again.

I pluck the torch off the ground, draw a deep breath, then slide my foot over the flickering line.

It only takes two beats of my heart before the fire starts to sputter, but I carry on ... pushing further.

Deeper.

With each echoing step, my dancing bulb of light shrinks a little more, yielding to the plummeting temperature that's turning my breath white.

I time my steps with every exhale, sweat breaking out across the back of my neck despite the biting chill ...

Surely the next sconce is only a few steps away ...

Step, *breathe.*

Step, *breathe.*

Step, *breathe.*

My flame sputters, lungs falter, and I pause ... letting my next breath leak out of me in a milky haze that somehow still snuffs the torch entirely, plunging me into a sea of darkness.

I forget how to move. How to breathe or think or blink.

The torch clatters to the ground and seems to bounce and bounce and bounce, like it's descending a flight of stairs. The echoing assault shoves me into action, and I pivot, racing toward the promise of light, every hair on the back of my neck standing on end as if something is watching me flee.

When I finally merge with the light, I spin, collapsing against the unpainted wall—chest tight, lungs battling for space, heart catapulting little bolts of fire through my veins.

"You win again," I rasp, throwing the darkness a side-eye.

CHAPTER 6

ORLAITH

I descend the grisly, obsidian steps cut into the vertical cliff that leads to Bitten Bay, soft squeaks protesting from my bag every time it bumps against my thigh. Stony Stem stands sentry in the sky, casting a long, slender shadow across the pale ocean.

When I'm almost at the bottom I leap, landing ankle-deep in black sand that seems to gobble up the light. The gentle breeze salts my skin as my eyes sweep shut, and I'm lulled by the soft lap of waves, picturing myself as a plant delving its roots into the silky sand ...

Why anyone wears shoes, I'll never understand. They cut you off from *this.*

When I open my eyes again, they're instantly drawn to a perfectly round rock nesting on the shoreline, as if the ocean just offered me a gift.

Smiling wide, I dash forward and pick it up, imagining all the things I can paint on its smooth surface while tucking it in my knapsack for safe keeping.

I jog toward the cove's right hook without even *looking* at the long, wooden pier across the bay that'll finally see some use when Rhordyn hosts the ball; something I'm trying not to think about since I'm currently evading a dress fitting.

The rocks are the same color as the sand, though less forgiving on the naked soles of my feet. Luckily, I know where to step so they can't sink their teeth in too far.

I'm nearing the water's edge when a familiar head pushes above the froth, white hair slicked back from the sharp angles of his face.

"Treasure? You never come down here at this time," Kai says by way of greeting, voice deep and silky.

The constant, invisible pulse that echoes off him gently taps my skin like little bursts of air. I call it his *beat,* and I can always tell exactly how Kai feels by the way it interacts with me.

I swing my bag off my shoulder and lower it to the rocks, pulling the length of my hair forward and playing with the end. "Don't I?"

His eyes narrow and his long, silver tail slithers beneath the surface as he slides forward. "What are you avoiding?"

"A gown fitting." I dust off my pants and shrug. "Don't look at me like that, I hate dresses."

"Oh, I'm aware. I clearly remember you ordering me to stuff a poofy number at the bottom of a chasm so you'd never have to look at it again. What ... ten years ago? Seven? Five? I lose track."

Last time I attended a Tribunal.

I'm all for outfits that smudge my shape, but I could barely fit through the door in that thing. There wasn't a single pair of eyes it didn't draw.

Dropping to a crouch, I pick a piece of seaweed from his hair and flick it away. "You look good in frills. Me ... not so much."

"I don't believe you. And I saw you pluck something off the beach. What was it?"

"I did!" I pull the perfectly round rock from my knapsack and brush off the sand. "Look at this glorious sight. Have you ever seen a rock so smooth?"

He takes it from my hand, examines it from all angles, then scrunches up his nose. "Not my favorite."

I gasp. "Take that back!"

His liquid laugh ripples over the water, and I roll my eyes, snatching the stone. I retrieve the fat, red apple and wave it through the air, causing Kai's laughter to stop.

Instantly.

He follows the movement like a charmed serpent, eyes dazzling emeralds caught in the sun ...

Hypnotized.

"I'm sorry," he pleads. "I love you, and your treasure hunting skills are just as glorious as your perfectly smooth rock."

"That's ... a fantastic apology."

I toss the apple, and he's so swift to whip it from the air that all I see is a blur of motion.

"Be right back," he spouts before diving in a churn of steely scales and long, rippling frills. He returns a minute later, empty-handed, apple stashed somewhere beneath the glossy ocean surface.

Head cocking to the side, he drifts closer, fixated on my now cupped hands as if he can sense the treasure tucked within. "What do you have there?" His beat taps against my fingers—a gentle, inquisitive nudge for me to unfurl them.

Chewing my bottom lip, cheeks blazing, I open my hands and push the object toward him.

His eyes widen—whirlpools caught in a globe. *"Is this—"*

"The rock you gave me last week? Yeah," I murmur, sitting. "I, ahh ... I painted it for you."

His beat stops, as if it just choked on a breath.

He stares at me for long enough that I start to sweat, so I grab his hand and stuff the rock into his palm, then watch my own hands mash together. "To get the right tone of red, I had to use a little blood. A bit archaic, I hope you don't mind. And the paint is actually waterproof. You know that tree milk I told you about? The stuff that leaks off the wood when I peel the bark off a rubber tree? I mixed some of that with my regular blend. So yeah, the paint repels wa—"

He clears his throat and I glance up, getting caught in the glaze of his eyes.

My rambling thoughts stutter to a stop.

He's *never* looked at me with such reverence before ...

"Kai?"

"It's ... the kindest thing anyone's ever done for me," he whispers, turning his attention to the rock.

He once spoke of an island he holds close to his heart—said it's made up of big, iridescent rocks with millions of smaller ones crumbled around the shore. That a geyser leaks a ribbon of blood-red liquid into the mirror of water surrounding the place.

"I hope I got it right."

"It's perfect." He traces the glittery shore with the tip of his finger. "Thank you, Orlaith. Truly. It would have taken days to paint such a treasure ..."

I roll the hem of my pants and swing my legs into the chilly sea, tilting my face to the sun, eyes closed. "You're my best friend." My nonchalant tone masks the fact that I'm speaking around a lump in my throat the size of an acorn. "I'd do anything for you."

"Be right back," he calls, and I open my eyes to see him

disappear with a splash, leaving me alone with the warm, sleepy day that's reflecting off the ocean in fractals.

I smile, remembering the many times I've heard those three words before Kai's darted below the surface to stash something away. Being an Ocean Drake, he can't fight the urge to bank his treasures at his earliest convenience, even if it means momentarily breaking away from such riveting company.

He's like an ocean broom—the ultimate collector of things that'll probably never see the light of day again. I picture a large, underwater cavern brimming with a king's bounty, and the mental image of him dusting all those trinkets clean with his long, billowy tail has my grin widening.

Kai's head breaks the surface, and he lifts a hand, smiling. "I have something for you, also."

My brows knit.

Pinched between his thumb and forefinger is a dainty shell that twists around itself in a delicate swirl of pink and opaline. It has a silver ring pierced through its lip, and attached to that is a latch no bigger than my pinkie nail.

"It's beautiful," I whisper. "What sort of shell is it?"

The only ones that wash up here are gray, rugged cups the size of my hand, their inside scoop a dazzling mix of purples, blues, and pinks. Ground down, I use them to make a metallic paint that glimmers like a haunted rainbow.

"A baby conch," he answers with glee, washing me in his rich, briny scent as he glides forward. Clipping the charm to the silver chain around my neck, he settles it next to the big, black stone I've always worn. "The small ones usually get broken against the rocks, so this was a rare find, Orlaith. *Very* rare."

I look down, toying with it, loving the way it tinkles

against my gem; two treasures, opposite yet so perfect together.

"They're sea whisperers. If you speak into the hollow, the ocean will carry the message. So if you ever need me ..."

"I love it," I blurt, catching his stare. A smile splits his face like the crest of a glistening wave curling toward the sun—there one minute ... gone the next.

His nostrils flare, gaze dropping to my right leg. "You're bleeding," he murmurs. "What have you gone and done this time?"

Why all the men in my life seem so caught up on my lacerated skin, I'll never know.

"Cut myself during training." I shrug, still toying with my shell. "It's not major. I was supposed to get it looked at, but I got busy with other things."

His smile is all teeth—sharp canines exposed in their full, feral glory. "Lucky for you," he purrs with a mischievous lilt to his words, "I'm somewhat gifted at healing wounds."

I lift a brow.

He rolls my hem further, revealing the messy slice across my thigh, only barely missing my heart-shaped birthmark.

Well.

"Admittedly, that's worse than I thought it wa—" Kai tips forward and sweeps his tongue down my raw wound in a warm, wet caress. "What are you doing?"

All the blood in my body seems to rush to my cheeks.

"You're licking me. You're licking my cut."

He makes this amused, muffled sound, continuing to paint my hurt with long, precise swipes. By the time he pulls back, my cheeks are aflame, though all that heat swiftly drains away as both sides of the laceration knit together, leaving a pale pink line.

I stare at it, mouth full of words and no breath to speak them.

My surprise ebbs when I glance up and see the way he's looking at me—brow creased while he smacks his tongue against the top of his mouth.

"What?"

He shakes his head, swallowing. "You taste weird."

"That's not a very nice thing to say! I bet you don't taste great either," I chastise, tossing a scoop of water at him. "And *by the way,* now that I know you can lick my wounds away, I'll be down here every time I get a paper cut, stuffing my finger in your mouth."

I can't believe he didn't tell me this sooner.

A smirk softens the sharpness of his bladed cheekbones. "Stuff your finger in my mouth whenever you like, but starting a water fight with *me?* Orlaith, that was terribly unwise."

He rises out of the ocean one foreboding inch at a time, revealing the long, powerful slant of his sun-kissed muscles. My mouth pops open, head tipping back, eyes widening as toffee skin gives way to the round, steely scales of his mighty tail.

Shit.

I scuttle back like a crab seeking shelter. "No, Kai ... no. *No!* Don't you dare, you big, slippery *hellion—*"

His arm sweeps out, and he whips me against his cold, wet chest, then dunks us both into the brisk sea.

The bastard.

CHAPTER 7

ORLAITH

I purposely drum my footfalls down the hallway while wringing out my hair, mulling over all the creative ways I can spike an apple with enough senna to leave a fourteen-foot Ocean Drake shitting undigested seaweed for a week.

Rounding a corner, I almost charge into Rhordyn planted like a boulder in my path, and I squeal, stumbling back.

His swift hand weaves around me before I lose my footing, and I peep up through the wet mess of my unbridled hair, instantly flayed by argent eyes.

My thoughts turn to smoke.

And just when I thought this day couldn't kick my ass anymore.

I pull a breath, almost choking on air heavy with the smell of leather and a frosty morning. It sifts through my lungs and infuses my bloodstream, kicking my pulse into a churning rhythm that can't be healthy.

He's chillingly beautiful, otherworldly in stature. Just the sight of him has a crippling effect on my ability to function properly, and I hate it.

I hate it so damn much.

Rhordyn's head cants to the side, and a midnight brow

lifts, but his hand stays firmly locked between my shoulder blades while he punishes me with his silence.

Something deep inside screams for me to *run*.

Not that I ever listen.

A breath puffs out of me, and his chest inflates as I glide back a step—that hand falling away and leaving a chilled stamp of skin in its place.

Despite the height he lords over me, I hold his austere gaze, refusing to drop my chin or show even the slightest hint of submission. He may be well over six feet of sculpted, virile poise, but my rioting nerves can go to hell.

"Orlaith." His voice is a velvet purr that blows up my heart rate.

I dip into a slight curtsy and slide to the side, intent on shifting around him like water averting a river rock, but he moves with me.

My eyes narrow.

The entry to Stony Stem is *just behind him,* and I'm dripping the ocean all over the floor.

"Excuse me," I mutter, taking another sideways step. Again, he mimics the movement, causing me to shoulder the stone door that's always locked—the one Rhordyn uses some nights before he leaves the castle grounds.

Next to The Keep and The Den, *this* door annoys me the most.

Intrigues me the most.

I've twisted many hairpins trying to break into the damn thing. It's probably a glorified broom closet, but not knowing ... it's a certain sort of torture I don't particularly enjoy.

I sigh, leaning against it, arching a brow and pointing my thumb at its stony face. "Are you finally taking me on a tour?"

Hands sliding deep into his pockets, he fixes me with an icy stare. "Your cut."

"What about it?"

There's the seed of challenge in his eyes. "It's been healed."

I feel the blood drain from my face.

Can he ... can he smell that? Was he *watching?*

Hell ...

"Kai's tongue is multi-talented," I blurt, suffering a sudden wave of verbal diarrhea that's sure to earn me a prompt eviction.

"Is that so?" He steps forward, voice drilling beneath my skin and gripping hold of my heart.

Squeezing it.

I retreat a larger step, struggling to find even an ounce of air to nourish my suffocating lungs. "Don't you, ahh ... have to visit one of the local villages this afternoon?" I ask, my voice somewhat raspier than usual.

Both brows lift this time. "Barth. Yes. Why? Do you want to come?"

I blink at him.

Hasn't he pecked at me enough for one day? I've already agreed to attend his ball.

"No, thank you."

I swear I hear the words thump on the ground between us.

There's the slightest twitch at the corner of his mouth, something that almost softens one of his many hard edges.

Almost.

"You know," he starts, rolling his sleeves, exposing powerful forearms and a wealth of tawny skin branded with a tease of silver scripture I wish I could see more of. "There is a bakery there that supplies the best honey buns in all the territories."

I frown.

"Can't you just bring some back for me?" I almost suggest he stash them in The Safe in exchange for my offering, but we don't talk about that.

Ever.

He shrugs, the smooth movement somehow lethal enough to crush a man's spirit.

Crush *my* spirit, if used in the correct setting.

"Their ... *rules* don't allow for the exportation of honey buns."

I'm no expert on things that reside outside the castle grounds, but I'm sure that's a crock of shit.

"So?" he pushes, pinning me with his full, undivided attention, making me feel like I'm standing trial, awaiting punishment for something horrific.

I thieve another backward step and find a small amount of air to soothe my staggered breathing into something more rhythmic, yet he continues to ruin me with cunning eyes that make my skin feel translucent. Like he's seeing straight through me, watching my cogs whirl.

Does he see how they rely on the circles they spin? How one delicate shift could break me apart and scatter my bits all over the floor?

"I'll stay here," I whisper, and a shadow shutters his eyes, the muscle along his jaw feathering.

"Live, Orlaith. All I'm asking is that you *live*."

"I *am* living," is my lackluster answer, one that's met with a sigh that pushes out of him as if it's been bottled up for a while.

Perhaps he's growing tired of this game. Well, that makes two of us.

He jerks his chin at me. "Aren't you supposed to be wrapped in measuring tape right now?"

Fuck.

Dropping my stare to his chin dimple, I go back to wringing out my hair like it's the most casual thing in the world. "Oh, *damn*. Must have slipped my mind."

He does that beckoning gesture with his finger again—making it bounce like a lure.

Just like a stupid fish, I snatch the bait, only to see that he's still looking at me like my skin's transparent.

I return the favor, though Rhordyn's waters are so muddy I doubt their sediment will ever settle enough for me to truly garner his depth.

"Slipped your mind, Orlaith? I didn't realize it was slippery."

I shrug and make a small grunting sound, staring forlornly at the entrance of Stony Stem ...

"Lucky for you," he rumbles, gesturing in the opposite direction of my refuge, "I'm heading there now. I can escort you."

Of course he can.

For a fleeting moment, I consider making a dash for my tower. He never goes up there unless I'm behind the door that separates us and a droplet of my blood is flushing the water in my crystal goblet.

I think better of it when his head tilts to the side, as if he *knows.*

A shudder rakes through me at the predatory gesture—one I try to hide by lifting my chin, tossing sodden hair over my shoulder, and stalking off in the direction he's motioning.

I know when to pick my battles, and *this* one ...

It already has me beat.

I hate this place with its rolls of fabric stuffed into corners and mannequins crowded around in various stages of undress. I have no appreciation for fine things and exotic fabrics—no interest in parading around with my feathers fluffed like some of the men and women who attend the monthly Tribunal.

I behold my daily attire pegged on a wire strung between two walls, dripping water all over the ground.

That's all I need. Movability without the frills. Clothing that helps me blend in.

I sigh, towel-drying my hair, ass perched on a seat and jammed in the corner of the room like some inanimate object. Beside me stands a mannequin with similar features to a doll I used to have ... before I tossed it over my balustrade because its wide-open eyes kept staring.

Unseeing.

There was something satisfying about watching it shatter on the stone at the base of my tower.

The robe I'm swimming in slips off my bare shoulder, and I pull it back up, attention diving between the three-inch gap in the doorway again.

Rhordyn is in the next room, standing on the stage while Hovard's pretty assistant flutters around him in a swish of silky, black material, stretching the measuring tape along his arms, across his chest, down the inside of his leg ...

I glimpse those silvery tattoos that wind around his side —a fine scripture sketched across his skin, tapered around muscles like the shading on a painting. Words I don't recognize, understand, or even know how to pronounce.

I arch my neck, seeking a clearer view, cheeks heating. My gaze drifts up, only to catch on one quicksilver eye pinned to me through the gap like a perfectly shot arrow.

Sucking a sharp breath, I look away.

"Are we done here?" Rhordyn asks, tone so hard I flinch.

"Yes, Master," Dolcie blurts, her voice gentle as a summer breeze.

I envy her that.

"And you're after the black cashmere imported from the alps?"

"Yes," Rhordyn answers. "But it's a neutral ball, so Orlaith isn't bound to Ocruth colors. She's welcome to pick something different."

Frowning, I glance up as the door creaks open.

Dolcie's oval face pushes through, blue eyes stark against her frothy curls the color of soil. "Your turn," she says with a sweet smile that looks forced.

"Lovely."

I follow her through to the other room that's steeped in sunshine spilling through large, square windows, instantly struck by the robust, earthen scent of *him.*

It's a tight-lipped battle to maintain my composure.

Fiddling with the robe's belt knotted around my waist, I step onto the fitting platform, trying to ignore Rhordyn weaving buttons through their holes, chin pressed against his chest.

Hovard sweeps in like a blow of autumn leaves, his fiery hair standing up in all directions. He has the creamy complexion of someone from the East, though he boasts the black garb of a Western resident, plus a few add-ons like frills around his sleeves and the swarthy lace appliquéd over his waistcoat. Small spectacles sit halfway down his nose, their shape matching his beady eyes that flick over my form.

He flaps a hand in my direction, attention turning to the rolls of fabric stacked in the corner. "Robe. Off."

Rhordyn clears his throat and turns, staring out the window while finishing with his buttons, but making no move to leave the room.

Right.

I draw a shaky breath and loosen the bow around my middle, chewing my bottom lip. Silky fabric slithers down my shoulders, exposing the corset that's barely containing me.

I have no idea how I'm supposed to move in this thing—or breathe properly—but this ... *torturous* article of clothing that shows far too much of my too-tight skin is apparently fashionable.

Dolcie scowled the entire time she was stuffing me into the awful contraption, likely because it wasted half an hour of both our lives. And now here I am, standing on a platform, feeling like a tree without leaves to smudge its shape.

Hovard rests his hands atop his swollen belly, eyeing me the same way I assess a rock before I slick paint across it. "You've gotten slimmer through the waist, my dear. If you're not careful, you'll snap in two."

I open my mouth—

"Tut-tut! It wasn't a question." He flutters his hand about, retrieving a roll of lush, green fabric. It's held against me, swiftly replaced with one the color of my wisteria, his gaze hopping from my eyes, my damp hair, the exposed parts of my skin, finally landing on the necklace draped around my neck.

He taps the stone with the tip of a pencil previously caught behind his ear. "You will be wearing these, yes?"

My hand shields the round, inky gem and baby conch in the next heartbeat.

"Yes," Rhordyn says, spinning, and I meet the chilling intensity of his all-pervading stare.

I don't take this necklace off. Ever. Rhordyn gifted it to me when I first came to this castle, and I've worn it ever since.

Some of my earliest memories are from when I was so small that climbing Stony Stem felt like scaling a mountain, even with Baze or Cook holding my hand, easing me up each step, my necklace a comforting weight around my neck.

Though it felt heavy back then, this stone taught me to walk with a stronger stance. To keep my head up and *move*.

I'll be wearing it in the ground one day.

Rhordyn rests his back against the wall beside the window, looking very much at home with his feet crossed at the ankle. I almost roll my eyes when Dolcie bends over to retrieve some pins off the floor, peeking back to check if he's watching.

"Very well. We can work around it. Now, I like the green." Hovard pulls a long slice of fabric close to my eyes. "This tone compliments the shade of your hair. Or there's the rose gold; a gentler approach," he muses, replacing the sample. "More innocent, too."

How can he say that when my breasts are practically jumping out of this torture suit? I miss my chest wrap.

"Then there's the red, which would look *stunning*, but it's likely to draw ..." he tips his head from side to side, "*mature* attention."

He continues stuffing information in Rhordyn's direction

while holding different swatches near my face. As he speaks, Dolcie drapes a stiff, creamy fabric across my skin. Piece by piece, it's pinned against my body, forming a pattern that exhibits me in a way that leaves very little to the imagination.

The garment begins to take shape, and my stomach twists a little more with each panel of fabric she fits into place, my gaze dropping every few seconds to see just how much skin she's *not* hiding.

When she drops her pincushion, she again shoves her voluptuous curves in Rhordyn's direction, and I jump on the opportunity to maneuver some of the fabric so it's not so revealing.

She's quick to set it back the moment she stands up again.

"Can't you make the neckline a little higher?" I whisper, quiet enough that only she can hear.

"Oh, honey, no." She drops her voice low, stealing a glance at my hands wrung together. "There's nothing *endearing* about a woman who dresses like a little boy and constantly has dirt beneath her nails. That's no way to become a promised lady."

My cheeks heat. "Excuse me?"

She shrugs, tucks a twirl of hair behind her ear, and throws me a coy smile. "*Everyone* parades their breasts at fancy gatherings these days. If you don't, you'll have no hope in standing out amongst the masses, and you'll be stuck in this castle until you're an old crone." I grit my teeth as she threads another pin through the thick fabric. "I'm doing you a favor. Trust me."

I'm about to tell her to shove her *favor* up her ass, along with her pincushion, when Rhordyn's voice rents the air.

"Less cleavage."

Hovard's ramblings are severed mid-sentence, and my

gaze darts to Rhordyn's face, but he's not looking at me. He's looking at Dolcie, giving her cherry cheeks and bedroom eyes his full, undivided attention.

"Master?" she asks, tone light and innocent, hands still against my breasts that are rising with every sharp pull of breath.

He pushes away from the wall and strides forward, head tilted to the side. "Do you need me to say it clearer?"

Dolcie looks up at him through her lashes. "But I thought—"

"You thought *what?*" The last word snaps out of him, and Dolcie pales, her mouth falling open but failing to shape words.

"That you'd be p-pleased. That you'd want her to look appealing for any potential suitors."

He stares at her, unblinking, the tense moment lasting long enough that Dolcie withers. Beads of sweat collect on Hovard's temples, and his eyes dart between the two.

"It's fi—"

Rhordyn cuts me off. "Orlaith told you exactly what she wants, and you blatantly ignored her request. Unless you want to find yourself out of a job and lose your residence within this castle, I suggest you fix the pattern. Now."

Dolcie drops into a curtsey so fast you'd think her knees had given way. "Yes, Master. S-sorry, Master."

She gets back to work, rearranging the fabric across my bust with trembling hands, and I hiss when a sharp sting has me staggering back, shielding my left breast. "*Ouch!*"

"Out!"

Rhordyn's destructive tone causes a riot of movement, and Hovard ushers a pale-faced Dolcie through the exit—hand to her lips, pincushion discarded on the floor.

Rhordyn holds my gaze until the door snicks shut behind them both, and I'm acutely aware of his chest rising and falling to the same rhythm as my own. He makes a small clicking sound with his tongue before charging toward a table stacked with a jug and crystal glasses. He pours one half full, then peers at it, silent and still while my heart sits in my throat.

I know what this moment could grow into. Can feel the weight of potential pushing on my chest, stifling my breaths.

That inner voice, again, is screaming for me to run.

He clears his throat and spins, stalking toward me.

Perhaps I'm a fool ... but I'm a curious fool. And *this* has never been done in person. There's always a door separating us, slapping a mask over the act.

He stops only when we're sharing breath, eye to eye, on the verge of something *transcending.*

For the very first time, there is no door separating us. Nothing but thin air that's a blend of both our scents.

"May I?"

Please do.

I nod, refusing to blink as he pinches the edge of the mock-up dress, peeling it down like the corner of a book page.

Every inhale brings my breasts closer to his chill, every exhale pulls them away again, much like the internal tug-of-war I wage with myself daily.

Part of me wants to be closer, the rest of me knows I need to stay the hell away—that Rhordyn's an ocean that would plunge into my lungs and drown me if I fell into him.

He looks down, his icy trail of scrutiny landing on the freckle of pain on the swell of my breast that's acute enough to draw a bead of blood.

I should know.

My chin tips, nipples pebbling, flesh anticipating his touch so much it's almost uncomfortable.

His ragged exhale agitates my skin.

I blink, and the air shifts.

Suddenly his back is turned, and I'm listening to him stir the water ...

Looking down, I see nothing but a red prickle of damaged skin.

No blood. No smear.

Gone.

And I felt *nothing*. Not a single brush of contact. As if he did everything he could to make sure his touch didn't linger.

This heavy rock in my stomach feels a lot like disappointment.

He walks toward the door, not giving me a single look at his face. Is there pleasure in his eyes? Dissatisfaction?

Disgust?

Would it be so bad to let me see?

"I won't be needing your offering tonight."

My heart is thrown like a snowball, the swelling lump in my throat hard to draw a steady breath past.

Those words ...

They're acid to my bones.

He's stealing that sadistic thrill from my nightly ritual, replacing it with *this*—something equally refined, as if the door were still separating us as he took my offering.

He pauses with his hand wrapped around the handle. "Lilac."

I shake my head, glazed attention lifting to the back of his head. "What?"

"To match your eyes," he murmurs before tugging the

door open, and then he's gone.

My lids flutter closed, shuttering me away.

I was bleeding at the breakfast table this morning, and he certainly didn't demand I dip my leg in a bucket of water.

Is this some sort of *punishment?* His way of forcing me to break my routine? Because that's what it feels like.

He dealt his blow and left.

There's a soft knock, and I look up to see Hovard bowed around the doorframe, assessing the space with his marble eyes. "He's gone?"

"He is." I clear my throat, watching him inch back in like the ground is littered with hot coals. "And he liked the red."

Hovard pushes his glasses further down his nose and studies me over the rim of them. "Oh?"

I nod. "And I want the dress cut low in the back and more fitting around the hips."

His brow pinches, eyes going wide, cheeks sponged red. "But ... but Orlaith, my dear ... you wouldn't be able to wear your underbones. That would be considered *very* informal for such an occasion!"

"That's the point," I bite, unpinning the rest of Dolcie's monstrosity from my frame.

If I must attend this ball, I refuse to be stuffed into something impossible to breathe in.

"So long as the neckline sits around my throat, I'm giving you artistic license, Hovard. You've always said you'd love to dress me like a doll. Well ... have at it."

He stares at me for a long moment before he bursts into a foray of movement and chatter and expressive hand gestures that make me smile.

Rhordyn wants to punish me? Well.

Two can play that game.

CHAPTER 8

ORLAITH

The sun is sinking, turning ribbons of cloud a soft shade of violet.

Standing amongst the ever-changing masterpiece of color and light, I watch Rhordyn stalk toward the labyrinth of trees that sweep around the castle grounds ...

My Safety Line.

He reaches the far corner where forest meets the plunging cliff and begins his survey of the perimeter—a walk that will trace my Safety Line until he disappears into the forest. Goes places I'll hopefully *never* go.

Beyond those trees, bad things happen.

Wide, unseeing eyes.

The smell of burning death.

Beasts that tore into—

I clear my throat, hating him for hacking such a huge hole in my routine. Now I'm up here in knots, chewing on excess time, and I doubt he gives a shit.

He got what he wanted.

Hearing a sharp squeak, I glance through the balcony doors to my knapsack hooked on the corner of my ornate bed frame. After my afternoon got eaten up by Hovard, I never made it down to see Shay ... meaning I've still got a mouse in my bag.

Poor thing.

I peer back over the balustrade, watch Rhordyn trail the treeline, and my brows tuck into a frown.

Despite my bubbling well of curiosity, I've always stayed up here while he makes his evening rounds—figured the closed door between us extended to *this* part of the routine, too.

But today is no regular day.

He screwed up my schedule, threatened me, demanded I attend a *ball,* and took away my evening thrill. If he can't respect my boundaries, why am I respecting his?

I draw a deep breath, scan the brassy rays stretching across the fluffy forest, and decide it's the *perfect* time to visit my friend Shay. The fact that I'm exploiting the task to garner an up-close view of Rhordyn's perimeter sweep should be entirely discounted.

I pull on a sweater, repack my bag, and dash out the door, taking the steps of Stony Stem two at a time until I reach the base, exiting into the castle's fifth floor corridor.

When I enter The Tangle, I take a shortcut that spits me out just behind Rhordyn, and the rich scent of blooming night lilies has me breathing deeply, capturing the spicy perfume that always makes the back of my throat tingle.

I dart across the small stretch of grass, merging with a pool of shadow that fringes Sprouts—the greenhouse. Taking advantage of a manicured garden shrub, I use it as a shield while peeking around the corner of the cold, glassy building I love so much.

Watching.

His shoulders are rigid, barely shifting with each smooth step he assaults the ground with.

There's nothing strange about his actions. He's simply walking the same trail he always does, brushing a hand across the odd tree trunk here and there.

Parting from my line of sight, he lures me to leave the safety of my perfect hiding spot. I stick to slabs of shadow as I trail him, silent as a leaf being pushed along by the chilled evening wind.

The stars are beginning to wink, the moon a crescent barely holding much light by the time Rhordyn reaches the path that cuts into the forest—one framed with dense, twisting vines petrified by a long life.

It almost looks like a tunnel, dusted with little white flowers that smell sweet and fresh.

He pauses at the entrance.

Something about the way he's holding himself has me edging behind the stump of an ancient tree clothed in moss, dropping low and pressing flat against the ground. Cool grass cushions my cheek as I ease forward just enough to glimpse his profile.

It may be the swiftly fading light, but I swear I see him whisper to the flowers right before he disappears into the forest.

I sigh, roll onto my back, and look to the stars prickling the darkening canvas, drumming my fingers on the ground.

The hairs on my right arm lift ...

I let my head fall to the side and scan the inky forest depths.

Shay is harder to see at this time of day, and it's not like he makes it easy for me by leaping around and waving a hand. But I can sense him—can feel the air around me shift as if it's cleaving a path for my friend to move through.

I push to a stand and edge toward a bush of night lilies. The white dust on the tips of their inky petals shimmers brighter by the second, their luster brought to life by the fading light.

Courtesy of these flowers, some of my paintings glow in the dark; like the stars and the moon on my bedroom door.

Barely two inches from the black line of rocks I've planted to mark my Safety Line, I kneel, foraging through my bag for the jar with holes in the lid. I untwist the top and stuff my hand inside, pinching the mouse's stringy tail before gently easing him out.

He wrestles the air, squeaks sharpening, and I catch movement in my peripheral—a lanky, wraith-like creature flitting between elongated pockets of gloom, dressed in a smoky sheath that seems to gorge on the light.

My smile grows.

I can feel his eyes on me, akin to a paintbrush dipped in oil that flits across my skin.

He reaches a particularly thick piece of shade, its sharp edges blurring as the nest of night lilies brightens, releasing more of their spicy scent and spilling a soft glow that gives my gaze something to cling to.

There, he hovers—no more than two long steps away.

I lift the mouse higher, bringing him eye level.

Whiskers twitching, the rodent arches his back and reaches for my nose, like he thinks I'm going to save him.

I cock my head to the side and watch him struggle. Watch him stretch and stretch until he's turned himself into a fluffy pendulum; one that counts down his final heartbeats.

I usually just fling them over the line, but—

I'm not seeing any effort to overcome your fears.

I sigh, failing to tame the heavy roll of my heart.

Dammit, Rhordyn.

Before I can think it through, I grit my teeth and shove my hand across the line of rocks, breath held, body stilled, doing everything in my power not to crumble into a ball and release a sawtooth scream.

I should probably be afraid of the messy shadow inching forward, crouched low and making that clicking sound in the back of his throat ...

I'm not.

My fear is a wild thing pointed in other directions.

I last four seconds before I drop the mouse and snatch my hand back over the line.

Shay pounces in a snap of smoky ribbons and skeletal fingers. There's a final, tortured squeak before his blackness begins to ebb, and wet, suckling sounds ensue.

I shake my hand, stretch my fingers, inspect my skin ... half-expecting it to bubble and split. Part of me *wants* it to—wants the world beyond my Safety Line to be so poisonous the only option is to stay right here forever.

Safe.

I guess I can't exactly claim this as a victory when I'm hoping for such things.

Shay rears back, and all that's left of the mouse is fluffy skin sucked close to a small, angular skeleton. I once used a stick to nudge a corpse back over the line so I could inspect the thing, and it was hard like a pebble.

My friend and I watch each other while the moon owl hoots his eerie wake-up call, and I can feel the hum of Shay's appreciation.

Despite the fact that he can probably hunt his own food, I

think he enjoys the fat little gifts I provide. Or perhaps he just enjoys the company while he dines.

Something I can appreciate.

In an unceremonious spurt of movement, he darts off through the darkening forest, leaving a chill that nettles my skin.

I shiver, peering at the path that swallowed Rhordyn whole ...

He could be down there all night.

For not the first time, I wonder where it leads. A curious seed I refuse to plant or water or feed light into.

My world is right here, on *this* side of the stones. Out there belongs to the bones of my broken past and beasts that stalk my nightmares.

Pushing to my feet, I brush off my pants and make for the castle, certain dozens of eyes are pinned to my retreating form.

This stairwell twists deep into the ground, the way lit with torches held by rusty metallic sconces. The flames look like dancing blooms, and the further I descend, the more they hiss; the thicker the air becomes with steam that curls the loose veil of my hair.

Reaching the bottom step, the stairwell yawns into a vast cavern ...

I could wash in my room, but I much prefer it down here in Puddles—the communal bathing chambers.

Sconces cast the wet stone in a gilded glow and illuminate mineral fangs that hang from the ceiling, reaching for a dozen steaming springs, some with no more than a thin vein of rock casting them apart from their neighboring pool.

Each is filled almost to the rim with water that looks like black ink in the low light, a rich contrast to the haze that whorls off them in ghostly wisps.

The springs are big enough to house over ten people, but are always empty at this time, a luxury that allows me to strip.

My pants and panties go first, then my muddy, paint-stained blouse, before I get to work unbinding my breasts. Every untwist of the stretchy bandage allows me to breathe a little deeper, but even as I let the material flutter to the ground, my skin still feels too tight.

Always.

Stretching my arms this way and that, I tiptoe toward my favorite spring at the far end—the one pressed against the wall. I edge down toothy steps, letting the water scald my bristling skin. After a few seconds, the burn yields to a restful numb, and I dip further ... further ... until the floor gives way to the endless deep.

I'm not sure how far it goes, or if it even has a bottom. But the deeper you dive, the hotter the water, as if it spawns from the belly of the earth.

Hair dragging behind me, I tread toward the far side.

This spring doesn't have the most comfortable sitting spots, but *this spring ...*

It's my guilty pleasure.

Reaching the wall, I ply my fingers between a crack and grip hold, peering down to where years of erosion have worn a hole through the rock. A hole that allows the faintest flow of water to push and pull from whatever's on the other side, like it's sharing breath with a separate spring not caught inside the chamber of Puddles.

I dove deep and explored the breach once—felt its jagged edges, as if someone kicked it into existence. I tried to see what's on the other side, but it's dark down there. Gloomy.

Still gripping the rock, I rest my forehead against the wall and close my eyes.

A rich, leathery musk perfumes the air, making me moan. I empty my lungs before drawing them full, holding onto the ambrosial breath as if it alone could sustain me for eternity.

Feed my hungry heart.

The reason I love this spring so much—the reason I bathe here rather than relying on the convenience of the tub in my tower—is because sometimes ...

Sometimes the water smells like *him*.

CHAPTER 9

KAI

The ocean here is ice cold and always still, as though the wind is afraid to ruffle its surface.

Dead End. That's what I've heard some topsiders call this part of The Shoaling Seas. But to me, it's not a dead stillness.

It's a *waiting* stillness.

I skirt around the edges of a turquoise iceberg so big it's hard to see where it starts. Where it ends.

Bodies are trapped within, locked in a catatonic eternity —creatures who did not get the chance to decompose before the ice caught them.

Hundreds of these bobbing graveyards litter this part of the ocean, immortalizing a great deal of things I'd rather forget.

I push on, hands speared at my sides, churning my tail in a slow, rhythmic dance.

I'm not here to dwell on the past. I'm here because my hoarding drako decided there's a corner of our trove that could do with a little extra sparkle.

'Almost there. Set Zykanth free.'

He's pushing at my skin from within, making it itch, threatening to shred it apart. My jaw aches, as if it's about to pop from its hinges—

'Stop it. You're too big. She'll see.'

'Big ... but fast. Tail bigger than yours.'

I roll my eyes and power on, gritting my teeth. There is no reasoning with him when we're close to everything we both treasure.

The ocean bed drops away in a sudden cliff that always reminds me of my own insignificance. Here, the water is deep and black like a starless night, and feels just as empty.

No fish pock the water, and the sharks are far too cunning. The dolphins and the whales journey well out of their way to migrate around the trench.

Only the truly desperate brave this part of the ocean.

The desperate and the *stupid.*

Every cautious swish of my tail makes my chest tighten as I plot a path between the bergs, flinching each time two collide and mimic the crack of lightning. I pause periodically to ensure I'm not being followed.

That something isn't reaching from below to snatch me.

I dart skyward, slow when I near the glassy surface, and gently break through. The breath I release from the gills scored behind my ears is steady.

Controlled.

Which is a lot more than I can say about *him.*

'Get the rock. Get the rock!'

'Calm. Down.'

My eyes feast on the masterpiece before me—the small island caught in a shard of morning sunlight cutting through the clouds. All the colors of the rainbow ricochet off magnificent crystal spires that pierce the sky, bathing the island in a glimmering halo of light.

A geyser protruding from the center leaks a river the color of blood that cuts a skewed path into the sea, painting some of the water pink and tainting the air with the smell of sulfur.

I'm hit with a dose of serenity, remembering how I used to bathe in that warm, nutrient-rich water. It always made my scales gleam—

'Get the rock!'

I sigh.

'You're a pain in the ass sometimes.'

My regard darts to the waveless beach and the jagged band of shore littered with smaller pieces of crystal ... along with the bones of creatures *she* decided to spit out closer to the surface after she'd finished gnawing on them.

I survey the crystals from afar, studying their shape and the way they catch on the sun, trying to decide which one shines the *brightest.* Though my eyesight is good, it doesn't beat the ability to touch the marvelous, the fragile, the unique ...

The *treasured.*

It doesn't allow me to hold those gems to the sun and twist them this way and that to see their facets come to life.

'Nearer.'

'Okay. Just ... keep your shit together.'

I slide through the water slower than a setting moon, then pause, gaze flicking, senses sharpening.

'Don't stop.'

'Choke on a clam,' I growl, and Zykanth finally shuts up.

I resume my advance in peace, though he continues to bounce around, whipping against the walls of my insides.

The closer I get to the scintillating shoreline, the more his excitement infects me.

Orlaith likes round rocks, but the ocean isn't wild enough in this part of the world to polish anything smooth. However

... I think she might appreciate a crystal that catches the sun and spits it out in all the colors of the rainbow.

What she painted for me was truly special. She managed to capture the essence of this island without sighting it or understanding its significance. Or its heartbreaking history.

Though the baby conch was nice, it didn't show her my full gratitude.

Resolve hardens my features.

One for our trove, another for her.

Zykanth hums his agreement, and I inch forward. My hands bunch, release, bunch, release. Every frill tests the water for the slightest shift in flow. I draw a breath, my hand stretched out as though I'm much closer than I really am ...

A chill slithers down my spine, stilling the swish of my tail and the blood in my veins, blasting apart my impulse.

'She's watching.'

'Get it!'

'No.' I begin a slow, steady retreat. 'Today is not the day.'

My skin itches, scales threatening to pierce through. He tries to shove me forward from within, rattling the cage of my ribs, and my entire body shudders from the impact.

I snarl. 'You want to end up dead on that beach?'

He doesn't have to answer for me to know he thinks it's worth the risk.

I spin and bolt through the open ocean so fast I barely have a chance to draw another breath before I'm retracing my path through the icebergs, his chaotic roars pulsing through the water.

It's not until I'm free from the trench that I no longer feel as though I'm being followed. Still, I don't dare loosen my hold on my thrashing beast. Probably won't until I can find something else to distract him with.

It never used to be like this.

These waters were once safe and peaceful.

Teeming.

Now, they have a mind of their own, and they're angry, vicious ...

Deadly.

Standing guard over the ruins of a once-thriving relic—a job that used to belong to *us.*

I should be used to the taste of failure by now.

I'm not.

CHAPTER 10

ORLAITH

A blade of sun strikes my face, rousing me, and I unleash a raspy groan. Though I shield my eyes with a limp hand, I steal a moment to bathe in the soothing luster before rolling in the direction of my bedside table.

Something hard thuds to the ground, and I frown, cracking an eye open as I peer over the edge.

My wooden sword lies nestled amongst bits of discarded clothing.

"Shit."

I'm late.

Groaning, I tumble out of bed in an ungraceful heap, my tender brain bouncing around inside my skull.

My stomach twists, bile threatening to erupt up my throat.

Eyes slitted, I peel the rug, shift the stone with trembling hands, and dig into my hidden compartment. I twist the lid off the first jar my fingers collide with, retrieving three nodes and jamming two under my chalky tongue before flopping backward.

The cool stone eases my sins while I gather the will to move again.

Crawling to my refreshment table, I pull myself up and

pour a glass of water, tossing it back before gripping the vanity and braving the mirror for the first time in a very long while.

Another groan cracks out of me.

I pinch my pallid cheeks, lick my chapped lips. My braid is matted, eyes flat and gray rather than the usual lilac that sometimes lures me strange looks, the skin beneath them dark ...

Hell. I look like hell. Probably because I dosed up before I went to bed, then twice again when I woke throughout the night, hoping to avoid another nightmare.

Stupid, considering I'm on the last of my caspun, but I wasn't thinking about that at the time. I was too preoccupied with my determination to escape for a bit.

I stuff the third node beneath my tongue for good, counteractive measure. I've never taken three before, but if I go to training looking like *this?* Well. Baze will make me eat stone.

I'm dressed, watered, and lugging my sword behind me like an anchor when the drugs kick in. By the time I'm pushing open the doors of the large, circular hall with a glass roof and absolutely no purpose other than my daily torture sessions, my heart feels like it's shooting little bolts of lightning all through my veins.

I sway into the room, a cocksure grin splitting my face. Spotting Baze standing by the window, I fling my sword into the air and swipe it up. "Watch out, Baze. I'm feeling it. You won't be riding *my* ass today ... it'll be the other way around."

I toss the weapon again just as Baze turns.

That's not Baze ...

The sword clatters to the ground, making me flinch.

"Is that so?" Rhordyn snips, stalking forward, his own wooden sword swinging from his hand.

"Fuck."

I slide back a step, trying to swallow my heart that somehow managed to worm its way up my throat, and take a second to peer around the room.

We're alone.

Double fuck.

"Where's Baze?" I squeeze out, crouching to retrieve my sword while Rhordyn circles me with long, prowling strides.

"Probably using the spare time to ride someone else's ass," he burrs, and I leer at the roof. "Don't roll your eyes at me, Orlaith."

He sure knows how to set a tone.

I peek at the door, contemplating a quick dash to freedom. I'm more jacked than I've ever been. If I flap my arms fast enough, I could probably flutter out of here like a mail sprite.

I draw a deep breath, trying to calm the erratic sledge of my heart ...

Our gazes collide like rocks smashing together, and his nostrils flare, eyes narrowing. "You'd make it halfway to the door if you're lucky. But by all means," he says, gesturing toward the exit with a wave of his hand, "give it a shot."

My head kicks back as if I've been slapped.

Am I that transparent?

"Yes."

The word punches down my throat and lands a weight in my stomach. Apparently my opiate-smeared brain didn't realize I asked that question aloud.

"How long have you known?"

"About your ... training camp?"

There's an edge to his voice that wasn't there before.

Balancing on it feels dangerous. *Deadly* even.

"Yes." I pivot slowly, sword perched at the ready. "And just so you know, Baze said you wouldn't like me learning to fight. I was the one who begged him to let me do it."

Rhordyn's eyebrow pops up, but I keep talking. Keep attempting to climb out of this deep, gloomy hole I dug for Baze and me.

"He was just following my orders. I swear."

Ish. I swear-*ish.* There was certainly no begging involved, but the last thing I want is to drag Baze under. Only one of us needs to take the fall, and I'd rather it be me.

"Interesting tactic ..." Rhordyn muses. "Though not nearly as interesting as the fact that it worked."

What?

My overstimulated mind churns, trying to unscramble his riddled words. "I ... I don't get it. You're not angry?"

"I am, but not for the reasons you might expect. And you can save the martyr bullshit." He crosses through a slice of light, the morning sun glinting off his eyes as if they're hard, polished surfaces. "The training was never your idea. It was *mine.*"

My mouth pops open.

Baze, the bastard, is going to die.

Rhordyn launches, his wooden blade flaying the air so fast it sings.

I block his strike with the swift twist of my upper body and a delicate flick of my wrist, but the hit is *hard*—clanging through the air.

Through *me.*

Somehow, I resist the urge to clamp my hands over my ears and scream.

Perhaps the Petrified Pine is finally growing on me.

Face to face, weapons locked, we hold our ground. From

my vantage point, I can see beneath the weave of Rhordyn's hair to brows kicked high on his forehead.

"Sharp refle—"

I shift, ducking and wheeling around until my chest is flush with his back, the sharp part of my sword kissing his throat with dispassionate vigor. "Apparently I'm a natural," I spit, not wanting to hand him credit for something he barely lifted a finger for.

"You're *cocky,*" he answers in a razor voice that makes me picture an arrow being notched. "And high functioning."

What?

He spins out of my hold like smoke on the wind.

I'm still swallowing my shock, blinking at the feline smile pretending to soften his features, when he *unloads.*

In three swift strikes, he has me disarmed and stretched on the ground, wrists pinned to the stone with one powerful hand, my sword lying discarded somewhere behind me.

I gasp as the sharp edge of his weapon comes to rest across my throat.

Though his eyes are half-hidden behind the flop of his hair, I still feel the chill of his invasive gaze, his breath a frost on my face.

"What the fu—"

"*Pathetic,*" he growls, sword digging in. "Perhaps I finally understand."

My heart flips a beat.

"Understand *what?*"

"Why you cower from the world like it has you beat." He dips down until his lips are brushing my ear, then whispers, "Perhaps you did die that day, after all."

How dare he.

"*Get off,*" I hiss, thrusting my hips.

His own pull back, and he makes this low, vexing sound.

A *disgusted* sound.

"Or," he spits, tightening his grip on my wrists, head canting to the side while he guts me with his narrowed eyes, "perhaps I'm wrong. Perhaps you're fighting like a corpse because you're high as a *fucking* kite right now."

Never has a sentence landed such a pulse-scattering blow.

I can't breathe. Can't speak. So instead, I slam my knee toward his junk.

If he's focused on the fact that his balls feel like they're going to explode, perhaps his brain will empty.

He buckles the moment I make impact, something between a groan and a laugh grating out of him. "Cheap"—he tips heavily to the side—"*shot.*"

I kick off the ground and slide backward, snatching my sword before I leap up. "It was."

It was also an *impulsive* shot. One I blame on the fact that I am, well ... high as a fucking kite.

"Need a hand up?" I ask, watching him unravel in slow, ungraceful increments.

"*No,*" he grinds out, pushing to a crouch, drawing a few deep breaths before he rocks onto his heels and stands. He clears his throat and advances, hobbling only half as much as I'd expected him to, the wide breadth of his shoulders swaying with his advance. "But I *do* require you to hand over your stash."

My heart stills. The blood in my fucking *veins* stills.

He can't possibly know about that.

Somehow, I keep my features smooth, voice steady. "I have no stash."

He makes a clicking sound with his tongue and prowls closer. "Such a pretty lie. Under the carpet?" He flicks his sword into the air, then snatches it and points the tip at my face. "In that little hole you think is so well hidden?"

Motherfucker.

"Screw you."

He releases a dark, humorless laugh that boils my blood. "No, Orlaith. The sentiment points in the *opposite* direction."

Something inside me goes deadly still.

He flashes a cruel, unmerciful grin. "But you live under *my* roof, and you will hand over the Exothryl."

No.

I need it to bring me back from the dead every morning. To remind my body how to function after the anesthetizing balm I glug down night after night to ease my terrors into submission.

It's a delicate balance, and he's snatching the pin that holds it all together, assuming he knows what's best for me.

He doesn't.

I launch, snarling, slicing through the air, letting all my rage and pain and pent-up hatred bubble to the surface as I swing and swing and *swing*—immune to the sound and the weight of this sword I hate so much.

My vision narrows on his wide, quicksilver eyes ...

In my mind, they're black.

They're the eyes of those feral, circling creatures who choke my subconscious, because he's restoring their power to ruin me.

He dances back, smooth and dextral, like he's reading every move before I decide to make it.

I swing, he shifts.

I swing, he shifts.

My sword is an extension of my body, lashing at the man who's standing between me and the pretty lie I paint over the jagged surface of my heart. And I don't stop. Don't relent.

But neither does he.

He's just as hard, just as unbreakable as he always is, while my flesh yields for him every single day.

I'm not seeing any effort to overcome your fears, and my string of patience is thinning. Fast.

Something inside me *snaps.*

A haunting sort of calm laces through my veins and sets like mortar, lining my insides with that concrete grace he wears so well.

I *blur.*

Leaping forward, I drag the tip of my sword through his top. The material splits like a severed wound, and I slam to a stop, sobering, the weapon slipping from my hand.

My mouth falls open ... *nothing comes out.*

I've wounded him.

I stagger forward, splayed hands colliding with his warring chest, frantically peeling fabric back to inspect the damage.

There is none.

No cut exposing his insides ...

No blood.

Glancing up, I become hooked on his chilling stare, almost buckling under the weight of it.

His heart is a hammer against my palm, his beat slow.

Too slow.

Whipping my hands away, I stumble back.

He lifts a brow, drops his gaze to the bare skin exposed from my brutal strike, and grunts. Crushing the tattered material in his fist, he snaps his arm down, ripping the shirt right off his back and tossing it aside.

I stare at him, unable to look away from the smooth slabs of muscle he's made of—like every piece is a perfectly crafted stone. Stacked together, they form a work of *art.*

He reminds me of my wall in Whispers, but instead of mortar holding him together, there are *words.* Delicate words I don't recognize, the script stained silver like the ocean goes when the sky is crammed full of clouds. Lines yield and interact with the phrases, linking them, so if I were to transfer his body art to a sheet of parchment, every detail would be connected in some way.

"Your tattoos," I rasp, hand hovering in the space between us.

An illuminated pulse is throbbing through the markings, as if they have their own entity.

Their own *soul.*

It's a slow, sludgy beat I find myself timing my breaths to match ...

Thud-ud.

Thud-ud.

Thud-ud.

A wintry perusal scores across my face, luring me to seek the source.

My hand drops.

In those stony eyes I see more than just the hard man who stalks these halls and rules with a rigid regard.

I see a predator. I see my own morose oblivion.

He strikes.

If I thought my movements were quick, I was kidding myself. He's *lightning*—sharp and sporadic.

Impulsive.

There is no rhythm to his crippling lines. They're all power and destruction, meant to maim and disable and *kill.*

I swerve the advancing storm of his body, dodging blow after blow, retreating from wild, reflective eyes I don't recognize. Steered further and further from my sword lying discarded on the ground.

My back collides with stone, and he's *on* me, his blade a cold line across my throat, our shared breath intoxicating in its own malignant way.

My chest rises and falls in erratic bursts, mind racing. But though he has me caged between him and the wall with a death strike at my throat, something inside me has my chin lifting ...

His upper lip curls back, exposing teeth I picture ripping into my neck.

My gaze snags on them and struggles to unstick, until he growls low, weakening my knees, threatening to leave me hanging on the line of his sword.

"That was—" my tongue darts out, tasting the icy air as I flounder. *"You're ..."*

Something flashes in his eyes, reminding me of a thunderstorm rolling off the ocean.

The space between us shrinks. "I'm what, Orlaith?"

Dangerous.

There's a cough, and my eyes chase the sound, though I can still feel the chilling brand of Rhordyn's stare tacking me in place.

"What?" he snaps.

Baze, standing by the entry with his hands dug into his pockets, seems entirely unfazed by the fact that Rhordyn has me pinned against the wall with a killing blow at my throat. In truth, he looks far more amused with the glare I'm practically flaying him with.

Not the response I'm looking for.

Rhordyn's been orchestrating my training for the past five years, and Baze led me to believe it was our little secret. The bastard.

He doesn't even have the decency to look sorry about it.

"You wanted to be notified when the High Mistress crossed the border," Baze states, chocolate eyes detangling from my threatening stare.

Rhordyn releases an almost indiscernible sigh.

He pulls back, tossing Baze the sword while looking me up and down. "You finish up with *this,*" he says, jerking his chin at me before retrieving his shredded top off the ground.

"But I agreed to this under false pretenses!" I protest, eyes darting from one to the other. "I *quit.*"

Rhordyn stops cold.

A few long seconds pass, feeling like a small eternity. He finally unravels, shirt held in his white-knuckled fist as he looks my way. "Then your training will be replaced by daily trips to nearby villages. Escorted by *me.*"

Not a single cell in my body escapes the attack of his words. Even my bones want to crumble from the blow.

I find myself mouthing the word *no* ... unable to draw enough breath to say it.

Rhordyn's eyes harden. "Training it is, then. I'll be back tomorrow night."

My heart drops.

Tomorrow night ...

He's reneging on a blood-letting. Possibly two. Something he's *never* done before.

"But ... but don't you need me?"

"No," he growls. "I need you to sort your shit out."

Asshole.

"Ride her ass, Baze. Keep going until you can see the color in her eyes again."

"I hate you," I manage to whisper, watching him stalk toward the wide-open doors.

He grinds to a halt the moment the words slip off my tongue.

A small, humorless smile curls his lips into something almost painful to witness—a wicked sharpness that reminds me I don't know this male despite all the years we've lived under the same roof.

All the droplets of myself I've shared with him.

"Oh, precious," he says, surveying down, then back up the lines of my body still pinned to the wall by his phantom touch. "You don't even know the meaning of the word."

And then he's gone.

CHAPTER 11

ORLAITH

I hold a lungful of floral air, attempting to soothe myself from the inside while I ease the greenhouse door shut. A bunch of blooms are caught in my fist, boasting vibrant petals of every color but the one that depicts my current mood.

Blue.

Not the crisp, clear blue the ocean goes when it's not being stirred by wild weather, but the color of the bruised sky right before the last bit of light is pulled from it.

I twist off the lid on an empty jar and ease my fingers open, exposing the stems of my fresh haul and all the raw, weepy blisters vandalizing my palm.

That's what hauling fifty-six rocks across The Plank will do—make you look diseased.

The old tree that fell across the stagnant pond at the bottom of the estate twelve years ago used to be harmless enough ... until Baze started using it for training and corporal punishment. There are piles of rocks at each end, all bigger than my head, and if I lose my footing while ferrying them to the other side? Well, then comes a plunge in the selkie-infested pond.

I should have just faked a fall the moment blisters started

forming and risked a mad dash to the edge, but I was too busy nursing the chip on my shoulder.

That chip has only grown since I climbed Stony Stem and realized my entire stash was cleared out. Now I have to re-collect all thirty-four ingredients to make a fresh batch of Exothryl—most of which are currently out of season.

I'm pissed.

Tomorrow, when I wake feeling like my head's been crushed between two boulders, I'm going to be even more pissed. Something I'm certain Rhordyn considered before he deserted the scene of his crime, took off for a couple of days, and left me to salvage the scraps of my composure.

I huff out a sigh, pushing the flowers into the jar more forcefully than necessary, causing a few stems to snap.

A gardener walks by dragging a clipping sack, tipping his hat as I bag my hoard. I grunt a greeting in return, then stop and yell, *"Wait!"*

I swear I hear him groan.

He undoes the drawstring on his sack as I approach, baring the contents, stepping back and brushing off his jacket while I drop to my knees and sort through his stash of boxwood clippings.

"Gail, is it?"

The young man tips his hat again. "Yes, ma'am."

I come across some loose holly berries rolling around the bottom and click my tongue. Folding them amongst a piece of cheesecloth, I push to my feet and tuck the parcel in my bag. "You haven't snipped the heads off any bluebells have you?"

I don't intend for the question to come out so accusatory, but I can tell I've toed that line by the way he pales. "N-n-no, ma'am. I wouldn't dare! I'm just an apprentice hedge trimmer."

"Well, what about the other gardeners who are always buzzing around"—I wave a hand at the perfectly curated garden—"*snipping* things?"

If I had it my way, the entire place would be overgrown. Wild and unruly and sprinkled with flowers.

"I, ahh, I can't speak for the others, but I think it's fair to assume everyone knows better," he says, pulling the drawstring tight.

He's probably referring to these random bag checks I perform weekly to ensure nothing valuable has been beheaded. He'd do the same if he'd raised most of the garden from seeds.

He hitches the sack over his shoulder and slides back a step, tipping his hat for a third time. "If we're all done here, I have lots of work to do in preparation for the ball ..."

I sigh.

That damn *ball.* It's haunting me. And my plants.

"Just ... don't over prune."

"Wouldn't dare." He scurries off while I massage my temples.

Scanning the grounds, I drag my feet toward the eastern castle wall that's lined with nesting shrubs, hoping to find some bluebells that escaped the frost. The bulbs in Sprouts only yielded a single blooming bounty. The small amount of paint I derived from it has since been used, the stems dried and powdered and added to my confiscated stash of Exothryl.

Yes, it's one of the many ingredients I now need to recollect. Just salt to the wound. But more importantly, without blue paint I can't finish the stone I chipped from the wall in

Whispers. The thought alone is enough to make my head hurt.

My foot hooks on a rogue rock poking out of the ground, and I fly forward, landing face first in the grass and uncomfortably close to a pile of horse manure.

Groaning, I move to push myself upright when my eye catches on something tucked behind the shrubbery, glinting in a ray of sunlight.

I crawl forward and part the branches to find a small, circular window close to the ground, the glass so filthy it's impossible to see through. I spit on my sleeve, polish the surface, then press my nose against the pane and peer in.

Huh.

The interior, dimly lit by shafts of afternoon light, is packed full of large pieces of furniture covered in ghostly sheets.

I've never seen this space before, and that's rare. I've explored most rooms in Castle Noir aside from Rhordyn's den, that locked door at the base of Stony Stem, and whatever's in The Keep. The entryway to this room must be very well disguised, and that makes it even *more* intriguing.

My never-ending well of curiosity is frothing.

I reach back and pry the stone I just tripped on from the soil, biting my tongue as I prepare to toss it through the window pane—

"Laith."

I squeal, almost leaping off the ground.

Spinning, I narrow my eyes on Baze and drop the stone like it's made of fire, hand pressed to my bludgeoning heart. "What the *hell* are you doing here? You're the last person I want to see right now!" My brows crunch together. "Did you see me trip?"

"Yes," he says, arms crossed, wearing a cocky half smile. "And I was rooting for the pile of shit."

Of course he was.

"And I'm here because it's my job to keep an eye on you." He drops to a crouch, trying to steal a peek through the window. "What are you doing?"

I veer to the side, blocking his view while fiddling with the end of my braid. "You, like many others in this castle, take your job far too seriously. Maybe you should take the day off. Go find a maid to ... I don't know ... do things with. I'm still mad at you for lying to me for the past five years, so I'd appreciate the peace."

His brow lifts and he ticks off his fingers. "One, I've apologized for using a blatant lie to motivate you into learning self-defense. And two, in my *very* extensive Orlaith experience, this sort of reaction usually means you're up to no good."

Well, he's not wrong.

He gestures for me to move, pushing a stake right through my curious heart. I roll my eyes and shuffle aside, only because I can't possibly sit here all day guarding my find.

He parts the shrub and peers through the window. "Looks uninteresting."

"Are you *kidding* me?" I shove him out of the way and flatten my nose against the glass. "It looks the *opposite* of uninteresting!"

"It's just a dusty storage room," he says, tone bland.

"And in my very extensive *Baze* experience, you only speak like this when you're trying to hide something." I throw him a side-eye. "Is this what the locked door leads to? The one at the bottom of Stony Stem?"

His lips thin and he rocks to a stand. "You're much too observant for your own good."

"*Is it?*"

He sighs, brushing off his tunic with a few brisk strokes. "It's not where it leads to, no."

"So ... you know where the door leads." I scrunch my nose and turn back to the ... well, who the hell knows what. "Interesting."

A stretch of silence ensues that drags just a little too long, and I turn, seeing him halfway across the field. "*Where are you going?*"

I leap to my feet and dash after him.

"Away!" he yells over his shoulder. "Those questions have spikes, Orlaith. Spikes that will make you *bleed.*"

"I bleed every damn day," I say on a loose breath, jogging at his side to keep up with his long, agile strides. "And I can handle the answers. I'll be twenty-one in four weeks."

"Exactly!" he snarls, spinning so fast I slam into his chest and stumble back, barely managing to catch myself. "You're still a child. A *sheltered* child who never leaves the grounds."

My blood chills.

The words create wounds far deeper than the ones on my hands, and from the softening of his earthen eyes, I'd guess he knows it, too.

He sighs, glancing up. "Come on, it's getting late. The krah will start shrieking soon. And shitting everywhere. You know how much I hate those things."

Frowning, I look toward the darkening sky.

It's said that if a krah shits on you, your days are numbered—your death-date staked in the soil.

Baze runs for cover whenever he hears them flocking across the sky. I'm more concerned that I'm soon to close my lids on my first full day without pricking my skin. Dripping into a goblet.

Giving myself to *him.*

To me, that's far more damning than a smattering of poo.

I thought Rhordyn needed me ...

Now, I'm not so sure.

CHAPTER 12
RHORDYN

Fog curls around my ankles, collecting at the base of ancient trees, the fringing forest a clash of jeweled tones and deep pockets of shade. The clearing is large enough to offer a peek of plum-colored clouds slashed across the sky.

Krah glide through the bruised murk, squawking their wake-up call as I plunge my dagger deep into the boar's stomach. The spill of thick blood coats my hands and steams the icy air, and I drag the blade down, carving a grisly seam, stabbing the weapon into the felled log I'm using as a table.

The atmosphere is smoky from the blazing campfire centered within a noose of charred rocks, bridled with a makeshift spit I built using a few thick branches.

A gentle breeze whistles through the trees, bringing forth more hints of that musky, feral odor that makes my hackles rise.

But there's something else, too.

I pause, elbow deep in gore, smelling the air ... picking up on a fresh array of *other* scents; one masculine, one feminine, one new and sweet and—

"Fuck."

I hadn't counted on anyone being out this late. Not all the way up here.

This clearing is a thoroughfare—the moss, the grass, the trees all marked with a mottling of scents. It's the main reason I chose this spot.

Forest dwellers come to clean their kill in the brook that cuts through the middle, or to cook their meat to avoid drawing unwanted attention to their homes or villages. But most know better than to be out this close to sundown, and whoever *those* people are—the owners of the three fresh scents being shoved toward me—they'll want to be far away when I start cooking this beast.

I grip hold of warm, wet organs and rip them free, lumping them on the ground next to me with a heavy splat.

The flies descend like they're starving.

I can't begrudge them that, not when I know the pull of true, unrelenting hunger.

A few minutes later, a male threads through a veil of leafy vines. He's tall, dark haired and broad shouldered—his hand darting out the moment his gaze lands on me, preventing a petite woman from fully emerging through the same fall of foliage.

I watch them from beneath the rim of my hood, hand wrapped around the boar's still-warm heart.

The female is pretty with shoulder-length hair, a dusting of freckles on her cheeks, and slanted eyes that look familiar. A squirming bundle is strapped close to her chest, shielded by one of her soil-stained hands.

Neither of them moves as I rip the heart free and toss it to the ground, then push my hood back.

The man lets out a startled sound and falls to his knees, dropping his wooden bucket. The woman lowers much slower; a cautious curtsy, likely to avoid disrupting her young.

"Master," the man blurts, voice strained. "I'm so sorry. I didn't instantly recognize you."

I study them, noting their lack of weapons other than a small blade hanging from the male's belt.

A low rumble agitates the back of my throat, threatening to spill.

"Are ... are you just passing through?" he asks, pine-green eyes meeting mine. They widen, his gaze flying to the carnage littering the ground next to me.

"I was," I respond, tone low and even. The last thing any of us need is for them to panic. "Do you have a bunker?"

He frowns, the woman raising her other hand to her squirming bundle.

"Ahh, we do ..." He gestures to the bucket tipped on its side, spilling white, tumor-like lumps over the ground. "We use it to store the truffles." His eyes flick to my kill, back again. "Do you ... do you require use of it? To store your kill? That's a lot of meat for one man."

"No," I mumble, yanking my bloody dagger from the log and tossing it through the air. It plunges hilt-deep into the ground at the man's feet. "Take the blade. Go straight there and don't come out until sunup."

They both pale, and the wide-eyed woman falls back a step.

"Of course," the man says with a brisk nod.

They collect the truffles with frantic, trembling hands, retrieve the dagger, and then the couple darts off, leaving nothing but the stark scent of fear.

I finally let my growl spill, giving it weight, making sure it ripples through the forest. It's a possessive sound that finds berth in the trees and the shrubs and the very ground I'm standing on.

I toss some offal closer to the tree line and in the bubbling brook, then smear my face, chest, and neck with the blood of my kill. Impaling the carcass with a wet, sturdy branch, I suspend it over the flames, then sit on the red-slicked log, pull up my hood, and wait.

The sun dropped a while ago, leaving the forest cast in a darkness that seems heavier than usual. The only reprieve is the crackling fire throwing off a deluge of heat and smoke.

I reach forward and spin the stick, letting the flames lick at the boar from a different angle, making the skin bubble and boil, hissing in protest as juices dribble onto blazing logs and red-hot stones.

It was a well-fed beast, and it's letting off the strong, heavenly musk of roasted game. A scent that makes my mouth water as I watch the fat drip, and drip, and drip ...

The breeze picks up, feeding the smell into the lungs of the forest while I rotate the boar to the rhythm of my slow, churning thoughts.

Perhaps because of the late hour and my body's internal clock surging with anticipation, but I think of those lilac eyes glaring at me with unguarded rancor ...

I hate you.

Oh, precious. You don't even know the meaning of the word.

Better her hate than those heated looks she's been blind-siding me with recently.

Another turn of the bubbling, spitting, sacrificial animal.

The boar was foraging for truffles in a glen—at least until I put my blade through its heart—and truffle is a strong flavor; one which has infused the meat, adding a botanical depth to its roasting smell.

It's staring through wide eyes as it spins its circles, tusks still jutting from a wide-open mouth. It squealed at me as it died, and I can see the echo of that sound on its half-charred face.

In hindsight, lobbing the head off might have been prudent.

I grab a pointy stick and give the pig a prod, freeing a squirt of fragrant juice the exact color of the liquid Orlaith offers me in her goblet every night.

I sigh, shoving the thought aside.

Fucking hate that color.

The krah stop squawking, the songs of the forest coming to a silent crescendo, and I twist the boar again, hearing a twig snap from just outside the tree line.

There's some sniffing and an almost inaudible growl.

The hairs on my arms and legs lift, a violence threatening to arc up inside me.

Another twist of the meat, the thick branch groaning under the weight. Another mouth-watering drip splashes onto the blazing wood.

Another snap of a twig.

It goes against my nature to keep my back to a threat, especially one with such a potent musk. But I weather the pull of my instincts, waiting ...

Listening.

I sense a presence step into the clearing behind me. Can scent his desire to *slay*. I move off the log, kneel, and rip a chunk of meat free, layers of it shredding apart as ripe juice dribbles down my fingers.

The air shifts.

I snatch the pommel, whip my sword off the ground, and whirl on the Vruk galloping forward in long, powerful strides. In the same motion, I slash through the animal's exposed chest and throat, spilling him before he even has a chance to roar or push talons from those huge, feline paws.

Leaping sideways, I watch him continue to amble forward, drop to his haunches, and collide with the spit.

Sparks and coals and rocks scatter.

He lets out a gurgling lament, then tips, and the ground absorbs his hefty weight with a shuddering protest.

He jerks once, then stills, black blood pumping from the gaping wound, muddying his thick, winter pelt and buttering the entire boar with oily muck.

I toss the piece of shredded meat, listen to it *thwap* against the dirt as I turn from the beast and scan the tree line.

Two ... four ... *seven* hulking, snarling Vruks prowl free from the bush, heads low and talons out, pelts thick like the one I just slew. Their lips are peeled, ears flattened against their bulky heads, drool dripping from sharp, exposed fangs.

I sigh, slide my foot back, and draw a steady breath.

All at once, they charge.

CHAPTER 13

ORLAITH

I wake before the sun has hatched, the sky still a velvet blanket freckled with stars, though it's hard to appreciate when phantom nails are being hammered into my skull.

Glued to the bed by the weight of my body, I smack my tongue against the roof of my mouth, feeling like all the moisture has been leached out of me ...

If I ingest another drop of caspun, I might never wake. And if I stay in bed, staring at the roof, I'll just tie myself in knots over the fact that The Safe is housing my crystal goblet, filled to the brim with Rhordyn's nightcap, all because I couldn't let go.

I just *couldn't.*

Because even though he's not here to accept my offering, I still did it—like leaving food out for a stray that never came.

Best I just roll out of bed, run laps around my balcony once the exo kicks in, then paint some rocks until the sun rises.

Groaning, I hang my arm off the side and thud to the floor in a heap of listless, jutting limbs. I peel the rug back, lift the stone, and reach into the hole, slapping around the edges of the smooth, *empty* base ...

"No. No, no, no." My heart lurches into my throat as I dig a second arm in and scour the barren fucking tomb.

Gone.

The realization trips a memory surge, and I roll, face crumbling. I sling a belt of vile words at the roof, massaging my temples and hating Rhordyn just a little bit more.

Hating *myself* just as much.

For one nonsensical second, I consider searching the entire castle by candlelight for my three-year supply, coming to the conclusion they're likely destroyed or hidden in his den. Probably the former.

I curl into myself, shaking ...

What a waste.

If Rhordyn were here, I'd march to his den, pound my fist against his door and give him the sharpest, most poisonous piece of my mind.

Letting my head tip to the side, I stare out the window through slitted eyes, trying to find some sense of calm in the winking stars and crescent moon. But they're too close—the ground too far away.

I need my feet dug into fleshy soil; need to pull some peace from the earth and pretend I'm not fraying at the seams.

I just *need.*

Pushing onto all fours, I crawl to my refreshment table, toss back two glasses of water, then clamber up and shuffle toward the wooden bench littered with jars. I plunder one brimming with dehydrated ginger and peppermint, stuffing my mouth half full in hopes of taking the edge off the pain in my temples.

At this stage, I need all the help I can get.

Trying not to gag from the sharp explosion of taste, I pull

on some pants, then shrug on a coat to ward off the chill frosting me from the inside. I shoulder my bag, open The Safe, and grip the glass by its long, fragile neck, then tip the flushed contents all over the floor with a sneer.

Shame to waste such a pretty shade of pink.

The steps of Stony Stem are unkind to a caspun hangover, and I flinch with each featherlight footfall that feels the exact opposite. The passageways are endless, The Tangle relentless, but after cursing Rhordyn and Baze every step of the way, I finally pop out on the eastern side of the castle, drawing a lungful of crisp, morning air as I plant my feet on the grass and bore my toes into damp soil.

The relief is instant.

I release a sigh, shoulders loosening, head tipping back to stare at the dazzling sprinkle of stars. Closing my eyes, I bask in the stretch of peace only fractured by the odd chirping cricket.

The pull of the earth eases my pain, shoveling substance into the hollow space within me. It's a relaxation method I relied on before discovering the recipe for Exothryl, but that feels like a lifetime ago.

I barely remember that girl anymore.

If I could bottle this feeling and constantly sip from it, all my problems wouldn't feel so heavy.

Glancing down the wall, I realize how close I am to the little round window ...

How convenient.

I tiptoe toward it, hiding from the moon in a pocket of shadow pooled at the wall's base. Though I can't see any creatures crawling around the forest at night, I know they're watching. Can feel their eyes on me, leering from behind my Safety Line.

Incorporeal fingers walk up my spine while I hunt through scrub for the rock I discarded yesterday, a smile curling my lips when I locate it.

Hauling my arm back, I picture Rhordyn's face and toss the stone, causing an explosion of glass ...

Shit, that's loud.

I pause to see if Baze is going to leap from the shadows. When I'm certain the coast is clear, I use a spare jar from my bag to chip off any remaining glass before I turn and edge my feet through the hole, then my body, hanging there by strained fingers for a few tense moments.

Bracing myself for the fall.

Landing with a dense thud that rattles my tender brain, I delve through my knapsack for a candle and match. I spark the wick, casting the ghostly objects scattered about the room in a fiery glow—a stark contrast to the stretched shadows that creep up the walls and dance to life.

Nothing shrinks back. Nothing moves or makes a scuttling sound.

It's just me.

The air feels almost syrupy, like it's been trapped down here so long it's become lazy with its movement.

Clearing my throat, I tiptoe between broken bits of glass and edge toward a large shape, its veil of white weighed down by pockets of dust. I lift the corner of the sheet and peer underneath. Frowning, I pull the whole thing off and swat the air while I study the freestanding wardrobe.

It's the softest shade of pink, embossed to look like a sketched garden.

Gripping the delicate handle, I tug, releasing a puff of dust that threatens to blow out my candle. The door creaks open, and I peek inside the cupboard's hollow interior ...

"Perhaps this *is* just a dusty old storage room."

I move to the next sheet and fold it back, unveiling a set of side tables to match the wardrobe. Next is a headboard, then a pretty bassinet that cradles a stack of crochet blankets yellowed with age. They're soft like butter, and I dig my nose into one, noting the faint, unfamiliar scent of vanilla beans and a hint of damp soil.

Did these belong to one of Rhordyn's ancestors?

Frowning, I refold the blanket and reveal the next item: a chest adorned with the same intricate design as everything else. Sitting on the ground beside it is a stoppered urn and a littering of jars no bigger than a finger.

I lift the lid—heavy and curved and groaning in protest. My eyes widen, and I gasp at the hoard of fat gems glinting in the flickering light.

Rhordyn isn't one to flaunt his wealth. Aside from my diamond tools, the only jewels I've ever seen around the castle have been dripping from other people's lobes at the Tribunal.

My eyes narrow on a clear one partially hidden beneath a large, black gem, and I pick it up, holding it close to my flame so I can assess its clarity. Warm light ricochets off the many flat edges, scattering a confetti of color and light all around the room.

Something inside me twinges at the sight, like a lute string plucked too hard.

I return the gem to the pile, sweeping my hand through the treasure to reveal the front of an old book with gold writing pressed into its leather-bound face. I pry it from its grave and set my foot on the edge of the chest, resting the book on my thigh while I trace the scripted title.

Te Bruk o' Avalanste

I repeat the phrase three times over, working my tongue around the new sounds, testing their feel. My gaze darts to the chest, back to the book, and I shrug, deciding it's of no use in a dusty, old storage room. I slide it into my bag and close the chest, sealing all those pretty gems in a tomb that'll probably never see the sun again.

The birds begin to chatter, alerting me of the cresting sun, and I turn, looking for something to wedge against the wall so I can climb out the window easier.

The galvanized corner of a picture frame otherwise covered in cloth catches my eye. No dust has settled on the sheet, suggesting whatever's hiding beneath it has been recently viewed.

Frowning, I do a tight spin, peering into the darker sections of the room.

No door. Nobody standing in the shadows.

Returning my attention to the cloth, I give it a tug, hand fluttering to my chest as it pools to the floor ...

I'm fearful to blink lest I sever the view, my serrated breath a tribute to the masterpiece before me.

Trapped within the confines of the ornate frame is the most beautiful painting I've ever seen.

A male and female, knee-deep in grass, are walking side by side atop a rolling hill. There's a storm brewing in the distance, wind pushing the woman's long, raven hair to the side. The detail is so delicate, I feel I could brush the individual strands with the tips of my fingers—smooth them out or plait them into a long braid to keep it off her face.

The man is half cast in shadow from the approaching storm, stance strong, shoulders broad. The real beauty lies in what's strung *between* the adults, swinging through the air, caught in an oily eternity; a small girl with long, gray hair flicking about her in suspended animation.

I feel her happiness bubbling inside me, as tangible as the hammering organ in my chest.

It bleeds away in the very next moment.

Who are these people? What happened to them? Why is all this stuff packed in a room nobody uses?

I scan the space ...

It feels like a crypt where beautiful things came to be forgotten about, at least until I snuck in and poked my nose around.

I don't belong here.

My curiosity has taken a step too far this time, and there's no covering my tracks. No unseeing the happiness in this painting; a bliss that feels empty like the bassinet, the cupboard, the bed.

Guilt has a taste I'm far too familiar with—bitter and biting.

I replace all the sheets while that taste sours my stomach, making the already sickly organ turn. Leaping, I grip the bottom of the bare window frame and haul myself free of the room.

The Grave ... that's what I'll call it.

A grave for happy things.

The climb back up my tower seems longer, a weight pushing on my shoulders with every silent step.

Shame.

Shame for breaking into that reliquary. For having the book stuffed in my bag ...

I should return it. Probably will.

After I've read it.

My door clunks shut, and I slam the deadlock into place, sealing myself inside a different sort of tomb. One I intend to stay in all day while I nurse my throbbing, lethargic brain and search for the desire to move again.

Everything weighs too much. My feet, body, mind ...

Heart.

I stack the fire full of wood, guzzle another glass of water to ease my chalky tongue, then stack pillows behind my back to form a comfortable nest. Nose stamped against the leather-bound book, I draw a breath, releasing a raspy moan as the aged smell attempts to cradle my sins.

I shouldn't have taken this.

Even so, I open the front cover, peel page after page, and pour over the book's secrets.

Try to decipher them.

An hour later when there's a brutal knock at my door, I ignore it—shifting onto the balcony where I can read in the morning sun striking through puffy clouds. Minutes later, Baze screams up at me from the castle grounds, to which I reply by tipping my pitcher over the edge to shower him with my distaste.

If Baze thinks I'm training after everything he put me through yesterday, he's sorely mistaken.

If he wants to treat me like a child, I'll act like one.

CHAPTER 14

ORLAITH

I've never been so frustrated with a picture book in my life.

Sighing, I close the front cover and stare out across Vateshram Forest. *Te Bruk o' Avalanste* was not written in the common tongue, so I spent all morning trying to decipher its contents from the drawings littering some of the two thousand gossamer pages. My instincts are telling me this is much more than just a collection of pretty sketches, and I need answers.

Now.

Thankfully, my hangover has almost run its natural course, and though I doubt I'll look at food the same for a while, I'm stable enough to face another being without the risk of spewing verbal venom.

I wedge the book inside my bag, then change into something more appropriate for the cool breeze blowing off the ocean. Hair trailing behind me in unkempt disarray, I make quick work of Stony Stem and the hall that leads me to the western wing, one destination in mind.

Fresh ocean air salts my skin as I land ankle-deep in the sand and sprint toward the jagged rocks. I'm just dangling my legs in the water when Kai emerges by my feet—hair slicked down, jewel-toned eyes giving away his signature smirk before his mouth even crests the waterline.

"Two visits in one week? Treasure, you flatter me."

I shrug. "What can I say? You're my favorite fish."

He frowns, sharp gaze flicking over my features. With a splash of his powerful tail, he's half out of the water, looming over me and wearing concerned eyes. "What's wrong? You don't look well."

This day hates me.

Avoiding his stare, I pick up a shard of rock and toss it in the water.

"Orlaith ..."

"You know that sugar kelp I asked you for a year ago?" I risk a peek at him.

"Yes. You said its chalky texture was perfect for a special project you were working on. That you intended to grind it down and use it for paint."

I lied.

I *did* grind it down ... but I certainly didn't use it on a rock.

His eyes narrow, then go so wide I swear they almost pop right out of his head. "Do not—" he shakes his head for long enough that I realize the chance of convincing him to collect more is probably next to none. "Do *not* tell me you used the sugar kelp to make Exothryl, Orlaith. Do not."

His disappointment is just as punishing as Rhordyn's lashing anger.

I consider lying ... then think better of it. Perhaps if I'm honest, slap on some pleading eyes and tell him his scales gleam like ocean gems, he'll take pity on my hungover ass and gift me another stem or two.

"What would you say if I told you I did, in fact, make Exothryl with it?"

Kai makes this low, caustic sound that seems to expel from the delicate gills tucked behind his ears, then his fingers are in my mouth, forcing it wide while he has a poke around.

Not the best sign.

"Gid I kell you how glowious your kail wooks koday?" I garble around two digits that taste like the ocean. He seems to ignore my spontaneous flattery, manhandling my head and pulling my lids, inspecting my eyes. He even sniffs my hair before making another sound that has me wishing I had a shell to scuttle into.

"You've got it bad." He pushes away from the rock, leaving a wake of disdain, his eyes a pair of fishing hooks gouged in my skin. "How long? Six months? A *year?*"

He's definitely not getting me any more.

"Let's not get tangled in the detai—"

"Did you know overdosing on those things can lead to heart failure? They pop, Orlaith. Like bubbles. *Poof,* dead."

My blood ices.

The handwritten recipe I discovered in the back of an old herbs and medicines book didn't go into detail about the side effects. Simply said that exo was good for 'boosting one's morale post *klashten*' ... whatever the hell that means. Everything after 'boosting morale' felt like unnecessary scripture.

There was certainly no fine print about hearts popping.

Now I regret taking three at once. No wonder I felt like I was about to sprout wings and flutter off like a sprite.

"Rhordyn found my stash and took it all," I mutter, kicking at the water perhaps a little too ferociously. "So my heart's safe."

At least in a physical sense.

Kai drops low into the water, gaze seeming to assault the castle. "Well, that's *something*," he says, and there's a bitter shadow to his tone I'm not familiar with.

I consider asking about it, but he jerks his chin toward my bag. "Got anything interesting to show me today?"

His voice is still cold, but I latch onto the change in conversation like it's a streak of sun breaking through the clouds on a gloomy day.

"Actually, yes ..." I reach behind, peel back the lip of my bag, and reveal *Te Bruk o' Avalanste*—the pressed pages bookmarked in places by leaves, feathers, and various other bits now poking out the top. "I found a book."

Sort of.

Kai spears forward into my personal space, planting strong arms either side of me as he lifts enough to inspect the book still nesting in my knapsack.

My breath catches.

He's so close I can feel his beat thrashing against me, wild and unleashed. Like the air around him has its own violent pulse.

"A pristine, intact, *original* copy of the Book of Making!" he blurts. *"Is it? Is it intact?"*

"Ahh ... I think so. I didn't find any damaged pages while I was flicking through."

He makes a trilling sound that pebbles my skin, and I clear my throat, setting the book on my lap as Kai lowers into the water.

"The Book of Making ..." I trace the engraved text with the tip of my finger. "So that's what this means?"

"Yes!" He grabs my hand and plants a kiss on my knuckles. "It's a *very* rare find, Orlaith. Quite remarkable. The last time I saw an original was *years* ago, and it was half eaten by moth larvae. I never expected to see another so well-preserved."

In Kai language, that's: *you pissed me off, I'm disappointed in you, but I'm impressed by your treasure hunting skills.*

"It's written in ancient Valish, unlike the recent translated versions."

Huh.

"Well ... I found it in a barricaded storage room. I've never seen anything like it before."

His brow puckers. "Not even one of the modern editions?"

"Not that I can remember, no." I split the book at a spot I'd earmarked with a dried mulberry leaf. "But this is beautifully illustrated, so I was able to make out bits and pieces. Sort of. Where's this?" I ask, pointing to the pristine sketch I just revealed.

I wish I could draw like that. My own freehand, emotion-driven style has nothing on the finer details that make this illustration so incredibly lifelike.

I feel like I could step right onto that volcano and touch the stone spires reaching from its crown. Clouds flirt with the tapered tips of the sharp, toothy fence that guards over the crater lake nesting in the center of it all.

"Mount Ether. Home of the prophet Maars. Frightful creature, but he transcribes the future through riddles he carves into stone," Kai says, pointing to the twelve surrounding spires.

Something climbs up the length of my spine and leaves me battling a shiver.

"There's a band of hardcore worshipers called the *Shulák*. They hang off his every chiseled word like a suckling babe."

I frown, peering up, but his eyes are still cast on the text he can apparently decipher. "Like a ... a *faith?*"

"Yes. Many believe he speaks for the Gods."

Canting my head to the side, I tuck a lock of hair behind my ear. "Gods?"

His eyes narrow, a line forming between the white strokes of his shapely brows. "Yes. Surely your tutor taught you religious studies?"

"Ahh, no. I wasn't aware that was a thing. I figured Gods only exist in the fantasy worlds I read about ..."

Kai looks toward the castle, expression grim. "You're far too sheltered up there," he growls, and there's an unbridled storm in his frosty words. One I try to temper by placing my hand on his cheek to divert his attention back to me.

He lifts a brow.

"I'm not *that* sheltered, Kai."

A lie. Of course I'm sheltered, but I built the walls of my own prison.

I flip the page, seeking distraction, and my mouth twists in a cloying smile.

"So, wait ..." I tap the illustration of a slender female with hair that sways to her knees. She's tossing a piece of kelp into the volcano's basin of water that appears to be spitting out a version of ... well ... *Kai.* "Does that mean Ocean Drakes were made from—"

"Seaweed," he interrupts, voice monotone. "Yes."

I peek at him, catching his lackluster stare, chewing my bottom lip to stop myself from spitting laughter ... though a little manages to bubble out.

"You're terrible," he flips to another leaf in the book. "And you were made from stones, so you're not much better off."

"I think that's perfectly appropriate, actually."

He tips his head and laughs, the sound a splash of joy I wish I could swim in. His beat has calmed to that of a lapping wave by the time his chest stops shaking. "You're right."

Smiling shyly, I divert my attention to the book, running my fingers over the drawing of an Ocean Drake rising from the water—the frills that adorn the length of his long, powerful tail slicked flat against his scales. Beside it is another image of the same drake walking on two muscular legs.

The smile slips off my face as I lick my lips and peer up through my lashes. "Is this true? Can your kind walk on land?"

There's a bubble of hope in my heart that pops the moment Kai shakes his head, eases my hand away, and flicks to a different part of the book. "Not all. The originals could. And some of their direct descendants."

My shoulders droop. "Oh ..."

"What do you garner from this page?"

I look to the woman plucking a fallen leaf from the ground, her hair seeming to blend with the clouds. In the adjacent picture, she's blowing it into the volcanic basin. From there, a swarm of sprites are emerging.

"Um, that sprites were made from falling leaves by the Goddess of"—hell, I don't know—"*air?*"

"Correct," he says, leaning closer, his briny scent washing over me. It's a smell like no other, as though the entire ocean has been boiled down into a thick, perfumed syrup.

He's the sea incarnate. Rich and wholesome and—

My best friend.

He points to the feathers sewn into the Goddess' bodice. "Falanthia can take on the form of an eagle."

I nod, my exo-starved mind clinging to the information as he turns a few pages.

The corner of his mouth kicks up. "And this?" he asks with a wicked lilt to his tone. "Forest nymphs from ripe plums by the God of ..."

My blood turns molten, and I cast my gaze on the sprinkle of whitecaps crumbling the ocean in the distance.

That page ... *well.* When I first looked at it, I felt all kinds of strange feelings I've never felt before, and now that picture is branded in my mind, destined to be the source of impromptu blushing until the day I die.

It wasn't the nakedness that threw me. Not even the way the woman was stretched out, back arched, pinching her nipples and chewing her bottom lip.

It was the way her thighs were parted.

It was the man holding them open, face buried in their apex. It was his posture—half crouched like a feasting cat—and that long, hard, naked length looking ready to drive up into her.

"Fertility?" I ask, hating the way the word squeaks out of me.

He turns me to face him with a grip on my chin, and I note a gleam in his ocean eyes that wasn't there before.

"Correct," he purrs. "Clever girl."

"I doubt my tutor would have congratulated me for such a feat."

"No," he chuckles, releasing me. "Probably not."

Cheeks scalding, I turn the page.

"I don't know what that one is," I say, pointing to a man cloaked in black, the handle of a sword poking over his shoulder. All you can see of his features are a sharp jawline and the slash of a mouth that's pinched in a frown.

Except he's not a regular man.

There are three different versions of him melding together, and each has a different face, the two either side less vivid but no less chilling.

The one in the middle is carving off a piece of the blackness falling from the wide breadth of his shoulders, letting it flutter into the volcano's crater lake.

"Kavth. God of Death," Kai rumbles. "He can take on the many forms of the dead, and he made the Irilak with a piece of his shadow." He taps the illustration of a wraith easing from the basin—a *familiar* shadow with a face that looks like it was carved from a bleached piece of wood.

"So that's what they're called," I whisper, tracing the creature's chalky features.

I'm so caught up on that new slice of information—of *finally* having a species name to attach to Shay—that I don't notice the tension strung between Kai and myself until his finger slides under my chin.

He guides it up until I'm staring into narrowed eyes. Pinned by his keen attention.

"*What?*"

"Orlaith. Don't go getting close to an Irilak." His tone is hard like the rock I'm sitting on, edges just as sharp. "They're temperamental. Deadly."

"How so?" I ask, pushing a loose ribbon of hair off my face.

"They feed on fear ... among other things. They've been known to lure children into the forest, leaving nothing but a husk of skin clinging to skeletal remains."

I repress a shiver at the crude picture he's painting, thinking about the hard, fluffy lumps left behind after Shay's finished feasting on my offerings. But aside from ... *that,* he doesn't seem all that frightening. He's never once tried to attack me in all the years I've been flinging mice his way. I practically hand-fed him the other night, shaking with fear as I shoved an arm over my Safety Line for the very first time, and he still preferred the mouse.

The moment stretches while Kai searches my eyes, then sighs, transferring his attention to the book. "I'm guessing you brought this down for other reasons?"

He knows me so well.

"Thing is, I recognize a number of the creatures in here just from illustrations I've seen in other books," I say, turning to a page marked by a dried flower, "but there were plenty that threw me. Like *this* one."

The Goddess on this page is the most enchanting woman I've ever laid eyes on, with willowy lines and a dress that pours off her like petals. She's tossing a twinkly rose into the crater lake, and from it, the creature climbing out is no less striking than the deity he was made by.

His pale skin holds a light shimmer, his eyes like buffed crystals. Poking out from amongst the strands of whitewash hair is not a regular ear, but one with tiny, delicate thorns lining the shell that slims to a point.

"I was wondering if you could tell me what they are?"

Kai's voice drops to a low, almost mournful whisper. "In Valish, they're called *Aeshlians*. It means 'eternity without a shadow.' There are very few left."

My brows pinch together, and I glance up. "Why? What happened to them?"

He drives himself out of the water in a torrent of long, tapered muscles, scales, and ...

I swallow.

Why am I only now noticing that my best friend has so

much ... *allure?* It's a wonder he doesn't have females chasing his tail all day long.

"That's a very long, very sad story," he says, parking himself on the rocks beside me, silver tail sweeping back and forth through the water. "One I wouldn't taint your pretty ears with."

He pinches my nose, and I gaff him with a glare. "But you tell me *everything*."

All mockery drips off his face, and he cups my cheek like it's made of glass. "Not that, Orlaith. Never that."

It's a common misconception that Ocean Drakes are tidal —easy to sway.

Not mine.

I know Kai well enough to know that when he says no, he means it. He'd sever his own tail before going back on his word.

I look at the picture again, choosing not to bring up the déjà vu it strikes me with. The fact that a little boy who wears the same eyes comes to me in my dreams.

Always reaching.

Never catching.

Ignoring the tightness of my chest, I turn to the page marked with a toothy blade of shadow grass. "And what about that?"

There's something very unusual about the lithe, powerful-looking man emerging from the basin. I barely noticed his pointed ears or impeccably sculpted cheekbones. Even his guarded eyes didn't strike me at first or the way they're peering out of the page with some obscure war waging behind them.

There's just an air about him. A sense of primal prestige that locked my spine the moment my gaze flew over the picture.

Some innate part of me wanted to close the book in the very next moment. Still does, like a flower closing up in the face of a blistering storm.

The silence between Kai and myself stretches on a little too long, and I meet his eyes, shadowed by a pinched brow.

"What?"

"Did your tutor have a bad case of selective teaching? How do you not know any of this stuff?" he asks, slashing his hand through the air. "Some of the races in this book forged your way of life!"

I stare at him blankly. "I'm afraid you're going to have to be more specific."

"Well, take the Unseelie for example"—he indicates the picture—"pulled from the volcano by Jakar, God of Power. Thousands of years ago, they were the dominant, over-lording race, driven by their compulsion to sow seed and strengthen. To nest, *fuck*, and breed."

I flinch at the rawness of his words, cheeks burning at the way he emphasized that crass four letter word.

"The *plague* of their archaic beliefs still echo in your society," he continues. "For example; slaving was a very serious problem back then. As a result, bleeding one territory to bolster another is now forbidden, which is why changing one's territory colors must be a voluntary choice."

Tongue a chalky lump in my mouth, I shake my head, wondering if I should have waited to ask these questions when my brain is fully functional. "I don't get it. If they were so transcendent, why aren't they still around today?"

Kai lifts my hair, sweeping his fingers down the length of it, sending a shiver across my scalp. He tucks the weight over my shoulder so delicately you'd think he was handling a weave of spun gold.

"Their voracious hunger for control planted the seed of their demise," he says, eyes bleak. "The Unseelie *devastated* races, Orlaith. Even their own. Ripped each other to shreds in a great battle that destroyed an entire territory and threatened global extinction. Some believe Jakar himself tore apart the sky and exterminated what was left of his ... *miscreations,*" he growls, attention falling back to the page. "The reek of that wash of power still taints the sea in some parts."

I frown, studying the picture again.

Perhaps I shouldn't have asked. My world, it seems, is getting smaller by the second.

I look upon the next marker, and a ball of tension gets lodged in my throat, making it hard to breathe.

Slowly, I peel back the leaf of paper.

"And him?" I ask, barely able to look at the man depicted across a stretch of two pages.

He's built from powerful slabs of brawn, his hair dark gray, eyes black like the night sky. He's unrefined, beastly in his bearing, as if all that's stuffed inside him is almost impossible to contain.

He reminds me of the storm clouds that chew on my tower sometimes.

There are *five* versions of the man, each more haunched and distorted than the last, showcasing his gradual metamorphosis into a monster.

One I recognize.

"Bjorn. God of Balance. As you can see, his form is depicted similarly to the common day Vruk."

Sharp shrieks echo through my memory, and I nod,

remembering the ground trembling so much I thought it might crack open and swallow me whole.

"His ... his talons," I bite out, jerking my chin toward the long, black hooks glinting off a shaft of sketched moonlight. "Does it say anything about them?"

Kai taps a slant of script riddled across the page. *"Klahfta des ta ne flak ten.* Simplified, it means something akin to *unparalleled."*

"Oh," I whisper, nodding, thankful I didn't try to stomach breakfast or lunch. "And the common day Vruks this depiction was based on?"

"A Vruk's talon is lethal." Kai clears his throat, stare casting out across the bay. "To anyone."

I frown at the turmoil failing to hide in the depth of his ocean eyes.

"Kai?"

"Safety is important to you, yes? Above most other things?"

"I guess so. Why do you ask?"

His tongue slips out, sweeping the glitter of sea salt off his lips. "Be right back."

"Wai—"

He dives, disappearing beneath the water, his gossamer tail a slash that sends a string of seaweed topside.

I sigh, waiting patiently for his return.

When he reemerges, his arms are burdened by a small, tarnished chest he lumps on the rock beside me before prying the lid open. He digs around inside and reveals what appears to be a curved blade sheathed in leather. Its unworn hilt is forged from a dark metal, unadorned but for the end—tipped in ebony stone.

"What's that?" I ask, eyeing the thing like it's about to leap out of his hand and bite me.

Kai hesitates, then suspends it between us. "Something that can protect you from *anything*. Always."

Unease spills through my chest.

I reach out, hand shaking as if my body knows something my mind is yet to catch on to. I grip the curved sheath in one hand, the hilt in the other, and *tug* ...

Only a few inches of the weapon are exposed before I slam it shut, stomach churning, heart beating hard and fast.

A talon.

It's a fucking *talon*.

"W-wow ..."

"I just thought, well, you said you hate your new sword, and I ... Are you okay?" he asks, tone tender, his beat tapping around my edges.

I stuff the thing in my bag. "Never better," I lie, closing the book and placing it atop the talon so I can pretend it doesn't exist. "I just want to make sure this special gift is nice and safe in my bag."

"Treasure ..."

Looking up, I paint my face with a grin. The big, dazzling sort that usually gets him right in the gills. "I'm fine. Really. And thank you. It's such a thoughtful offering."

He frowns. "You're lying. I can feel a rise in your core temperature. You don't have to accept the gift if you don't li—"

I grab his face, pull him close, and plant a kiss on his wet, salty cheek, making his eyes glaze the way they do when I'm offering him an apple or something coveted. "I love your gift, Kai. I really do. Now, tell me the tale of when you got a fishing hook caught in your ear again?"

A slow, watery smile lights up his face. "You like that one, don't you?"

"I really do. And you tell it so well."

I manage to make it to the end of the story, back to the castle, and through a side door that spits me out by a bed of ivy before I vomit. When Baze finds me knotted on the ground with bile strung from my lips and asks if it's the withdrawals, another lie slips off my tongue.

Truth is, withdrawals have *nothing* on the extra weight tucked in my knapsack. A weapon that may or may not carry the weight of many lives taken. Slain. *Destroyed.*

The weight of families torn to bits and feasted upon, scattered across the soil.

And now it's mine ...

CHAPTER 15

ORLAITH

I'm trapped.

Flames spit and shadows churn, moving in wild jerks that cleave the air with ease.

Striking. Slashing.

I cover my ears with clawed hands, my body a ball of bunched muscle and protruding tendons threatening to snap.

Will I unravel, then? Will my skin split as my body ceases to hold together?

Will everything spill?

A cold seed is pitted inside me, turning my organs solid. My heart is heavier, weighted by the sludge of a pulse I resent. What happens when it can no longer push blood through my veins? Will a strike land? Will the beasts chew on me, just like they chewed on them?

Death is gripping my insides with hands so cold they burn, but there's a comfort in it. A safety that feels eternal.

Don't let me go.

The scene shifts, the ground falls away, and I'm perched on the edge of a chasm, looking into a well of darkness that echoes with muted screams, making me want to crack open and weep.

Something grabs me, jerking back and forth, threatening to toss me over—

Jolting awake, I stare into brown, overburdened eyes while warm hands cradle my face, adding fuel to the roaring well of flame inside my chest.

Baze pets me with smoothing strokes that fail to tamp the pressure filling my skull. The scream pouring from my throat rips with the force of a withdrawing blade—sharp like the talon stuffed in the back of my drawer of jars.

Rhordyn's presence crams the space full, pushing all the air from the room and leaving nothing for my lungs to grab.

Nothing for them to *shove*.

I gasp, wrestling for shards of breath ...

"Leave, Baze." Rhordyn's thundering voice battles my unbridled pulse, every beat a bolt of wood shot at my bulging brain.

Deadly.

Destructive.

Baze's sudden absence allows more space for *him* to fill.

Less air for me to breathe.

Rhordyn's rifling through the bottles atop my bedside table, cursing as cork after cork is popped. "Is this all you have left?"

His sharp words gouge my temples, and I groan, wishing he'd judge me with his inside voice.

"Orlaith, *where is the rest of it?*"

My legs churn, bunching the blanket at my feet. "That's all there is ..."

"*Fuck.*"

The atmosphere seems to squirm, trying to wriggle free from the crushing maw of his outrage.

My body is an inferno, every surge of blood shooting through my veins another lashing of liquid fire. I pull at my clothes, attempting to shred them, desperate for cool air to blot my sizzling skin.

If I rip, will flames spill out? Will my tower turn to ash?

The bed dips, and something cold slides beneath my knees, something else banding around my waist and gripping tight. I'm eased into a sitting position, perched against the glacial plains of Rhordyn's body—a winter sea that lugs me into its icy pall.

I'm lava in his grip. There is no sizzling sound, but I feel it in my blood.

We rock, smooth and docile, so at odds with my fire.

Another cork pops, and the sound almost splits me down the middle.

The pain—

"I know. I need you to tip your head and open your mouth."

No.

If I do that, my brain will bulge and burst.

A warm wetness dribbles from my nose, sluices over my mouth, and drips off my chin.

"I won't ask again, Milaje. *Now.*"

The depthless command has my lips parting; a weak, pathetic sound gushing out with the motion. But I don't have the power to tip my head.

He does it for me with a firm hand clamped around my jaw. A cool liquid splashes my tongue, and I choke it back.

"One more."

When the next drop lands, my tousled mind unravels enough for me to register the cold eddy swelling inside me, tempering the fire in my veins.

My treasured ease. My *release* from this ... this angry, swollen thing that's trapped inside a layer of too-tight skin.

I leave my tongue out, waiting for more.

"Enough."

It's so *far* from enough.

I need to drink until this volcanic hand no longer has my heart in its fiery fist. Until my brain no longer feels like it's stuffed into a tiny space where it doesn't belong.

I pop my eyes open, snatch the bottle, and tilt—mouth open, tongue lolling.

Nothing lands.

It's empty.

I toss it to the side, hear it shatter. Hands bunched against my ears, I wait for the pain to ease; for me to feel less like blown glass ready to burst.

"I'll send for more caspun," he says, blotting my chin, my lips, my nose. Pressing his frosty hand across my forehead.

I lean into his touch like it's the only thing tethering me to this world.

"It could take a few weeks to get here. You should have told me."

"You're *never here ...*"

He makes a sound akin to a rumbling thunder storm, molding my body so I'm curled to the side in a comfortable position that offers no content.

I'm still broken. Still splitting at the seams.

Still trapped on the edge of a cliff, trying to see past the endless sea of darkness at my feet.

I know I have to jump, but I have no idea what's down there. No idea what I'll see.

What I won't be able to *un*see.

"And you're taking too much at once. Is that why you've been relying on the Exothryl?"

I squeeze my eyes shut, figuring my silence is answer enough.

He growls, the sound a tangible flutter against my skin. "I'll be rationing you from now on."

I open my mouth, but he pins it shut with the stamp of his hand. "Don't argue with me on this. You will lose. I've obviously been far too complacent."

Complacent? How about *nonexistent*. A shadow in a room. A specter that only shows when you least expect it to.

Like now.

Why is he here? He never climbs Stony Stem for any reason other than to receive my blood or confiscate my heart-popping narcotics.

I'm about to ask, but he tugs the wool blanket up and tucks it over me, then nails it down with a powerful arm wrapped over my body.

"You're h-h-hugging me," I chatter out, feeling as if I've been dropped into an icy lake with stones tied to my ankles.

Caspun may be effective, but it has its repercussions.

"Yes," he grits out, like he had to force the word past the bars of his teeth.

I peep over my shoulder, throwing myself into wells of quicksilver lit by the gleam of a slow-dancing candle flame.

"Why?" I rasp, and I hate how pathetic my voice sounds.

Something dark slides over his face—a mask slipping down—and I know I'm getting nothing else from him.

He might as well be behind that door. Down in his den. Anywhere but here.

"Go to sleep, Orlaith."

Sometimes his orders make my hackles rise. Other times they make me fold at the stem like a flower crushed by the weight of a gusty wind.

Tonight, I have no energy left in me to fight, and ... I don't even think I want to.

He's hugging me.

CHAPTER 16

ORLAITH

He's gone by the time I wake, leaving no sign he was here aside from the hearty musk of his lingering scent infused with my pillow slip. Stuffing my nose in the silk, I draw a deep breath, filling my lungs and easing the painful eddy in my temples.

A memory of me tipping an empty bottle to my lips hits me like a plank, and a nervous flutter bursts in my belly ...

I'm all out of caspun.

Crap.

I've been dependent on the arcane bulb for so long. If I knew it was going to take forever to source more, perhaps I'd have plucked up the courage and come clean weeks ago. The repercussion of Rhordyn discovering I've been exceeding the recommended dose wasn't nearly as bad as I thought it'd be.

He was angry, yes ... but he still *hugged* me, then stayed until I fell asleep.

Closing my eyes, I remember his arm—big and strong like a shield. Remember the feel of his presence at my back, his weight dipping the mattress.

It was impossible not to roll into the small cleft between us. Bridge the space.

A shiver rakes through me.

I draw another calming breath, pulling my face from the pillow before I exhale, not wanting to muddy the slip with my own scent. Then frown when I realize it's *laundry* day.

Tanith will be up in a couple of hours to strip my bed ...

She can't have it.

Dragging the slip free, I bounce my gaze around the room, seeking the perfect hiding spot.

Easier said than done.

Tanith is thorough, never leaving a single dust particle unaccounted for, and I don't doubt she'll find this treasure no matter where I hide it. Except maybe *one* place ...

Rhordyn knows about my hidden compartment, but he's the only one. And it's not like he has any more reasons to dig around in there.

I peel the rug, shift the stone, stuff the compartment full of *him*, then slide the lid back into place. Something inside me calms to a light simmer, and I sigh, posture buckling.

After changing into my training gear, I run a brush through my calamity of hair and work it into a loose braid. Bag slung over my shoulder, I take on Stony Stem with delicate footfalls, trying to glide down each step so as to nurture my tender brain. By the time I step into the dining room, white dots are clouding my vision.

I'm half tempted to turn around and head straight back to bed.

"If you wanted to train, you're two hours late," is my morning welcome from a frosty Baze lounged in his regular spot, sipping from a steaming cup of tea.

"I slept in."

He looks up from the scroll spread beside his breakfast plate, weighted by a glass of juice and a large black stone I'd love to paint. He draws another mouthful, eyes meeting me over the rim. "And you still look tired."

"You're the one who tipped him off, aren't you? Told Rhordyn about the Exothryl?"

It's the only plausible explanation. Last night aside, Rhordyn never sees me, especially not in the morning when I'm jacked. If we bump into each other in a hall, nine times out of ten the chance encounter swiftly dissolves.

A guilty glint sparkles in Baze's eyes, that right dimple appearing. He sets his cup on the saucer with a delicate clink that belies who he is. How he looks.

There's nothing delicate about Baze aside from the way he tapers down like a finely crafted wooden weapon. When used correctly, and in the right situation, he's *lethal.*

"I take that as a yes. How'd you work it out?"

Baze shrugs, sets his elbows on the table, and fits his hands together. "How do you think, Orlaith?"

The question is *crooned*—bait for my fraying patience.

I massage my temples. "Can't you just tell me?"

"No," he says, motioning for me to sit. "Think I'll keep that information to myself." He takes a large bite of his apple and tosses me a wink that plucks at my nerves.

In other words, if I somehow manage to gather all thirty-four ingredients required to make more Exothryl ... *he'll know.*

I plod to my seat and ease into it, looking through the open doors to the window-lined hallway. There's no morning sun spilling through—nothing to fill the murky innards of Castle Noir with light.

Days like this generally start me off on the wrong foot, so the fact that I even made it to the breakfast hall despite my delicate condition should absolutely be noted on my *effort* chart.

"How are you coping?" Baze asks, staring at the morning report while stirring a sugar cube into his tea. Pretending the question is casual when we both know it's not.

I shrug, scanning the spread of food, stomach twisting. My gaze snags on Rhordyn's spare place setting and my chest tightens.

Part of me hoped he'd be sitting here after what we shared last night. Foolish, now that I think about it.

But he hasn't had my blood in a while ...

I know he said he doesn't need me, but after falling asleep in his arms last night, there's a hopeful spark in my chest. A warmth I want to nourish.

Oil for those precious cogs that keep me spinning.

A servant fills my glass with some zesty juice the color of sunshine. I wait until she's returned to her spot at the wall before my attention drifts to my empty plate. "I'm out of caspun."

Baze's cup clatters to the saucer. "You're fucking with me."

I catch his wide-eyed stare, saying nothing.

There's nothing more *to* say.

His mouth works like a fish out of water before he finally finds his words. "How the hell did you go through three years' worth of caspun in *three months?*"

I continue to stare, waiting ...

He throws his head back and looks to the roof, hands threading behind his head. "You've been using it as a preventative, then relying on exo every morning to counteract the comedown."

"I've been ensuring I get a good night's rest," I say, gripping my glass of juice—the only thing on this table I can think about consuming without wanting to dry heave.

"Does Rhordyn know? That you've been using it as a preventative?" I can feel his glare burning the side of my face as I take small, tentative sips from my glass.

"If he didn't work it out last night, I suspect he's about to find out."

"Well, you've got that right." He lifts his own glass of juice, pretending to clink with me.

No point being bitter about it.

"So ..." I jerk my thumb at the empty seat on my right, "is he gone again?"

Baze takes a bite of his apple, watching me with a shrewd gaze as he slowly chews, then swallows. "He's around. Now, since you're dressed for the occasion, we can spend a few hours training on The Plank. Unless you have some rocks to paint?"

The bottom of my glass practically assaults the table, making me wince from the bite of sound. "Really, Baze? You think I look capable of walking The Plank right now?"

"No," he shrugs, "you look like death. But perhaps a swim with the selkies will do you the world of good?"

Yeah, like losing a toe ever benefits anyone.

I pluck a grape from a pile and toss it at his face, but he snatches it out of the air with his teeth.

Rolling my eyes, I shift in my seat, not entirely sure the juice was a good idea after all. The few sips I took are sitting like spikes in my belly.

"You should eat before everything gets cold."

"I'm not hungry. And your collar has rouge on it," I say, spotting the smear of red matching the blush of the blonde, busty servant standing at the wall behind Baze, her gaze cast on the floor.

He pulls on his collar, inspecting the stain. "Well, I do love a good souvenir." Throwing me a wink, he buffs his jewel-encrusted ring. "And look at you, artfully diverting the conversation."

"Who gave you that?" I ask, admiring the way light refracts off the polished faces of all those tiny, ebony gems. "I've always wondered."

He watches me from beneath raised brows. "Who do you think?"

He really needs to lower his expectations of me for a while.

"Just ... give me multiple choice answers so I don't feel inclined to toss a melon at your head."

"Well," he drones, tone mocking, "let me give your sludgy, hungover brain a hint."

I'm going to murder him.

"The same person who puts those clothes on your back and pays Cook to keep you brimming with honey buns. Speaking of which, want one?" He gestures to the pile stacked in front of me.

My stomach knots.

"Not unless you want me to vomit all over you. And how long ago was that?" I ask, massaging my temples again, trying to ignore the dull throb.

The corner of Baze's lips sweep into a hook. "You know what, the years kind of ... *blur together* under his management. Now," he slams his hand on the table—the sound a blade through my skull, "let's get moving. If we're lucky, we might catch a few rogue rays of sunshine before the rain hits."

And if *he's* lucky, he might survive the day.

CHAPTER 17

ORLAITH

"Wait, what about our swords?" I ask, trying to keep pace with Baze's long, determined strides. Hard when I keep getting distracted by all the fluffy rose bushes.

The spurt of sun has done them good.

"We'll grab them later. Rhordyn wants me to spend an hour or so focusing on hand-to-hand combat," he mutters, chewing the end of a long piece of grass.

I scoff. "Funny that, seeing as I managed to kick him in the balls the other day."

Baze's head swings around so fast, I'm surprised his neck doesn't snap. "Excuse me?"

I shrug, massaging my temples, trying to draw comfort from the spongy grass beneath my bare feet. "He called it a cheap shot—"

A smooth, melodic giggle tinkles through the garden, attacking me with its sweet harmony. What swiftly follows makes my heels dig in—a deep, robust, *familiar* laugh that rolls like thunder.

I take off at a run through the labyrinth of botanical pathways with Baze cursing after me, something that only serves to accelerate my search.

Rounding a lush, perfumed bend, I slam to a stop.

There, standing amongst the roses—*my* roses—is the most striking woman I've ever seen.

She's tall and statuesque, her ochre cloak doing nothing to conceal her shape. Its split yawns from neck to foot, creating a window for long legs accentuated by brown pants that could pass as body paint, and a sandy top tailored to move with her curves.

If her clothes are anything to go by, this woman is comfortable in her beautiful, creamy skin.

Her hair is a tumble of strawberry wine, the fall of it tucked behind an ear lined with little rust-colored gems. Her pouty lips are pink, cheeks dusted with freckles. Long, thick lashes brush her well-defined brows as she looks up at *him.*

Rhordyn. Roughly hewn perfection. The man who wrapped himself around me last night and lulled me to sleep as if it *meant something.*

He offers her a smile that almost looks tired, but it's still a smile.

His smile.

Something inside me goes white-hot and deadly still.

Baze's hand lands on my shoulder, fingers digging in like hooks. I send my foot flying back and kick him in the kneecap, earning a guttural groan that has Rhordyn's attention whipping our way.

That smile falls, leaving nothing but a stone slate.

No smile for me.

Today, they all belong to *her*.

I shrug Baze off and stalk forward, bunched hands swinging at my sides.

"Laith," Rhordyn says, pebbling my skin as if he just tucked his lips against my ear and whispered it.

My next breath is nowhere near as sharp as the previous.

He never calls me Laith.

Even so, I plant myself in front of him—a tree with roots that bore into the soil like claws.

A bud of anger sparks inside me, and rather than tamp the erratic flame, I want to blow on it. To cradle and *grow* it until he and I are nothing but piles of ash. Let the wind sweep us up and tangle us together. Let our demise finally put some reason to this endless fucking riddle.

Because I'm tired. So, so tired, and I'm *not* okay with this—with that female standing amongst my roses, luring smiles from a man usually as apathetic as a gravestone.

His brow lifts.

A long, stiff moment hangs, our gazes locked as if we've just crossed swords. It's a battle, yes. A war even.

I'm just not sure what's at stake.

Overhead, the sky rumbles, but I refuse to blink. Refuse to break away. It's as if something deep inside—that still, silent part that's painfully aware—knows I'm standing on the edge of a different sort of chasm than the one that haunts my nightmares.

One that has the potential to ruin me.

The pushy ocean breeze assaults my back, shoving loose tendrils forward.

Reaching.

Rhordyn's nostrils flare, stare darting to my neck and a low, silky rumble eases out of him.

The sound infuses me like a dose of Exothryl, hurtling my heart against too-brittle ribs, pumping blood that's honey thick—heating my cheeks, plumping my lips, making my breasts feel hot and heavy.

Around us, the world seems to still ... or perhaps its significance simply falls away.

I let out a short breath and, despite my anger, find myself leaning forward like a flower stretching into a shaft of sunlight.

From somewhere behind me, Baze coughs.

The ball in Rhordyn's throat rolls, and he slides back a step, shattering the tension. It feels like some of the shards ricochet and slice into my fervid, vulnerable flesh.

Part of me wishes those wounds were physical—that my blood was spilling, making him react the way he did when Dolcie pierced my flesh. Reminding him of my value and fortifying that crumbling bridge between us.

My sight veers, catching on a bare bush that's always failed to yield anything but moss-green leaves.

Rhordyn clears his throat as if to dislodge the last of our tension. Or perhaps he's trying to dislodge *me.*

Either way, it hurts.

"Orlaith."

The sound of my full name lands like a slap to the face, almost buckling my knees.

"Yes, Rhordyn?"

By the way the muscle along his jaw ticks, I'd say he doesn't appreciate my challenging tone. But I refuse to be wounded game in front of this woman that exudes such feminine poise. Especially when I'm standing here looking like that bare rose bush.

"This is Zali"—he gestures sideways with a brusque sweep of his hand—"High Mistress of the East."

I stare at him for another long beat before I finally sway my attention toward the woman hanging from his personal space.

I notice her hand is notched inside the cloak that's falling off her like a dune, her head canted to the side. She has this look on her face—as if she's listening to the unspoken words between us, perhaps waiting for me to detonate.

"My apologies. I didn't see you standing there," I say, shoving my hand in her direction.

The corner of her mouth kicks up, something akin to shock igniting her eyes, and she pulls her hand free.

Her grip is firm, palm surprisingly calloused—

She knows how to fight, then.

She's a strong, composed woman who can obviously look after herself—a woman who wouldn't suckle off Rhordyn's hospitality like a newborn lamb.

Will he let her into his Den?

... Will she *bleed* for him?

Acid fires up my throat like a torch, all the air slipping through my fishnet lungs.

"Laith. I've heard so much about you." Her friendly voice is silky smooth, umber eyes veiling the wariness I don't miss. "I'm hoping we'll become well acquainted."

"I highly doubt that," I reply, dropping her hand. "And it's Orlaith to you."

Behind me, Baze chokes.

Rhordyn snatches my upper arm, and I'm dragged away, bag thumping against my thigh as I struggle to keep pace with his long, powerful strides.

"Ouch!" I gripe, being pulled past Baze who simply stands there, arms knotted over his chest, shaking his head.

He's either embarrassed by me or he pities me. Neither option is ideal.

Rhordyn lugs me behind a tall hedge and spins, stepping right up into my personal space, eyes a silver storm that devastates my skin. "That was rude, immature, and so very—"

He stops mid-sentence.

Just ... stops.

"So very *what,* Rhordyn?"

His eyes harden.

"Pathetic," he says with cold, steady precision. "It was just a hug. Nothing more. Don't get caught up on it."

My heart drops, a breath puffing out of me as if he stuck me through the lungs with a pointy stick.

Of course. How silly of me.

He folds his arms and my gaze darts to the inky cupla caught around his wrist—two bands that click together but can split to form separate cuffs.

He never usually bothers to wear the thing unless he's at the Tribunal.

A heaviness settles in my stomach.

"Are ... are you courting her?" My voice is a harsh whisper.

His shoulders drop an inch, and my heart mimics the motion. It's the smallest dent in his armor, but such a telling one.

He cares, but only because he feels a sense of responsibility.

No wonder he's always trying to get me to step outside my boundaries. He wants to move on with his life without this lovesick stray shadowing the insides of his castle.

He pinches the bridge of his nose and sighs. "Laith ..."

My name sounds so tired when he says it like that. Even so, it makes my stupid heart gallop, and I hate him for it.

"Just answer the question, Rhordyn."

I pay my way, one droplet at a time, so I deserve to

know if there's going to be someone else living here, walking the halls that have become my crutch. I deserve to know if a woman will be sharing his den, muddying it with her scent. Or if I'll be seeing her lure him to the dining table, sharing food with him ... something he's *never* shared with me.

It's that final thought that snaps me like a twig.

"Answer me!"

Rhordyn doesn't even blink at my poignant display of discomfort. He simply studies me for a long moment, like he's considering how, exactly, he wants to slice me up. Which part he'll toss to the crows first.

After a small eternity, he takes a smooth step back, cleaving us apart with an ocean of chill.

I don't like the way he's distancing himself. It makes the ground beneath my feet feel unsteady, as though it could split apart and devour me.

"I'm considering giving her my cupla," he says, voice monotone, words matter-of-fact.

My lungs flatten.

No.

Fuck, no.

I stagger back into dense foliage, vision blurring, heart in my throat.

Something inside me rears up, wild and ugly, urging me to stalk around this hedge, grip Zali by her strawberry hair, and tear out her jugular with my teeth.

The aftertaste of that errant thought is bitter.

But he laughed with her. *Smiled* at her. Not just a small, mocking smile ...

An unguarded one.

The only male who's ever smiled at me like that is Kai, so

whatever Rhordyn shares with this female must be special ... But his *cupla?*

In the stories I've read, a male only offers a female the other half of his cupla if she's his mate. His true love. His *destined.*

For a moment, I think I might collapse.

"Is she—is she your mate?"

His eyes widen before he tips his head and laughs, the breadth of his chest shaking with the roll of it, but it's not a happy sound.

It's dark and brutal, like stones clanking against one another over and over again.

The vicious sound tapers off, and he skewers me with his icy regard. "You do read some crap, don't you?"

"*Gypsy and the Night King* is not crap," I counter, leading him to shake his head.

"It *is* crap, Orlaith. *Mates* are a pretty lie that farmers tell their daughters so they won't settle for the local bard."

"The local bard?" I scoff, wondering how the tables flipped so quickly. "Right."

"Yes," he snarls, stepping closer, making my skin smart from the crush of his frosty aura. "A bard who may know how to sing a charming tale and lather you up with the promise of love, but in the end, will shred your virtue before staking your heart on a metaphorical spike."

I frown. "I thought we were talking about farmers' daughters ..."

"*Mates*," he snarls with a flash of his teeth, "is the tale they spin so an adolescent female will wait for *true love* to come along. So she'll accept a cupla before spreading her thighs and letting her maidenhood get torn apart." He offers me a wicked smile that sculpts his face into something I don't like.

Not one bit.

Well-trimmed branches jab me in the back with each labored breath, and I have nowhere to go. Nowhere to hide from that sharp smile that's carving me up.

"*Mates,* Orlaith, are a fairy tale. A tragedy painted with the pretty face of a happily ever after, but at its core, it's still a fucking tragedy. If you believe everything you read, you'll be disappointed when you finally step into the real world."

All the blood drains from my face.

When you finally step into the real world ...

I turn my head to the side, desperate to avoid facing the truth laid out before me. I dug into the soil, made myself a home, and now I'm one wrong move away from being ripped out at the roots.

A hot tear slips free, carving a path down my cheek and smacking the air with the briny taint of my unrequited emotions.

Firm fingers pinch my chin, forcing me to face him again.

"You're better than this."

The hollow statement guts me, and when paired with those tombstone eyes ... I'm six feet under, pushing daisies from my rotting corpse.

Because I'm *not* better than this. Once again, he's setting me a challenge, one I'd already failed the moment he led me to the starting line.

His gaze darts down, and I can almost feel his featherlight perusal of my lips before he spins, whipping away like a sail snapping with a push of wind.

"Dinner tonight, Orlaith. All four of us," he bellows over his shoulder. "Bring your appetite and don't be late."

His words fan my grief into red-hot flames of fury.

He's telling *me* to be punctual when I've stared at his

empty place setting three times a day for the past nineteen years?

My lips peel back, and I stalk in the direction of the stables, deciding Baze can spend the morning icing his kneecap rather than training me. I'm going to go shovel some horse shit, seeing as that seems to be the winning theme for the day.

CHAPTER 18

ORLAITH

I saunter into the dining hall, littering the floor with muddy footprints, hips flicking with each swaying step.

The servants, backed against the walls like potted plants, somehow maintain their straight-spine posture. None of them even *glance* at me, though I do notice a few begin to breathe through their mouths.

The room is empty of furniture other than the long dining table, its left end boasting a hearty spread. But it's hard to fully appreciate the smell of roasted game and herb-encrusted root vegetables with this pungent, sour-smelling waft clinging to me like a cloak.

Most of the chairs have been removed from the room, leaving four packed at the end like this is some sort of *intimate* gathering ...

A decision Rhordyn will no doubt live to regret once I take my seat.

I focus on the empty chair on the far side, avoiding eye contact with the man sitting at an ornate place setting he's never bothered to eat at.

Zali hasn't even received his cupla yet, and she's already got him joining our ... *dysfunctional* family dinners. The thought leaves me wishing I'd rolled in horse shit a few more times.

I settle into my seat and assess the spread that does nothing to stimulate my hunger. In fact, all it does is knot my insides further.

"Well, isn't this cozy?" I look to Baze seated opposite me and beside an empty chair. He's got an elbow perched on the table, head propped by two fingers prodding his temple, eyes wide like a moon owl. "What?" I ask, tucking a lock of hair behind my ear. A dusting of dried shit sprinkles my lap, and I brush it to the floor while I wait for him to answer.

"*What?*" Both brows reach for his slicked-back hairline. "Really?"

I shrug, relaxing into my seat, well aware that we're one person short for this little celebration dinner—not that I intend to let that dampen my mood. I, myself, was half an hour late. The fact that she's even tardier reflects poorly on her character, and she should absolutely saddle a horse, get the hell out of this castle, and never return.

I look sidelong at Rhordyn, the picture of elegant prestige in his inky garb that's pieced together with fine, silver thread. The jacket is left open to his sternum, revealing a black button-down beneath. He's reclined in his chair, elbow notched on the armrest, thumb painting paths across his bottom lip.

"Wow. You're both so well dressed. If I had known this was a tailored affair, I might have worn shoes."

Unlikely.

Baze clears his throat before the sound of delicate footfalls echoes on the stone.

I glance up to see Zali looking fresh as a blushing rose, dressed in a neck to floor gown that hugs her athletic figure.

Its rusty color compliments her skin tone and the spirals of hair falling over a regal shoulder, almost reaching the dip of her tapered waist.

She's the epitome of exotic wrapped in a perfect, well-presented package, and it occurs to me the manure was quite symbolic. Anyone would look like crap sitting next to that woman.

I look to Rhordyn, still watching me—still running his thumb across that bottom lip. Something about his unwavering stare has me wiggling in my seat, as if the action alone could shake him off.

"Where's that smell coming from?" Zali asks, drawing closer, and I let Rhordyn bear witness to the smile I whip up as I lift my hand and wave.

"Me." I turn my attention to Zali, now standing near the empty seat beside Baze, her honey eyes taking in my soiled cheek, the straw hanging from my hair, the muck caked to my clothes. "I've been bagging manure for my plants."

I expect to see her face twist, or perhaps even a gag; instead, she's looking at me with something akin to reverence.

She peeks at Rhordyn, smiling a little.

My chest tightens.

I'm outside the circle of some personal joke they'll probably laugh about later when they're tangled between the sheets. The thought sours the remaining scraps of my appetite.

Fingers strum against the table—an impatient tune that has my hackles rising a little more with each flourished beat. It takes me far too long to realize the tempo matches the frantic drum of my heart.

Suddenly—almost violently—it stops.

"Orlaith."

"Yes?" I answer, batting my lashes like I've seen the maids do when they pass him in the halls.

"I see you've brought half the stable to the dinner table. Would you like time to freshen up? I wouldn't want the smell dampening your appetite."

"I'm fine. And I'm sure the High Mistress doesn't mind," I say, looking at Zali seated close enough to kick under the table. "Do you, *Mother?*"

She chokes on a mouthful of wine, and I watch it dribble down her chin like a line of blood.

Leaning forward as far as I can, I snatch the goblet out of her hand and slog the entire contents in one large gulp. It burns a trail all the way to my stomach, and I wince, hating the taste. But that doesn't stop me from hailing the servant for a refill.

Baze moves to stand, but Rhordyn stops him with a slight bat of his hand, chin resting on his bunched fist like he's enjoying the show.

Well. Lucky for him, that was barely the first act.

"You know, I once read that anxiety can stem from a lack of maternal support. Considering I was raised by these two," I rasp while waving my glass between Baze and Rhordyn like a crystal war flag, giving Rhordyn *far* too much credit for someone who was never here, "it's no wonder I've got issues."

The servant fills my glass from a silver chalice, and I look deep into the pit of Zali's perfect, almond-shaped eyes ... wishing I could gouge them right out of her head. "But now I've got *you.*"

It's Baze's turn to choke on his drink.

"Yes," Zali replies, an amused smile playing on her lips. "Now you have me." Reaching for a goblet of water and leaning close, she uses her other hand like a shield to block Rhordyn as she waggles perfectly manicured brows. "And for what it's worth, I agree. I think you deserve a medal for putting up with them for so long."

My sail loses all its rigidity.

Damn.

A young servant begins placing bread rolls atop each of our place settings, but Rhordyn plucks his up the moment it lands on his plate and relocates it to mine.

The room falls into a fragile stillness.

I study that bun like it's the sum of my salvation and ruin all rolled into a well-seasoned lump of dough.

"Eat, Orlaith." The command is not gentle, but despite my lack of appetite, I know he's right.

I *should* eat.

I've never had wine before, and it's left me feeling a little light-headed. Likely because I've barely eaten since the withdrawals kicked in.

"I have manure on my hands ..."

Zali clears her throat, and I lift my gaze to the napkin she's suspending over the table. "I've dampened it for you." Her words are accompanied by a gentle smile that's almost tentative.

I set my glass on the table and take the offering, mumbling a thank you as I wipe my hands clean and split the bread.

Warm, yeasty steam puffs up and I sample the smell, expecting it to curdle my insides. Instead, it's a gift for my starved lungs, and I draw deeply, moaning as the intake awakens every nerve ending in my body.

Suddenly, any air ungraced with the delicious aroma feels entirely inadequate.

A small plate of cinnamon-nut butter slides into my peripheral, and I steal a peek at Rhordyn.

"Thanks," I mutter, using my finger to daub it onto the warm flesh, waiting for it to melt down before I take a bite.

Soft, fluffy goodness yields a wholesome, decadent flavor —the perfect mix of sweet and savory somehow meeting in the middle to form divinity incarnate.

My lids flutter closed, shoulders softening as I chew, nice and slow, trying to savor the taste. I'm not sure how it's possible, but Cook has improved her perfect recipe. I doubt anything but these *exact* bread rolls will satisfy my hunger for the rest of my entire life.

I glance up to see Baze and Zali watching me with awed intrigue. "What?"

They tuck their heads down and start ripping apart their own rolls.

Shooting a glance at Rhordyn, I'm stilled by the haunted look in his eyes. He's watching me with such primal intensity, I doubt a single strand of hair could shift out of place without him noticing.

"Is something the mat—"

I'm cut off by the sound of a blade loosening from the confines of its sheath—the hiss short and sharp, yet still managing to slip a hook through the flesh of my lungs and *pull.*

My gaze collides with the small, metal blade Zali is using to butter her bread, spearing my heart with the urge to flee.

The room closes in, evicting air I so desperately need as I struggle to convince myself I'm not the epicenter of three circling beasts; that they aren't slashing at me with talons that *scrape* every time they land a blow.

A Vruk talon is longer than that blade. It's black, and hooked at the end.

Not the same. This is not *the same.*

I drop the bun in the same instant Rhordyn's hand snaps out, gripping the sharp end of the dagger.

A rich, coppery tang permeates the air.

The weapon is snatched out of Zali's grip and folded amongst his napkin, as if out of sight equals out of mind.

He knows better.

He's seen me fall apart enough times to know that particular sound is my weakness. It strikes a match inside me—leaves my blood boiling, brain bulging.

Leaves me in a pathetic, coiled, screaming heap.

The side of my face feels to be carved by his stare, much sharper now.

Colder.

He's waiting to see if I unravel.

"Do you ne—"

"I'm fine," I snip, lifting my chin and shoving my shoulders back. "In fact, I've never been better."

Lie.

A scream is on the tip of my tongue, *begging* for me to cut its leash. But this time, it has little to do with the surge of pressure flirting with my head.

Things are changing. And I don't like change. I'm not *comfortable* with change.

I grit my teeth so hard I'm surprised they don't shatter.

"Are you sure about that?"

The question is flat, but so is my answer.

"Yes."

"Well," he bites out, "I'm glad to hear it."

I stand, staring straight through the wide-open doorway,

doing my best to ignore the blatant scour of his scrutiny and the stark blanket of silence that's befallen the room.

"Excuse me. I've suddenly lost my appetite. Probably all the ..." I swallow thickly, "shit."

I walk the long way around the table and head toward the exit, begging the silence to hold.

"Orlaith."

Rhordyn's voice casts my feet in stone.

"I'll be up in thirty minutes," he rumbles. "Since you're feeling so *fantastic*."

I'm still useful, then.

My lids flutter closed, blood frosting from the feral lilt in his tone—the underlying tune of *need*.

Well, I have needs, too.

My eyes pop open, and I continue walking, hands balled at my sides.

I don't answer.

CHAPTER 19

ORLAITH

Wrapped in a robe that's too dense against my fervid skin, I pace back and forth, wearing a path into my fluffy rug while I clobber myself with questions. The roaring fire glints off the sharp piece of metal pinched between my thumb and finger ...

The one that knows the softness of my flesh; the taste of my blood. The one that helps me drip into this goblet sloshing with an inch of clear water.

Do I feel safe in this tower?

To a certain extent, yes.

Do I want to leave my safety circle?

Never.

But I'm suddenly wondering how much of that has to do with me bleeding into this goblet every day for the past nineteen years, giving little pieces of myself to a man who was never mine. A man who's given *nothing* of himself in return.

Nothing

Rhordyn's simply a shadow that sometimes drifts through this castle. Just a specter that has a voice dense enough to make him seem real. And now he's downstairs, sharing a meal with another female while I'm preparing to stab myself in the finger. For him.

I sigh, bottom lip caught between my teeth, looking down at the pin like it's a sword about to pierce my stupid, vulnerable heart.

White-hot fire blazes through my veins.

Screw it. Screw him. And screw his fucking needs.

I let the pin fall to that little porcelain plate and set the goblet on the table. Stalking to my bed, I snatch *Te Bruk o' Avalanste* and crack it open to a random page, pretending my insides aren't churning.

Minutes pass, eaten by the constant tick of my bedside clock while I pretend to read, though I haven't turned a single page by the time that long, slender hand kisses the thirty-minute mark.

Footsteps echo up Stony Stem—dense, thunder-clapping ones that could only belong to one person.

I hear the little wooden door being unlocked, then opened.

Silence.

The waiting sort of silence that's deafening, stretching for over thirty seconds before the door slams shut and those same footsteps hurriedly descend.

I expel a mighty breath.

Five minutes later, more footfalls approach—as I'd expected them to.

They're rushed. Frantic.

Familiar.

Knuckles rap against the wood, and I tuck a lock of hair behind my ear, the silky strands damp from my bath. "You may enter."

The door opens and Baze strides in, gaze darting around the room before landing on the book open in my lap. His brows bump up and he quickly catches my eye. "Sorry to, ahh ... interrupt. Are you okay?"

Interrupt?

"Better than ever. Just enjoying a bit of light reading. Why?"

He clears his throat and steals a quick glance at the pin still cradled by my plate. "Have you—have you forgotten something?"

I lift a finger to my lips and tap, pretending to think while my heart bruises itself against bone.

"No," I finally answer, eyes dropping back to the page of ... *God of Fertility. Crap.*

Cheeks ablaze, I swiftly turn the page. "I absolutely have not forgotten anything."

He retrieves the pin and walks over, waving it in my face.

I peek up, mouth popping open, hand coming up to cover it. "Ohhhh, that!"

Baze sighs, all terseness melting from his shoulders as he sets the pin on my bedside table and retrieves the goblet of water.

"I'm not doing that anymore."

He stumbles a step. It's quite funny, actually. I've never seen him do that before.

"Excuse me?"

I shrug. "Yeah. Tell Rhordyn he can go fuck himself. Or her. One or the other."

He takes a risky step closer. "Orlaith, you're acting extremely out of character. Is it because I caught you looking at dirty pictures? It's nothing to be embarrassed about."

I don't think, I just *do.*

The book flies through the air, almost clocking him in the cheek. It would have, too; my aim is superb.

Unfortunately, so are his reflexes.

With a sharp hiss and a hand that strikes with the poise of lightning, he snatches the book from the air. "What the hell was that for?" He barks, studying me like I've suddenly grown a tail.

"Out!" I scream, leaping up and herding him toward the door, seizing the goblet.

He slides back until he's over the threshold. *"Laith—"*

"And don't forget to pass my message on!" I slam the door in his face and stalk back to bed.

It's not until I'm nesting amongst my pillows, the red, misty anger ebbing from my vision, that I begin untangling the past few moments.

Regret lumps itself into my belly.

I just threw that beautiful book through the air. Tossed it like it was nothing more than a hunk of trash. And now Baze is in possession of the ancient, stolen relic ...

"Shit."

I set down the hairbrush, lifting my gaze above my vanity to the stout, timber-framed mirror—the only thing that doesn't bend to fit the curve of my walls.

The reflection staring back shocks me, as it always does. Makes me wish I hadn't looked.

My tutor used to say eyes are windows to the soul, but no matter how much I've searched mine, I've never found myself.

Eventually, I stopped looking.

They're large and soft lilac flecked with gold, and they dominate my other features.

My nose is small with a dusting of freckles that skip across my cheeks, giving my otherwise fair complexion a sun-kissed glow. I touch thin, shapely lips, fingers drifting down my sharp chin before pushing the mass of golden hair behind me. Untying my robe, I ease it off bladed shoulders, exposing honed collar bones and slight arms despite Baze's grueling training regimen. I let the material drop a little more, reveal my budding breasts, and tilt my head to inspect what I've been flattening with my wrap since they first appeared ... as if controlling my body meant I could control *everything else.*

My entire *life.*

Rhordyn wants to inject me into society, but there's a reason I don't attend monthly Tribunals anymore.

Tried it. Don't like it.

You can't control a crowd. Can't control the way they look and whisper and unravel you with their words.

"Why her?"

"Why not our mothers, daughters, brothers instead? What makes her *so worthy of being spared?"*

Questions I've asked myself so many times, the echoes have left an internal scar.

But my eyes don't hold those answers. It's as if my soul slipped free of them long ago, leaving nothing but a shell that doesn't quite fit.

I blink, spilling tears I smear over my cheek. With a sigh, I look away, foraging through my dresser for something to sleep in.

The sound of heavy footsteps blasting up Stony Stem has me sucking a sharp breath, tugging my robe across my breasts moments before the door flies off its hinges and skids across the floor.

A whimper escapes me as Rhordyn pours into my room with eyes shaded black. He slams into me, corralling me against the wall, locking me between what feels like two unyielding sheets of ice.

I swallow thickly, all too aware of the tensed panes of his powerful body. Of the way his head's dipped, nose grazing my neck, his cold breath an assault on my prickling flesh.

"You deny me," he snarls, tone menacing.

Wild.

"I—"

"It wasn't a question," he snaps, and my spine locks.

His smell is a drug clogging my throat, stopping me from drawing a deep gulp of air lest I get high and pass out.

"I ... I forgot."

"Don't lie to me."

Two sharp points punctuate the thumping flesh of my neck and I gasp, mouth dropping open. The pressure increases, as if he's about to break the surface and bite into me.

Spill me.

Something has me tipping my head to the side, like a flower exposing her brittle stem to a pair of clippers.

He makes a low, rumbling sound that stays trapped in the tomb of his chest.

My lids flutter closed.

His every breath pushes him closer, and I find myself timing my own just to lessen that slice of space between us, allowing me greedy sips of his body—equally as foreign to me as my own.

But where he's hard, I'm soft like butter and so damn vulnerable. Right now, he could tear me to ribbons, and like the supplicating creature I've become in the shadow of his presence, I wouldn't even fight.

Suddenly, almost *punishingly*, the sharp pressure abates, leaving nothing but the tender chill of his lips against my carotid. "Tell me the truth," he murmurs, catching my breath.

The truth ...

"Now."

"I—I was jealous."

"And why were you jealous, Orlaith?"

The question skates over my fervid flesh like the smooth slide of a blade, dropping my thrashing heart into my stomach.

"Because in the gardens, when I first saw you ..."

I pause, knowing I shouldn't say what I want to say. Knowing that's crossing a line that should be left uncharted until I draw my last breath.

"Go on," he commands, and the simple slash of it almost brings me to my knees. Probably would if I weren't tethered to the way his lips move against my skin every time he speaks.

"I saw you *smile* at her ..."

His body locks. Though it only lasts a fraction of a second, I revel in the brief drop of his shield.

"Greedy girl," he whispers, voice akin to the wind shaking my window panes in the dead of night. "You want them all to yourself?"

I shiver all the way to my toes.

Always.

"Yes." The word is syrup slipping off my tongue, heated like the dull ache between my legs. One that has its own desperate heartbeat, screaming for him to pin me to this wall with a different part of his body—

Breath crumbles out of me.

"Well," he rasps, then swallows. "I'm greedy, too."

He whips back, forging a hollow chasm between us, luring long tendrils of my hair to chase his presence.

He storms toward my bedside table and snatches something off the surface. I don't realize what it is until he rounds on the hearth and those dancing flames reflect in his platinum glare as he fires my needle.

Shadows frolic across his sculpted face, highlighting his foreboding expression, brows drawn so close they're almost meeting in the middle.

I study him while my lungs battle their confounds.

It's so strange to see him crouched in my room, firing my needle—not dancing around the act but *involved*.

This is what I've always wanted, for there to be no door between us. And the fact that he's here, now?

It's a bucket of icy water dumped atop the angry flame threatening to turn my heart to ash.

He waves the pin through the air, retrieves my half-filled goblet from my bedside table, and stalks toward me. I swallow, our gazes locked as he lifts my hand and drags it close.

I've forgotten how to breathe. How to move or function or even *think*.

My fist is unfurled, one stiff finger at a time, and he picks his target—my pinkie finger—stretching it out like he's flattening the coiled petal of a pretty bloom.

I usually avoid the pinkie, only because it's small, the skin so soft and delicate.

"That one hurts the most," I whisper as he works his thumb up and down the base until the tip is red and aching.

"I know," he murmurs, piercing the flesh.

The sharp, sobering sting makes me wince, and I watch a

droplet of blood bulb to the surface. Rhordyn slips the needle between his teeth as the cherry tear blooms and blooms until it's dribbling down the side, threatening to drip.

He dips my finger in the water, blushing it rosy pink, tainting it with my need to give to this man. With his strange compulsion to *take.*

Lids sweeping shut, I try to ignore the smell of blood distilling the air while a question bubbles in my chest again —*desperate* for freedom.

Tonight, I've lost the energy to keep it contained.

"Why do you need it?"

His tightening grip bunches my knuckles.

Silence stretches, finally shattered by the scrape of Rhordyn's commanding voice. "Look at me."

Slowly, I open my eyes, assaulted by a vision nothing short of punishing. He's all hard angles and bitter resolve—a beautiful nightmare made flesh.

There's death in those silver eyes.

"This, Orlaith. This *right here* is why we have the door."

My pathetic heart drops so abruptly, my next words come out choked.

"No. I just want to know *wh—*"

"You're not ready for that answer," he bites out through tight lips and a stiff, almost unmoving jaw. "And for your own sake, I hope it stays that way."

He drops my hand and spins, taking the goblet with him, leaving my arm hanging at my side and dripping water all over the ground. Like a cow who just got milked and has now been sent back to the field to regenerate her udder.

"Don't forget again," he growls, putting my needle on the tray and walking straight out the door, disappearing without a backward glance.

It's a slap to the face.

"I can't make any promises!" I yell. "I have a lot on my plate, you know!"

I hear him grunt, then nothing but heavy footfalls winding down Stony Stem. Once they fade, all I'm left with is a hollow silence dented by the rapid beat of my fragile heart.

Deflating, I stumble back, colliding with the wall ...

I gave in.

What's more, I set the question free and got nothing but riddles and a verbal scalding in return. In fact, all I have to show for it is a sore finger and this lingering ache between my legs—one I try to ignore as I blow out my bedside candles and crawl into bed, robe and all, for what I hope will be a shadowless sleep.

It's not.

I dream of giant creatures that bite into my skin, shake the life out of me, and send my blood splattering.

I dream of things that make my flesh their own.

Things that make me *break.*

CHAPTER 20

ORLAITH

I wake drenched in sweat, hair plastered across my face. The fire is out, and it takes all my energy to peel the sheets back and roll out of bed.

Seems the hangover from a terrible night's sleep is almost as bad as exo withdrawals.

The sky rumbles, loud and boisterous, making my mirror rattle against the wall. I rub sleep from my face and pace to the window, seeing shaded, high-hanging clouds preventing any light from filtering down.

Waking to a heavy sky that holds nothing but the promise of rain always leaves me feeling like an unoiled hinge.

I rinse the nightmares from my face, change into leather pants, a button-down, and a loose-fitting sweater, then weave my hair into a hurried braid while the bath tap fills my sprinkling can.

Fourteen seedlings nest on the windowsill above my painting station, drinking what they can of the low light. Their small clay pots are handmade, varnished with bold colors that pay tribute to the paint I'll eventually make from some of their flowers.

I test the soil, dribble water where it's needed, then step

onto my balcony to tend the bigger ones camped against the wall beneath the overhanging roof on the western side.

"Look at you guys!" I splash their dirt, fawning over their bright green shoots and unfurling fronds. "You're all doing so well! Except *you,*" I mutter, crouching, narrowing my eyes on the fig tree that seems to sag every time I take my eyes off her. "Having another down day, I see."

I give her a healthy dose of water and peer up at the rumbling clouds again, scrunching my nose. We both miss the sunshine, and by the looks of things, I doubt that'll change any time soon.

I may have to graduate her to Sprouts before she goes and dies on me.

"Hang in there, Limp Leaf."

I work my way around the curved balcony, past my box of herbs and the lemon tree I've been raising for the past five years. Its branches are laden with vibrant yellow fruit that will eventually be juiced and used as a preserving agent for my paints.

Next is my wisteria—the only plant that's been here longer than I. It's so large, it weaves through the balcony and down the tower's edge, and can be seen from almost anywhere on the castle grounds.

I tend the flock of rose bushes yet to show their first bursts of color, then pause by the willow sapling I grew from a seed. Not only is willow bark an excellent pain reliever, I also love the way they mature from gangly saplings to such proud, majestic trees.

I crouch and check his roots, seeing them peeking out through the holes in the bottom of the pot ...

A smile fills my cheeks.

This is *exactly* what I needed to pull me from my funk.

"It's like you've grown up overnight," I whisper, feeling a little less heavy for the first time in far too long.

Planting Days are my *favorite* days.

"It might just be me, but independence suits you," I say, patting the soil around the base of my freshly planted willow, loving the feel of dirt on my hands. I push to my feet, glancing out across the rippling gray pond enclosed with a wreath of swaying reeds. A fallen tree slices its center—The Plank—its underbelly decorated with a carpet of dark green moss and curly white mushrooms.

Weepy should like it here. The soil is irrigated enough, and bonus points for being able to check his progress every time Baze makes me train on that death trap reaching across the insidious water.

I rummage through my bag for a jar and spoon, creeping toward the mucky fringe of the stagnant smelling pond. Kneeling in the black mud I use to make my mortar, I scoop big globs of it into a jar, then dart away from the reeds, putting ample space between myself and that body of water before bagging my plunder.

This place is frightening. I never know what's going to leap out at me from the shrubbery.

Hands wiped on my top, I sigh and make for the castle.

A lump of dread sits heavy in my empty stomach as I weave through cold hallways and ascend vacant stairwells on my way to the breakfast hall.

Will *he* be at the dining table? Will Zali be there, too ... smiling up at him and luring him to laugh?

The poisonous thoughts propel my pulse into a hurried, resentful tempo.

Shoulders shoved back, I stalk into the room, my strong stance almost buckling the moment I feel Rhordyn's frosty stare threatening to tack me in place.

Clearing my throat, I glance at Baze in his regular spot, hunched over the morning report.

His eyes roll up, and he frowns, face half lit by orange light spilling from the roaring hearth on the back wall. "Are you in a better mood this morning?"

I try to ignore the spike of fire that sizzles my veins, but then I remember the vision of *Te Bruk o' Avalanste* almost colliding with his face and my mood improves dramatically.

"I have no idea what you're talking about."

"Really," is his lackluster response.

Tanith fails to stifle a giggle as I brush past her on my journey toward my seat, and I offer her a wink. She doesn't have to attend my meals, but I think the ample entertainment keeps her coming back for more, and I don't begrudge the moral support.

Sitting, I search the long table for an extra place setting.

There is none.

"Where's Zali? I thought these family meal times were going to become a ... a *thing?*"

"She had to leave in the middle of the night," Rhordyn rumbles, the tenor of his voice demanding my reluctant attention.

He's going to ruin a perfectly good Planting Day, I just know it.

Slowly, I look his way, struck by his catastrophic masculinity. He's all brooding composure wrapped in finely crafted garb—so at odds with his six-day-old stubble.

"Urgent mail-sprite. She'll be back for the ball."

That damn ball. I want to scrunch it up and throw it in the bin.

"Too bad," I mutter, gaze momentarily dropping to his empty plate.

Always empty.

His eyes narrow, and mine mirror the action.

"Do you have something you want to say, Orlaith?"

Yes.

A million words but I have no tongue to speak them.

I pluck a plump, purple grape off a gnarled stem. "Nope," I reply, slipping the fruit into my mouth and biting down. Saccharine liquid explodes across my tongue, and I let out a soft, purposeful moan as I chew ... nice and slow.

His fingertips strum against the tabletop, eyes hardening a little more with each precise beat.

I wonder if he can see the challenge in my stare—wonder how it feels to have the shoe on the other foot for a change?

"Is that nice?" he asks, toying with the question.

"Positively *delicious*." I pop another in my mouth and watch the muscle in his jaw feather. "Best thing I've ever tasted."

Lie.

I'm not even hungry, and this grape is threatening to turn my stomach inside out. Honestly, that bread roll was the best thing I've ever tasted, but I'm not about to tell him that. Not when he was the one who handed it to me in the first place.

"I'm so glad." He tips to the side, reaches under his chair, and straightens before he lumps *Te Bruk o' Avalanste* onto the table between us with a hefty thud.

I almost choke as icy shame slams into me and turns my muscles stiff.

Shit.

I should really stop snooping around his castle before he boots me out on my ass. Or perhaps that's exactly what he's about to do.

"I thought I'd return your ... *weapon*."

Gaze lifting slower than a rising sun, I almost wither under the weight of his scrutiny.

A waiting calm sits between us—a breath held hostage while Rhordyn reclines in his chair, chin on the balled-up pedestal of his fist. That stare intensifies, sending a droplet of sweat rushing down the length of my spine.

"I-broke-into-a-storage-room-below-ground," I blurt, the words a hot coal spat off my tongue.

"I'm aware. I had the window replaced yesterday."

Crap.

"Oh," I squeak, cheeks burning, though it might be from the fire blazing at my back, assaulting me with its sudden, relentless heat.

"And tell me," he purrs, planting his elbows on the table. "Did you get a chance in your very busy schedule to have a read?"

Baze clears his throat.

"Just a little bit." I instantly regret my understatement when that raven brow almost jumps off his perfectly rendered face. "*Three times*. I flicked through it three times with a fine-toothed comb before I took it down to Kai to decipher some of the language."

I stamp a hand over my mouth.

Oops.

Rhordyn peers down the table for the briefest moment, pinning Baze with a guarded look that's impossible to decipher.

He pushes to a stand, the movement akin to the draw of a sword. "And tell me," he grits out, retrieving the book and prowling around the table, strong thighs tensing with each assaulting step.

Te Bruk o' Avalanste thumps on the tabletop beside my plate, and I squirm as his hands connect with the back of my chair. "Do you believe anything in there, Orlaith? Do you believe sprites were made from *fallen leaves?*"

I release a shuddered breath, feeling like the room is too small, too hot. Although Rhordyn's blocking the fire's boisterous flames, it's not enough.

I'm going to burn.

I spin, looking up into his eyes, searching for any hint of reprieve.

All that's staring back is a cold disconnect.

It should chill me to the bone. On a normal day, it would. But my insides are throbbing with this hot, intimate pulse I can't seem to douse.

"Rhor," Baze warns but is silenced with a bat of Rhordyn's hand.

"Answer me, Orlaith."

I feel like this answer will determine my fate; whether I'll be burned at the stake like some of the women in books I've read or if the flames licking at my feet are only temporary.

"I don't know," I admit. "I was confused that my tutor never taught me religious studies or even spoke about these supposed *Gods*. I've never read anything about them in Spines."

"That's because it's all *bullshit*," he says, and I flinch at the slash of his tone. He reaches around me, and I almost choke on his deep, manly scent as he snatches the book off the table and waves it through the air. "Why do you think this ended up in a dusty old cellar?"

I daub my brow with my sweater sleeve. "I don't know, Rhordyn."

"Well," he purrs, and although his voice is treacle, I get the sense of a snake preparing to strike. "Consider this your religious lesson for the day. Believe me when I tell you, any *Gods* worth worshiping would take more pride in their position, and they certainly wouldn't leave it to someone else to clean up their mess."

He flicks his wrist and the book goes fluttering over his shoulder.

I squeal, jolting as it lands in the belly of the mammoth fireplace atop a stack of blazing wood. Sparks explode, embers crackle, and I feel like it's my heart he just lobbed into the raging inferno. Flames gobble up the rich tapestry of ancient culture and beliefs, and my eyes sting as I watch the pages blacken and curl—all those beautiful, telling pictures falling victim to a fiery demise.

"That was a beautiful book," I whisper past the lump in my throat, feeling a tear dart down my cheek.

"And it made *fantastic* firewood," Rhordyn snips before charging back to his seat.

I wait in patient stillness, watching the pages burn, listening for sounds of him filling his plate. It's a hollow hope —the sort that's aching for sustenance to fill its void and give it something to feed on.

The sort of hope that leaves me winded when those sounds never come.

Unable to watch any longer, I turn from the book, haunted by the hungry crackle behind me as I wipe the swells of my cheeks. I clear my throat, lift my chin, and try to focus on a platter of fruit, searching for any sense of appetite. Trying to ease my mind from the heartbreak flaming at my back and the internal smolder that's threatening to offer me a similar fate.

"Eat, Orlaith."

I very nearly scream the same thing back, but think better of it. He just burned a relic of ancient lore as if it were nothing but trash. Who's to say he won't toss me in the fire, too?

That's a bit dramatic, but his extreme demonstration set the trend.

Hand trembling, I pluck a peach from the pile and rest its furry, sunset skin against my parted lips ...

Rhordyn's stare is a cube of ice being dragged down the side of my face, a vast contrast to the fire blazing in my belly; shifting lower ... *lower* ... spreading across my belly button like the stretching wings of a bird.

Perhaps the Gods are punishing me for leading *Te Bruk o' Avalanste* to a fiery demise?

Battling to keep my hands steady, I set the peach in the center of my otherwise empty plate and roll the sleeves of my sweater. When that doesn't cool me down, I peel the entire thing off, seeking an ounce of relief from this small sun dawning in my abdomen, setting my skin alight.

"Laith. Are you feeling okay?"

I look to Baze watching me with narrowed eyes, a slice of meat pinched between his fingers that seems to be forgotten about. He's dressed in a thick sweater while I'm considering whether it's socially acceptable to strip down to my chest wrap and panties at the dinner table. Because this button-down, these pants ...

They're *suffocating* my skin.

"It's just a bit hot this morning. Can someone douse the fire? How are you bearing this heat wearing all those clothes?"

I wiggle in my seat, trying to temper some innate itch I can't seem to pin down. The friction makes me quiver from the tips of my toes all the way to my fluttering lids, but does nothing to quell my smoldering skin.

If anything, it makes it worse ... although now I've started, I can't seem to *stop*.

"I'm not hot," Baze murmurs, frowning when I clear my plate and start using it as a fan.

Rhordyn makes this low, abrasive sound that arcs my spine, shoving my breasts forward. I glance at him, lungs compacting when I see his hands gripping the arms of his chair like they're the only things binding him to this world.

His nostrils flare, eyes full-bellied moons, and there is no color in his cheeks. No light in his features. Nothing but cold, astute awareness.

Something in those depthless eyes reminds me of Shay; of the way he perches in a slab of shadow, waiting for me to toss his fleshy feast so he can pounce.

"What's your problem?" I ask, working my plate-fan to a frenzy.

Baze makes this high-pitched choking sound. "Oh ... *fuck*."

"*Out*," Rhordyn snaps, but Baze just sits there, watching him with wary eyes.

"Do you think that's wise?"

"I said *out*."

His brutal command vandalizes the air, and Baze curses, eyes to the ground as he stands and pursues the door.

I pause my fanning. "Why are you—"

"And clear the north wing of all males!" Rhordyn bellows, his voice a clap of thunder.

"Was already on it," is Baze's nasally response before he disappears.

I frown, glancing at Rhordyn. "What the hell is going on?"

Ignoring my question, he waves a hand at Tanith. She peels off the wall and sways toward him, her movements a dance I usually admire—

I don't realize I'm snarling until Rhordyn growls, long and menacing, and I pry my gaze off the approaching female.

"*No,*" he berates, eyes skewering me in place.

He seems bigger—broader—his pressing essence commanding me to yield.

I'm just about to stand when he rises like a mountain shoving out of the ocean. "*I said no.*"

The words power out of him and snip the flame off a candlestick in the middle of the table.

Though my chin is jutted, something inside me curls.

"Tanith," he grates, keeping me impaled with his emphatic regard. "Cast your eyes to the floor. Now."

I study the pretty female who is staring at the ground, paused a respectable distance from the table. The sight has my shoulders softening, upper lip no longer peeled back from bared teeth that were ready to chew.

"A cold bath needs to be drawn in Orlaith's tower," Rhordyn flings at her, attention aimed at me. "Notify Cook that she'll be taking meals in her room for the next week; simple, palatable food. And she'll need some rags prepared and brought up, seeing as she won't be able to retrieve them herself when the time comes."

Hang on ... "*What?*"

Tanith curtsies, then hurries from the room.

"But I don't want to take meals in Stony Stem for the next week," I plead as Rhordyn sinks into his chair. "Whatever this is, my answer is *no*."

Silence stretches. The man's not even breathing. So, I take the chance to validate my point while rocking back and forth against my seat.

"Look, I know you think I don't have much of a life, but I do. And I have things that need tending. There's just no way I can spend an entire *week* trapped in my tower. Much as I like it there," I quickly tack on. "Wonderful view. Fantastic housekeeping service. The stairs are a bit much after a long day, but who am I to complain?"

His eyes drift shut, lips stamp together. Even his shoulders look heavier ... but I disregard that in light of my own barreling emotions.

"I'm sorry. As thankful as I am for Stony Stem, it's just not possible for me to cloister myself up there. I mean, I'm not sure how you were expecting Baze and I to find the space to train." I fan myself with the plate again, matching the beat of my jerking hips. "We'd be right on top of each other."

Rhordyn's eyes open, and I suck a breath.

His face looks sharpened by a whetting rock, his eyes flat like twin sheets of slate.

Suddenly, I feel like a fat, overfed kitchen mouse hanging by its tail.

"There will be no training."

My head kicks back as if he just slapped me. "Why the hell not? You're the one that said—"

"Because you're going into heat."

My heart stills.

The breath in my lungs becomes heavy like mortar, and

even the sensual fire boring deep into my groin seems to abate a few degrees.

I know what a female's heat is, only because I stumbled on an anatomy book when I was thirteen.

But that's about *all* I know.

Two paragraphs into the chapter, I skipped to the next, cheeks aflame. The medis who wrote about the experience made it all sound so ... so ...

Sexual.

I thought I'd avoided it. That perhaps the caspun had successfully warded it off—one of the side effects I'd noted while studying the herb in a medicine book I found in Spines. One of the only adverse side effects I was actually *pleased* about.

Suddenly, my chest wrap feels too tight. Too constricting. My body's desire to mature despite the hurdles has cast light on the fact I've been punishing it for far too long, blind to the nail-biting pain that comes with having my budding breasts flattened.

"Can I ... can I stop it?"

Please say yes.

"No, Orlaith. You can't."

The words land like rocks in my stomach, certain to weigh me down for the rest of my life.

"I need you to walk out of this room, go straight to your tower, and stay there."

Stay there ...

Not only is my body rebelling against my mind, but I'm also being shunned to my tower—being ordered to *stay* for the first time in my life.

I need something normal to cling to or I'm going to fall apart. Maybe not straight away, but eventually the noose of anxiety will slither in and steal my breath, just like it always does when I feel like I've lost control.

"Surely exceptions can be made? I'm not asking for much. Just an hour a day for me to ..." hell, I don't know, feed Shay ... collect flowers ... visit Kai ... "*wander?*"

The wooden arms of his chair groan.

"*Now,* Orlaith!"

Guess that's a no.

My hands fall to my lap, bunching into fists as I glance at the door, lips pursed.

What if Tanith comes back?

"I'll be in my room. *Alone,*" Rhordyn grates out, and I slide my gaze back to him, weighing the value of his words. "With the door locked," he swiftly tacks on.

I try not to over analyze the fact that his statement seems to tame my volatile nerves. The last thing the mural of our relationship needs is another layer of paint. It's messy enough as it is.

"Fine," I snip, knowing *exactly* how stubborn that lock is.

Nothing is getting through that thing without a key.

I stand, making to walk around his side of the table when a low warning sound rumbles out of him.

My feet cement in place.

He jerks his chin in the other direction, and I sigh, diverting my path, heading toward the exit while fanning myself with a silver plate that doubles as an unrewarding mirror for my flushed face.

"Your handmaiden will be up to tend to your needs and collect your nightly offering," he says when I'm halfway across the room.

His words peck at me, though I try not to let my discomfort show.

Likely fail.

Half my enjoyment comes from listening to him ascend those stairs, open The Safe, remove the goblet, and collect that little part of *me*. I use his sounds as a stencil to create a physical picture in my mind, and now he's taking them away, too.

I quicken my pace.

"Orlaith."

My name is bitten out like it's some sort of curse, and I spin, seeing an ocean of unsaid words in his catacomb eyes.

"Yes?"

"Do not, under any circumstance, leave your room. Do you understand me?"

Swallowing, I nod.

"Say it."

"I understand, Rhordyn."

"Good." I note a softening of his tone—detect an easing of the tension in his features. "Go."

I don't wait for him to tell me again.

CHAPTER 21

ORLAITH

Chunks of ice chase my movements as though caught on a line, dissolving to become one with the water in this deep, galvanized tub hidden behind a fall of black velvet. There's a sconce above my head spilling light over my flushed body, illuminating curves that have never looked so plump and pink and—

I sit up in a dash of water and rage.

Hugging my knees close to my chest, I rock in little hammering motions that fail to distract my restless mind. The movement stirs water around *that* part of me and a moan slips out; one that scalds my cheeks because just behind the curtain, Tanith is changing my sheets.

But I just can't help it.

I'm so sensitive—untouched need pulsing with its own carnal heartbeat, something that seems directly connected to the torrid roots digging low in my belly.

Demanding.

"Are you ready for more ice?" Tanith asks, her voice reminding me of a wind chime.

"I think so," is my hollow response as I rock and rock and rock, bunched in a knot, letting the icy water strike that chord of pleasure in a delicate way.

I'm so far out of my comfort zone that I want to burst at the seams. Want to dip my head below the water and *scream*.

Thunder rumbles all around my tower, like I'm the beating heart of the storm. Usually, I'd enjoy bunkering down with a book or the blank canvas of an unpainted rock during this sort of weather, but my mind's a riot of hyper-sensitivity, bored with my limited resources. This aching, bone-weary boredom, like my muscles are crammed full of energy I don't have the space to expel.

My forehead prickles, and a bead of sweat trickles down the side of my face. My rocking motions turn sharp and desperate, sending water sloshing over the side of the bath.

Tanith draws the curtain, rolling linen sleeves to her elbows. She doesn't seem to hold my previous behavior against me, and I no longer want to grip her by that glossy, chestnut hair and snarl in her face until she folds with submission. Thankfully.

Without her, I'm not sure how I would have survived the last three days.

"Warming up again?"

"Mmmhmm."

She hefts a black bucket off the ground, cheeks reddening as she tips it over the edge. I watch the waterfall of ice tumble into my tub, those thick shards shrinking the moment they pierce the steaming surface.

Ice has nothing on this fire in my veins.

"Would you like me to scrub your back?" she asks, placing the bucket down and tucking a few loose strands of hair behind her ears. She smiles, her pretty brown eyes warm pools against her tawny skin.

"Thanks for the offer, but not right now," I murmur, empathizing with my sacrificial ice. Those shards shrink, giving everything of themselves until there's nothing left to give.

But my fire continues to take and take and *take*.

Tanith dribbles more oil into the water and the sharp, spicy smell of bergamot perfumes the air—a robust scent supposed to aid in masking the potent bouquet of my heat.

Too bad it's not all that effective.

I can still scent my desire to be filled. It's a floral musk—like a field of roses in full bloom—and it's mortifying.

"There's a fresh robe laid out on the bed," Tanith informs me as she retrieves the empty bucket with one hand, the other notched on her hip. "Hopefully this lot of ice cools you down enough that you can finally get some sleep."

"Maybe ..."

She crouches next to the bath, looking at me with big, empathetic eyes. "I know it's rough, but I promise it gets better. Once the fever breaks, you'll feel like you own your body again. You just have to get through these next couple of days."

"That feels impossible right now," I admit, hating the lusty tone of my voice. It doesn't matter that I'm speaking to my handmaiden—every word that's come out of me since my heat struck has sounded like a proposition.

"I know. Look, I'll let you get some peace," she says, pushing to her feet. "Unless there's anything else, I'll return in a few hours to collect your goblet and deliver your evening meal."

Actually ...

I sit a little straighter, movements suspended. "You haven't seen any bluebells around, have you? I need more blue paint to finish my rock. If I can't sleep tonight, it'd be nice to have something *else* to focus on." To be fair, having the stems handy in case I manage to collect every other ingredient required to make more Exothryl would be a convenient bonus.

Tanith shakes her head. "I heard the gardeners complaining about the frost killing them all this year. But there could be some in the greenhouse?"

I deflate, chin resting on my knees as I jerk back into motion, sending more water splashing over the edge. "I've already cleared it out. Never mind."

She gives an apologetic smile, lays another towel on the ground to sponge up the overflow, then leaves, my door closing behind her with a jarring clunk.

My spine stiffens, attention spikes, body stills.

The sound reminds my restless soul that there is a door. I'm not locked in.

... I can *wander*.

I'm not sure where I'll go. I just know I don't want to be *here*.

My hands dart out and I cling to the edge of the bath, white-knuckled, teeth gritted, muscles triggered to *move*.

I shouldn't. I know I shouldn't. My heart is telling me I shouldn't ...

But other parts of me disagree, and right now, those parts have a stronger sway.

I wait another few minutes, frozen with feline poise while I listen to Tanith's pattering retreat down Stony Stem. The moment the sound tapers off, I drive out of the bath and am through the door on my very next breath, two steps down the spiraling stairwell before I realize I'm naked.

"Shit."

I spin, leap onto the top landing, and sprint back into my

room, snatching my robe off the bed. It's light and airy, the perfect weight for my ... condition.

Not even bothering to dry myself first, I pull it on, tie it loosely around my waist, then I'm back out that door and barreling down the steps.

Self-restraint has never been my strong suit; neither has my ability to follow orders. To be fair, I'm surprised I lasted this long. Rhordyn should be proud.

It's dark outside, shaded by the boisterous storm blanketing the sky, striking the ground with fluorescent bolts that illuminate my stairwell.

Honestly, I shouldn't be in the tower during a storm like this. I might get electrocuted. Anyone in their right mind would agree my actions are entirely justified.

Each step matches the dull, carnal throb between my legs that only seems to intensify with the friction of my frantic motions. I'm moaning by the time I amble onto the bottom landing, robe hanging off my shoulder, the tie around my waist having lost tension from my hurried descent.

I glance down, figuring I should fix myself before I pop out into the main hall, then collide with a barricade of rock and go stumbling—all the breath hissing out of me as my back slams against a wall that's equally unforgiving.

Sucking large gulps of air, I sweep sodden hair off my face and gasp at the vision of Rhordyn stretched out in the doorway.

His hands are gripping the archway's peak, and he's leaning forward, hanging all his weight on the corded brawn of his arms.

His *bare* arms.

He's topless, his tattoos iridescent in the low light leaking off a nearby wall sconce, contouring the bricks of his body into a beckoning work of art. The bulk of his upper body tapers to a V, punctuated by a fine trail of black hair that disappears beneath the low-cut waistband of form-fitting pants.

Pants that do *nothing* to hide the powerful lines of his legs and the large bulge between them.

I press my knees together, the sutures of my composure stressing.

He's a casual wall of flexing might, his features savage, and there's war in that stare scoring across my skin.

He shifts his weight, hands dropping to his sides.

The action alone feels monumental.

"You told me you wouldn't leave your room," he rumbles, the cadence of his voice bruised with warning.

He stalks forward, and the air seems to shift, accommodating his advance. He plants his hands either side of my head, two physical barriers as solid as the wall at my back.

Every cell in my body surrenders to his closeness, like the ocean tiding to the moon's hungry pull.

Inch by inch, my eyes brave the voyage up the regal planes of his body until I'm peeking from beneath a fan of lashes, knees almost buckling from the wrath stamped across his face.

"You told me you understood." His head cants to the side. "So why are you here, Orlaith?"

I swallow, the sound a splinter in the silence. "Because I ... I need to move—"

"*No*," he replies on a bestial growl that attacks my exposed shoulder. The upper swell of my breast. "You need to *fuck*."

I pant hot, shuddered breaths, that fire dealing sensual blows between my legs that almost leave me incapable of holding my weight.

Yes.

Yes, that's exactly what I need.

His gaze flicks down as he makes a low, abrasive sound, coaxing my skin to pebble. My hips push forward, lured by his closeness ...

His *smell.*

It's there ... somewhere between us. Something my body needs.

Something it's *desperate* for.

Rhordyn draws deep, his expanding chest pinning me to the wall, the world seeming to hold its breath with him. Even the sky stops rumbling for a few tense moments.

His eyes close, face twisting, and though we're pressed together by what feels like gravity, it's as if there's an impassable abyss cleaving us apart.

When he opens his eyes again, they're sheets of cold, black ice.

"Go back up those stairs. Now. And lock the fucking door."

... *No.*

My entire body screams it loud enough I swear the silence quakes.

"But—"

"*Now,* Orlaith! My patience is unbearably thin."

With a large strip of my naked body bared but hidden by our closeness, I don't dare do as he asks, instead pushing my hips *forward.*

He whips away so abruptly I almost fall into his current, willingly or not.

Back pressed against the opposite wall, he watches me like I'm all of his worst nightmares rolled into one inconvenient package. "Five ... four ... three ..."

My stomach drops.

For once in my life I listen to that voice inside and *run,* taking the stairs two at a time, robe slipping down my body.

With every step, another louder, more violent one follows, landing my heart in my throat and sending lashes of fire to every inch of my skin.

I whimper.

His brutal footfalls clap with the thunder and the rain and the bursts of light, getting louder ...

Louder ...

There's a slickness between my thighs that makes each ascending step feel like a punishment, and my knees are quaking by the time I make it to the top.

A cold breath hits the back of my neck seconds before I dart into my room, slam the door closed, and dash the deadlock into place. My forehead lands against the star-freckled mural, pinched nipples exposed to air that's nowhere near cold enough, because those flames are no longer dancing inside me ...

They're a hungry, raging inferno that's threatening to ruin me.

Turning my head to the side, I dissect the silence between the heaving beat of my breaths, listening, listening ... until Rhordyn's heavy footsteps begin a glacial descent down my stairs.

I spin, letting my back drag down the door. Skin grates off my spine, but I hardly feel the pain over the ache between my legs.

My bare ass settles on the cold, stone ground, and my entire body jolts with the contact as I picture something else grinding against that part of me. Spreading me. Sinking in.

Claiming.

My trembling exhale is *his,* though he's not here to receive it.

The Safe is right next to my head, empty like this feeling low in my stomach, and this *thing* inside me is not okay with the latter.

In fact, it's *furious.*

That fury knows only an insatiable hunger, forcing me to grind against the ground in stiff, jerky motions that do nothing to suppress this agony—rather fueling it into something wild and unleashed.

It's not until a droplet of moisture lands on the swell of my bare breast that I realize I'm crying.

CHAPTER 22
ORLAITH

My paintbrush swirls over the rock from Whispers, leaving threads of teal that clash with ... *everything* else.

"Dammit," I hiss, tossing my brush at the table and watching it spit color all over the wall.

I was hoping the waterproof paint I mixed for Kai's stone would be the answer to at least one of my problems. Though it's not deep-ocean blue, I figured it would suffice for the final whisper in my mural.

But it's not right. I'll have to wait until next season to place this final piece.

I scan the collection of colorful rocks lined up on my table, all different shapes and sizes. Some are painted to look like miniature gardens; some are scenes from around the castle or from the books I've read. Some are bits of my nightmares—the stones I paint when my subconscious continues to peck at me long after I've woken.

It usually brings me a sense of calm, but right now, that's not the case.

I shove wet hair off my bare shoulder and push off the stool, releasing a moan, that intimate part of my body that's flushed and swollen instantly mourning the cold, slate surface I've been grinding against since my last bath.

My breasts are so achy and heavy and full, I can't bear to look down. My skin flares with a parched sort of heat, thirsty for even the slightest brush of a fingertip.

I didn't ask for this, I don't want this, and I *hate* what it's doing to me. How it's tied me into an animalistic knot, reprogrammed my mind into thinking there's only one thing I need to survive: hot, feral sex. *Deep* sex. Crippling sex that digs up into me and wets my insides.

This heat can go to hell.

I look through water-streaked windows to a misty Vateshram Forest. To the wild ocean being lashed with wind and a whitewash of rain.

Five days of being stuck up here, out of routine. Five days of being naked, hot, and constantly *wet.*

Wet with sweat, bath water ...

Wet between my legs.

A crack of lightning opens the sky and I frown, thoughts turning to Kai out there at the mercy of the elements. He once told me that he lost a friend to a lightning storm, and it planted a permanent seed of concern.

I miss him. Wish I could swim with him—get tossed around by those angry waves until I feel *normal* again.

I've forgotten what that's like.

Pushing past the heavy door, I step onto my balcony, the rain rinsing my scorched, naked skin.

There is no sizzle, but I feel it. Shudder from it. *Feed* from it.

I grip the balustrade and tip my head, letting the fat drops cool my face. My shoulders. My bare breasts. I even open my mouth and swallow some down, hoping it will chill me from the inside.

But those roots low in my belly are still seeking somewhere to delve. Still demanding my hips to loosen.

I don't like feeling as if I have no control over my body. And without all my daily tasks to occupy my mind, I have too much time to *think*. That path always rouses the anxious creature sitting heavy in my chest—the one that shrinks and swells at his own leisure and beats me from the inside. I just want to crack my ribs and set him free, but I can't ...

Time after time, he lures my mind to the edge of that gloomy chasm. Forces me to look down into the murk, then holds my eyes open when I try to squeeze them shut.

Screams for me to *jump*.

Despite my unwavering curiosity, I can't bring myself to make the leap ... certain I'll be spat back out in pieces.

I let my chin fall, hands balled into fists, that carnal fire seeming to simmer from an endless supply of fuel. Another reminder things are changing, and I hate it. Wish I could cut this sensation right out of myself, and that's how I know things are really bad.

Fingers flexing, I draw a deep breath meant to loosen my chest.

A vicious howl rips through the forest, gouging the air. My eyes pop open and I freeze—chilled to the bone, colder than I've been in days. My throat constricts, breaths coming in short, sharp sips that do nothing to sate my sudden urge to *scream*.

I don't have the air in my lungs to belt it out as a different sort of scream shatters my ability to stand.

My knees collide with stone.

The very human sound is snipped like a blown candle

flame, but still the wail echoes in my mind, joining a chorus of phantom cries that ripple up from my internal chasm.

Not real. All in my head.

But that initial sound ...

There's a Vruk down there somewhere, and Rhordyn needs to know.

I stumble to my feet and stagger inside, snatching my robe off the bed on my way past. I'm nearing the bottom of Stony Stem when Baze's voice chisels the air, and I stop short of the doorway to the fifth floor corridor, back pressed against the wall.

"It's an entire pack. Shattered a hole in the fence and tore through that small village on the outskirts of Lorn. The sprite said it was over before anyone even knew it had started."

There's a responding grunt that's like an ice-pick chipping off parts of me, and I slide into a slab of shadow I doubt will cloak the scent of my pheromones, but it's worth a shot.

I hear a lock clanking, a door dragging open, heavy footsteps that still too quickly. I don't have to peek around the corner to know where they are. There's only *one* door opposite the base of Stony Stem—the lonesome one that has borne the unsuccessful brunt of my hairpin too many times to count.

"Fuck. You didn't tell me it was this bad."

"It's not your concern," Rhordyn says, his voice nothing short of lethal.

Something inside me goes deathly still.

"Rhor ..."

"*No.*"

Baze clears his throat, and even from here I can feel tension stiffening the air. "Well, why don't you as—"

"Do *not* finish that sentence, Baze. I refuse to take more than the bare minimum. End of conversation."

I peel off the wall, arching like a flower seeking the sun.

Baze is emerging through the doorway, eyes heavy as though he hasn't slept in days. Rhordyn appears next, wearing his signature black pants and a loose button-down rolled to his elbows, hair pushed back from the chiseled structure of his face.

The vision of him has hot blood rushing to my lower abdomen; has me biting my lips shut to trap the mortifying moan that's sitting on my tongue.

He begins to push the door closed, and I stretch a little further, squinting, trying to see what lies within the hollow of darkness that's swiftly disappearing.

He pauses, chest expanding, head snapping to the side. A growl rumbles out of him, almost tangible, and he slams the door shut—his muscles seeming to press against the confines of his shirt.

Baze curses below his breath, and I dart back, fusing with the puddle of shadow.

"You go," Baze snips. "I'll deal with *that*."

"Not a single fucking finger," Rhordyn grits out, and something about the cut of his tone has that fire scalding me with a whole new level of heat.

My lids flutter closed and a dewy bead darts down my temple. My fingers itch to reach between my legs and press into the source of wetness I can feel slicking my inner thighs.

"You forget I rather value my cock," Baze replies with a jovial tone that sounds forced.

There's an awkward beat of silence, the clank of a lock sliding into place, before footsteps assault the rock and taper off. When I can no longer hear any sign of life, I peek around the corner, squealing when I see Baze reclined against the wall, legs crossed at the ankles, arms knotted over his chest. A lounging predator with a bemused expression on his face.

"You scared me!" I shriek, hand slapped across the hammering organ in my chest. "You should try breathing louder. I can't tell you how much it would benefit my nerves."

"You're supposed to be in your tower."

I peep down to make sure all my bits are covered before mirroring his stance, stifling a moan when the action brushes my pinched, tender nipples. "I heard sounds. In the forest."

"Rhordyn will have it under control."

My heart almost leaps out of me. "*Just* him?"

Baze banks his head to the side. "Of course."

Of course ...

Does he know what's out there? What's *really* out there? Because if he did, I'm certain he wouldn't be so blasé about our High Master dealing with it by himself.

My hands twist together, bottom lip pulled between my teeth as I peer off in the direction Rhordyn just disappeared ...

"You have that look on your face."

"What look?"

"The look you get when you're about to try and break into a door with your hairpin."

I frown, casting my gaze on the audacious bastard. "You pay far too much attention."

"Paid to." His offhand tone is an utter contrast to the russet pins of his eyes. "Which lock are you contemplating an assault on this time?"

I tap my temple, fingers like a woodpecker's beak. "*This* one," I say through clenched teeth.

The one that prevents me from leaving the castle grounds.

His eyes flare as he no doubt realizes what I'm implying. "No," he commands. "Forget it, Laith. It's not happening. If he catches you over that line in your current state, things won't end well."

"And if he *dies*, you'll be the one I—"

Baze groans, tips his head against the wall again, and starts to tick off his fingers.

"Wait, what are you doing?"

"Tallying the number of threats I've received today. I suspect I'm about to hit double digits. Quite the milestone."

That fire in me flares, flogging my insides with relentless belts that leave me struggling to maintain my composure. He's not taking this seriously, and I'm all out of patience. No one survives what Rhordyn's going out there to face head on.

No one but me.

That line my mind has sketched around the castle grounds pales in comparison to the thought of Rhordyn falling victim to those merciless creatures; to him no longer assaulting these halls with his presence or collecting my offering night after night.

A vision of him flashes—one where he's broken on the ground, bleeding out.

... Wide eyes that stare at nothing.

I flinch.

Not him. My nightmares can chew on me, but they can't fucking have him.

I don't register my forward step until Baze is at my front with the pointy end of a wooden dagger poised against my throat, his handsome, statuesque face hardened by a mask of austerity I've never seen before.

Not on him.

"Are you serious?"

"Deadly," he utters with a flash of teeth that appear sharp and vicious in the low light.

"I thought you were supportive of me stretching my wings?" I force out through a clenched jaw.

"Always, but I'm not supportive of hormone-induced stupidity. You're not ready to face what's out there. Certainly not like *that*."

"I've survived them before," I reply, trying to ignore the tremble in my voice—that battered part of me that's agreeing with him. Because the raging inferno low in my gut is threatening to turn me into a torch if I don't chase Rhordyn right *now*.

"I'm not talking about the *Vruks*," Baze growls, sliding forward until barely an inch of space separates us. "Now, I'm awfully sick of breathing through my mouth. So either turn around and climb that tower or I'll pick you up, toss you over my shoulder, and carry you up there myself."

"You wouldn't dare."

"Oh, I fucking would." He puts pressure on the blade and my eyes flare, cauterizing the urge to swallow lest I drive the thing into my own damn throat. "And I'd pay for it dearly. So why don't you be a good girl and do what you're told for a change."

There is no room for movement in his command, and it occurs to me that he's learning some terrible habits from our bossy High Master.

"Fine," I hiss, slamming my hands against his chest and shoving.

Hard.

He stumbles back a few steps, gaze locked on his pectoral. The spot I just touched him. He releases a long, dramatic sigh, resheathing the blade down the inside of his boot and muttering words I don't understand. When he unravels ... his eyes are pitch black.

He jerks his chin toward my stairs. "*Now*, Laith. Before you do any more damage."

There's something unbridled in the scrape of his voice, and I feel it scour every inch of my skin.

He glides forward a step—the motion so smooth it reminds me of the mountain cat I once saw prowling through the forest—and my heart leaps into my throat.

This time, I have the good sense not to argue.

I can hear the howls from my tower—a sound derived straight from the pit of my nightmares. Not even my dense, feather-stuffed pillows can stifle the racket.

Rhordyn's down there somewhere. With *them*.

Another pained moan slips out.

Eyes squeezed shut, robe clinging to my sweat-slicked body like a second skin, I tuck my knees up close to my chest and stuff another piece of night bark into my mouth. My third in just as many minutes.

It tastes like dirt and is corrosive to your teeth, but it's my last resort. A fast-acting sedative that wears off not long after you've been dunked into an inky sea of sleep. Though the effects don't last long, I'm hoping the kick is all it takes considering I've barely slept in days.

I just need to be free of this yearning ache between my legs and the sounds I can't escape; need to be rid of this hollow desperation urging me to race down Stony Stem and dart across my Safety Line. For me to follow Rhordyn into the forest.

I stuff my face into the balled-up pillow slip that smells like him and close my eyes, waiting for sleep to ease me out of this living nightmare. Praying the monsters don't follow me into the abyss.

But they do.

They always do.

I dream of their vicious talons, of fire licking at my toes and wide eyes that never blink. I dream of a little boy with glistening irises and stretched-out arms, but he's so far away I don't think I'll ever be able to reach him.

I dream of an unyielding hand wrapped around my throat, belonging to a man I think I recognize.

Most of all, I dream of *him* ...

Rhordyn.

Somehow, that's the most frightening dream of all.

CHAPTER 23

ORLAITH

Too much blood—the metallic scent so potent it clogs the back of my throat. The ground shakes, again and again, like giants are stomping.

If I can't see them, they can't see me.

I tuck into a ball and hide in a bubble of protection I don't want to leave. But is it enough? Will it split like an egg as they fall through the roof and tear me limb from limb?

I wonder if I'll bleed the same color as the others, or if something inky will leak from my severed bits?

Will the monsters chew on me like they chewed on the boy with a face freckled with stars? The one who reaches for me in the darkest corner of my dreams ...

I hide, go elsewhere in my mind, someplace I can't smell the lingering scent of agony. But I can still hear the scratching, like something sharp is being dragged down a dinner plate over and over and over and—

A honed sound powers out of me, the tapered edge a spade forged from the fragments of my pain ... and I dig, shoveling velvet nothing. Forming a chasm that grows and grows until it feels eternal.

Something is following. Slithering after me. Watching me work.

My throat hurts, and still that chasm grows while I scream and scream and scream, digging down, down, down ... deep into the core of my mind.

Like a seed, I plant my hurt at the bottom of the gully, cover it with dirt, and pat it into place.

My relief is instant.

It's gone. Buried in a ravine so dark and vast that light will never cast a ribbon of life onto that wretched seed. Won't let it shoot up and show my colors in a bloom born of death.

My scream tapers off ...

Their sounds are gone. So are their howls.

There's nothing but bone-chilling silence, but I'm cold. My heart is ice. One tap from a chisel and I'll shatter—

I feel myself being pulled from the mattress, settled against something hard and wet, like silk-wrapped stone.

Opening my eyes, I see the edge of Rhordyn's jaw through a curtain of tears. Realize I'm tucked against his chest, screaming, the sound a rusty rasp that tastes like blood.

I let the knowledge of where I am settle, smelling the deep, earthen musk of his scent. Usually a comfort.

Right now, it's the opposite.

I'm sizzling. My head feels like it's about to burst. There's an ache between my legs that's going to kill me—an emptiness I can't shake no matter how much I roll my hips.

I try to speak, and his grip tightens when all that comes out is a curdled cry for help.

"I'm here. You're okay."

I'm not.

"M-my head," I force out, something warm and wet dribbling from my nose, down my chin.

"Fuck."

Rhordyn lifts me, holding me close while he carries me through the balcony doors. A blanket of falling droplets drench us both, and he sits on my sodden balcony, settling me between strong thighs so my back is resting on his chest.

I can feel his breaths—in and out.

Vaguely aware that my split robe is baring my breasts, I close my eyes, waiting for the crying clouds to tame the pressure in my head. The ember in my core.

Rhordyn eases me forward, removes his shirt, then settles me against his bare skin that's cold as slate. He covers me with fabric that's wet, heavy ...

Oppressive.

"No," I rasp, clawing at it. "No, no, no ..."

I don't need to cover my body. I need to expose it.

Ruin it.

In my mind, my fingers are long, merciless claws. I use them to shove fabric, baring the flushed, tender skin of my belly—*untarnished* skin I gouge and slash with strikes of unrestrained wrath. Because I can't do this anymore ...

I'm done.

This heat has boiled me down to nothing but a lump of wanton need, and I have to choke this feeling. Need it to die so I can get back to being *me.*

"*Stop*. Orlaith, you're hurting yourself."

"I'm fixing myself!" I scream. "I'm going to rip it out with my bare hands!"

A serrated growl saws out of him as he snatches my wrists, pinning them against my warring chest. I try to pull them free so I can hollow myself and end this agony but his grip tightens.

"What are you—"

"No more."

I whimper, desperate to extinguish this furnace inside me.

My hips roll, seeking ... searching ... until a surge of pressure threatens to crack my skull open, and a shriek belts out of me in jagged spurts.

"Fix me!" I plead, and his chest stills. "*Please*. I can't take it anymore. I need ... I need ..."

Something. *Anything.*

I wrench against his hold, determined to snap my wrists if that's what it takes to free myself.

"Fuck, *Milaje*. Stop."

"*Please ...*"

He groans; a sound of deep-seated torment. "You're going to be the death of me."

"So long as you take me with you," is my strangled reply, and for a fleeting moment even the rain seems to hang in the sky, as if the world is sucking a gasp through parted lips.

"*Never.*"

The word is bitten from the night and spat with distaste, landing on my chest like a rock that threatens to stop my lungs from drawing breath. Something about his declaration eases the pressure in my head but fuels that fire into forking spikes that lash out, making my hips jerk and jerk.

My skin itches from the fervid fury trying to flee through my pores, and I want to scratch at it. To tear off big chunks of flesh so I can release the heat in plumes of fire and steam and—

I wail, the sound flawed by my sliced-up throat, overriding the symphony of splatters.

I thought I was in agony before ... but this? This is something more. Something *deadly.*

In a surge of adrenaline, I manage to wrench an arm free, but he snatches it up, hands clamping around both wrists like manacles.

My next breath is acid.

"You're killing me *now.*"

He releases a feral growl that threatens to cleave me down the middle.

Still holding firm, he maneuvers my wrists into a bundle held within one of his hands, freeing the other.

My heart skips a beat.

Fingers lingering on the delicate curve of my clavicle, his breath quickens to join mine, but we're out of sync—as if our lungs are playing tug of war.

I've never wanted to win something so badly in my life.

A small eternity sifts by before his fingers trail down, pebbling my skin, pausing briefly where the plump flesh cradles my vulnerable, eager heart.

My breath hitches, back arching.

His hand is calloused and worn, cold like the bolts of rain hitting my skin and those shards of ice that danced across it in the bath. For a moment, I wonder if he, too, will fall victim to the fire in my veins. If he'll dissolve like the milky breath puffing out of me with every fevered exhale.

His hand continues to rove at a glacial pace, perhaps waiting for me to make a sound; scream at him to stop.

I'm frightened to move lest he do just that.

He chases raindrops down the slope of my breast, the ladder of my ribs, bypassing the sodden ribbon knotted around my waist and pausing just below my belly button.

Don't stop.

Please don't stop.

I hear him swallow over the pound of rain, feel his chin rest on the top of my head as if he lacks the energy to hold it up.

My muscles spasm beneath his hand, and my insides do the same, clamping around nothing.

Anticipating.

I roll my hips, an unbridled answer to my body's plea, desperate for his touch to explore the hot wetness between my legs.

He's so close ... *inches* from crumbling that barrier between us.

"You're going to promise me you won't try to hurt yourself again."

"Yes, whatever you say ..."

Right now, I'd give anything he asked.

I'd give him my soul. The breath in my lungs. I'd lump my heart on a silver platter and let him drink straight from the source.

"Say it, Orlaith. Or I go no further."

"I promise!"

A soft, rolling growl makes his entire chest vibrate.

His hand descends those final few inches, fingers cupping that most intimate part of me, providing a cool perch for me to grind against.

My entire body shudders—threatens to turn inside out, all my blood seeming to rush to that one point of contact. I unfold for his drugging touch that's loosening my joints, making my hips tide like the ocean.

Smooth. Confident.

Drawing my own strokes of pleasure from his resting hand, I feel myself start to pulse from the inside, my legs drifting wider as I stoke that heat into something that roars with its own fiery heartbeat ... *but it's not enough.*

I need him filling me, stretching me, chilling me from the inside. I need him to make those flames wink out.

"More ..."

His chest quakes, and something hard presses against my spine.

"You're going to regret this," he grits out, his deft touch sliding up my slit. Spreading me apart.

Threatening to stake a claim.

I need it like I need the breath in my lungs.

His finger swirls around my entrance, stirring me into a frenzy of tight, desperate need before it dips into the heart of my hot, sensitive core. It happens so suddenly my head kicks forward, then back again, body aching to coil around the connection.

It's everything and more. So much more.

I never want this moment to end.

Eyes stinging, I gasp aloud as he eases out, making wet sounds while he swirls around, then slips back in, again and again, striking me with bolts that never go further than his second knuckle.

I drive my hips forward in hopes that he'll dig into me until I'm raw and full, but his reflexes are swift, retreating with the same dexterity.

"Stop it. If I go any deeper, I'll break you, and I'm not leaving here with your blood on my hands."

"Then *don't leave.*"

My words are met with an icy growl that threatens to shatter me.

He inserts another finger and quickens the pace, pumping in short, exquisite strokes, pushing me higher, *higher* ... until I'm a knot of carnal need—flushed and swollen and spread.

Something inside me is about to burst.

"Rhordyn ... I need ... I *need* ..."

Lips tucked close to my ear, his thumb slides up my slit,

swirling around, then stamping against that vulnerable bud of nerves. "*Come,*" he growls, and I'm struck with a surge of lightning, body lurching forward as I convolute in an explosion of ecstasy.

There is no up. No down. There's just him and me and this current surging between us, threatening to tear the world apart in a clash of fire and thunder.

At this moment, I couldn't care less. All that matters is *this.*

Us.

Just when I think I can take no more, everything loosens; my body and mind and anxious soul. I unravel, drawing what feels like my first full breath in days, my fire a sated beast.

Rhordyn's fingers are still inside me as I fold upon his chest, heaving, recovering in his arms while my aftershocks pulse around the welcomed intrusion.

I no longer want to jerk my hips or rip my skin and gut myself. I no longer want to scream my frustrations at the sky.

I'm *free.*

But more than that ...

This moment of stillness is *bursting* with possibilities. Perhaps that door between us will no longer be necessary. Perhaps he'll finally let me in—talk to me and share a meal with me.

Let me into his Den.

Perhaps he'll spread me out on this balcony and stoke that dozing well of pleasure until it's a hungry inferno, only to be assuaged when he thrusts other parts of himself inside me.

Perhaps his plan to gift Zali his cupla no longer exists ...

I draw a deep, unbridled breath, picking up on the hint of

a wet dog smell. A scent that blows into my conscience and flares a memory to life—reminds me where he's been.

My muscles tighten.

"You went out there with the ... with the Vruks," I whisper, struck with the echo of stress I felt while ascending this tower earlier, swiftly followed by a belated surge of relief.

Rhordyn survived.

So enmeshed in the revelation, I barely register his stillness until he draws a deep breath, expelling it with a coarse sigh. "Yes."

His clipped answer chips at my content, but I dash those thoughts away, fanning life into this wistful feeling lightening my heart, making it swell.

He's here, with me, quenching my body and planting hope in my chest.

"How are you still alive?"

"My sword got to them first."

He releases my wrists, and I'm lifted, limp and listless. Held against his chest with my head rested atop the sludgy beat of his heart, he carries me inside where I'm struck with the botanical medley that lingers in my room. That, and the overriding fragrance of my heat.

My cheeks warm as he winds around the space, past my bed and vanity, until he reaches the tub. He sets me in the icy water—robe and all—the liquid a balm to my flushed skin.

I have to stop myself from pulling him in with me.

"Their talons—"

"Are useless if they don't land a blow."

He spins, leaving the curtains gaping enough for me to watch him stride toward the door—bared muscles rippling with each brutish step, his sodden shirt strangled in the tight ball of his fist.

"Wait, where are you going? You're not leaving, are you?"

He stops mid stride and turns his head so I can see his side profile over the wide breadth of his shoulders.

No eye contact. Nothing but cold detachment.

My stomach gutters before he even starts to speak.

"Remember your promise. And I suggest learning to fuck your own fingers. You won't be using mine again."

The words land a crushing blow that bursts my hope into a million mangled pieces.

My next breath is choked.

Knees hugged close to my body that suddenly feels too bare, too vulnerable, I watch him pursue the exit like it's his salvation.

He pauses at the threshold, a figure of shadow and seething brawn. His head tips for a second, and then he leaves, slamming the door shut—thumping that barrier back into place between us.

My body jerks from the onslaught.

I listen to his descending steps, each beating another nail into my bruised and battered heart. By the time he reaches the bottom, I'm choking on a bouquet of noxious emotions, *one* eclipsing the rest enough to leave me shivering despite my fever ...

Shame.

CHAPTER 24

ORLAITH

Outside, the world is gray and gloomy. The rain has abated, but the high-hanging clouds are preventing even the tip of my tower from catching light.

I miss the sun; the way it fills me up. I feel like my soul is dripping away—like I'm wilting.

Empty.

It doesn't help that I woke this morning to a broken fever, which I celebrated for all of two seconds before I realized I smelled like bloody death.

Feeling like I'd peed myself, I'd peeled back the quilt, mortified when I saw a red stain that had seeped through to the mattress. Not only did the entire thing have to be replaced, but I now have a wad of thick, absorbent material stuffed in my undergarments.

Sighing, I cast my gaze across the lumpy clouds and slide off the windowsill, locking eyes with the mannequin standing by the far wall, swathed in a neck-to-floor, blood-red gown.

Wide eyes that stare at nothing.

I bristle.

Tanith delivered it this morning, and now it's in my personal space—a constant reminder the ball, Tribunal, and

Conclave are just around the corner. A trifecta of obligatory torture.

The monthly Tribunal is necessary for Rhordyn's people to have a stage to voice their woes, but with people coming from all over the *continent* for the ball and Conclave, too? It's going to be a challenging few days.

The less I think about it, the better.

I snatch a throw off the end of my bed and cast it over the mannequin, hiding the proof of Rhordyn's insistence to inject me into society against my will. Retrieving my bag, I tip it, scattering its contents across the bed. I'm about to repack it with the bits I need for the day when all the energy sputters out of me, and I let the crochet tote fall to the bed in a heap.

I just ... don't have it in me.

Peeling off my nightgown, I tug on some flowy pants and a loose shirt, and head for the door.

Kai will cheer me up. He *always* cheers me up.

I'm just settling on the rock's edge when Kai's head pops out of the water; hair slicked back, eyes glistening jades. His nostrils flare, brow pinches, and he wades close—powerful shoulders rising above the silvery surface as his beat taps at my edges. "You're bleeding."

I sigh, rolling an apple around in my hands. "Not the sort you can lick better, I'm afraid."

His brows jack up, and he tilts his head, exposing the three delicate lines on the side of his neck. "You sure about that?"

It takes me a moment, but when it finally clicks, I toss the apple at his head.

He plunges below the surface, and the apple dunks a second later. Kai re-emerges right in front of me, fruit in hand, assessing me as he takes a crisp bite.

"What's that look for?" I murmur, churning the water with my feet.

"You look sad."

"Reaching sexual maturity and going back to wearing diapers in the same week will do that to you."

"No doubt." He smirks. "No swimming for you—"

"Don't say it."

"Might attract the sharks."

I groan, and he laughs, moving closer, biting down on his apple and leaving it there. He rolls the hem of my pants until they're at my knees, then grips me by the hips and lifts me with an impressive feat of strength for someone half submerged. Setting me down on the edge of the rock, he perches between my wide-open thighs.

Feeling like I need to draw from someone who's not all frosty hardness, I lean forward and tip my head to the side, enjoying the way his silky skin kisses my cheek while I draw on his rich, briny scent.

There is no pause. No moment of awkwardness to pinch bits of the comfort. Though from different worlds, we've smudged that vivid line and made a warm, cozy home for our friendship.

My happy place.

He sweeps his arms around and locks us together, pulling me closer.

"Have I told you lately that you're my very best friend?"

"You have," he rumbles, fingertips brushing up and down

the length of my spine like the sweep of a paintbrush, decorating me with his affection. "And nobody can *ever* take that away."

Moments pass with us wound together in peaceful ease, his tender embrace making me feel a little more whole.

"Orlaith ..."

"Mmm?"

"I think I know what you need," he whispers, hand stilling low on my waist. There's a raspy layer atop his voice that I haven't heard before.

"You do?"

"Mm-hmm." His chest rumbles with the sound, and I peel back, snagged by his mischievous grin.

My heart does a flip-flop.

He tucks a ribbon of hair behind my ear, leaving his hand resting around the side of my neck, and I notice a touch of red pinching his cheeks. "It's a gift ... of sorts."

The skin beneath his touch tingles, sending sparks across my shoulder and around my ear. "I do like your gifts ..."

"I know you do." He smiles, eyes glinting with a roguish sparkle as his thumb sweeps along the sharp of my jaw. "And I like *giving* you gifts."

I nod, though I'm not sure why.

Perhaps it's the bubbling nerves in my stomach—the ones that have me sitting a little straighter, conscious of my breath, thankful I had the foresight to brush my teeth before I ventured down Stony Stem.

Perhaps it's his body—a pillar of refined brawn shored between my legs, as if he's staking his own sort of claim.

Or maybe it's the fact that he's my safe space. And right now, pitted with a vulnerable heart, bound with skin that doesn't feel right, brimming with a fiery soul yet somehow feeling utterly empty, I don't want to be anywhere else but here. With him.

These are my thoughts as I stare up into sea-green eyes. "Well, come on," I whisper, feeling my pulse quicken. "Hit me with it."

A deep rumbling sound shudders out of him, and I swear his eyes flash fluorescent green. It's the only warning I get before his lips clash with mine—roving and moving in a hungry dance that's far from delicate.

I'm thankful for that. If he were gentle, my inexperience would be entirely exposed.

His hand slips around the back of my head, tongue spearing, and there is no room for self-conscious thought as he feeds me a hungry growl that turns me liquid.

I quake in his arms, yielding.

Exploring.

With the taste of salt on my lips, I let him fold me to his will. Let his hand burrow into my hair and teach me how to move. How to *let go.*

When he finally breaks the kiss, he hovers an inch from my face, breathing hard, spilling ocean essence all over me. "Now," he pushes out, his tiding breath matching the beat of my own. "That's how you kiss someone you *love,* Orlaith. Anything less and they aren't worthy of your heart or the power to break it. Understood?"

I nod, tipping forward until our foreheads meet. "Understood."

Climbing the jagged stairway etched into the cliff, I drag my thumb back and forth across my lower lip that's puffy and tender and tastes like the ocean.

The taste reminds me of Kai—of playful, happy things; moments that are light and wholesome. That taste is a reprieve from the strange emotions that have taken my body hostage over the past few days.

I want to go back to being invisible. Back when I could pretend I was still just a kid in desperate need of a roof and a bed and a warm meal every night. Someone who couldn't possibly be old enough to survive on her own outside the castle grounds.

But I'm no longer that same passive child who couldn't defend herself. I'm a sexually mature *woman,* old enough to receive a cupla and leave the safety of my nest.

The thought makes me shudder.

Unfortunately, my crop of excuses to stay are growing thin.

I step through the door at the top of the stairs and nudge it shut with a backward kick, the dull thud chasing my steps down the dimly lit hall. Rounding a corner, I tuck my thumb between my lips and again I taste the sea, drawing from its calming reassurance.

Something plows into me with such reckless force that the wind is knocked from my lungs. A powerful, unforgiving mountain of muscle drives me back and slams me against the door, my head saved from the impact by a hand wrapped around the back of it.

I gulp for air, eyes wild and darting, looking up into Rhordyn's cyclonic stare.

Pure, unrestrained fury is lashing off him like the virulent beat of a storm. I can taste its sharp, sour tang in the air. Can feel it collecting at the back of my throat.

He's studying me—a scathing regard so cold it burns.

I finally draw a wheezing breath, but it offers little reprieve. "You bast—"

"Did you enjoy it?" The question is fired.

"Enjoy *what,* Rhordyn?"

He cups my jaw like I'm made of stone—not flesh and bone—then kicks my feet apart and pins me in place with the spear of his hips.

I gasp, the intake so sharp I swear it cuts my throat on its way through.

"Having him between your legs," he growls, voice savage, and now it's more than his hips holding me against the door.

It's something else hard and just as brutal.

A sensual, organic warmth throbs to life in the unguarded junction between my thighs.

His thumb slides up my bottom lip, and he rolls it, watching it fold as if he's bending the petal of an immature bud and forcing it to bloom. "Having his tongue in this mouth."

My blood chills.

His gaze flicks up, catching me off guard and making me jump. He takes the opportunity to weave his other hand into my hair and grip.

Hard.

A little sound leaks out of me as he tugs my head to the side, baring my throat and the heaving rise of my breasts. "Having him grab you like this and take the fucking reins."

Perhaps it's the way he's holding me, like I'm the adult I've been pretending not to be, but I spit the truth at him like it's a pebble on my tongue.

"Yes. I *enjoyed* it."

He makes a guttural sound and burrows his face into my neck again, dragging his stubble over the sensitive skin—firm enough to leave a graze. "An interesting choice of truth to serve up, *Treasure*. Especially when you offer so few."

"*Fuck. You.*"

The assaulted skin blazes when he finally pulls back.

"No," he purrs, tucking his lips close to my ear. "But you won't be scratching that itch with *him* either."

His words are ice and disturbingly direct.

"I—"

He nails my jaw shut, slaying me with that unforgiving glare. "And just so you know, if I catch you kissing Fish Boy again, I'll gut him from chin to cock, poach him in milk, and serve him with a side of mash."

The threat injects stone into my spine.

I snarl, ripping my chin from his grip. "You do that and I'll be gone from your life forever."

My words land a serrated blow, and I picture it sawing through his intentions, leaving them in a pile of bloody carnage between us.

I mean it. I'd be gone—something that would probably thrill him to the bone. Though I wonder if he hears the underlying implication of my threat ...

He'd *never* get another drop of my blood.

He snaps back, perhaps expecting me to fall to the ground without the pin of his hips holding me in place. But with the threat on Kai's well-being, I'm more composed than I've been in days—my feet firmly rooted even as I watch him stalk off down the hall.

"Try it, Milaje. Just fucking try it."

CHAPTER 25

KAI

Once upon a time, sleeping with one eye open was a must. A necessity. Close both and who knows what could slip past and thieve your most prized possessions.

Old habits die hard.

But we're not sleeping. We're trying.

Failing.

Curled in a knot within a rocky nest at the mouth of our trove, my drako surveys the ocean, watching shadows drift by.

Large shadows. Tiny shadows. Shadows with long, wiggly arms, and some that chase others at an alarming speed.

Zykanth isn't roused by them. Big or small, fast or slow, he knows there's not much out there to fear.

Not anymore.

A jarring sound comes to us from above. A strident summons.

Tap ... tap ... tap ...

Drawing our lungs full of chilly water, Zyke releases a great, disruptive rumble that ripples through the ocean, scattering a swarm of Bala sharks that were nibbling the algae off our scales.

My drako doesn't move; not a single fin. Doesn't even crack our other eye open.

'He won't stop.'

As if to prove my point, the sound repeats. Faster this time.

Tap-tap-tap.

Zykanth flicks our serpentine tail—an abundance of silver frills dashing through the water. *'Eat angry man?'*

'No. We cannot eat him ... Unfortunately.'

He huffs, expelling a scalding plume of water, making a zealous effort to close the other lid.

Tap-tap-tap-tap-tap-tap-tap-tap-tap—

We snarl in unison, upper lip peeled back from the arsenal of our fine-tipped maw.

'Angry man have no rhythm.' Zykanth begins to unfurl. *'Angry man better off dead.'*

'Zyk—'

He shoves off the ledge with a great beat of our tail, skirting around sharp rocks and through swaying forests of waterweeds. Swarms of fish scatter, the ocean holding its breath as we spear skyward.

I sigh, snatching control moments before he breaks the surface.

Our jaw dislocates with a painful *pop* that never gets any easier, and the entire length of our spine convolutes as we shrink and shrink, one compacting vertebra at a time. Bones crack and crunch and splinter, our skin tightening, herding Zyke into the cage of my chest where he thrashes against my ribs—the painful thuds casting ripples through the water.

He really was going to eat him.

Head rising above the surface, I arch a brow, taking in the shadow of a man standing atop a small mound of jagged stone. He's dressed in black, eyes twin moons peering out from the darkness.

"Isn't it past your bedtime?"

"Get out," he growls with a flash of teeth, tossing a metal rod aside—the one he just used to rouse us with.

It clatters against the stone in an erratic beat that makes me bristle. Makes Zykanth do the same.

Crunching my nose, I battle to keep my top lip steady. "Only because you have such *impeccable* manners."

I pull the last of Zykanth's essence into the shell of my chest, and my tail splits, bones solidifying, joints bending. The last of my scales peel inward as I dig freshly formed toes into the grooves of the rock, grip hold, and lug myself free from the ocean's secure embrace.

Unfurling before Rhordyn, I look down on him, brow raised, manhood hanging heavy between my bare legs.

"Put the shorts on." He tosses a wad of material at my chest, and I let it fall to the rock.

"Intimidated?"

He doesn't answer. Simply crosses his arms.

"I'll take that as a yes." Bending, I hold his stare as I retrieve the pants. "Can't have that now, can we?"

I step into them, button up, and pocket my hands.

The moon breaks through the clouds, casting a beam of silver light upon us while we marinate in a stretch of silence that goes on and on and—

"You going to talk, *bruák?* Or are we just going to stand here watching each other?"

No answer.

"Guessing game it is. Let me see; surly frown, those creepy eyes ..." I let my gaze drag down his body, and

Zykanth ricochets off my ribs as I notice a bulge in Rhordyn's left pocket.

'Treasssure,' Zyke trills, tapping his essence around the confines of the mysterious object.

I quickly avert my line of sight, drawing a couple of long sniffs.

"The reek of rage that tells me if it weren't for"—I wave a hand at the silver scrawl peeking above his collar—"all *that* under there, I'd be bleeding out at your feet." Shrugging, I drawl, "Another notch in your belt."

Rhordyn steps forward, putting us almost eye to eye, and I push my shoulders back.

"That was an accident. A casualty of war."

Zyke pauses, and I have to lock my spine as he slams against my ribs and lungs and heart, straining my next breath.

"If it makes you sleep better at night, keep telling yourself that." I look down ... up again. "What's in your pocket?"

The question lures my drake back to his previous mission of surveying the shape and size of the curious item while Rhordyn's features harden.

"You think I sleep, Malikai?"

"Hope not. I hope you can't close your eyes without wanting to gouge your own brain out." I feign a yawn, dragging it out before I continue. "Come to think of it, perhaps that's *exactly* what you should do. I wouldn't mind watching blood dribble from your eyes and your mouth and your fucking ears."

Just like *her.*

"Asha was my friend, too."

Behind me, the ocean stills.

Listens.

"She was more than just my *friend.* Did you know she was the last female?"

His eyes widen; the slightest tell that's oh so telling, gone the very next second.

"I'll take that as a no." Kneeling, I pluck a shard of rock off the ground, inspecting its cutting edges before pushing to my feet, gaze catching on his pocket again. A momentary lapse I try to hide by flinging the stone, watching it skim across the water's surface. "You doomed the fate of my entire species with that blow."

Casualty of war ...

It's half tempting to set Zyke on him, then sit back and watch the carnage unfold. Rhordyn would put up a good fight, but that's half the fun.

'Treasure in his pocket. Can't eat angry man with treasure in his pocket.'

'Don't be silly. You'd just have to chew gently for a change.'

Rhordyn clears his throat, crossing his arms again. "Did you give her the talon?"

"I did. And I hope she guts you with it."

His chest shakes, and a bout of deep laughter rolls out of him.

"Is something funny?"

All humor seems to melt off his face, transforming it back to the sterile starkness I'm used to. "Not really, no. Believe it or not, you and I are on the same side. At least until you drift further across that very vivid line." He jerks his chin at me. "You know the one."

He saw the kiss, then.

Good.

"We're not on the same side, Rhordyn. Not since you

doomed my people." I steal a glance at the tower poking high in the sky, half glazed by a lick of moonlight. "And Orlaith needs me more than she needs you. All you do is knot up her head, then leave me to untangle the mess."

He looks out across the ocean, and I take the opportunity to study the lump in his pocket more thoroughly.

Zykanth perks up.

It looks heavy. Sizeable. The edges are perhaps a little jagged, but sometimes it's those sharp bits that really define a piece. Set it apart from the others smoothed by the polish of water and time.

I bunch my hands, stuff them in my pockets.

Take them out again.

"When was the last time you took a trip to the island, Malakai?"

My heart lurches.

I follow his gaze to my outstretched hand, unwittingly reaching for his pocket. With a start, I snatch it back and knot my arms, mirroring his stance.

"I said *when?*"

I don't answer. Don't dare spit a lie that will no doubt be picked apart. Don't give him the glory of dissecting the pieces.

Rhordyn shakes his head, a low growl caught in the back of his throat, a look akin to disgust splashed across his face. "I didn't doom your kind. You did that yourselves."

A hiss rips out of me, lips peeled back to expose sharp incisors and even sharper canines—teeth threatening to lengthen and duplicate until my jaw is packed full of a deadly cavalry.

"It's only a matter of time before the wrath of The Shoaling Seas takes a bite out of you, and then what? That girl has lost *everything,* and you have the nerve to offer her something so temporary?" He cocks his head to the side, eyes narrowing. "Or are you prepared to give up your beast for her?"

Fury bubbles inside me with the force of a thousand waves.

My muscles bulge, bones splintering under the pressure of keeping Zyke contained, jaw popping over and over. Even my skin begins to itch and sting, and I know that if I were to glance down at my legs, I'd see patches blooming with scales. I'd see frills sprouting from my ankles, maybe even my toes.

Rhordyn clicks his tongue, looking me up and down. "I didn't think so."

I crack my head from side to side. Bunch my hands into fists.

"We are on the same side, Malikai. The side that's no good for *her.*" He steps close, until I can see the smoky swirl of his unsettling eyes, like a storm cloud just swept over them. "So, next time I catch you kissing Orlaith, I'll stick you through the heart. I don't care if you're the first or last of your kind, if you're on two feet or none. Consider this your first and final warning."

It's not the threat that catches me off guard, but the conviction in his tone. It's his eyes that look more empty than full, despite his keen attention. A look I've seen too many times in Orlaith's wisteria stare.

But there's something else, too ...

"What have you got to lose, Rhordyn?"

He lifts his chin. "*Everything.*"

Something glimmers in my peripheral; a gem held aloft in his white-knuckled fist—too big for him to fully enclose his fingers around.

But it's not just any gem.

It's iridescent. The unrefined heart of a pre-storm rainbow. And there's only *one* place it could have come from.

Zykanth trills, peering through my eyes, tapping his essence around Rhordyn's fingers in a command to drop the treasure.

He doesn't.

Instead, he pulls his arm back and lobs it through the air, watching me with that condemning gaze as I fight to keep Zykanth contained.

It's the distant *plop* that shatters my self-restraint.

My skin rips, bones crack and grind and swell, muscles pull and stretch, and the water eats us up in a single gulp as we plunge into the sea.

By the time we return to the surface—our priceless treasure stashed deep in the most protected corner of our trove—Rhordyn's gone.

CHAPTER 26

ORLAITH

I'm going to die.

Baze's sword whistles through the air, nicking my shirt and sending me stumbling down The Plank—the felled tree that stretches from one side of the deep, ashen pond to the other. His follow-up jab has my foot sliding too far to the side, and my arms windmill.

The glossy water may look serene, but the lofty marshes circumnavigating the lagoon are a fence that contains the sinister truth. Something I'm trying not to think about as I totter on the ball of my right foot.

I find my center of gravity and fall into a crouch, chest heaving, sweat dripping down my temples.

"Orlaith, *focus.*" Baze points his wooden sword at me. "A little blood is no excuse to slack off."

I doubt he'd have the same attitude if his dick was bleeding.

"You're not playing fair," I rasp, unfurling like an emerging fern frond ... though nowhere near as glamorous.

His eyes widen, upper lip peeling from his teeth.

I shuffle back.

"And *you're* not shielding your weakness." He makes another dextrous stab for my innards, but I leap out of reach.

"And I'm playing more than fair. I didn't make you wear a blindfold, though I have one on hand in case you continue to move like molasses," he purrs, donning a sharp smirk.

"I am not moving like molasses!"

"Are too."

I hiss, bounding forward, swinging so fast I nick a hole in *his* shirt. I smile, reveling in the win ... forgetting my flank is wide open until his sword collides with my ribs, knocking the air out of me.

My foot slips and the last thing I see before I strike the surface of the pond is Baze tipping his head to the sky.

The water snatches me with an icy grip, the stark chill of it shocking my lungs and almost convincing me to suck a breath. I kick, sword still captive in my closed fist, legs churning.

This pond isn't like the ocean. It's not salty and swirling and home to my best friend. It's still and stagnant and it smells just a little bit like dead things.

I break the surface and gasp, dashing a slimy piece of weed off my face, caught in the crossfire of Baze's cutting glare. "*Help me up!*" I shriek, trying to ignore the splashing sounds that certainly aren't coming from me.

"Did you keep hold of your sword?" he drawls, as if we have all the time in the world.

I wave the thing above my head.

"Lucky ..." He crouches, watching me with a bemused expression. "But really, I should make you swim to the edge for leaving yourself so open."

Something brushes against my foot.

"*Hand!*" I squeal, and he finally reaches out. I lunge forward, grasp his palm in mine, and curl my legs as he hauls me free of the frightening water and plonks me on the log.

I gulp air, sodden hair an anchor down my back.

Baze kneels, features hard, eyes frosty like the ground on a stark winter's morning. "That was sloppy, Orlaith."

"You almost left me for selkie bait," I sputter.

He frowns. "You do that in a real battle and you're dead. It won't be a wooden sword smacking you in the ribs. It will be a very real, very metal one sliding through your *heart.*"

"I know that."

"Do you? Because this"—he gestures to me with a bat of his free hand—"is not the girl I've been training for the past five years. I know you're still getting used to the new sword, but that was a *novice* mistake I haven't seen you make since you were seventeen."

I hate every word coming out of his mouth right now, mainly because they're so painfully accurate.

Rolling my eyes, I pluck a piece of weed from my hair and lob it at the pond that's now deadly still.

Too still. I swear I can feel countless pairs of eyes assessing me as the wounded prey I certainly smell like.

"You're awfully haughty for a man with a black eye," I mutter, glancing toward my freshly planted willow, hunting for happiness in its shooting branches.

Nothing.

Baze pushes to a stand, casting me in the long line of his shadow. "This isn't about me, Laith."

"And my care factor is at an all-time low."

"I can tell. Is it because you kissed the Ocean Drake?"

I turn so fast I almost lose my balance. "How do you kno—"

"Is that why you're out of sorts?" he continues, brow so arched it's almost hidden behind the mess of hazel hair hanging over his forehead. "It's the tail, isn't it? Or maybe his pretty scales? Some girls like shiny things."

"You're an ass," I spit, cheeks burning.

"That's not very nice," he drones, wearing a frown that does nothing to hide the glimmer in his eyes. "I just saved your life."

If looks could kill, he'd be selkie chow, and I'd be free to go check the nabber and gift Shay his first mousy meal in days.

"You're the one who told Rhordyn, then?"

He shrugs. "Rhordyn doesn't really need me to tell him anything."

"What's that supposed to mean?"

"Exactly that." He gestures for me to stand, and I groan, pushing up, a little light-headed from blood loss and certain I'm about to slip straight back into the pond without the slightest bit of coercion. "Now, *left* hand."

My shoulders and heart drop in unison. "But you know that's my weak one. And I'm *bleeding*."

"Correct." He jerks his chin, and I reluctantly trade hands. "Let's pretend it's from your arm and not your"—his gaze darts down, then up again as he clears his throat—*"nether regions."*

I nearly drop my weapon and cost myself another chilly dip in the pond of death to retrieve it. "How about I stab you in the crotch so we're equally disadvantaged—"

He strikes too fast for me to trace, but I move on pure instinct and slide back.

"That's it." A lopsided grin curls his lips and rinses me with rapture. It's the one that breaks across his face whenever he's semi-proud of me, and I *live* for it.

He strikes again, but I arc to the side, and his sword

breezes past my ribs. His next move is swift—a brutal shot for my neck—but I manage to defy gravity and swerve the attack, ducking low before I shift all my weight onto one foot and kick the other out ... straight at his feet.

He goes down hard, his splash so boisterous I'm sure every selkie in the pond heard it.

My smile is smug, sword swaying through the air as I stare down at the churning water. After a few seconds, he breaks the surface, eyes wider than I've ever seen them.

Embracing the log with one long arm, he reaches his other out to me. "Quick, before they eat me."

I roll my eyes and extend my hand, then realize his *own* is empty ...

"Wait, where's your sword?"

His mouth pops open, then he's launching up, snatching my hand, *yanking*—

I fly through the air.

The cold water is just as unmerciful the second time round. Just as daunting—rife with the threat of pin-like teeth that latch onto your vulnerable bits and *shake.*

I break the surface, gasping, both hands empty.

"You *fool.*" My gaze snags on what appears to be a pale rock breaking the surface not too far away, wearing a wig of brown waterweed.

It's deadly still ... at least until its large, inky eyes blink open.

"Now we have to swim to the edge," I hiss, watching the slitted nostrils on the selkie's flat nose flare.

"And fast," Baze mutters, luring me to glance in the direction he's looking—seeing six, eight, *twelve* more heads break the water's surface and cast their gloomy eyes on us. "Seems they're attracted to the scent of blood ..."

"But what about our swor—" My heart leaps into my throat, clogging my spill of words as they dunk below the surface in unison.

Selkies ... they attack from *beneath.*

"Forget the fucking swords," Baze grates out. "Our toes are more important."

He churns toward the reeds, leaving me choking on the wake of his double standards.

If it were just *my* sword, he'd have me underwater, hunting through three feet of muck while fending off the swarm with my bare hands. Big commitment for a sword I'm not particularly fond of.

I take off after him, all too happy for it to stay down there and rot. Fingers crossed the next pair Baze pulls out of his ass is made of a softer, less strident wood ...

A girl can hope.

CHAPTER 27

RHORDYN

I lower the heavy lid on the wooden chest and clank the deadlock into place, feeling Greywin's nervous assessment, hot like the heat spilling from his kiln. I taste his tempered excitement in the dense, smoky air.

Despite the sweltering atmosphere, I've always liked this space. The smell of grit and determination has seeped into the stone walls and the wooden tables nesting about. You can see it in the worn utensils and the battered anvil—in the old, weather-beaten man who has a cot set up deeper in the cave so he never has to leave.

Greywin's looking at me over the top of his cluttered workstation, a bushy mantle of silver brows shadowing his eyes. The forge is blazing behind him, casting the cavern chamber in a red glow.

Okay? he signs with fingers knotted from old age.

His entire family was slaughtered in a Vruk raid over forty years ago, after which he gouged his own eardrums with a stick as self-punishment for not being there.

This is all he has left. His craft.

I make a fist and nod it, pushing to a stand, stamping my thumb to the flat of my palm then twisting both hands in opposite directions to signal how impressed I am.

He grunts.

Barely smothering a smile, he slips his gloves back on and turns, using tongs to remove a long, fiery blade from the kiln before forcing it into submission with a hammer.

Ting-ting-ting.

Clang.

I lean against the wall, watching him work. His quarters used to be stationed on the castle grounds until I moved him out here nineteen years ago. This cave digs deep underground, so none of his sound spills into the forest or makes its way up to Orlaith's tower.

Heavy footfalls echo down the throat of the cave in alternate rhythm to the jarring, metallic strikes. The reek of whiskey and whatever female wet Baze's cock last night hits me before he emerges into the workshop glow—hair a mess, dark circles beneath his eyes. His top is loosely buttoned, and he didn't even bother with his boots.

Two days off, and he's fallen into old habits.

I arch a brow. "Good night?"

He avoids eye contact, scratching the back of his head and repressing a yawn. "You wanted to see me?"

I watch him for a long moment.

Clang.

Clang.

Clearing my throat, I push off the wall, reaching for one of the two swords laid out on Greywin's work table, both made from an almost black wood with leather-bound pommels.

Simple, well-made weapons.

I hand the smaller one to Baze, his brow buckling as he studies it with eyes more vigilant than they were seconds ago.

"Wait ..." He steals a glance over his shoulder to our master plan—different colored logs stacked against the far wall. Stepping stones to edge Orlaith closer to an eventual metal blade. *"Ebonwood?"*

I nod.

He looks at the blade like it's going to twist out of his hand and slit his throat. "You're pushing her too fast."

He's right, of course. But patience is a luxury I've been sipping on for years; a luxury I can no longer afford.

Not when it comes to her.

"No. I'm not pushing her fast enough."

He sighs, weighing the weapon in both hands. "She barely withstands the draw of a metal blade at dinner, and you think she's ready for *this?* It's over double the density of her last sword. The sound difference—"

"May be jarring," I finish for him.

He looks at me through his tangled mop of hair. "Exactly. We agreed to move onto walnut after she got used to the Petrified Pine. Which she wasn't, by the way. If we hadn't lost the set to that selkie hovel, I'd have kept her on the pine for the next six months."

Six mon—

"She seemed to cope just fine the other day."

"Because she was fucking *jacked."*

An image I'll carry to my grave.

I clear my throat.

"Be that as it may, we don't have time for walnut anymore. We barely have time for Ebonwood. I was tempted to move right onto Silver Olivewood ..." I shrug; the heavy pelt draped around my shoulders having nothing on the weight that's been stacked there for years. "I had Greywin thin the hilt on hers instead."

"I can *see* that," Baze replies, swinging the blade and making it sing. "She'll grumble ..."

"Undoubtedly."

He picks up the slightly bigger sword I had forged for him in the same wood, and strikes them against each other, splitting the air with a sharp sound.

He winces.

Internally, I do the same.

"And I'm free to hold *you* accountable?" he grits out, eyeing me over the crossed weapons. "I'll be taking full advantage of that because I'll tell you now, she is *not* going to like this."

I fold my arms and lean against the wall. "My decision. I'm happy to take the fall."

Take her *hate*.

"You say that now," he mumbles, inspecting the swords from all angles, "but last time we changed, she spiked my tea with something that made my piss turn green for a week. Just so you're aware."

Greywin lets out a hearty chortle, leading Baze to narrow his eyes on the old man.

"I thought he was deaf."

"He can lip-read just fine ..." the corner of my mouth threatens to bounce up into a half smile, "though he rarely bothers."

Clang.

Clang.

Clang.

"I'm going to take that as a compliment."

"Good for you."

He jerks his chin at the chest. "What's in there?"

"A contingency I hope we don't require," I mutter,

sweeping past Baze on my way into the cave's gloomy length.

He swears, low and sharp, before his hurried footsteps follow.

"She needs to know, Rhor." He shadows me through the waterfall of vines that act as a natural door into the dewy forest lit by blades of dull morning light.

"About?"

He slays me with a condemning glower. "*Everything*. Or at least the fucking basics."

"No."

I let the vines fall back into place behind him and spin on my heel, stepping over mossy boulders and tree roots that twist out of the soil.

"You're fucking brutal. I was hoping you'd soften with age, but every year that passes, you just seem to get worse."

I brush my hand against a tree. "I'm choosing to take that as a compliment."

"Good for you," he says, matching me stride for stride while we marinate in a stretch of silence. "I hope you're prepared to pick up the pieces if everything unravels."

"That girl has been in pieces since I lifted her from the rubble," I mutter, watching him veer around a deeper pocket of shadow. "There's nothing nearby. You don't have to dodge the dark."

He takes the long way around the shadow of a boulder taller than us both, traipsing knee-deep through a rushing brook. "With all due respect, I'm not prepared to take my chances. Have you seen the one she feeds on the edge of your scent line recently?" He shivers, leaping onto dry land. "It's almost doubled in size."

"I have, yes."

"And you're still not concerned?"

Catching the sound of a distant flutter, I look east, seeing a small, misty orb darting toward me. "It won't hurt her," I tell him, shoving my hand out like a perch.

A female sprite no taller than my index finger lands in the middle of my palm, pointy ears poking through her straight, white hair. With skin so pale it's almost see-through, her inky eyes make a bold statement on her small face.

Opaline wings stick out from her back like tapered leaves, dusting my hand in powder as they flick about, then sink to garnish her gauzy dress.

She pulls a scroll from her chest holster and hands it to me, bouncing up and down, clapping her hands.

Baze snort-laughs from his spot perched against a tree in a muddy beam of light, swords resting against a rock before him. "You spoil them."

I reach into the pocket of my cloak, retrieve a pale gem no larger than a pinhead, and hold it out.

The sprite makes a sharp trilling sound and snatches the gift so fast I can barely trace the movement. "Happy sprites make for reliable service," I say, watching her dart off through the forest with her plunder. She'll go straight to her den in a tree somewhere and grind that diamond down to dust, use it to coat her wings, then spend hours admiring her reflection in a pond somewhere.

"An *aggressive* service. I got bitten the other day because all I had to offer was a nut."

I drop my attention to the scroll, unraveling it. "I hardly see how that's *my* fault."

"They're spoiled from your pocket diamonds. Anything important?"

"An update from the regiment. It was a hard winter, and they're running low on game. I'm having them shift closer to

Quoth Point." I roll the scroll and pocket it. "They can make use of the old barracks there, and there's plenty of fish in the ocean to keep them fed."

Baze's eyes widen. "*Quoth Point?*"

"It's precautionary."

"*Precautionary ...*" he mimics, drawing a deep breath and pushing it out fast.

I let the silence stretch while he digests. When he finally shoves off the trunk, his shoulders appear heavier. Even the smudges beneath his eyes look darker.

"Well, in that case, the Ebonwood was a wise choice," he says, looking at the swords. "Speaking of which, I better get back."

He retrieves both weapons and heads west, weaving between ancient trees that bear their shadows down around him.

"Baze?"

He pauses, regarding me over his shoulder, brow raised.

"Clean yourself up. You smell like a tavern."

Get a handle on it before I end up scraping you off the masonry.

He lowers his eyes and nods, continuing toward the castle.

He'd never admit to it if I asked, but he relies on *her* just as much as I do.

CHAPTER 28

ORLAITH

I wake to the *whoosh* of my curtains being drawn.

Groaning, I pry an eye open, using my hand as a shield against the mottled beam of light, though I'm pitted with regret when the motion sends shards of pain lancing through my shoulder.

I feel like I've been trampled by a horse.

"It's too early," I mumble, watching Tanith flutter about, boasting a smile that looks like it was carved from a moonbeam.

"It's past nine," she chirps, dancing her feather-duster over my collection of painted stones with one hand and cranking a window open with the other. "Baze requested I wake you for train—"

"*Shh,*" I hiss, jabbing a finger in her direction and earning myself a glare of feigned innocence. "Don't say it. Don't use that word, Tanith. You know it hurts me."

"Training," she says, and I make a sound like a dying animal, glancing at the swarthy sword on my bedside table that's taunting me with the promise of strident blows. "In Hell Hole ... or whatever it is you call that place."

It didn't have a name, but it does now.

"I'm going back to sleep," I mutter, sandwiching my head between two pillows. "Maybe forever."

I consider the implications of spiking my offering with something that makes Rhordyn suffer just as much as I am.

Fucking Ebonwood sword. That thing's loud, heavy ... I *hate* it. It makes Petrified Pine seem like paper in comparison.

"You can't go back to sleep. I've also been instructed to ensure you get some sunshine."

"From who?" I ask, my words muffled by the pillow.

The question is a little acidic, I'll admit.

"The High Master himself. He said if you complain, I'm to remind you that he owns the roof, and is quite within his rights to remove it should you abuse its privileges."

And *he's* about to find out what happens when you overdose on senna.

Peeling the pillow back, I peep out the window at the hazy clouds drifting past. "But it's not even sunny." I breathe deep, scenting the promise of a shower on the breeze ruffling my curtains. "In fact, it's going to rain."

Tanith shoves the balcony door open and scans the sky, fists pinned to her hips. "Then you best get out there fast."

Think I'd rather stay right here where I don't have to see anyone. Especially not bull-headed males who refuse to let me dive to the bottom of the pond and retrieve the swords we lost the other day—swords that were a *dream* compared to the new ones. Yes, Selkies are scary, but in my very biased opinion, the reward far outweighs the risk of losing my toes.

Sighing, I glare at the thing ...

Tanith prances toward the bed and whips my blanket off, exposing me to a slap of cold. "Up!"

"Ugh ..."

I toss the pillow at her, earning a laugh as I swing my legs over the side of the bed.

Unraveling the long, golden plait hanging heavy over my shoulder, I wander outside and lean against the balustrade, getting my prescribed dose of *non-sun* while looking down on the world. On gardens churning with people dressed in not only the signature black garb of the West, but also rust-colored cloaks of the East and a few dark blue tunics of the South.

"I think I've lost track of the days. Is the Tribunal today?"

"This morning," Tanith calls, bundling my sheets. "But a Conclave is being held this afternoon, remember? And the ball is tomorrow."

My heart plummets.

I take a few steps around my balcony, past Limp Leaf and over a branch of my wisteria, gaze dropping to the ships grouped within Bitten Bay's watery smile. I count twenty-four in total, made up of three flotillas, the largest consisting of dull brown ships with open-mouthed lizards protruding from their bows.

A smaller fleet anchored further in the bay is made of several black, sturdy-looking boats, their hulls wide and sitting low in the water. The third group—the minority—are white and sleek with slender hulls made for cutting through rough water, navy blue sails wrapped around their masts.

I look through the window to the mannequin, untouched since I tossed my throw over it, and frown at the glimpse of blood-red silk spilling across the floor.

Well, shit.

"Your sheets are clear. You should start feeling more yourself," Tanith calls out.

"That's something," I mutter, returning my attention to

the cluster of people exploring the lush castle grounds. Smelling *my* roses. Picking *my* flowers.

Frowning, I focus on a woman with long, raven locks as she plucks a salmon-colored rose from the bush I grew from a seed.

"Why do they always target *Peachie?*"

Tanith comes up next to me on the balcony, her arms laden with dirty laundry. "What's wrong?" She blows a tendril of hair from her eyes and scans the grounds below.

"Peachie." I point at the brazen woman tucking the pretty loot behind her ear. "I *never* see her fully fledged because every Tribunal, someone snips at her. I'm sick of it. And of course, she took the only one without bruised petals."

I shake my head.

"How ..." Tanith squints, face scrunching up. "*Wow.* You must have *very* good eyesight."

"Why do you say that?"

"I certainly can't make out that sort of detail from this far up." She shrugs and spins, heading back inside. "Now I understand why the gardeners do most of their pruning during meal times."

"*What?*"

Lumping my laundry in a basket, she plants her hands on her hips. "They say it's the only time they feel like they're not being eyeballed."

I blink at her, feeling a little nauseous, wondering if she knows she just tossed me a jar of worms I intend to bust the lid right off of. "Thank you, Tanith. That's *very* interesting information—"

"That you didn't hear from me," she tacks on, leveling me with a hard look.

Ahh, she does *know.*

"That I absolutely did not hear from you."

She smiles and throws me a wink, and I turn back to the scene below.

Those deceptive bastards aren't going to know what hit them.

Finger-combing my hair, I survey the border, snagging on a small patch of navy that makes my heart flop around. Squinting, I focus on the cluster of bluebells growing at the base of an ancient oak tree ... four long paces past my Safety Line.

Might as well be on a different continent.

"Tanith?"

Receiving no reply, I turn to see she's slipped out, and consider chasing after her before I come to my senses.

Sending my handmaiden across my line of rocks would be rather selfish of me considering I'm unwilling to step over it myself.

I sigh, gaze lured to the trickle of people atop horses and carts clattering through the front entrance—a monumental, black stone archway smothered in crawling vines.

Better get to training or Baze will be on my case for making him miss the Tribunal.

Bag bumping against my hip, I take a route less traveled to avoid the unfamiliar people bustling around, having a nosey about the castle. I understand their desire. Curiosity is a natural thing—or so I tell myself every time I find something new to explore in this big, old labyrinth of intrigue that doesn't belong to me. I repeat the internal mantra as I watch a man boasting the Southern garb approach, strolling down the narrow, well-lit hall I thought would be abandoned.

A hall with no nooks or shadows for me to hide in.

He moves with a confident swagger, shoulders pushed back, hands dug deep into his pockets.

I lift my chin, reminding myself that to turn around and run would look awfully suspicious. I need to act normal, pretend I'm not freaking out ... though my galloping heart knows otherwise.

As we draw closer, I notice he's deeply handsome with swarthy skin and golden, sun-kissed hair that's pulled back from strong, masculine features.

He looks down at my bare feet, and his brow almost hops off his face.

Warmth floods my cheeks, and I look to the walls, the floor ... *anywhere* but him, until I can no longer avoid the awkward tension strung between us.

Our gazes collide.

Once I stare into those glacial blues, I can't look away no matter how hard I try.

There's a magnetism I don't understand, like he's rummaging through the pit of my soul, examining me from the inside out.

My breath catches, held in the grasp of paralyzed lungs.

The slightest line forms between his brows, and his steps slow, while mine become a frantic, churning beat, passing him like wildfire breezing past a stone.

I don't dare look back and seek the source of the burning point of perusal between my shoulder blades—a red-hot poker threatening to push through me. He's likely realized who I am and is drawing his own conclusions about the girl who lives in Rhordyn's tower and never leaves the castle grounds.

The child-survivor.

Perhaps Rhordyn will count this toward my progress chart.

It's not until I veer around a sharp bend that I can finally breathe.

Ahead on my right is a wooden door, and I steal a glance over my shoulder before pressing into it, letting it swing on silent hinges that have always allowed me to move into this elbow of The Tangle inconspicuously.

The pokey tunnel is roughly hewn rock, and very few torches line the wiggly hall. Those that do burn as though barely clinging to life, choking on air that's thick and damp.

I don't waste time checking to see if I've been followed. Whoever that man was, I doubt he knows this castle like I do.

I pick my way along the tunnel until I come to a fork in the path, then steal a torch from a wrought metal sconce. It gives me a bobbing aura of light as I veer left, rounding on a sudden dive almost steep enough to slide down, but not quite.

I've tried.

Once the path flattens out, I stop and lift my torch, illuminating the tapestry hung across the wall to my left. Hundreds of vibrant, delicately stitched flowers pock a lonely hill, sprinkling it in bright pops of color.

The solemn vision of beauty almost makes me cry every time my eyes hunger over it.

It's exotic and so full of life ... yet it's hidden in this dark tunnel.

The center of the masterpiece dips as if the hall behind it

just took a breath, and I peel the corner back, thrusting my torch into the throat of darkness beyond.

I step into the gloom, let the tapestry thump back into place behind me, then make my way down the long, slender hallway that's as dusty and unkept as the first time I walked along it.

Discovering this passage just shy of my thirteenth birthday was my most exciting find in years—something I knew from the moment I stepped past the heavy tapestry and saw the distressed state of my surroundings.

Neglected tunnels always lead to interesting finds.

I round on a small booth pressed into the wall with a seat skirting its length. It could easily pass as a strange little resting spot, but it's so much *more* than that.

I can hear the distant burr of a voice radiating through the wall, and I stab my torch into the empty sconce, freeing my hands.

Kneeling, palms flattened against stone, I seek the wound in the wall—a hole the size of a large plum, perfect for garnering a full, overhead view of the people crammed into the throne room. They fill the entire room to my right, bar a crescent of space that separates the dais from the crowd.

Separates *Rhordyn*.

Ceiling aglitter with hundreds of chandeliers that sit not far above my eyeline, the room looks like it was carved from a slab of night sky. It's beautiful, I've always thought that, but beautiful things don't always bring you happiness.

Somehow, and despite the ocean of bodies all garbed in Ocruth black, the room still gives me the sense of a vacant chest cavity.

My gaze darts to Rhordyn, sitting atop a throne made of cleverly placed silver stems soldered together to form an elegant dais. Beside him is a pile of offerings almost taller than himself: crates of chickens, jewelry, fine materials, baskets of herbs, and much more.

A man's standing within the arc of empty space—years etched into his face and stacked upon his shoulders in bricks of brawn. A farmer perhaps, considering the crate bulging with fat, yellow fruit on the ground beside him.

He's dropped to one knee, shoulders hunched, revering Rhordyn with dull eyes rimmed in shadow.

"It was a monster that destroyed the fence. A great beast of a thing. And now there's a gaping hole welcoming *anything* to slip through!"

Rhordyn nods, chin notched on his fist. "And it will be fixed, Alstrich. I will see to it."

Plucking a sack off the floor, he loosens the silver drawstring, digs through the clattering contents, and retrieves a black chip he then extends.

Alstrich lifts his crate and places his offering next to a leashed goat. He then takes five steps up the dais and drops to a kneel to receive his token. The currency of promises.

Made from a near-worthless metal and stamped with a Master's sigil, a token can't be used to purchase grain or stock or to buy yourself out of debt with a neighbor. It's worth so much *more* than that.

To hold a token means you're owed a promise, and it's only revoked once that promise is fulfilled.

A scribe at a nearby table scratches notes onto a roll of parchment as Alstrich backs down the dais and, with the vow held in his white-knuckled fist, merges with the crowd.

Rhordyn waves for the next person to come forth: a young woman I recognize from a previous Tribunal as being the medis from a nearby town.

Her eyes are large and tawny, cheeks flushed, hair long and brown and fastened in a low ponytail. Her black, ankle-length dress flatters her curvy form, its long sleeves drawing my eye to her porcelain hands and the deep blue and gold cupla secured around her left wrist.

A shackle of promise. One that wasn't there last time I saw her.

She curtsies, head bowed in a sign of respect.

My attention slides to Rhordyn—to his straight lips and stony eyes—and I can tell he's noticed the cupla just by the way his brow pleats.

"Mishka, what is your query?"

She straightens, worrying her bottom lip, smoothing the front of her dress. "High Master, I come to you with a full but heavy heart." Her words are spoken softly in a reluctant cadence. "I've accepted a cupla."

Rhordyn's gaze doesn't waver from hers as he says, "Congratulations. May you be blessed with a long and happy coupling."

"Thank you, Master." Her hands settle over her lower belly like a shield, then swiftly fall to her sides. "I ... I come today because my male is not from the West."

There's a slight lift of Rhordyn's brow—a ruse of shock that doesn't reflect in his stormy eyes nor the tone of his reply. "Oh?"

"N-no. He's from the South. The capital."

Murmurs ripple through the crowd.

"Quiet," Rhordyn says, his voice a low command.

Starched silence sweeps over the room.

Mishka clears her throat, though it doesn't stop her next words from coming out rusty. "My placement in Grafton as the town medis has been my greatest honor, Master. It has brought me so much joy over the years, but with my change of circumstances, I ..." She pauses, hands twisting before her. "I must ask you to bequeath me the sanction to cross the wall into the South."

There's a collective gasp from the crowd, and even my own hand claps across my mouth.

People don't often search for love outside their territory, but on the off chance of it happening, the male generally relocates so the female can remain close to her family for support in raising their eventual young.

Not the other way around.

And for a female medis who loves her post? Who I'm beginning to suspect is already with child? It makes little sense.

"Mishka, I must ask. Is this decision your own?"

There's a silent threat in Rhordyn's question, and the crowd goes dead quiet, as if their intake of breath is hinging on Mishka's reply.

Just like mine.

A territory's strength is in its people's ability to breed strong men and fertile females. Therefore, the law protects women, preventing them from being coerced into crossing walls and trading colors against their will ... by penalty of death.

Mishka's feet shuffle, her almost tangible well of nerves serving as fuel for my hammering heart.

"It's my decision, yes. But as I say, it's been made with a heavy heart." Her hands settle over her lower abdomen again. "I'm seven weeks pregnant. Although the thought of raising our young without the support of my mother is daunting ... the thought of staying in Grafton is *frightening.*"

The last word cracks out of her, and I lean closer to the wall, pressing my face against the cold stone.

"Frightening?" Rhordyn asks, tone even.

Too even.

There's murder in his voice.

"Y-yes, sire. After the attack on Kriesh a week ago, I had to feed liquid bane to any who were left breathing. A short while back, a bard passing through Grafton sang of other incidents very close to home. Sang of the Vruks growing in numbers and strength. Of *children* disappearing."

Children ...

I taste bile, and even from here I can feel the air chill.

"Go on."

The ball in Mishka's throat bobs.

"My male says the attacks haven't yet hit the South, so with great respect, we feel this move is the safest choice for our swelling family."

Rhordyn shifts forward on his throne, hands steepled, eyes like chips of ice illuminated beneath a full-bellied moon.

There's a waiting sort of stillness about the room—a silence stretched too thin.

It's Rhordyn's job to keep his people safe, and right now ... they're not.

His hands fall and he straightens. "Another medis will be found to fill your absence. Do what is right for your family."

Though the words sound genuine, it's like they've been bitten from a slice of slate.

Mishka bows so low her hair brushes the ground, then rises and slips into the murmuring crowd.

I pull back and spin, spine hitting rock.

Children are missing. Vruk numbers are swelling. People aren't feeling *safe* anymore ...

I close my eyes, picturing my invisible line of protection hard like a diamond. Hard enough to keep me in. Keep the monsters *out*.

But it's all a pretty lie I tell myself, because they're already here ... in my head.

They already got me.

CHAPTER 29

ORLAITH

Still no bluebells. Still just withered stems that bear no bursts of that deep ocean blue I desperately need.

With my knapsack slung over my shoulder, I slip out of Sprouts and dart behind a thick shrub. My hands squeeze into tight fists, fingernails almost gouging the flesh of my palms as I mull over the little bunch of blooms I spotted past my Safety Line—so close, yet so far away.

My bag squeaks, and I lift my gaze to the sky packed with dense clouds threatening to spill again. I frown, scanning the border where tailored, lime-green grass meets the sheer rise of bedraggled trees ...

Perhaps it's just overcast enough that my friend will come out and play.

Mindful of the many strangers visiting the castle, I dash between well-trimmed shrubs, rose bushes, and moss-covered boulders. I'd never usually attempt such a risky maneuver on a busy day like this, and it's something I'll absolutely pin to my lapel next time Rhordyn pecks at me about *effort.*

Merging with the shadow of a large oak tree just shy of my Safety Line, I look left and right, checking nothing has scattered my border of irregular sized stones before I scan the world beyond.

The forest is gloomy beneath the canopy, its floor a canvas of mossy trunks and rebellious roots that twine out of the ground like tentacles, illuminated by the odd shaft of light.

Those little blue buds are staring at the ground, hanging off hunched stems.

Worrying my bottom lip, I reach inside my bag and pull out the jar containing the fat rat I found tucked inside my Nabber this morning.

Cook was so pleased when I caught the vermin that she promised me a pile of honey buns, despite her busy, pre-ball schedule.

The birds stop chattering and a silence consumes the woods; the air seeming to hold its breath. My sacrificial offering pushes his nose through an air hole, whiskers twitching.

The hairs on the back of my neck lift ...

I glance up to see a dark shape using the shadows of ancient tree trunks like a pathway to approach.

Shay.

He moves fast, a dusky flicker stopping only when he draws near enough that I can sense the void of his body. Feel his pull to be less ... *empty.*

It always makes me picture a vacant lung trying to inflate.

Kai may be right about these creatures, but my experience with Shay is much different. I don't see him as a weapon or something fierce and deadly. I see him as my lonely, skittish friend.

A smile teases the corner of my lips as he hovers, the shadow about his head folding back like black smoke yielding to the wind. A face emerges, not dissimilar to the blanched skull of a dog long dead.

His forehead is wide and flat, eyes inky balls set in too-big sockets. His nose is a pallid hook, mouth a toothy slash barely covered by lips the color of milk.

Most would balk at his unveiled appearance, but I've seen too many monsters in my nightmares for his face to frighten me.

His lips curl up in a jagged smile, exposing an abundance of serrated teeth. Gaze stabbing at the jar, that smile falls, and he makes a sound I recognize—like a tambourine is clogging his throat.

Hunger.

Nodding, I grip the lid. "All for you, Shay. But"—I look to the bluebells—"I was wondering ..."

Shay regards the plant, then me, head tilted to the side. A long moment slips by before he turns and drifts toward them as if snagged by the hands of a gentle breeze.

My heart trips over a foray of ecstatic beats.

He curls over the precious flowers, stare sliding sideways, eyes clinging to me.

I nod and lower to a crouch, arms banding around my knees to cage my welling excitement.

Shay regards the blooms again.

His ivory, fleshless fingers emerge from his cloak of dense vapor, teasing the air with cautious, clawed strokes. His digits clink together as he reaches for the flowers, and I smile when he grasps the curved stems.

The flowers turn brown, then shrivel until nothing is left but a small bundle of straw-like husks.

My smile fades, lungs empty.

Dead ... *just like that.*

Shay hisses and snatches his hand away, head whipping to the side, sooty gaze seeming to plead with me.

The sadness in those eyes is a bitter, unnecessary poison. I don't need to see his sorrow. I can feel it in the atmosphere; see it in the fading of the forest's jewel-toned luster.

Kai was right about one thing: Shay *is* a predator, but I doubt my friend enjoys what he has to do to survive, bar the brief satisfaction of sustenance.

"It's okay," I say, tone gentle, offering a warm smile I hope touches my eyes. "They weren't important."

He looks at the husks again, and I'm reminded of Rhordyn. Of the way he regarded me before he left for the East—like I'm the sum of his own self-loathing.

I hate you.

Oh, precious. You don't even know the meaning of the word.

Or perhaps he's just sick of me creeping around his castle, rifling through his shit.

I clear my throat and waggle the jar, making the rat squeak.

Shay's keen, predatory gaze snaps to me, and he makes that rattling sound again, leaving my bluebell corpses at the base of the tree.

He draws near, and I feel the pull of his hollow form trying to suckle air from the surrounding space. For a moment, I wonder how it would be to fall into his void ... if it would hurt or feel like drifting off to sleep in the arms of a friend.

I close my eyes and untwist the lid, keeping it atop the jar as I seek out my non-existent bravery. It takes longer than I care to admit for that tiny surge to hit, but once it does, I shove my hand out and tip.

A fleshy thump breaks the silence, and I snatch my hand back, holding it close to my galloping heart.

I open my eyes to see Shay ascend on his prey in a surge of shadow. There's a suckling sound—a gentle *whoosh-whoosh* —his body moving with the tempo as he feeds.

When he retreats, a hard lump of fur and bone and nothing much else is revealed, and he looks up as he sniffs the air, watching like he's waiting for me to run or be afraid.

He'll be waiting forever.

I open my mouth to speak, but the words are left unsaid as the shrill sound of a metallic blow jars me to the bone. Another swiftly follows, the sonic a tangible force hacking through the air.

Clang.

The hits aren't aimed at me, but they strike nonetheless, assaulting like nails hammering into a soft piece of wood.

Clang.

My spine curls, hands cup my ears as the telltale ebb of brain-bulging pain begins to bloom.

It's relentless. Excruciating.

It's going to kill me.

Shay swarms forward, doubling in size, stopping just short of the invisible barrier that separates us. He releases a sharp hiss I try to focus on, but it does nothing to soften the blows.

Clang.

The scream threatening to push out of me finds its own tenor. It swells and swells until it's almost louder than the sound of warring swords, ripping my throat raw and making me taste blood.

I rock and rock, holding Shay's stare as if it could keep me from bursting into a million pieces.

Something dribbles from my nose, travels down my chin, and drips onto my bunched up limbs ...

I don't check to see what it is. Don't dare tear my gaze from Shay's until his mouth falls open, spilling his own horrific screech. All those sharp teeth seem to slice the sound, fragmenting it into hundreds of piercing shrieks pushed out at once.

It's an icy blast to my bloated brain.

The taste of blood thickens, my scream bubbling as I tip ... leaning toward Shay. Wanting nothing more than to fall headfirst into the pall of him. Perhaps he'll take me into a painless splendor where I cease to exist? Somewhere I'm no longer at war with myself.

Shay darts away, and I squeeze my eyes shut, spilling a whimper along with more warm liquid down my chin.

I would have done it. Would have thrown myself at him just to escape the pain.

I'm trapped.

There's no way out ...

I'm suddenly crowded—touched by unfamiliar hands, surrounded by exotic smells I don't recognize. Fingers stroke my limbs, and I wail so loud the sound becomes me.

If I open my eyes, will everyone be in pieces? Will their blood be wetting the soil?

Away. *Get away!*

The ground seems to shake, convincing me I've fallen headfirst into one of my nightmares. There's a deep snarl, somehow tangible over my tortured sounds.

They're here.

They've finally come for me.

I scream louder.

Strong hands weave under my knees, around my back,

and I'm pulled against a hard chest that smells like leather and a cold winter's day.

It's not a comforting sort of hold, but a cage of arms that pin me in place. It claims and commands ... the sort of grip that can only belong to one person.

I peel my lids open to see the man from the hall standing with his feet shoulder-width apart, his sight trained above my head, set on the person carrying me.

There's a seed of hate in those cerulean orbs, mildly veiled by a wash of confusion.

A flash of light lures my attention to the silver sword hanging from his white-knuckled grip, and my mouth tingles, stomach threatening to spill.

But I can't peel my gaze away.

A hand sweeps over my eyes, severing the sight, creating a protective bubble that allows me to pretend there aren't countless bystanders watching me unravel.

My next scream is muffled, absorbed by a cold, robust chest, and it's not until the sound tapers that I realize Rhordyn's heart rate is no longer slow and sludgy ...

It's *violent.*

CHAPTER 30

ORLAITH

"You're okay," Rhordyn murmurs, as if he's trying to soften his voice.

An impossible task.

He's rocking with me while warm, sulfur-smelling water laps at my body. It's a balm to my blazing skin, though it does little to temper the throb of my bloated brain.

I'm convinced it's about to cleave open and spill my thoughts, my essence ... *me*.

I try to open my eyes, but a wall sconce sends light knifing into the smudge of my vision.

"*It hurts,*" I moan through my sandpaper throat, palms bracketing my temples.

Rhordyn's hand sweeps across my brow, and I nuzzle closer to his chest, breathing hard, searching for that calm spot inside me.

I jolt from another wave of pressure, and a wild scream belts out of me as my spine volutes like a squirming snake.

"Orlaith, I need you to relax."

"*I can't,*" I force out through clenched teeth.

"I can put you to sleep if you think it'll help. There's a spot right here"—firm fingers probe the cleft between two taut muscles in my neck—"all I have to do is push."

"No."

If he knocks me out, that doesn't fix the problem.

I keep running ... hiding ... and I'm sick of it. I need to learn to handle myself.

I press my hands to his chest and *shove,* shocked when he allows me to fall out of his sturdy grip.

The water teases past my breasts as I stagger to a stand. Inhaling deep, I dunk below the surface, dropping through water that grows progressively warmer.

Darker.

It's only when my bum hits the ground that I open my mouth and *scream,* releasing a stream of bubbles that assault me on their rush to freedom.

I kick off the stone, darting to the surface and drawing deep, not even bothering to open my eyes before I sink and punch out another scream.

The process is repeated over and over until all the pressure dissipates and I'm listless, suspended, uncaring whether I float to the surface or not.

Strong hands shackle my upper arms and yank me free of the water's grip, forcing me to stand straight before my back is whacked by the flat of a palm.

"Breathe ..."

I draw a raspy breath and fold forward, resting my forehead on a shoulder that's more rock than flesh. I suck on Rhordyn's scent as I'm drifted back against a wall, pressed between man and stone, each equally unyielding.

But it's *Rhordyn* I'm leaning against. Drawing from. Using like I do my tonic.

Dammit.

I always end up seeking comfort from him when I'm at my most vulnerable, and it never does me any favors.

Cursing myself, I tip my head back and suck a ragged breath, cracking my eyes open.

What I see has my lungs flattening.

Rhordyn's eyes, usually metallic plates that bounce light, are *absorbing* me. His brow is pinched the slightest bit, and there's something about his mouth that makes it look far less dispassionate than normal.

The concern in his eyes is unfamiliar. I've never seen anything but the hardness he wears—his impenetrable boundary.

He's like that locked door opposite the entrance of Stony Stem. Like The Den and The Keep.

Just something else I want to crack open and explore, though I've never been given as much as a peek through the keyhole.

Until now.

Our warring chests collide with every draw of breath; mine bound and clothed, his covered by a thin, black shirt that's clinging to him like a glove. He's taking me in as if he's trying to see past a mask that isn't there.

I'm an open book, and that's where our power balance is so very off.

I give too much away, what with how I shiver every time his voice cuts through the air. With the way his closeness snags my breath, and how he makes me feel like I'm safe and protected in the boundary of his castle grounds.

It has nothing to do with the castle, and everything to do with *him*.

"I'm okay," I whisper, instantly realizing my mistake.

The words were too soft, too placating, stiffening Rhordyn's aura like a sheet of ice the moment they left my lips.

Clearing his throat, he casts his gaze to the ceiling. After a few drawn-out breaths, he drops his chin and looks at me through the eyes of that ice-cold mask I'm far too familiar with.

Gone.

Suddenly, looking at him is painful.

I roll my head to the side, veering from the sight.

Four sconces cast the room in a soft, golden glow, illuminating chiseled walls that plunge into the *single* large spring …

There's nowhere to walk around the edges—nothing but a stairway that rises from the water, filling the chamber's entirety. Even the roof is lower, those mineral fangs much closer to piercing the water's surface than they are in the room I'm used to bathing in.

Confused, I turn to Rhordyn.

"This isn't Puddles …"

"No, it's not."

He holds my stare, a small lock of hair grazing his forehead.

"Where—"

"My personal bathing chambers."

My stomach drops.

I look below the surface to the hole in the wall I'm pressed against, a gentle current swirling at its entrance …

It's like the one in Puddles. In *my* puddle. The one I'm lured toward on the off chance I'm gifted a streak of Rhordyn's scent.

My guilty *fucking* pleasure.

Slowly, I peer up at the stoic male standing over me.

The air has changed—become charged with the mix of our scents. But it's more than just that …

It's the way he's looking at me now.

There's a hunger in those eyes that's so potent, it's scalding my cheeks, pooling liquid heat in that intimate spot between my thighs.

I release a shuddered exhale, choking the sound by biting down on my lower lip, tongue glazing across the plump flesh as if to taste his breath on it.

The ball of his throat bounces, and my gaze travels up the strong line of his neck before traversing along his sharp, masculine jawline. I get snagged on his chin dimple and that dark frosting of stubble, remembering how it felt grating on my neck. Recalling the mark it left—a rash that branded me for two days.

And then his mouth: sculpted, sensual, lips barely parted. If I tip my chin, I could taste him. *Really* taste him.

With that thought heavy in my head, the treasured scraps of his breath on my face feel utterly insignificant. Because I want it *all.*

I want that mouth to hunger over me with the same primal veracity that he seeks my blood when he's gone too long without it. I want him to nip at my lip, to feed from me while I reciprocate in an entirely different way.

Sustain my hungry heart.

Pulse whooshing in my ears, I lean into the small space separating us—

My mind splits from the *now,* and I'm back in a freezing bath, tears sluicing down my cheeks. He's walking away, leaving sharp words protruding from my heart.

I suggest learning to fuck your own fingers. You won't be using mine again.

The memory jolts me from my lusty smog, and I see this situation for what it really is ...

Me, leading my heart to the whipping post.

I place a hand on his chest, looking at the spread of my fingers, thinking about how small it looks against the breadth of him ... then I draw a deep breath and *push.*

He slides back like a blade through butter, and I let my hands ball into fists that suddenly feel too delicate. Too weak.

"I'm okay now," I rasp, though the words taste like the lie they are.

I'm not okay.

I haven't been for years. I've just been hiding; keeping myself occupied. Now the perfect symphony of my routine has lost its rhythm, and I'm adrift.

Lost.

I wade toward the throat of stairs that rise up from somewhere below the waterline and disappear into the gloom. An exit that probably leads through The Den.

My galloping heart betrays my nervousness.

His scent is everywhere—an intoxicating elixir that clings to me, *fills* me ...

Will I smell someone else up there, too? Will Zali's essence be thick and heady? Fresh?

... Will I smell their scents mixed together from the joining of their bodies?

Fuck.

I'm almost at the stairs when I'm struck from behind and shoved against the wall—chest first, cheek pressed to stone. Rhordyn's fists nail either side of me, his granite body flush against my back.

He dips his face into the crook of my neck and my entire body trembles, the delicate flesh yearning for more abuse from his sandpaper stubble. *Other* parts of me yearn for the same claiming cruelty—throbbing and desperate.

He draws deep, like he's feeding from the inhale, but it's

blown back out like an unwelcome guest. A low rumble sets every one of my nerves on edge, as if they're expecting something *more.*

Three times, he sucks little breaths that sound like the seeds of words.

Three times, those seeds fail to sprout.

"What, Rhordyn?"

Another breath, this one sharp and intentional.

I wait for words that do not come, but rather a harsh huff that lands its blow and bathes me in the unwanted perfume of his scent.

"Exactly what I thought." Prying myself from the cage of him, I drag my front across the stone until I can breathe without choking on his musk.

I'm over thirty paces up the stairs when he calls my name. It almost sends me tumbling back down where I'd no doubt end up in a crumpled heap at his feet again.

So, I run.

I run until I'm spat out in a room I refuse to take in. It's not until I reach the door, hand wrapped around the handle, that my fire-breathing curiosity burns through her restraints.

I peep over my shoulder, eyes widening as I survey the panorama of his quarters.

Not what I expected.

The room is bigger than my personal space, sparsely furnished with a black four-poster bed. A side table carved from the same material nests beside it, topped with an unlit candelabra.

A crackling fire casts his space in a buttery glow, warming his scent so that it coats my throat and leaves my mind churning through molasses. But what really has me staggering, despite being anchored to the doorknob, is the *easel.*

Almost as tall as Rhordyn and wide like the breadth of his shoulders, it's set by the window, a table by its side heaped with bowls of coal.

The rest of the room loses its luster because all I can see is the canvas it's boasting.

The half-finished sketch.

A delicate pair of hands are immortalized on the cloth. One is palm up, the other resting with the tips of four fingers perched in the cradle of it, like they're drawing sips of comfort from an absent well.

They harbor a restful sort of peace that makes my heart feel far too heavy for my body to contain ...

He draws. Rhordyn *draws.*

But not just that.

He *sees.* He's caught this moment of such mournful beauty, and it's hooked me—caught me in the back of the throat and cast little prickles in my eyes.

Rhordyn spills into the room like a storm, and our gazes collide, holding for a few drawn-out seconds. Quicksilver swirls threaten to consume me, as does the sight of him standing there, soaking wet and fully clothed, yet somehow looking so incredibly exposed.

Every muscle in his body is outlined by the sodden material, and I find myself envying that long-sleeved, button-down shirt for the way it has a hold on him.

His eyes are wide and wild, every fleck in the metallic pools glimmering like stars cast in a smoke-filled galaxy. The twists of his hair fall in such nonchalant disarray they bear their own sort of perfection, dripping water upon his powerful shoulders.

He's beautiful. Heartbreakingly so. And it's my turn for words to be caught behind my teeth.

I blink a few times, severing my sight of him in a gentle way. Because I deserve gentle.

I deserve gentle when this man is so boldly destroying me.

Nose blocked, I tug the door and stumble into the long, cold hallway that lacks a heartbeat. A hallway that leads only to and from The Den—a path I've walked too many times to be healthy.

It's not until I'm all the way up Stony Stem, body lumped on the floor against the closed and dead-locked door, that I breathe through my nose again. With it comes the unbridled tears that pull straight from my pitiful heart.

I'm in love with a man who'll never be mine—who's unavailable in every way, shape, and form—and I'm certain it's going to ruin me.

CHAPTER 31

ORLAITH

Firm knuckles assault the door.

I feel it down my spine, all the way to my toes. I feel it in my bones and in my fucking soul.

"What?" I whisper, knowing who it is. I knew from the moment I heard his heavy feet ascending my stairs slower than normal, as if he were being cautious for a change. "It's not feeding hour yet."

Silence stretches so long I picture being tossed through the castle gate like a sack of grain.

There's the faint clear of a throat, and then, "Funny."

I thought so.

"I'm here to escort you to the Conclave," he commands, and every muscle in my body tightens.

Nobody told me I was expected to attend. And the thought of facing all those people after what just happened in the gardens? Fair to say, attending the Conclave is at the bottom of my priority list.

"I think not," I reply, gaze pinned to the open window. To the blanket of heavy clouds refusing to allow even a shaft of sunlight to split through and warm my skin.

Make me feel less *numb.*

"You think not?"

"Don't sound so surprised. I made your *effort,* and it didn't turn out so great. Hard pass."

"Then I guess you'll be hitching a ride over my shoulder."

This asshole.

"My door's locked for a reason."

"And it wouldn't be the first time I've busted through it. Should I call the carpenter in preparation? It's his birthday, and he's spending the day off with his family, but I'll tell him it's urgent."

"Leave the poor man out of this," I mutter, glancing down at my clothes and realizing that in the time I've been sitting here, staring at nothing, they've almost entirely dried.

"Is—" I clear my throat, scanning the clouds again. "Is that male going to be there? The one who ..."

I grind my teeth, mind staggering back to the memory of those sounds splitting me apart strike by strike—of the familiar man with azure eyes and a sword hanging at his side.

I feel ... *rattled.* Not myself. I don't know if I have it in me to face *him* most of all. Not after he saw me unravel like that.

And it wasn't just him. It was an entire crowd of people previously roaming the castle grounds; a crowd Rhordyn no doubt carried me through once he plucked me up and bundled me against his chest like a child.

"Yes, but you'll be at my side the entire time."

My heart leaps into my throat and flutters about.

At his side ...

He really shouldn't use that sort of language around me.

"Won't Zali be there?" I ask, tone flat, and he puffs out a sigh.

In that sound, I hear exhaustion.

"Orlaith, I need you in that room with me," he insists, leading me to release my own exasperated sigh.

"I'm not dressed for it ..."

"You look perfect to me."

I peel off the door and twist around, staring daggers at it. "You can't even see me."

"Don't need to."

I roll my eyes, then hear him rumble—a deep, throaty sound that ignites every cell in my body. But that fire is swiftly extinguished when I remember where this discussion is leading.

"Do I have to talk?" I ask, eyes squeezed shut.

"You don't have to do anything you're not comfortable with."

"Can I get that in writing?"

No answer.

I blow out a breath, run my fingers through my hair, and shove to a stand, straightening my blouse with a few firm tugs. Sweeping damp hair off my shoulders, I lift my chin and whip the door open, catching a glimpse of his posture; bent forward, head bowed, as if he were leaning with his forehead pressed against the grain.

He arches a midnight brow and moves back until he's three steps down Stony Stem, his eyeline just below mine.

He's the picture of savage regality, dressed in a fine garb that contours to the grooves of his chiseled physique—so impeccably tailored, it's as if Dolcie dipped him in shadow ...

I glance away before my mindset erodes any further. Dolcie and her measuring tape can drop in a ditch.

Rhordyn's shoulders square and he offers me the crook of his arm.

Ignoring it, I sweep past, careful to breathe through my

mouth—the sound of his hearty chuckle grating my nerves as I stomp down the stairs.

He's giving me his smile again, but it's tainted now.

That smile belongs to somebody else.

The distressed-wood door does little to soften the chattering coming from behind it.

People.

My twisted fingers betray my skittish nerves, as does the sweat collecting down my spine.

Rhordyn severs my sight of the door, a galvanized shadow slipping into place. But I don't want to look into his unnerving eyes right now, so I stare at his chest instead ... only mildly less intimidating.

Reaching for the stone and shell hanging around my neck, he tucks them down the front of my top, pinching buttons through their holes until they're secured all the way to my throat.

I swallow, painfully aware of his closeness—his paused fingers.

The silence between us seems to draw its own breaths, bearing a full-bodied weight and pressing against me, demanding attention.

He shifts, hands landing on my shoulders like weights, and I dare a peek at his eyes ...

There's a sincerity there—an openness that binds me with his attention, tending wounds that were beginning to turn septic.

I can't help but revel in it.

Does he know he sustains me? Gives me everything and nothing all at once?

My next breath is nowhere near as satisfying as the last, as if nothing compares to the sips of *him* he feeds me.

Tortures me with.

"Orlaith," he says, voice a little raspy. "Are you ready?"

No.

Beyond those doors, we cease to be alone.

Beyond those doors, what we have in this small, disencumbered moment becomes overburdened with the weight of reality.

Even so, I nod.

His hands fall and he spins, shielding me while he tugs the door open, the rusty hinges releasing a pained groan.

The rush of chilled air hits me.

Gray light spills from the expanding void as Rhordyn steps forward. I follow, leashed to his essence—a puppet to every shift of his booted feet.

Murmurings abate as we move into the room crammed full of restless energy. I glance around, taking in the rocky dome of space that's much like a tomb, or at least how I picture tombs to be from the books I've read; a gloomy void, dull and dramatic.

A blade of muddy light shafts through a single open window cut from the peak of the dome, landing on the round stone table dominating the room. The light penetrates the rusty grate covering a hole in the middle of it, piercing down into the guts of who the hell knows what.

I hate this room—can feel the ghosts of past conversations caught in the crypt of it like they're tangible things. And it's cold.

Bone-jarring cold.

When I first cracked open that old wooden door to discover this place tucked into the castle's heart, I backpedaled like my ass was on fire.

One peek, that's all I needed to know this is not a happy space. It just ... bothered me. Still does, the feeling slightly overridden by my heart-cinching anxiety at the sheer amount of people seated around the huge, circular table, looking at me with barely veiled curiosity.

My skin pebbles, spine stiffening.

There must be over fifty pairs of eyes on me—one big circle of *nope*.

Rhordyn grips the back of one of the few spare chairs and lifts, walks it back a step, then places it on the ground again.

My gaze docks in his pewter eyes.

He motions for me to sit with a jerk of his chin, hands still gripping the seat. But my feet are mortared in place.

Chairs scraping across the ground only bother me a little, yet he must have noticed ...

"Milaje."

His beautiful, carved lips shaping themselves around the nickname has me jerking into action.

The chair shocks me with its chill, threatening to tug all the remaining warmth from my body. I shiver, tucking my hands between my thighs to conserve heat.

Rhordyn takes a seat beside me, and conversations start again.

In an effort to avoid the furrowed brows and stolen glances nipping at me, I look to the hole in the ceiling; to the peek of bulging clouds it allots me.

There's no glass to prevent the gentle mist of rain from entering.

I let my attention plunge to the halo of smooth stone

circumnavigating the rusty gate in the center of the otherwise unrefined table, directly below the hole in the roof ...

I wonder where the water goes.

Shivering again, I feel the cold brush of Rhordyn's stare and peer sidelong at him.

"What?" I whisper, and he releases me from his scrutiny, stare stabbing out across the table.

"Your lips are blue."

"That's because you dragged me into a *cellar*," I bite out, and he grunts in response.

The door opens behind me, offering the softest breath of warmth before it shuts again, and heavy footsteps preface the grind of wood against stone.

I grit my teeth, feeling a heat brush over my face, drawing my gaze to the man who just entered.

Twin cerulean orbs assess me in a way that feels far too intimate. Not a sexual sort of intimacy, but one that goes far, far deeper than that ...

The man from the garden.

He reclines in his chair like a cat lazing in the sun, draping a leg over the arm of it. The movement crumples his fine Southern threads—a tunic that accentuates his muscular physique and lends a drop of nonchalance to his already casual façade.

All the while, his stare doesn't waver.

So, I study him with the same unwavering intensity.

He's attractive, I'll give him that, harboring a strong, exotic sort of masculinity I'm not familiar with.

I've seen Bahari males before—there are two others currently seated around the table at various intervals—but never one like *him*.

I've not seen skin such a perfect shade of bronze.

I can tell he thinks highly of himself by the way he holds his chin, his shoulders. The way he so boldly examines me, as if he couldn't care less about the male by my side filling this space with his expanding essence.

A hand nails to my shoulder and I jerk, then relax into my seat as I tune into the calming presence behind me.

Baze.

Something about his touch makes me feel a little less hollow.

His companionship, I realize, is one I take for granted. Even his closeness seems to loosen my knot of anxiety and plant little seeds of fire in my veins, taking away just a smidge of this bone-jarring cold.

He leans in, breath cool on my ear. "You okay?"

I nod, resisting the urge to rest my head against his arm and use it as a comfort pillow. "I'm fine."

The conversations ease, and the room gradually becomes quiet.

Baze's hand shifts, but he stays standing behind me and Rhordyn. A sentry at our backs.

"Do we give him another hour?" someone asks, and I seek out the long face of a rusty-haired Eastern male. He's slight like a thistle weed and just as prickly looking, with a sharp, beady stare the color of pine needles. But there's power in the way he holds himself.

"No," Rhordyn answers. "He's not coming."

"Who's not?" I ask Baze, trying to ignore those crystal-blue eyes assessing me from the opposite side of the table.

"The High Master of Fryst," Baze whispers in my ear, and Zali rises from a seat four spaces away.

The vision of her makes my breath catch, her willowy beauty a stark contrast to a room filled with mostly men.

She's dressed in tan leather pants and a chestnut top, armor hugging her curves—a breastplate that's made from what appears to be bronzed scales. It looks impenetrable, yet the way it dips and bulbs enhances her lithe, feminine form.

Her rosy hair is pulled back and secured in a tight bun, cheeks flushed from the chill she's probably not used to—not with being from the Eastern Territory of Rouste where the sun burns the dunes into rolling hills of desolation.

I barely recognize her; awed by her confident stance in front of this room full of people.

"You all know why we're here," she announces, voice clear and lilting. "So I'm just going to cut straight to the point."

I glance at Rhordyn, who appears comfortable in his chair ...

Perhaps Zali is running this meeting.

"There's been an alarming number of Vruk attacks across Fryst and Ocruth over the past four years. Not only are their pack numbers swelling, but these beasts are growing in both size and cunning at a discerning rate. Equally disturbing is that entire families have gone missing without a trace, children snatched in other circumstances."

An icy chill slithers up my spine.

"These possible abductions often leave a scene too clean to be pinned on a pack of rogue, blood-lusting *mutts,*" Zali continues, spitting the last word with distaste. "Which means the disappearances and frenzied Vruk raids are either entirely unrelated or someone is governing *both;* weakening our smaller regions, instilling fear, and bleeding our populations." She plants balled fists to stone while she surveys every person sitting around the table.

Bodies lean forward as if lured by her pause ...

"I know it seems like a stretch after years of relative

peace, but we need to prepare for the possibility of a territory war."

A second of silence beats by before a riot of yelling erupts —Low Masters and Mistresses tossing verbal blows back and forth across the table. The sharp scent of fear makes me want to breathe through my mouth.

As far as I'm aware, the boundary fences have been in place for *years*. There have been small, regional battles between neighboring Low Masters and Mistresses, but nothing that has threatened the walls that bind us to our overriding territories.

Nothing that has threatened the *colors* we wear.

Blunt voices bounce off the curved stone walls, assaulting me from all angles. The Bahari male sitting opposite me is picking dirt from under his nails, wearing an expression akin to bone-deep boredom.

He obviously has very little skin in the game.

"What are you suggesting we do?" a man with chocolate hair and piercing green eyes bellows. I recognize him as one of the Low Masters from Rhordyn's territory who often shows face at the monthly Tribunal.

"Unite," Zali remarks without hesitation.

"And what about High Master Vadon?" someone yells from my left, and my brow buckles.

"He stopped trading with us four years ago," Rhordyn states, his low voice rolling through the room like thunder, cauterizing every other spill of sound.

He's reclined in his seat, arms knotted over his chest, not even looking down the table at the man who just asked that question ...

He's looking at the Bahari male.

"Neither he nor any of his Regional Masters are here

today, and every sprite I've sent his way since trading ships stopped traveling down the River Norse has not returned. You do the math."

"Perhaps he's simply been affected by the storms!" someone yells, and more chaotic muttering ensues.

Zali stalks to the edge of the room where she heaves a large sack off the ground, cheeks reddening as she hauls it over her shoulder. Once standing in front of her seat again, she lugs it onto the table with a heavy thud.

The noose of bodies seems to tighten as we collectively lean forward, even the Bahari male.

Everyone but Rhordyn.

A smell hits me, but it's not the chafing odor of partially rotten flesh that has my throat cinching. It's the underlying waft of wet dog—a scent that casts a line into my memories, hooking on something too big and vicious to pull to the surface.

I'm about to stand and walk out of the room when Rhordyn snatches my hand and pins it against his thigh.

I turn to hiss at him, but Zali grips the corners of the sack and *tugs*, sending a big, fluffy, frozen head rolling across the table.

My hand flies to my mouth in an effort to catch the garbled sound that rushes out.

People stand and point and gag, screams bouncing off the curved walls. Sour-smelling vomit spills across the table, though the putrid stench is swiftly lost to the cinder scent of pure, undiluted fear.

Rhordyn's hand tightens, offering me a frosty anchor while I'm caught in the crossfire of that vacant stare ...

Vruk.

I gawk at a wide, flat maw—at blood-stained teeth

exposed by its peeled back lips, as though the creature died mid-snarl. The gray, shaggy mane has been hacked through, leaving a slice of exposed meat and bone and dried blood.

A thick neck that used to be attached to a hulking body.

"*Breathe,* Orlaith."

I try, but my lungs are made of stone. If I force them to inflate, I'm certain they'll shatter.

The trembling ground.

That awful screeching sound.

No.

No, no, no ...

Baze's warm hands land on my shoulders, pinning me to the chair with their comforting weight, but it's not enough to tamp that pressure bulging inside my skull.

"*Look at me.*"

I can barely hear Rhordyn's voice through the ringing in my ears, but I can't do what he's asked. I can't peel my eyes from that devastating maw—worried that if I do, it'll come back to life and snap at me. Rip me up until I'm nothing but scattered pieces.

Rhordyn drops my hand, and for a second I'm adrift; floating without anchor. But then he grabs my thigh under the table, and a breath strikes the back of my throat.

"*Look. At. Me,*" he growls against my ear so ardently that it shoves through the haze.

I peel from my nightmare and stare into eyes that are ruthless. Stark, frozen lakes that take no mercy.

"It's *dead,* Orlaith. Nothing can hurt you so long as you're with me. Do you hear?"

I think I nod.

"You're going to breathe," he orders, fingers digging in, grip tightening to the point of pain, and I suck a sharp gasp.

The icy wave of oxygen barrels into my lungs, enriched with the scent of *him*. It's a balm for my insides, the instant relief tempering me.

The shrill sound in my ears tapers enough for me to hear the ongoing commotion, voices rioting back and forth.

Baze lifts his hands.

Rhordyn's throat works, and he loosens his grip, though he doesn't let go. His hand stays wrapped around my thigh as he surveys the room.

"Silence."

He doesn't have to yell for his voice to rip through the tumult.

Some sit, others continue to stand, our combined attention on the decapitated head. Swallowing thickly, I notice the stark difference to the Vruks that haunt me in my sleep ...

This one has a long, shaggy coat.

"Why is it so ... *fluffy?*" someone asks, pointing an unsteady finger.

"Almost all the Vruks I've been encountering over the past few years have the same thick winter coat, no matter what time of the year it is," Zali responds, gaze falling on me. A small line appears between her brows, and then she's rolling the frozen head back into the sack.

I try to avoid looking at the dark smear on the table as Zali treads to the edge of the room and lets the head thunk to the ground, swiping her hands on her pants. "These days, Fryst is almost entirely frozen all year round. Based on the evidence, it appears these mutts are growing in strength and numbers in the Deep North before venturing over the alps."

My stomach threatens to turn inside out.

More whispers spill from tight lips and bared teeth.

"What does that mean?" someone asks from the other side of the table.

"One of two things," Zali states. "Either Fryst is overrun by Vruks, to the point where they're running out of food and spilling across the mountains in search of fresh game ... or High Master Vadon is purposely breeding and feeding the mutts, then setting them free by the border and letting them do his dirty work."

The room goes so silent you could hear my needle drop. I can feel the weight of a thousand thoughts settling upon my shoulders; can see it in the many pairs of wide-open eyes—some staring at the High Mistress of Rouste, others at the empty space before them.

"Neither option is ideal," Zali tacks on, her honey eyes lacking their usual warmth. "If the Vruks keep growing in numbers, strength, and cunning ... then bunkers may no longer be enough."

"They're not enough *now!*" the thistly man yells, spittle flying, and a number of people mutter their agreement. "We're cowering when we should be fighting!"

"We should be *preparing,*" Zali corrects with a raised voice that silences the room. "Rhordyn recently sent a scouting ship down the River Norse, and there's now a gate larger than this castle barring the border entry."

Eyes widen and gasps spill. I try to look equally shocked, as if I'm not a cloistered hermit who has a limited sense of the world beyond my Safety Line.

"We don't want to be caught unprepared if those gates crack open and something nefarious spills out," she continues. "A territory war on anyone's terms but our own could shrink our borders, decimate our populations, and set us back *centuries.* Nobody wants that, and nobody wants to continue living in fear of Vruks tearing through our villages and ripping apart our loved ones."

People nod, eyes turning cold and grim, while I try not to wither under the darting glances that dare to pick at me: the living reminder of just such an attack.

"So, the question is ..." Zali pulls a tawny badge off her lapel and throws it at the table. It comes to a halt next to the rusted grate—only a few inches away from tumbling through one of the holes into the unknown abyss. "Do we sit back while our smaller villages are plucked off one by one? While our people are taken or left mauled in a field, and we're forced to feed liquid bane to anyone left alive but wounded? Or do we unite, combine our assets, strengthen our walls, and prepare to not only defend what's ours, but to stake the problem in the heart and ensure the thriving future of our lands?"

The grip on my thigh tightens.

Rhordyn tosses a black badge on the table—one stamped with his lone-sword sigil—and murmurs follow.

A stout man with red hair and a crooked spine stands with the help of two younger males wearing the same rusty-colored garb. Years are etched around eyes that regard the High Mistress of Rouste with tenderness, and he tosses his own tawny badge on the table. "My region is small, and I have limited resources since a pack of mutts tore through my village a month ago, but I'm happy to honor this pledge if it comes to it."

I glance at Zali, noting her smile that looks more sad than happy.

Badges add to the growing pile, and I find myself avoiding the source of a heated audit branding my face from across the table.

Rhordyn's like a rock beside me. I'm not even sure he's breathing as that pile grows and grows ... until there's nobody left but the Bahari male who wears the sun for skin.

My gaze finally lifts, breath catching when our stares collide, and I swelter from the scorch of his narrowed focus. I can't breathe under the force of which it's branding me, but I refuse to let that show.

He clears his throat and slips his leg off the arm of his chair before leaning forward. Seconds drip by, but they feel like minutes before his eyes flick to Rhordyn. "I request a private audience."

The words are deep, husky bolts that echo through the room suffering in otherwise stark silence, striking me over and over again.

I look sideways, hear Rhordyn grind his teeth, and something heavy lands in my stomach ...

"Fine."

CHAPTER 32

ORLAITH

I wiggle my fingers into the leather glove, another layer to help ward off the chill as I descend Stony Stem, seeing but not seeing, stepping but not stepping, mulling over *everything* I just heard.

A week ago, my world was *huge* ... at least in my mind. Now, it feels tiny compared to the bigger, overriding picture Rhordyn shoved down my throat when he dragged me to that meeting.

He must know I'm simmering. Probably the reason he had Baze escort me to my tower post-Conclave whilst he stormed down the hall in the opposite direction, leaving my curiosity to feast on that wealth of startling information like a starved child.

I have questions.

The man has me just where he wants me—interest piqued, rattled enough to want to know more. He's not forcing me over my Safety Line, but instead, threading his arm inside my cage and feeding me scraps of the outside world. Perhaps trying to prove how fragile the bars I've put around myself really are.

The bastard.

Battling my other glove, I'm exiting the stairwell into the

fifth-level hallway when the hairs on the back of my neck lift ...

I spin, drive my bare foot into an unprotected kidney, and corral a man twice my size up against the wall with my hairpin pointed at his carotid.

He puffs out a startled sound, cradling his abdomen, eyes wide with surprise.

The Bahari male.

"Well," he chokes, "I wasn't expecting *that.*"

My hair unwinds, seeming to realize it's no longer clipped in place, falling heavily around my shoulders.

"Do you make a habit of sneaking up on women?" I hiss, digging the weapon deeper, almost enough to draw a bead of blood.

It's tempting. I'm on edge, and this asshole keeps dropping in on my alone time, reminding me the castle is swarming with strangers—something I'm trying so *very* hard not to think about.

He lifts a brow. "If I'd wanted to sneak, we certainly wouldn't be in *this* position right now."

"You're suggesting you let me get the better of you ..."

Those eyes gleam like sky-born crystals, and from this close, I can see specks of purple around his irises.

"I'm suggesting that I'm not opposed to being pinned to the wall by a beautiful woman."

I shove back, leaving him lounging against the stone, a smooth smirk kinking the corner of his lips. There's a mark where my hairpin was dug into his neck, and the sight of it gives me an odd sense of satisfaction.

Baze would be proud, even if this male is insinuating he purposely let down his guard. No man would happily allow someone to kick him in the kidney.

His eyes narrow, head tilting to the side, revealing a glimpse of his undercut. I spot the scrawling lines that are barbered into it—like an artist took a blade to the half-shorn canvas and turned it into a work of art.

Suddenly self-conscious, I hold the clip between my teeth and sweep my hair back, twisting it into a heavy knot at the nape of my neck before securing it in place.

His gaze doesn't waver, hunting every movement like a shark who just caught the scent of blood. Though there's something ... *more* about it. Like those eyes are peeling back my layers, one by one, assessing me for flaws.

"What a pretty flower to keep locked in a big, rocky tower."

My head snaps back. "*Excuse me?*"

He jerks his chin toward the entry of Stony Stem.

I realize with a start that he's insinuating Rhordyn keeps me imprisoned.

"*No*—" I shake my head, tone adamant. "He doesn't. It's not like that."

"Doesn't look that way to me," he purrs, crossing his arms and ankles, looking far too comfortable at the foot of my tower. "Has anyone ever told you how striking the color of your eyes are?"

I ball my hands into tight little fists that hang at my sides.

"What's your name?"

"Cainon," he answers far too swiftly, like the word was already sitting on his tongue, waiting to be thrown. "But you can call me Cain."

"Do you want something, Cainon? Did you lose direction on your way to your meeting with Rhordyn? Or perhaps you require an escort back to the guest suites on the *ground floor?*"

He pushes off the wall and pockets his hands, shoulders

lax as he strides forward a step. There's a shift in his eyes—the lofty sharpness falling away, replaced with liquid swirls of a summer sea. "I wanted to apologize. For earlier."

My mouth falls open, closes again, throat tightening.

Oh.

My feet move of their own accord, sending me on a mindless trail down the hall underwhelmed by shafts of gray light diving through the windows, putting *that* particular conversation well and truly at my back.

I don't want his apology. I want him to forget it happened and leave me the hell alone.

"There's no need," I call over my shoulder as I walk like I have a destination in mind.

I don't.

I just don't want to be *here,* alone with a man who seems to care far too much about how I regard him. That's the only reason he'd be on the fifth floor, apologizing for something he surely presumes I'm embarrassed about.

He's suddenly right next to me, walking in long, lazy strides. "You walk very fast."

I frown, gaze still cast ahead. "Why did you come here?"

The question is spat out like an ember that was scalding my tongue.

"Why did I come here?" he repeats, and I grind to a halt.

We spin at the same time, chest to chest but a foot apart, my head tilted back so I can see into the whirlpools of his eyes. He's almost as tall as Rhordyn, but I don't let the fact that my chin is in line with his sternum bother me.

He's in *my* castle. In *my* territory. And his actions thus far have been questionable at least.

"Yes. You didn't pledge yourself to the cause," I say, prodding the badge on his lapel with my index finger—the one that's Bahari blue carved with the sigil of a mountain pushing from the ocean. "So why did you come here?"

Both his brows lift. "Not just a pretty face, I see ..."

Internally, I roll my eyes. "It doesn't take a genius to listen. And your flattery doesn't work on me. Neither does" —I gesture to his ... *everything*—"all that."

"Pity," he mumbles, an amused lilt to his tone that has my brow pleating. "And who's to say I'm not pledging myself to the cause?"

My frown turns into a scowl.

This male is just as difficult to read as Rhordyn. Perhaps I'm cursed to be surrounded by intense men who make very little sense.

"You didn't hand over your badge. I assumed—"

"Everyone else at the table has far less to offer than I do, and unlike Zali, I'm not fucking Rhordyn for compensation."

The words land like nails, the visual sowing deep into the soil of my brain, but I work hard to keep my features from betraying my internal flinch.

"So that's what you're after?" I cut him a glare, as if the look alone could convince him to spill. "Compensation?"

He shrugs. "I want many things, Orlaith."

"I didn't tell you my name."

"You didn't need to."

A retort gets jammed in my throat, and I clear it out before turning away. "I must be going. I've got things to do. Places to be."

You to avoid.

"Orlaith ..." His voice chases me down the hall, grips hold of my ankles, and bolts me in place.

Slowly, I turn.

He hasn't moved from where I left him, but the intensity

in his eyes has returned, solidifying those aqua pools into something that strikes a much harsher blow. "Will you be at the ball?"

A storm of unbridled energy swarms my heart, battering it while I consider the event Rhordyn is forcing me to attend. As if making me sit next to him in that room today wasn't enough for everyone to see I'm ... *just me.*

Nothing more.

"Yes," I bite out, watching his mouth hook at the corner.

"Your excitement is palpable."

"How very perceptive of you," I mutter, spinning. "Not just a pretty face, after all."

His deep, rolling laughter batters my back as I stalk away.

CHAPTER 33

ORLAITH

Clinging to the shadows, I peek into the ballroom, trying to blend in with one of two large urns gushing Night Bloom vines that creep across the wall, framing the grand entrance.

It's not often I seek Rhordyn out, but I need answers, and for once, the bastard is going to give them to me.

The huge space is half-dressed for tomorrow night's ball. Long, gossamer strips of silver material drape from the high ceiling, transforming it into a billowing cloud. Thousands of thin, metal strings shoot down from between the pockets, tipped with tear-drop bulbs of light as if the rain is something to worship.

A swarm of servants are buzzing beneath the pretty canopy, moving furniture into place—large, round tables I've only ever seen stacked in one of the many storage rooms. They're being swathed in inky cloth that puddles at the base, their surfaces decorated with gray flower arrangements too big and lush for one person to carry.

I frown, nostrils flaring, scenting the floral perfume the grand ballroom is bathed in.

Those flowers should have been left in the garden, but at

least they're using the grayslades. There's an abundance of them around the castle.

If it were any other, I'd be showing my teeth.

Noticing movement in my peripheral, I glance along the hall to see Sophia approaching—a maid with large, pretty eyes and midnight hair, arms laden with a stack of silver platters.

I wave at her. "Excuse me!"

She startles, almost losing her cargo, then drops into a tight curtsy that makes me cringe. "Miss! Good grief, I didn't see you there."

"Do you know where I can find the High Master? I expected him to be here ... I don't know, *overseeing*," I say, batting my hand toward the ballroom.

Her brows almost collide. "No, Miss. And I'm not sure, Miss."

She curtsies again, then hurries through the doors as if she can't get away from me fast enough.

The staff aren't usually so skittish around me.

Someone taps me on the shoulder, and I whirl to face a burly guard with dark eyes and a mop of ebony hair smoothed off his face with a lubricated sheen.

I lift a brow. "Jonas."

"Orlaith. What were you ..." He glances over my shoulder. "What were you and Sophia talking about?"

I jerk my thumb toward her. "You mean just now?"

He nods.

"I'm, ah, looking for Rhordyn. I thought Sophia might know where to find him."

"Oh ..." He expels a deep breath and rolls onto his heels, face softening. "That's all?"

"What else would it be?"

"Good. The High Master is busy." He turns and starts to walk away at a brisk pace, but I lumber forward and snatch his wrist.

"Busy *where,* exactly? I lack the patience to spend the next two days searching every corner of this castle." His gaze shoots down to my white-knuckled grip, and I loosen my hold. "Sorry."

He clears his throat, glancing at another guard stationed by the doors. Hard to be certain, but I swear they share an exasperated look.

"What do you think I'm going to do, wound the man?"

"Nosey in on our High Master's business."

... Justified.

Most of the guards don't trust me, though I can hardly blame them. I've caught the majority in compromising positions over the years. Apparently I don't walk loud enough—probably why I keep catching Jonas with his tongue down Marcus' throat, despite the fact that he's courting Sophia.

"Spill, Jonas."

He crosses his arms. "No."

I mirror his stance, narrow my eyes, and wait ... foot tapping the floor.

Silence.

When impatience gets the better of me, I lean in and whisper, *"How's Marcus?"*

His eyes widen, the moment stretching long enough that I shift back and find a comfortable spot against the wall.

I'd never snitch, but *he* doesn't know that. And it wouldn't surprise me to catch him pissing on my rose bushes after this little powwow.

He mutters something indiscernible and sighs. "Rhordyn's in his office on the third floor."

Should've considered that.

"Thank yo—"

"Having a *private* meeting." He emphasizes 'private' as if he's about to crack open a dictionary and point out the meaning right here and now. "He and the High Mistress of Rouste said they're not to be disturbed under *any* circumstances."

My spine stiffens, heart feeling like it just got tangled in a thorny vine.

Private meeting ... with Zali ... in his office ...

The bitter taste is hard to swallow. So is the vision that just got plunged into my brain like a stake.

Her spread out across his desk like that woman from the book—back arched; bare breasts being groped by masculine hands; Rhordyn bent over her like a silver-scrawled shadow, face between her thighs, rumbling ...

Feasting ...

Fuck.

"Right," I answer, trying my hardest to maintain a casual demeanor when all I want to do is vomit. "Guess I'll just ... frolic back to my tower, then."

He rolls his eyes and strides off down the hall, as if he's addled by the mere sight of me.

Heart in my throat, I make my way to the third floor, straight to the grand hallway that leads to Rhordyn's office.

Five times I almost turn around—telling myself this sort of morose curiosity is septic. Self-destructive. But my feet have a mind of their own, leading me down the path sure to ruin me.

Softening my footfalls, I draw closer, hearing the uneven burr of more than one masculine voice.

I pause.

That doesn't sound like a man and woman locked in the throes of pleasure.

The surge of relief is so abrupt I have to clamp my lips shut to catch my sigh.

I press against the far wall and duck behind a dense, velvet curtain bunched at the side of a closed window. It offers me the perfect vantage point that's near enough to hear every word being passed back and forth in Rhordyn's office, and if I peek my head out the far side, I can probably catch a glimpse through the wide-open door, too.

Honestly, if this meeting was *that* private, he should have closed the damn thing. If Rhordyn catches me snooping, that's going to be my exact line of defense. Everyone knows doors are my weakness. Leaving one open during a private meeting? Well, he should know better.

"Nice touch with the Vruk head, Zali. You never cease to surprise me."

Cainon.

"There was nothing *nice* about it," Zali snips. "I found that *mutt* feasting on a farmer and his son. The four other Vruks from the attack are now flayed and pinned to stakes as a deterrent. They weren't the first, and they certainly won't be the last.

Seems Zali just gained my respect.

Cainon clears his throat, and I can almost picture him crossing his arms or inspecting his nails like he's bored with the conversation. "As much as I enjoy your stories, I need to speak with Rhordyn alone."

"Fine," Zali snips, the word prefacing her heavy steps, as if she's wearing the weight of all her anger in the soles of her shoes.

Steps that are drawing in *my* direction ...

Shit.

I hold my breath and close my eyes, pressing myself flat against the wall, hoping she can't see my bare feet poking out the bottom of the curtain.

Her footsteps draw closer, and my lungs start to burn as I hold ... *hold* ...

She pauses, and seconds pass before the curtain peels back, allowing a slice of dull afternoon light to cleave apart my hiding space ...

I wince, squinting into large, honey eyes fringed with dark lashes, waiting for the verbal blow to land—the one which will likely earn me an armored escort back to Stony Stem.

Instead, she offers me a coy smile, throws me a wink, then lets the curtain fall.

Gaping at the thick material, I listen to her retreating footsteps.

"That dismissal applied to you too, Baze."

I sidestep to the left, peel the curtain, and peep into the study.

Cain has his back to the door, the wide breadth of his shoulders blocking half my view. Baze is out of the frame of my vision—probably propped against a wall somewhere—but I can see Rhordyn. He's stretched out in his chair, perched behind his large, sable desk.

"He's not going anywhere," Rhordyn booms, and something about the way he's watching Cainon has the hair on the back of my neck lifting.

Cainon clears his throat and widens his stance. "Very well."

"Very well," Rhordyn repeats. Aside from the shift of his lips, everything else about him is stone still.

"You want use of my ships?"

Cainon's ships?

Rhordyn taps a finger on the arm of his chair. "Only a hundred or so," he says with the slightest lift of a shoulder. "You have five times that. I'm sure you can spare them."

Five. Hundred. Ships.

Who the hell is this man?

"If Vadon has bent, he's going to be ... problematic," Rhordyn states, tipping his head from side to side. "He's vastly protected by the mountains. His only weaknesses are the River Norse which is now *gated* and the western cleft in Reidlyn Alps that's only accessible by boat. Our options are to either risk certain suicide by taking the mountain pass, or a much safer journey through The Shoaling Seas." He leans forward, steepling his hands and hammering Cainon with a gaze that would bleed the empty air between them if it had a heart. "We need those ships."

I squeeze my lips together ...

His words are the fortified walls of an impenetrable fortress.

Safe. Confident.

Unyielding.

Though I want to shelter behind their barricade, something tells me I should do the opposite. That I should run and never look back.

"Well, if your suspicions are correct, he's only an immediate threat to *your* pretty lands," Cainon responds, tone sharp. "Why should the Vruks be anyone's problem but yours?"

I lean further to the side, glimpsing Baze's face, his shoulder nailed to the wall, arms crossed over his chest. I search for any betrayal of expression, considering he's generally far more animated than Rhordyn is ...

Not today.

He's just as hard, just as stoic, looking at Cainon like a python ready to strike.

I notice the sword at his hip and my mouth goes dry ...

That's not his wooden sword.

I've never seen that silver hilt before, or the big, iridescent gem crowning the pommel, lording over the length.

"Soon it won't just be Vruks and the odd disappearance." Rhordyn's tone is like the pond in the middle of winter.

Smooth, cold, and deadly calm.

Cainon's head tilts to the side, barely enough for me to notice. "Is that a threat?"

"That's a *fact*."

"Well, The Shoaling Seas chew up a tenth of everything that passes through, so the moment I toss you my badge, I throw at least ten ships down the drain. If we have no *formal* tie," Cain counters, shrugging, "I can't make any promises."

The temperature drops so suddenly my breath turns milky, and I have to bite down on a shiver as I watch Baze's hand shift to the hilt of his sword.

Rhordyn's eyes grow dark. "Choose your next words wisely, Cain."

"The orphan charge you keep locked in that tower," he says without hesitation.

My spine locks. I'm so still I can hear the *whoosh* of my heartbeat thrumming through my veins.

"What about her?"

Rhordyn's voice is so monotone I picture death.

Cold, grisly, merciless death.

"I wish to gift her my cupla," Cainon responds, and it

suddenly feels like the castle is too small to house the disruptive energy rolling off the High Master of the West.

"Is that so?"

He stands, the motion slow, fluid smooth—like he's toying with time, striking each movement with an exclamation mark. He prowls around the edge of the table with a strong, steady gait, and Cainon shifts until they're standing chest to chest and I have a full, unperturbed view of two powerful profiles.

They're night and day. Sun and moon. One couldn't be more different from the other, but both own the sky in their own wicked way.

Rhordyn's taller, and he uses it to his advantage, looking down on Cainon like he's no bigger than a bug on the masonry.

"It's a very brash man who would come to a neighboring Master's estate and bribe him in such a way. Part of me is impressed, though that part is miniscule. The rest of me wants to peel the skin off your testicles and make you eat them—force you to ingest the seeds of your future offspring."

Cainon lifts his chin, sliding his hands deep into his pockets like this is a casual chat about the weather. "I wouldn't threaten me, Rhor. Certainly not when you're harboring a woman with such ... *distinct* Bahari attributes in your little rocky tower."

Huh?

Rhordyn slides forward until there is no longer any space cleaving them apart. "Do you need me to remind you who you're talking to?"

My heart is in my throat, the moment growing its own hungry pulse.

There's something *more* between these two—a history I don't understand.

Cainon drifts back a step. It's only a small concession, but it seems significant.

Rhordyn grunts and stalks back to his chair, reclining into it in the same way he sits atop his throne.

"You would lock her up and let her rot when she could be the key to your salvation?"

Rhordyn shrugs. "Orlaith will not suffer the weight of a political pairing. So, unless you've miraculously stolen her heart," he says with a flippant wave of his hand, "then you can kindly go fuck yourself. And your ships."

I swallow the lump in my throat and sag against the wall, letting the curtain fall back into place.

He needs those ships. The *people* need those ships.

"The offer expires at midnight tomorrow," Cainon states, and heavy footsteps follow. "Make the right decision for your people, Rhor. And for her."

The parting three words are rich with disgust, showcasing his displeasure at however he perceives my situation.

Our situation.

It's not until Cainon's footfalls fade that I slink away; body moving through the motions, mind churning.

That conversation exposed me—wedged a stick of guilt deep within my conscience. Because I survived a Vruk attack despite my tender age and was gifted a cushioned life, sat high and dry in my pretty tower while the world crumbled around me.

Yes, I suffer every time I close my eyes, but I'm the lucky one. I'm the one who got to *live*.

But what's that life worth if it's at the cost of others?

Most of the people who work at this castle have family in

the nearby villages. Mothers. Fathers. Children. *Grand-children.*

One way or another, my safety circle's encroaching—like hands sliding around my neck.

Tightening.

Could I bear the weight of watching Cook mourn her newly born granddaughter because I couldn't break through the bars I've placed around my own mind?

I know the answer to that question, and it's a frightening one. An answer just as deadly as that circle I've drawn around this castle.

Borrowed time. That's all these past nineteen years have been ...

And it seems that time is running out.

CHAPTER 34

ORLAITH

Despite the roaring fire pouring heat throughout my room, the stone floor is cold and unforgiving beneath my bare knees and shins.

It's fitting. A way to prepare me for my inevitable frosty encounter.

I study the pretty constellation on my door—a dusting of stars that surround the crescent moon like worshippers.

The echo of approaching steps reaches me, and my heart launches an attack as I look to The Safe ...

My hand tightens around the glass vial stoppered with a cork.

He's going to be so pissed.

Rhordyn's booming footfalls encroach, and I draw a deep breath, letting it crumble out of me, my hair a thick veil hanging heavy around me like golden armor. Not that I think it'll do me any good.

There's a pause before I hear his key shove into the hole. Hear it clank around and dash the bolt aside.

Hear him open the door and remove the goblet ...

Silence.

Nothing but bone-chilling silence.

I try not to smile, biting down on my lips to tame them.

I probably shouldn't find this so amusing.

A low, animalistic growl has my skin prickling, prefacing a shove of my door. It creaks inward and Rhordyn barrels through the opening, skewering me with an arrowhead glower.

His eyes widen before he shoots his gaze at the ceiling, punching fists to his sides, spilling crystal-clear water across the ground. "What are you doing, Orlaith?"

"I just want to talk," I say, waving the vial of blood at him before tucking it down the front of my chest wrap. "You're going to have a proper conversation with me in exchange for my offering tonight. One that involves *actual* speaking and not just brooding stretches of silence and the odd grunting sound."

He mutters something in that strange language I don't understand, then clunks the goblet atop a small table and pinches the bridge of his nose.

My eyes narrow. "What's wrong?"

"Nothing."

"Do you have head pain?" I ask, waving a hand in the direction of my stash of jars, each filled with various bits of dried flora. "I have the perfect antido—"

"If you try stuffing a leaf in my mouth, I'll bite your finger, get what I came here for, and be gone before you even feel the pinch of my teeth. Now get off your knees, and put some fucking pants on."

Rude.

"Would it kill you to use manners every once in a while?" I ask, pushing up and giving him my back. I dig through my drawers for some longer pants, seeing as my sleep shorts are apparently inadequate. "Besides, you didn't seem so disgusted by my thighs earlier when you had your hand on one."

No answer. Hardly surprising.

I wiggle into a loose pair of trousers, tie them at the waist, and gesture down my body with a dramatic sweep of my hand. "Better?"

He's staring at me, jaw so gritted I wonder if it's fused shut.

"Guess that's a yes. This two-way conversation is off to a strong start. I'll have to set you challenges more often."

He very nearly guts me with a glare, but I look away fast enough to avoid any major damage, pointing at a calico package peeking out from his bunched fist.

"What's in your hand?"

He lobs the parcel through the air, and I nab it, loosening the string fastenings and layers of damp cheesecloth, finally unveiling a tiny bulb that's such a deep shade of purple it almost looks black.

A familiar, potent smell taints the air.

"A single dose of caspun to tide you over for the night. Zali was able to procure a month's supply from a traveling merchant on her way across the border."

"That was thoughtful of her."

"It was also *lucky,* considering how hard it is to find. You'll no longer be using it as a preventative measure," he says, flexing his control and only succeeding in stapling nails into my nerves.

My upper lip peels back. "*Clearly.*"

I'm sick of these games. Sick of all these doors between us. I'm tired, frustrated, brimming with information that's chafing my insides, and I've had enough.

He widens his stance, arms crossing over his chest as he takes me in with overt curiosity. "Have at it, Milaje."

I *will* then.

"Well ... for starters, were you just going to put this in The Safe and leave without telling me?" I bark, waving the precious brain-pressure-relieving bulb at him.

"No. I was going to knock, inform you there was something in there, and *then* I was going to leave." He shrugs, eyes like silver-barred prison cells. "I know it's not ground down, but if you can make enough Exothryl to pop an army's worth of hearts in one sitting, then I'm certain you can manage dealing with *that.*" He stabs a hand in the direction of my caspun and boils my blood.

"You need a nap."

His left brow jacks up. "Excuse me?"

"*You* heard," I mutter, casting my gaze out the window.

Naturally, all I get is a grunted response that lands like a slap to the face. A stretch of silence ensues, lasting long enough that I consider smashing my vial of blood on the floor just to rile him. But then the quiet is broken by a sigh so deep it sounds like a mountain's rumble. "Ask your questions, Orlaith."

I look back to see Rhordyn massaging the bridge of his nose again, as if my very presence is making him want to prong a finger through his sockets and gouge his own brain out.

Right now, the feeling's mutual.

"Did you get the last badge?"

"Not yet," he states, dropping his hand.

The answer bites into my chest so hard I swear it reveals a window to my hammering heart.

Not *yet.*

Meaning he's either rethinking his response to Cainon's proposal ... or he's considering gaining his support by *force.*

Both options grate me.

I don't want to be tossed at Cainon like a sack of misshapen vegetables nobody wants to eat, and I don't want Rhordyn and Zali to be forced to thin their resources in order to gain the key they need to sail The Shoaling Seas into Fryst.

There needs to be another option. There *has* to be another option.

"Well ... what are you going to do about it?"

Tell me no action needs to be taken. Tell me you found a hundred ships crammed in a random, long-forgotten cove somewhere and you no longer need Cainon's help.

Rhordyn shrugs, the motion wary. "Anybody not with us is against us. Simple as that."

My heart slams to a stop—partially with relief, mainly dread. Because it's not simple.

Not at all.

It's wasted lives. Wasted resources.

Another nail in my coffin.

"And you can't just ... wait? Dig deeper bunkers? Batten down the hatche—"

"No," he bites out. "That's what we've been doing, and our people are being slaughtered. The longer we wait, the weaker we get, the less chance we have of withstanding whatever eventually comes through those gates."

I wrap my arms around myself in an effort to hold everything together, though it offers little reprieve. I'm already scattered, choking on that raging beat of chest-cinching anxiety.

There's only *one* option I can see ... and to pull it off, it's going to take every last ounce of courage I can scrape together. I'm going to have to lie to myself. *Deceive* myself.

Force myself into doing something I'd hoped I could avoid for the rest of my life.

I'm going to have to become somebody different. Someone bold and heartless.

Fearless.

"Why did you drag me to the Conclave?" I ask, glancing back up into his distant, rocky stare.

"To open your fucking eyes, Orlaith. The world out there is so much bigger than *this*," he growls with a sweep of his hand, gesturing around my room. My entire *universe*. "I needed to prepare you for the worst case scenario."

There are still words left on his tongue; I can sense them sitting there, ready to be flung.

"And?"

"And your tower may be high, but you of all people should know it's usually the tallest flowers that get targeted with a pair of clippers," he says with callous precision. "I figured you'd appreciate the heads up."

The blow is brutal, meant to wound and cleave me from the safety of my shell. Meant to leave me feeling *exposed*.

Right now, the last thing I need is a bitter reminder of how *exposed* I am. I already feel it all the way to my bones.

My fists bunch and I bite my bottom lip so hard I taste blood.

Rhordyn's nostrils flare.

His eyes grow dark and stormy, scouring me in a way that leaves me feeling naked despite my clothes and the thick shield of my hair.

"Anything else?" he drudges out through clenched teeth.

"Yeah," I snap, wanting him gone. Hating the indifference in his eyes when all I need is a hug—for someone to tell me everything's going to be okay.

A pretty lie to solder my spine.

"One last question." I dig my hand down the front of my top and retrieve the vial, chewing up the space between us in three short strides. "Why are you such a *dick?*"

His eyes widen.

I slam the vial at his chest so hard it would wind a regular person, but Rhordyn's no regular man. I'm reminded of that as I move to tug my hand away.

Not fast enough.

He grabs the vial, snatches my wrist like it's a wielded weapon, and pulls me so close I'm assaulted by the eddy of his icy breath—held at knifepoint by his rapier eyes.

"Who taught you that word?" His voice is a blade that cuts me in all the wrong ways. Leaves raw, tender trails down my body, where they meet between my legs and make me throb.

I swallow thickly.

Technically, I learned the word from one of his guards, though I doubt now is the right time to mention that. So I shrug, feigning immunity, draping a casual bravado over my wrought reality. "I'm not as innocent as you think I am."

He laughs, brutal and unapologetic. "One day you'll look back on this moment and realize how wrong you were."

Incorrect.

It will be the other way around, but he'll see that soon enough.

He drops my arm and spins, then lumbers through the doorway, pausing on the threshold of the stairs—the light spilling off a flaming wall-torch half-gilding him into a statue of dark, arrogant beauty. "You're no longer required to attend the ball," he announces over his shoulder, the words presented like a bowl of gruel.

A lackluster lie for me to choke down.

Unease settles heavy on my shoulders ...

"And why not?"

He turns a little, barely catches my eye, and shrugs. "People have seen more than enough. You're off the hook. Congratulations."

His words hammer that final nail into my coffin lid, plunging all the way through my soon-to-be rotten corpse, leaving me doused in dread.

Then he leaves.

CHAPTER 35

ORLAITH

I work tirelessly, pinning long sections of hair into golden rosettes that sit high atop my head. Fitting the final piece into place, I tame loose tendrils around my face, completing the bouquet hairstyle that's far too regal for my liking.

But it fits the mold—makes me look like a High Master's ward would be expected to look.

I hope.

I glance down, ensuring the pendants resting between my unbound breasts aren't obvious beneath the sheath of blood-red material.

Poor Tanith. I think back to the moment she came to collect the gown, only to find a naked mannequin and me, claiming to have condemned the dress to a watery grave during my visit with Kai this morning.

The lie slid off my tongue, and I'd felt a twinge of guilt when she paled, claiming she'd been ordered to retrieve it. But not enough for me to fetch it from beneath my mattress and hand it over.

Not once has Rhordyn offered me an easy out, which means he's purposely trying to keep me from the ball. Perhaps he thinks Cainon will poison my mind, but blinkers are bracketing his eyes, and he can't see that Cainon's the *antidote.*

I'm the antidote.

He's going to toss me out eventually ... it might as well be in a territory that hasn't been invaded by Vruks yet.

I pop the cork off a jar of lip lacquer I made from ground-up rose petals, scented oil, and a bit of lard. Women at the Tribunal often wear red on their lips, so I figured I'll blend in if I do the same.

Claiming a paintbrush, I draw a deep breath and look to my pale reflection.

Tonight, this mirror is not my enemy. Because tonight, I'm not the Orlaith who's spent the majority of her life hiding behind a make-believe line, using Rhordyn as a shield.

Tonight, I'm somebody strong, composed, and resilient.

"Strong, composed ... *resilient ...*"

I dip the tapered bristles, steady my hand, and stain my lips red with delicate precision. The color makes my lilac eyes pop and is the perfect tone to compliment my dress. But more importantly, it makes me look like somebody else, and tonight, that's exactly what I need.

A mask.

Next is a smudge of kohl around my eyes, turning them smokey and mysterious. I even use a sharpened stick to draw a line of it above my lids that flicks out beyond the corner.

Vision complete, I let the stick fall to the vanity.

I look so confident and majestic—nothing like the woman who broke down in the gardens yesterday. A pretty, sacrificial offering dolled up just enough to draw that pair of clippers Rhordyn was so intent on warning me against.

It's *perfect.*

Pushing to my feet, I smooth the material hugging my legs before retrieving my shoes off the bed.

The heels look like oversized thorns, and I have almost a hundred and fifty stairs to descend. With that in mind, I decide to put them on later rather than risk cartwheeling to the base of Stony Stem and breaking every bone in my body.

Stressing the limits of my tight dress, I edge down the tower in increments, one hand tracing the wall while the other grips my shoes and hem, every step announced by another bitten word.

Strong.

Composed.

Resilient.

By the time I reach the foyer at the base of my tower, I almost believe myself.

Bending to slip my heels on, I notice a dinner tray sitting on the ground near the open doorway, covered by a wooden lid with a small velvet pouch perched on top. Frowning, I reach for it ...

The door slams shut.

The sound of a bolt sliding into place has my heart diving into my stomach. I dart forward, grasp the brass handle, and push—

The door doesn't budge.

It's never been locked before. I didn't even know it *had* a lock.

"Hey!" I bellow, slapping my hand against the wood so hard my palm throbs. "Open the damn door!"

My only response is a convenient void of silence.

No retreating footsteps.

Whoever just locked me in here is standing by, listening

to me yell, and there's only *one* person I'd give that sort of credit to.

"*Rhordyn!* I know you're there! Open this door right now!"

Nothing.

I kick at it, slam my shoulder against it, search its hinges for a way to pry them loose ...

"*Rhordyn!*"

Heavy footsteps retreat down the hall while I kick and snarl and scream. Teeth bared, I unfasten a hairpin and dig it down the side of the door where I think the lock might be, but it's useless.

There's no weakness for me to manipulate.

Bent pin pinched between my throbbing fingers, I crumble to the ground in a frustrated, sweaty heap ...

How dare he.

Flopped on the bed, I stare daggers at the velvet bag hanging from my finger. The one I just opened to reveal a stash of healthy bluebell heads ... minus the stems.

I frown, seeing the gift for what it really is.

Placation.

Perhaps Zali told Rhordyn I was standing behind that curtain. Perhaps he's just being a controlling prick. Whatever the cause of my sudden jailing, the outcome is still the same.

I'm pissed, trapped, anxious ... and that's a dangerous mix.

I'm not silly. I know Cainon has seen something he likes in me—that he's using me as a bargaining chip. Something Rhordyn is obviously opposed to.

I know he thinks I'm better than a political pairing, but

what Cainon said to me at the base of Stony Stem suggested Rhordyn's own pairing is at least partially political. And what's good enough for Rhordyn is good enough for me.

I may not be a High Mistress, but I can do one better than Zali. I can secure Rhordyn a hundred ships and the means to put a stop to the carnage spreading across the land. I can help make the world a safer place just by accepting a simple cupla.

But I can't do that from up here in my tower, and the deal's off the table at midnight.

We're running out of time.

I hiss at the clutch of bells, half tempted to toss them out the window and see how fast they fall.

Actually ... *screw it.*

I roll off the bed and swing the door open, sweeping onto the balcony in a swish of red. Stepping close to the balustrade, I take in the castle grounds littered with people dressed in pops of color, decorating the grass like a field of wild blooms.

There are carriages parked about, hooked up to horses chewing on piles of straw. A line of torches leads to the front entrance, ready to light a path for the guests whose chatter comes to me on the still twilight air.

My isolation from such a crowd would usually thrill me to the bone, but I'm not that girl tonight. All I see are potential victims of a future raid I could have prevented.

It's not good enough.

I suspend the bag of blooms over the edge, gaze diving to the long, metal support beam that runs from the base of Stony Stem by the fifth floor, crosses a courtyard, and anchors itself to a sturdier wing of Castle Noir.

My heart flip flops. "*Of course.*"

I dash inside and set the velvet pouch on my pillow,

though not before I give it a sniff. I'm not searching for the bluebell's fragrance, but savoring the scent of leather and a crisp, icy lake.

Rhordyn handled this bag. Picked these buds. Somehow knew I needed them. Then went to the effort to remove the stems required to make more Exothryl, leaving only the goods to make more paint.

The bastard.

I stain my lips with another layer of rouge before grabbing my shoes and making a dash for the stairs. They're full of the murky light of sundown, the sconces not yet lit. They probably won't be, considering the door's locked and I'm supposed to be hiding in my tower. But again, I'm not that girl tonight.

I'm strong. Composed. Resilient. Someone who doesn't cower from the slice of a stare or the hack of a word.

Someone who wears her skin with *pride*.

I lean against the concave wall, one hand gripping the base of a tall, oblong window. My heart sits high in my throat as I glance across the canyon of empty space, tracing the thin, metallic beam that roots from just below the window, stretching toward a stout part of the castle.

A safe, sturdy destination, which is a lot more than I can say about the beam.

I cast my stare on the stone courtyard five stories below ...

That fall looks terribly unforgiving, but the way I see it, I either tiptoe across this lengthy plank and make it to that damn ball or more innocent people suffer.

There is no option.

I lift my leg, causing my dress to split from knee to hip along the side seam, leaving a gaping hole. I groan, rip it to the hem so it comes across as a risqué fashion choice, then clamber onto the window ledge and shift my grip to better support myself.

If I don't die now, I will when Rhordyn sees I'm flashing half my ass cheek in-front of the entire congregation.

Praying nobody looks up, I stare at the ground.

"Shit ..."

My one saving grace is my experience walking The Plank, something I hope will aid me to keep my feet firmly planted.

That's the theory, anyway.

Drawing a deep breath, I secure the train of my dress and cast my gaze toward the opposite window. I settle my first foot on the beam barely wide enough to support the full width of it and relinquish my grip on the sill, transferring a single shoe to my other hand to balance myself.

I push my arms out like I'm flying, my other foot moving on its own, sailing me away from the port of Stony Stem. The chasm of doom yawns beneath me as I settle into that corner of my mind that's quiet, calm, and entirely naïve.

My heart slows as I walk—paces long and delicate, body light as a feather.

I'm not five stories in the air with my life balancing on a shift of wind. I'm strong, steady, and there's *nothing* in this world that can stop me.

The air seems to cradle me as I walk the last few paces, and a laugh bubbles in the back of my throat. I transfer both shoes to one hand and grip the skirting, using it to swing myself through the open window, landing in a narrow hallway like an agile cat.

My smile is so wide it feels like my face is splitting.

I dart down the corridor lined with tall, peek-a-boo windows to my left. It takes a sharp bend, then a fall of stairs has my feet hammering the ground at a swifter pace. The steps flatten to a landing, and I slide my hands over the wall to my right, applying pressure until it swings open and reveals a secret entrance to The Tangle.

This elbow is tight, squiggly, and dark—a trail I have to work my way through by feel alone—but a short route that spits me inside a blanket box. I shove the lid open and clamber out, brushing myself off in the dusty storage room that's stacked full of old furniture. I pat my hair, secure any loose bits, then step out the door into a loud, bustling hall doused in the smell of baked seafood.

The kitchen is ahead on my left, a steady stream of servants flowing in and out.

I walk at a brisk pace, keeping my chin high and eyes trained forward as I pass the door, inserting myself amongst the river of servers clothed in black—

"Stop right there, missy!"

Dammit.

I spin to chase the source of the fiery inspection burning the side of me. "Hi, Cook ..."

She clicks her tongue, then herds me toward a quieter section of the hallway and eyes me up and down, dusting flour on her already chalky apron while I try not to fidget.

"I was told you weren't attending, and that I'm to serve a plate of honey buns at the base of your tower once the sun goes down." She reaches deep into her pocket and pulls out a black key that makes me cringe internally.

"Whoever told you that must have gotten the message wrong," I say, jerking my thumb toward the flow of servants. "I'm actually headed there now, so I'll jus—"

"The High Master himself told me."

Oh. Crap.

I nod, hating that I got caught lying to Cook, but her family lives in a nearby village ...

I'm doing this for *everybody*.

"Sometimes Rhordyn doesn't know what's good for him," I mutter, and her gaze softens.

"Well. That's something I can agree with." She stuffs the key into her pocket and motions for me to step closer. "Quick, let me help you put those shoes on. If you bend over, you'll tear that dress to your tit."

My cheeks blaze as I squash a sigh of relief, swinging my shoes into Cook's awaiting hands so fast I almost flog her with them. She kneels, holds them out, and I slip them on one by one.

As she fastens the buckles, I watch servant after servant rush past with round, silver platters encumbered by brimming champagne flutes, overhearing one of them natter about some announcement that's about to take place ...

I frown.

"What announcement?"

Cook stands, gives me a sweeping scan, and rearranges a few pins in my hair. "You and I both know which announcement they're referring to, my girl."

My heart drops as I glance down the hall, wishing the backs of my eyes weren't stinging. Wishing the extra surge of determination had everything to do with my will to do good —that it was untarnished by the thorn of resentment poking holes in my heart.

Yes, I know exactly what announcement they're referring to.

CHAPTER 36

ORLAITH

The lilting tune of a distant fiddle accompanies a riot of bodies flowing in and out of the grand ballroom.

Some are maids carrying those silver trays laden with champagne flutes; some are poised women dolled up in dresses cinched at the waist, their skirts flowing behind them like liquid. Their painted smiles and beaded hairstyles make them look untouchable.

Two are dressed in gray gowns that cover every inch of skin aside from their pinched faces—hair pulled back in tight hairstyles that showcase upside down v-shaped scars in the center of their foreheads.

Those people ... I make extra effort to avoid looking at their eyes.

Men are clad in tailored suits that square shoulders and taper hips. Suede suits. Velvet suits. Silk suits as polished as their slicked-back hair.

You can usually tell a person's territory simply by their garb, but this ball is a colorful, eclectic expression of personality.

Looking down at the ruby dress that's tailored to the dunes of my curves, I almost lose my nerve. Almost hightail it back to Cook so I can beg for the key to Stony Stem. It's only the sight of a raven-haired child notched on her mother's hip that convinces me otherwise; her big, round eyes anchoring me in place.

She appears to be the only one who can see me standing in the shadows, and she's looking at me like she *knows*—like she can see into the chasm of my soul.

If I skitter back to my tower, her breaths are numbered, and I can't bear the thought of the light bleeding from her eyes.

My hand whips up to the treasures hidden beneath a layer of red; a jewel that reminds me to strengthen my spine and a shell that shields my heart.

The lute changes tempo—becomes dense and beaty—and it jerks me into action. I peel from the slice of shadow clinging to the wall, my tormented toes bearing the weight of every step.

Heads turn and eyes widen, whispers dole out from between lips that barely move as I walk toward the grand entrance.

Admittedly, I didn't consider how much this dress would make me stand out when Hovard came up with the sketch. I was pissed, off-kilter, and desperate to rattle Rhordyn in any way I could. But now that I'm here, dressed in nothing but a yard of silk that coats my skin like a lick of blood, I'm drowning in regret.

Everyone's watching. Taking me in. And aside from the rouge and the powder and the kohl, there's *nothing* for me to hide behind.

I'm not wearing a bodice like all the other women. My back is entirely bare. There's a split in my dress that's inviting peeks of flesh from hip to toe every time my right foot kicks forward a step.

The crowd parts like a split book, as if I'm emerging from the gutter. Though it makes my cheeks scald, it does allow me a clear view of the elegant ballroom cast in a pearly glow. A straight shot to the man leaning against the far wall near a raised podium, arms knotted over his chest that seems to have paused in its labors.

The music stops as the crowd drinks me in, assuaging their curiosity while cool, steely eyes regard me.

Needle me in the heart.

My skin may be blazing with the collective focus of a room full of inquisitive eyes, but it's *his* that leaves a frosty scar. *His* I'm hanging off, despite it being barbed.

I take a moment perched on the threshold of my inevitable demise, certain I won't survive his wrath for what I'm about to do. Not when he's staring daggers at me simply for escaping my cage.

But he asked for *effort.* I'm simply following orders.

I watch his eyes flare as I lift my chin and push my shoulders back. Because right now, wearing this dress that clings to my curves and exposes a shape that's never been seen, I'm *not* damaged. I'm not the girl who's afraid to step foot outside the castle grounds, and I'm certainly not the girl who's uncomfortable in the sheath of her own skin.

I'm strong, composed, *resilient ...*

Rhordyn gestures to the musicians, and the music starts again, dissolving the spell of silence. The crowd slowly swirls into action, still pecking me with peeps while filling the empty space and cutting me off from Rhordyn's prying eyes.

Releasing a jagged sigh, I plunge into the breath-stealing scene thick with cloying, exotic smells, barely five steps in when Baze spears through a gap in the crowd, clad in a black suit that accentuates the strong lines of his formidable form.

"What do we have here?" he grits out, stealing my arm, his face split with a smile that shows too much teeth.

He's leading me with a hold so tight my arm loses circulation from the elbow down, so I dig my fingers into his side and pinch.

Hard.

"Ow," he mutters without moving his lips.

I feign a diplomatic smile. "Sorry I'm late. I had a slight wardrobe malfunction."

"I can *see* that," Baze says, steering me through the crowd, weaving between round tables embellished with floral centerpieces and platters of food. "And here I was thinking we were going to make it through the night without a hitch."

I snag a flute off of a server's tray and guzzle the contents in one thirsty drag, face pinching as the bubbly liquid wrestles its way down my throat. "Buckle up, buttercup."

He snatches the glass out of my hand and waves it at my face. "This stuff is *not* for you."

"And why the hell not?"

"Because you don't know how to regulate yourself."

I frown.

He's treating me like I'm a child again, and it's dampening my certitude. I'm just about to tell him exactly that when my other wrist is snatched up and tucked into the crook of Rhordyn's arm. I'm peeled away from Baze, who flashes me an unapologetic wink before disappearing into the crowd.

Traitor.

"Are you not wearing any undergarments?" Rhordyn asks, the pulse of his icy voice hitting the shell of my ear.

"You'll never know," I purr, pretending I'm not affected by

the strike of his words. By his manly musk twisting around me like greedy fingers, or by the way he's holding me against the strong pillar of his body.

He grunts, and I become all too aware of his black suede pants brushing the exposed slice of my leg ...

He's weaving me through the crowd, holding me like he doesn't want to lose grip, and it's messing with my head.

I don't appreciate this ... *effect* he has over me.

Especially not now.

A waitress buzzes close and offers us bite-sized slices of bread capped with roe and a creamy spread. I take one despite my churning stomach, my heart suffering the expected pinch of disappointment when Rhordyn waves her off, scowling as if the very sight of it repulses him.

Something inside me *snaps.*

Perhaps it's the fact that I'm wearing a roomful of curious stares I'm convinced are studying my mask for flaws. Perhaps it's that I'm treading the thin line between composure and another embarrassing public breakdown should something set me off. Perhaps it's simply that he's *here,* screwing with my head, but I shove the canapé at his face and glare into twin wells of scarcely veiled composure.

Wide. *Unblinking.*

Right now, this tiny, pre-dinner nibble is equally as threatening as a weapon poised at his throat. He knows it. I can see in his eyes that he recognizes the challenge I've staked in the ground between us.

The question is, what's he going to do?

A moment hangs, the silence between us roars, and it feels like we're the only two people in the room. Us ... *and this little piece of bread.*

His head banks to the side, and he regards me with the

intensity of an artist's chisel, like he's looking for something to chip away.

I make sure he sees nothing but the icy resolve I wish I hadn't learned from him.

A line forms between his brows, gaze passing to my offering.

I lift my chin, hand mimicking the motion, thrusting the food closer to his face.

Rhordyn clears his throat and snatches the canapé, shoving it in his mouth. I swear he barely chews before he swallows, and something sparks in his eyes that sends a chill shooting down my spine ...

Something akin to *hate*.

"Happy?" he bites out, and I release a captive breath, unaware I'd been holding it this entire time.

He just ate in front of me ...

It should be insignificant, but for me ... it's *everything*.

I nod.

"Good. Now that we've gotten that out of the way, how the *fuck* did you get out of your tower?"

It's hard not to wilt at the growl in his voice, his eyes churning with unsaid threats.

I break away from his scrutiny, feigning disinterest. "I have my ways."

He grips hold of my arm again, steering me in a wide arc around a waitress bearing a tray of flutes. "I'll be investigating."

"I wouldn't if I were you," I say, trying to wriggle out of his strict hold so I can steal another glass. That champagne was tasty, and I like the way it's warming my belly.

"Why not, Orlaith?"

His words cut into me, and I cringe, thinking back to my little trip across the beam ...

He'll work it out, and then I'll probably wish I'd fallen off the damn thing and plummeted to my death.

I glance over to see him staring at me with wide eyes. "Well, now I'm *very* intrigued," he bites out, steering me toward a corner fringed with large urns that are spilling potted night lilies, turning our backs to the wall so that we're looking out on the busy crowd.

Though his proximity chills me to the bone, it also sets fire to my skin. "Just remember, you're the one who wanted me to come."

"Perhaps it wasn't very clear," he mumbles, the baritone of his voice only serving to weaken my knees. "But me telling you not to come, trying to secure your dress, then locking you in your tower was my way of *uninviting* you."

Praying my cheeks aren't as flushed as they feel, I compose my features into what I picture is a vision of regal poise. "You took me to that meeting because you wanted to nudge me over my line. If you think I'm ready to face the world, why stop me?"

His eyes harden. "What I want, what I need, and what is *right* are three entirely different things."

I almost laugh, stabbing my gaze at the crowd giving us a healthy crescent of space. "How very cryptic of you."

Can he hear the hammer of my heart? Because I can. It's roaring in my ears, rattling me to the core.

It's telling me to push him further—to hack and hack until I break him apart so I can inspect his insides. See if he's just as stony beneath the hard surface.

I don't realize his grip on my arm has loosened until cold

fingertips graze across the bare skin at the small of my back …

I jerk from the contact.

"Despite how *murderous* I am," he mumbles, and there's a roundness to his words, like they had to veer their course to get here, "you do look ravishing in that color."

My breath hitches, head whipping to the side, blood rushing to my cheeks as he begins to trace little circles over my sizzling skin.

They're tight, taunting, and more delicate than the tapered tip of a paintbrush. They're stirring my insides, twisting a coil of nerves in my lower stomach like a living, breathing, hot-blooded serpent.

A dampness forms between my legs, and I tighten the press of my thighs, feeling that flush shift from my cheeks, down my neck, where it pinches my nipples into hard peaks.

I'm a stone statue, tentative to move lest I scare him away. Worried that if I shift, he'll smell my body's reaction to the small dose of attention he's gifting me.

"Thank you," I whisper, barely loud enough to stir the air.

"Though I'm not sure how I feel about everyone being privy to all … *this*," he grinds out, drawing his circles lower, *lower*, until they're dancing around one of the twin dimples stamped above my bum.

I clear my throat and try not to squirm.

He's *never* touched me this way—open and exploring. Like he's painting little secrets on my skin.

"It's just a back …"

"It's not just *any* back, Orlaith."

I swallow the tart taste of indecision, questioning *everything* I'm about to do.

With a few stirs of Rhordyn's finger, he's unwoven my

resolve and turned me into a pathetic puddle of need. I'm a slave to these sips of attention he feeds me—I need them like I need the breath in my lungs—and I can't afford it.

The cost is far too steep.

Strong, composed, resilient ...

"Why did you lock my door?" I ask, biting the words from my slate of hardened resolve.

For a moment, I think a line forms between his brows, but when I blink, it's gone.

"A kindness."

It's probably a bad time to tell him that while I appreciate the thought, his execution needs work.

"That's it?"

"Yes. But you're here now," he says, studying the crowd. He turns those eyes back on me, and I realize exactly why there's so much space separating us from anyone else—like there's a barrier physically stopping them from stepping too close.

There's a lethal dexterity in those silver-spun eyes that's *gutting*.

"Why are you here, Orlaith?"

I swallow, looking away before my insides spill. "Sucker for punishment, I guess."

His fingers pause.

The silence stretches while he carves my cheek with his icy blade of perusal, before he grunts and looks away, allowing me to finally draw a half satisfying breath as he begins painting those circles again.

"And what did you do with the bluebells?" I stab my stare at the side of his face, though he continues to survey the crowd. "Toss them over the balcony or hang them up to dry?"

"Neither," I bite out. "You're not as smart as you think you are."

"They're on your pillow, aren't they?" He meets my stare and steals my breath for a haunting moment.

How does he know?

"I don't miss much, Orlaith. Certainly not when it comes to you."

A gasp slices into me ...

"I know every glimmer in your eye, every rapture that makes your soul *sing*. I know that right now, your spine is locked not by your own accord, but because my fingers have you wound like a puppet on a string," he says, tightening their delicious swirl and making me throb in places that ought not to throb.

Not for this man.

He leans closer, his breath an icy assault on my ear, and I find myself arching like a flower—reaching as if he's the sun and not a bitter frost that'll likely leave me ruined.

And I'm angry. *So* angry at myself, because I'd probably enjoy it. Being ruined by Rhordyn would be better than never drinking the sips of his affection again.

"I know that your cheeks are flushed because you're embarrassed by the dull ache between your legs. By the wetness you can feel smeared between your thighs. You're worried I can smell it. I can."

My heart slams against my ribs, his stare flaying me, then picking at my insides.

"I know you're fighting some internal battle, because although I can smell your arousal ... I can feel your anger licking at my skin like a *flame*."

A beat passes—sweet, innocent limbo. A peaceful, stolen moment that's doomed to die a grisly death.

I know it. Can feel it in the air, like the ocean drawing a watery breath.

When his beautifully carved mouth opens, I almost reach up and slam it closed.

“Let the anger win, Orlaith.” His fingers stop their circles, that door slamming shut between us again. “Let the anger win.”

And then he’s gone, leaving me alone at the wall, crushed against it by his parting words.

A terse reminder that I may be his, but he’ll *never* be mine.

CHAPTER 37

ORLAITH

A tear darts down my cheek, and I bat it away with a swift hand, as if it doesn't hold the weight of my fractured heart in that one tiny bead.

Another swiftly follows.

Rhordyn steps onto the dais, followed by a smiling Zali who's dressed in a gown of swishing bronze that melts off her curves. The crowd turns their attention toward the High Master and High Mistress standing above everyone else like they were made to fit together. Made to rule and conquer and save the world together.

They wear no crowns or diadems of power. No need when they carry themselves with such regal poise that the very air seems to bow around them.

The skin on my left arm tingles, and I glance sidelong, seeing Cainon resting against the wall not a foot away, hands threaded deep in his pockets.

His hair is pulled back in a bun that shows off the fierce lines of his undercut, and his outfit is far more casual than anyone else's; tight navy pants and a white, form-fitting button-down, sleeves rolled to reveal his thick, corded forearms. Unbuttoned at the top, his shirt offers a window to smooth slabs of golden muscle.

He's a slant of sunlight cutting through the dim—the picture of casual elegance dressed in raw sex appeal with a dash of wild abandon.

"Why does the pretty flower cry?" he asks, rolling his head to the side, snagging me with a nonchalant stare.

But I sense a seed of sincerity beneath the hook of his rakish mouth, in the depth of those pale blue eyes. And the question, it's so ... *invasive*. Like he's gone fishing down my throat, trying to hook my heart on a line.

I'm not used to questions such as this from anyone but Kai.

His hand lifts, encroaching on the space between us, and I don't have the air in my lungs to object before he sweeps the pad of his thumb along my jaw, smearing a tear across it like a bead of paint.

Despite my surprise, a toxic form of gravity is luring my eye toward that podium. No matter how much I fight it, I break.

His thumb falls the moment my eyes flick away.

"I see," he murmurs. "The flower dug her roots in."

"The flower was *stupid*."

A *ting-ting-ting* splits apart the celebratory racket. The music stops, and a silence slips over the crowd, though to me, it doesn't seem silent at all. It's blaring, and not a single part of me wants to be here watching this story unfold.

I peel off the wall, determined to charge through the enchanted crowd and find a corner away from curious eyes. Somewhere I can compose myself into that resilient woman who's strong and grounded ...

Cainon's hand slips into mine and grips, anchoring me in place.

Anchoring me to *him*.

My stare stabs down at our twisted fingers, his skin so golden compared to the creamy tone of my own.

"Nope." The word is thick and incriminating, leading my gaze to slice up and dive into the waveless pools of his own. "You stand right here and *watch*," he whispers, pulling me back against the wall with a soft thud. "If you stay in this castle, *this* is what you'll see every single day. Except it'll be much, much worse."

My brows collide as he shrugs a shoulder. "You'll be able to smell her all over him. You'll see her swell with his child, because that's what will be expected of them to make this façade believable."

My breaths become sharp and short—my imagination painting a clear, concise picture.

And it hurts. It hurts so fucking much.

"And eventually ..." his expression softens, "eventually, those feelings will turn to love. It doesn't matter who you are, where you've come from; it's in our nature to fall in love with the shackle that *binds* us."

Another tear darts down my cheek, and again he catches it, sucking the residue off his thumb.

Something inside me twists at the intimate sight.

"And why the hell do *you* care?"

Cainon offers a consolation smile that doesn't reach his eyes. "Because there are other options that would benefit us both."

Honesty.

Well, that's something. I usually get nothing but corked answers.

"Tonight," Rhordyn rumbles, his barreling voice filling the room, "I address not just the people of Ocruth, but the entire *continent*."

My spine straightens, gaze coaxed to the podium by the deep tenure of his familiar voice threatening to undo me.

Rhordyn assesses the crowd for a long, haunting minute, capturing hundreds of breaths, tilting hundreds of chins, widening hundreds of pairs of eyes before he takes Zali's hand in his own.

My blood chills.

He might as well have busted the same hand through my ribs and grabbed hold of my heart. Because right now, he's controlling my beats, deciding whether to let the thing keep pumping or to yank it from my chest and toss it at the ground.

He doesn't look at me. Not once. Just squares his shoulders and says, "I found love in the secure roots of a friendship I've treasured for a very long time, much the same way I treasure the protection of my lands. My *people*."

The crowd cheers, filling the ballroom with a meal of merriment that starves me of breath.

He lifts Zali's left hand, parading her bare wrist like it's some sort of trophy.

It *mocks* me—makes me feel like my chest is caving.

Don't do it, Rhordyn.

Please don't ...

"Tonight, I make our most sacred promise to this woman beside me."

I can't breathe, can't think. I've climbed to the tallest branch in the tallest tree, snapping them all in the process, and now the only way down is to *fall.*

"But I also make the same promise to our people. Because Zali and I will not just be uniting in love, but also in *territory.*"

Love.

The word tears a hole in my heart; brings a fresh wave of tears that threaten to spill.

"We will be smudging the border between our lands in an effort to make them safe again!"

This time when the crowd erupts, it's deafening. A booming applause riddled with hoots and whistles and screams—the desperate pleas of people who have been living in fear for far too long. People who believe this coupling is the cure for their very worst nightmares.

And perhaps it is ... but it's *killing me.* Plundering my heart and planting a shadow seed amongst the fleshy mess of my insides.

My foot darts forward as Rhordyn reaches for the cupla secured around his wrist, and the hand anchoring me grips tighter.

"Don't," Cainon growls.

"Screw you."

I'm about to take another step when the bastard tugs my arm until it's locked against his torso.

"You're a dick," I bite out, watching Rhordyn cinch that obsidian oath around Zali's wrist, feeling part of me break away and wither at the sight.

"Undoubtedly. But you'll thank me later."

"Not likely."

The catch is fastened, and the crowd erupts in a riot of cheers, toasting frothy glasses while I resist the urge to rip my arm right from the socket and dash back to Stony Stem where I can lick my wounds in peace.

He did it. He actually fucking did it.

I whip a glass off a passing tray and down the entire thing in one gulp.

"Impressive," Cainon yells over the roar of the mob, and I murder him with a glare, my back to the dais ...

It's customary to seal the gifting of a cupla with a kiss—something I have no interest in seeing. By the way the crowd explodes with another round of applause, I know exactly when it's happened.

A few agonizing seconds pass before something deep inside me *tugs,* commanding my head to turn. I refuse, but the hook yanks harder, *harder* ... until I finally give in and steal a peek toward the dais.

Big mistake.

Rhordyn's gaze flays me as I slam the empty glass against Cainon's chest, and those wide, metallic eyes seem to harbor the buds of silver flames. I swear his presence expands—takes up more of the joyous vista, infecting it with an icy anger most people probably don't recognize.

Music starts, the crowd churns, and a blanket of merriment severs me from his stare.

I breathe a serrated sigh, liquid ire surging through my veins.

He did it.

There's nothing left to hold me back.

Baze emerges from the crowd, slaying Cainon with a rusty glare as he stabs a hand toward me. "Orlaith, may I have this dance?"

He's not really giving me a choice. He's giving me a *command.*

But I'm feeling untethered and brave—my stomach bubbling with liquid courage that's licking its way through my veins, making me feel weightless and warm.

Strong, composed, resilient.

"No, thank you," I answer, smiling sweetly, fluttering my

lashes up at Cainon who lifts a tawny brow. "*Cain* has already asked."

Cainon's lips hook at the corner, the gesture sharpening when Baze makes a rumbling sound somehow audible over the wash of merriment.

I don't dare look back at him as I'm led toward the large square of floor space, only a few dancers decorating its buffed obsidian surface.

My smile bleeds away the moment I'm spun into Cainon's chest. "I have no idea how to dance," I hiss, acutely aware of how confidently he moves with the music. There's a casual certainty in the way he grips my hip and holds my hand aloft, directing me to make the right steps like a puppet on a string.

"You're doing fine. Just keep following my lead."

He spins me out, and I'm careful to plant twin seeds of love in my eyes—to wear a smile that's lustful and convincing. I'm careful to show my feelings with long, lingering looks and in the way I posture myself toward him.

He spins me against his chest, and it shakes with a burrowed chuckle trying to break free. "You're an interesting thing." I'm spun out into another twirl. "And that *dress* ..." he purrs, watching the gush of red twist around my legs. "*Exquisite.*"

"Thank you," is my tight-lipped response as I hold my counterfeit grin. When I'm tugged in with my back pressed against his muscular chest, I notice all eyes on us—including Rhordyn and Zali, who are standing side by side at the edge of the dancing square.

Rhordyn's gaze grabs me from across the empty space, and there's violence in his eyes.

Cold, merciless violence.

He asked for this. He wanted effort.

I look away.

"Everyone's watching," I mutter, focused on keeping my vicious heels to myself. I doubt wounding the man is any way to acquire the ships he apparently has control over.

Cainon's lips brush the shell of my ear. "Indeed. And I've never seen a more convincing show."

"I'm glad to hear you're not fooling yourself into thinking this is something more," I say without shifting my perfectly painted smile.

He twists me out, then whips me in so we're chest to chest and I'm caged by the snare of his ocean eyes.

Eyes that are suddenly *serious*.

"I'm not too prideful to steal another man's treasure, Orlaith."

I paint an extra layer of love in my eyes, pretending there isn't a frigid arrow protruding from my scorned heart. "I know."

I'm tugged so tight against his body that my breasts ache. "*Do you*, though? How far are you willing to go to spite your wounded heart?"

Strong, composed ...

Resilient.

"*As far as it takes*," I bite out with all the conviction I can muster.

As far as it takes to secure those ships; to save more little girls from living the same nightmares that ruined me.

His lips curl at the corner again, exposing a deep dimple on his right cheek. "We'll see."

And then his lips are on mine, moving with mine—a strike intended to capture, wound, and claim.

The room chills as his tongue digs in and sweeps across

my own. As he probes and explores and steals the breath from my lungs.

It's fierce and predatory, unveiling a fiery wash of masculine want I wasn't prepared to withstand. It's like he just sat down for a meal, and something about his ravenous hunger has my body heating. Spine arcing.

There's fire in my veins but ice at my back, and the two are *battling.*

When he pulls away, I'm panting.

Scattered.

The crowd begins to murmur, the tips of my fingers grazing puffy lips tingling from his heated assault. Despite the restless onlookers, a sense of silence encroaches, and I peer out from the bubble of tension embracing us.

I realize we're the only ones on the dance floor. That we have a dense boundary of onlookers—some throwing hushed words at their acquaintances, some open-mouthed and gawking, some stealing glances at Rhordyn ...

I dare a peek at the man himself, a shadow of seething brawn staring at Cainon with something much worse than death in his eyes.

Deep inside me, something throbs—sharp and painful, as though an internal wound is leaking vital fluids.

His attention drops and I follow his scathing trail to the dark blue and gold cupla now secured around my wrist ...

My heart leaps into my throat.

Barely able to draw breath into my encumbered lungs, I glance up, but Cainon's not looking at me. He's looking at Rhordyn with the same menacing glare laden with the same menacing message.

"This is what you wanted, yes?"

All I can do is nod.

"Good. Then don't look so shocked. Stun the people with another one of those dazzling smiles."

"How about I stun you with another kick to the kidney?" I bite out through a forged grin.

"Later, when there aren't so many people watching. Shall I make a fancy speech, too? Declare my love with some ornamental verbiage?"

Gods, no ...

"That won't be neces—"

"Silence," he yells, buttoning a hundred pairs of gossiping lips with a single word.

Internally, my palm collides with my face.

He grips my hand and hoists it above my head, like he's erecting a war flag. "And raise your glasses to the future High Mistress of the South."

High Mis—

Wait.

The moment stretches, tension crackles, before a sea of flutes shoot skyward ...

Oh, shit.

CHAPTER 38

ORLAITH

Bare feet planted on the top step of Stony Stem, I peek down at my hand clutching a fiery torch. At the cupla secured around my wrist like a dark blue shackle.

The only color I ever pictured wearing was *black.*

My heart's lost its rhythm, composure nowhere to be seen. I can feel my strong, resilient mask smearing a little more with each droplet expelling from my eyes.

I'm not okay.

My tears may be silent but inside I'm screaming.

Staring at the door that usually separates Rhordyn and I during our nightly ritual, I drop my shoes, listening to them tumble down the steps behind me. The key to Stony Stem swiftly follows—the one I begged Cook for after I fled the ball.

My tongue sweeps across my bottom lip to find it's still smacked with the taste of Cainon—

I kissed Cainon.

I stab the torch into a wrought holster protruding from the wall and draw a quaking breath, choking on the smell of citrus and salt, realizing my dress is *drenched* in the unfamiliar scent. A whimper bubbles in the back of my throat, the silky, figure-hugging sheath suddenly *suffocating* me.

This gown was its own sort of mask ... and deep, deep down in the shameful corner of my mind, I'd hoped Rhordyn would see through it.

Peel it back.

That he'd take one look at me and see the dress for what it really was; a pretty tourniquet to hold me together while I fell apart on the inside.

But he didn't, and the dress worked too well.

Too fucking well.

Off. It needs to come *off.*

I battle the fastenings at the back of my neck, but my fingers are jittery, frustration bleeding out in ravaged sobs that betray everything I'm feeling inside.

A groan rents the air as my hands fly to the front, gripping tight. I rip the bodice, gasping at how easily it tears down the middle and bares my naked breasts.

I rip again, feeding off the sound of splitting seams, wishing my hands and *wrath* belonged to somebody else.

Somebody cold and brutal and—

Not mine.

He's not mine.

I take my ire, confusion, sadness out on the masterpiece I never wanted in the first place, the dress shrieking while I force it to release me in increments.

What I want, what I need, and what is right are three entirely different things ...

A twisted sound wrings out of me as the last scrap of material falls, the shredded ribbons decorating the ground like a bloody puddle. Heaving and raw, I stand on the steps with nothing to warm me but the roaring flame of my own self-hatred, my hatred toward *him*, and that stack of psychological kindling between us that finally caught light.

I pause, sheathed in uncertainty, staring down at the pile of ruin. I may have led myself to this moment, but the whiplash has left me spinning without direction.

I'm now tethered to an expiration date. My net will dissolve, and I'll no longer be welcome here in my carefully curated normal because I'm promised to another male.

The High Master of another territory.

By stepping into that dress tonight, I tore down the walls I've come to rely on.

I'm not okay.

I grip hold of the rusty handle and jerk my door wide, greeted by the sight of my room exactly as I'd left it. Nothing has changed.

Except me.

Shooting steel into my spine, I make for the crystal goblet sitting atop my side table, snatching it around the neck. I carry it to my workstation where I lay it sideways, using one of my unpainted rocks to hammer the rim.

Small, sharp bits of crystal crack free.

Spin, *smash.* Spin, *smash.* Spin, *smash.*

I keep going until every inch of drinking surface is sharp enough to slice. I hurt every damn night for that man—an act that now feels hollow—it's about time he bled for me, too.

Leaving a mess of shattered glass, I retrieve my needle and hold it in the bud of a candle flame.

The tip turns red, but still I leave it there, letting the heat leach up to the pinch of my fingers where it scalds my flesh like a branding iron. I close my eyes, holding, *holding* ... until the tears darting down my cheeks are from equal parts pain and heartbreak.

Let the anger win, Orlaith. Let the anger win.

"Fuck. You."

My finger and thumb are throbbing with bolts of fiery pain by the time I whip my hand back and blow on the needle, the smell of fried flesh tormenting me—trying to pull memories forth.

Dark ones. *Painful* ones I dash away.

I stare at the needle ...

My gluttonous curiosity has never been a deal breaker when it comes to giving Rhordyn my blood. Though desperate to know why he needs it, the simple fact that he *does* kept me pricking my finger night after night for *years.*

I built my life around the act. Clung to it with every bit of my being.

Hungered over it. Fed off it. *Relied* on it. Convinced myself it somehow made us special ...

But Rhordyn slaughtered that theory the moment he fastened his cupla around Zali's wrist.

I stab the needle into the tip of my pinkie, hissing when it almost digs all the way to the bone, but it's nothing compared to the painful pinch of my heart.

A bulb of blood swells, and I let it drip into the otherwise empty goblet, wishing I could drain my emotions just as easily. Turn the tap and let my undiluted anger, sadness, and heartbreak drip until there's nothing left of *him* inside me.

But he's still there, sitting heavy in my heart. Making my stomach twist and twist and twi—

I stab again, this time into my thumb, gouging deeper than I ever have before. The flow of blood is instant, but still that weight lingers.

So I stab again and again and *again,* only stopping once all ten of my trembling fingers have given to the goblet, adding to the little red puddle of undiluted *me.*

I hate that color—the color of secrets. The color of my past, my present, but no longer my future.

But I also *love* it.

In that heavy pool of blood, I can almost see Rhordyn's reflection—see the way he looked at me from the edge of the dancing square.

In his eyes, I saw betrayal. And if I peel back the layers of heartbreak I fed into by convincing myself we were so much *more,* I can see the sense in that ...

I've been safe in this tower for the past nineteen years. Been fed, clothed, and tutored. I've been trained—been allowed to freely roam a castle that belongs to someone who seems to value privacy above most other things.

Nothing has harmed me. Nobody has forced me to leave my comfort zone.

Yes, Rhordyn hurt me first, but I retaliated, and not just for the greater good. A smidgeon of my actions fed from that vindictive well inside—a bubbling desire to hurt Rhordyn just as much as he hurt me.

This ... this *thing* between us is turning me into a monster.

I walk to the stairwell and bundle an armful of my shredded gown, closing the door on the rest of the carnage. Kneeling, I open the hatch on The Safe to reveal the hollow, wooden tomb.

You do look ravishing in that color ...

My face twists.

I shove the dress inside the compartment, tuck the vandalized goblet amongst the shredded material, and slam the door shut.

Turning, I slide down the unforgiving grain, arms wrapped around my knees as if they could hold me together.

Part of me hopes Rhordyn will dash up Stony Stem

straight away. That he'll somehow sense I've dished up an ample, undiluted offering and come running.

The rest of me expects to be punished by his tardiness.

Minutes tick by and my churning well of emotions have me counting every second.

Is he even coming?

The thought of that tiny pool of *me* sitting in a goblet unwanted, unused ... It hurts. The thought of never again giving him a taste of myself *hurts.*

Despite everything, part of me enjoys the thought that my blood ends up inside him. That droplet by droplet, I find a way into his system.

Invade him.

But that's not proper thinking for a coupled lady; even I know that. I've read enough books to have a certain grasp on the veil of etiquette a female dons the moment she accepts a cupla.

I hear the faint sound of footfalls ascending Stony Stem, and my heart leaps with relief, then plunges as I realize this will be one of the final times I hunger over that sound.

Thump ... thump ... thump ...

Each step seems to land slower than the last, his footfalls far softer than they usually are.

Where has all his noise gone?

With a slight squeak of its unoiled hinges, the tiny door opens, and I draw a ragged breath, picturing my dress gushing out like the innards of a slaughtered beast to reveal my sharp and bloody offering.

Is he looking at the goblet, seeing all the pain I poured into its hollow? The edges honed as a silent plea for him to show me his *own* hurt?

With another squeak, the wooden door presses shut, then

silence. Nothing but an encroaching stillness that drags on for so long it feels like the room begins to sway.

Knock on my door. Bust in here. Scream at me. Tell me how disappointed you are.

Tell me you'll never forgive me for as long as you live ...

But he doesn't do any of that. Which means I'm forced to swallow my own venom rather than lash it at him, too.

He descends Stony Stem, and I release a sawtooth breath, still dressed in nothing but my too-tight skin and the shackle of my actions.

That, and a thick lacquer of disappointment.

I threw down, and he didn't even fight.

That fire in my belly sputters out like a spent wick when I hear his footsteps fade to nothing.

Gone.

He's gone.

I open The Safe to see a calico-wrapped package placed in the center of the wooden shelf. When I unravel the layers, I find an already ground-down lump of caspun I want to dump all over the ground.

I don't want this. It works, but *he* works better.

Not mine.

I stand on unsteady legs and pad toward my workstation, then mix my tonic in preparation for the nighttime horrors I can already feel clawing at my consciousness. Stepping onto the balcony, I look out to a velvet-clad night, imagining Rhordyn stalking across the castle grounds—doing his sweep around the perimeter before disappearing into the deluge of trees.

It doesn't take long for my teeth to chatter, sending me racing indoors where I pull a top from my drawer and drag it on.

Staring into the hungry hearth that offers no reprieve, I begin up-rooting all thirty-three hairpins, freeing my hair before piling it on top of my head and securing it with a band for sleeping. I wash my face, retrieve my candlestick off the mantle, then make for the bedside.

Dropping low, I peel the rug back, revealing my hidden compartment.

I may be broken, confused, and painfully disappointed by the man who's given me *everything* but the one thing I truly want, but none of that stops me from lifting the rock, pulling Rhordyn's pillow slip out, and digging my nose into the silky pleats ...

None of it stops me from holding it close as I climb into bed and blow out the candle, submerging myself into a pall of black.

Knotted in a heap, I reach behind my neck.

The silver latch is unfamiliar to my scorned and throbbing fingers because I've never removed this necklace before.

Never wanted to.

The metallic teeth finally give way, and the chain falls in a heavy heap amongst my sheets.

A sob bubbles out as my fingers trace the vacant path ...

My skin feels *bare* without it pressed against me—like a tightness just peeled off and left me raw.

It's strange. *Unnatural.*

But Rhordyn gave me the necklace, and I can't wear it anymore. Not with Cainon's cupla fettering my wrist.

Not with *Rhordyn's* cupla fettering Zali's.

My life is changing. The more I fight it, the more it's going to tear at my seams.

I set the crystal pendant and baby conch atop my side table and take cover beneath the sheet, nuzzling a pillowcase that harbors the scent of a man who's promised to another woman. Because tomorrow, I'll be lighting the fire and feeding it to the embers.

I'll be releasing him, something I have to do before I can release myself from this cage of my own creation.

Rhordyn was right ...

I'm better than this. Stronger than this.

It's time I grew up.

CHAPTER 39

ORLAITH

I roll onto my back and stare at a ceiling I cannot see, wishing it were lit with a fiery glow so I could watch light and shadow battle across it to the tune of crackling wood. A haunting lullaby that sometimes brings me a sense of peace.

At this rate, I'll never sleep.

I sigh, reaching for the jar of night bark on my bedside table when a distant churn of heavy footfalls has me jerking up, sheets pooling in my lap, pillow slip clutched close to my chest.

Something's wrong.

The boisterous melody swells until it sounds like I'm caught in the midst of an angry storm. Without even a pause in tempo, my door bursts off its hinges and crashes into my laden bookshelf, sending most of my books thumping to the ground.

A foreboding shadow charges through my room like a wild animal, snarling, tossing things around, the smell of leather and a winter wind smacking my senses.

My heart slams to a stop.

"*Where is it?*" Rhordyn roars, his silhouette lugging a drawer out of its socket and tipping its contents all over the floor. A box of knickknacks is the next tribute to his unbridled chaos; precious pieces I've collected over the years scattering atop the pile of clothes like pepper garnishing a meal.

My eyes narrow ...

This bastard.

"Where's *what?*" I hiss, watching him tug another drawer free—his robust shape barely lit by the light leaking into my room from the stairwell.

A barrage of my underwear arcs through the air, and my cheeks blaze.

Here I am, clinging to a pillow slip bathed in his scent like it's my most prized possession while he's tossing my delicates as if he's rooting around in a three-day-old pile of trash.

He strides toward the bed, dropping low and reaching under, before he pauses for a beat.

"Rhord—"

He leaps up and stabs his attention at my side table, the tense line of his shoulders seeming to soften as he snatches my necklace off the tray. Then, he's grabbing my upper arms, pulling me forward with unforgiving hands and trussing the chain around my neck.

"What the *hell* are you doing?"

He's never handled me like this before, like I'm nothing but a floppy doll.

The crystal bulb and conch shell land atop my chest, tinkling against each other while he manipulates the latch, fingers grazing my neck, sending shivers up and down my spine.

All over my skin.

He releases a deep sigh and pulls away, lumping onto the

edge of my bed, elbows planting on his knees before his head falls into the scoop of his hands.

I can hear the trampling thud of his heart. Scent the deep, salty musk of his desperation.

There's something so unsettling about seeing a man his size—a man who's usually all hard edges and sturdy resolve—bent over himself like a felled tree.

I don't recognize this male one bit.

"Rhordyn," I whisper, reaching ...

The second my fingertips brush the brick of his shoulder, he jerks away, causing my hand to retract.

"There's something I need to show you," he rasps, the crumbled tenor of his voice lifting the hairs on the back of my neck.

Rhordyn doesn't speak like that—like part of him is just as broken as I am.

Standing, he strides into the darkness, his heavy footsteps my only guide to his whereabouts. He strikes a match and lights a sconce near my vanity, bathing the room in a flickering light.

My eyes lap at his reflection in the mirror; his virile features pulled off an otherwise black canvas by the spill of golden light.

He drags a small, wooden stool out and gestures for me to sit.

My brow buckles.

"What are you doing?"

His gaze drops to the pillow slip I'm still clinging to, nostrils flaring, chest swelling. He exhales, his stare finding my own again—eyes hardened steel but slicing me in a gentle way, like the tapered edge of a shaving blade gliding across my skin.

"Come," he rumbles, jerking his chin at the mirror. "Come see."

For once, there is no challenge in the words. Just a simple request.

I wonder what hidden weight it holds for him to hand it to me so delicately.

I sweep my legs off the bed and stand, pillow slip clutched to my chest as I walk toward him.

There's no point trying to hide it now.

It's too late for that.

Rhordyn's black button-down is rolled to his elbows, and the vision of his corded forearms glazed in firelight has my stomach knotting.

Every cautious step results in the hem of my shirt brushing against my naked thighs, but his gaze doesn't drift to the bare show of skin, and I don't bother attempting to hide myself. Don't see the point when he's already planted inside me in ways I doubt I'll ever be able to explain.

I halt, staring up at his impeccably carved profile, internally cursing the world for sowing me in the presence of his baited beauty.

My attention roves to his bunched fists and white knuckles, as if he's holding every ounce of tension in the tight balls of his powerful hands.

"Laith."

Our stares collide.

There's torture in his eyes, and I fail to draw a single lick of sense from it.

Slowly, I lower to the stool, bare ass colliding with the cold grain.

A shiver rakes up my spine.

I peep at the mirror; take in the man now standing behind me. Study the unfamiliar softness in his eyes.

Frown when I realize it's not the sort of softness that tears down walls and lets other people see your true self ...

It's *sorrow.*

I've seen that look before, years ago, but I can barely grasp the memory. Or perhaps I just don't want to.

I clear my throat, hands twisting together in my lap.

Rhordyn draws a deep breath, then motions toward my hair. "May I?"

Curious, I nod.

My lids almost flutter shut as his fingers explore the heavy knot atop my head, unraveling the band, releasing a heavy curtain of flaxen locks that cascade around my shoulders and down my back. He gathers it all up, the calloused tips of his fingers brushing the delicate skin behind my ear, and I bite down on a shiver.

My thick waves are pushed forward over my left shoulder while he takes large gulps of my reflection.

I watch the ball in his throat roll, watch his chest swell, then deflate before he reaches for the latch at the back of my neck.

He fiddles with it, battles it, his regard finally splitting from mine to study its delicate workings, well-defined brows a pinched mantle above his stormy eyes. The chain falls, tumbles to my lap, and his gaze darts back to my reflection, those silver swirls becoming pools so wide they seem to dominate the room.

I hear his heart skip a beat, watch the color drain from his cheeks as a tightness peels off my face, down my neck, across my shoulders ... like paring the skin off a mandarin and freeing the fruit beneath.

Rhordyn releases a sigh that has its own chaotic tempo.

"Wh—"

Something glimmers in my peripheral, and I steal a peep at my own reflection, stilling the battered organ in my chest.

My stomach flops.

There's a person staring back at me from the world behind the mirror. A woman with opaline skin and a storm of iridescent hair cascading down the left side of her body like a waterfall glistening from the sun's touch. Her exposed ear tapers to a tip, the outer scoop lined with delicate prickles that shimmer. And her *eyes* ...

Her eyes look to be carved from crystal, glittering with an ocean of iridescent facets.

Freckles dust her nose like a miniature map of the stars, so similar to the ones I painted on my bedroom door. I reach up to brush one and my fingers collide with glass.

Fingers that belong to a hand I've never seen before.

The skin is fine and pale, like the petals of a delicate, ivory flower. I touch the back of it, recoiling from the feel—soft and silky and not like my own.

A sharp gasp cuts into me as realization empties my waning well of composure.

No.

Please, no.

The ground seems to tilt, and I grasp the edge of the vanity, eyes wide ...

"What ... what ..."

What the hell.

A tear rips a glistening path down my cheek, leaving a trail so bright and clear it's hard to look at. Batting it away, I notice a mark creeping up the side of my neck and across my right shoulder—a black, inky stain that looks like the tapered tip of a crawling vine.

Temptation to touch it fizzles in my belly as my lids sweep shut, blocking out the view, sending more wetness darting down my cheek ...

A nightmare.

I'm trapped in one of my nightmares.

"Orlaith ..."

My eyes snap open, but I ignore my reflection, turning my sharpened ire onto the man behind me.

I jab a finger at the mirror. "Who is that?"

"The girl I saved from a Vruk attack when she was two years old," he grates out, and I barely recognize his voice. It's just as hard as it usually is, but these words have cracks in their faces. They're tarnished with age and chipped in places.

These words have been chained inside him for so long they're wary of their freedom.

"This is you," he continues. "This is who you *really* are."

Who I really am.

I shoot to my feet and stumble a step. His left fist unravels, twitching at his side as I grip the vanity to steady myself, that silk pillow slip discarded on the floor.

"*How?*"

No answer.

"How did you hide me from *myself?*"

He responds with a hard stare that says so much more than his absent words do.

I swallow, like forcing glass down my throat, which I swiftly realize is the jagged edges of betrayal slicing me up on their way down.

"You lied to me."

"I would have lied to you forever if I thought I could get away with it."

The admittance strikes me like a stone to the head, and I waver, blinking rapidly, trying to clear my blurring vision.

The words were said with such cold, detached certainty.

"Why?"

"Because I made a promise to a dying woman." He slides forward a step, a half-lit shadow lording over me, boring through my ebbing stability. "A promise I intend to keep."

"And what was that promise?" I ask around the swollen lump in my throat.

"To keep you *safe*."

Safe ...

"And that's it?" Every cell in my body seems to pause. "That's the *only* reason?"

"Yes."

His reply is instant, the word a lash that severs something vital.

My eyes shutter, and I feel my heart do the same—the single word a needle that bleeds my bubble of uncertainty.

I lift my chin, watching his eyes widen as I harden my own. "Well. Consider this me formally releasing you from that pledge."

I stalk toward the bed, but a hand whips out and snags my wrist, halting my retreat and making my head whirl around.

"Lai—"

"Get your hand off me."

He drops it with a sharp hiss, then snatches the other and *yanks*—pulling me so close I can feel the beat of his anger in the rise and fall of his chest. He dips his head and plants his face right in front of mine, so I'm assaulted by the draft of his icy breath.

"You'll never be rid of me. You may not have a shadow, but you're chained to mine for eternity. You think *this* has any weight?" he says, waving my wrist around—the one shackled by Cainon's cupla—and a vicious sort of chuckle rolls out of him that smarts my skin. "You can run off and tie yourself to your pretty High Master, but I'll hunt you to the four corners of the continent. Not because I want to, but because I can't *fucking* help myself."

My wrist is tossed at me with such force that I stumble back three steps. He traces those same steps until my back collides with one of the poles on my four-poster bed.

I suck a gasp as he pulls so close I can feel the press of all his hard angles, all the bulging pockets of muscle. His thigh slides between my legs and notches into place, pressing against my most private area ...

That bare, exposed part of me that's suddenly flushed and aching.

I should be afraid, pinned to a pole by a man well over twice my size wearing eyes glazed with ire.

I'm not.

I'm trapped somewhere between wanting to claw his face off and wishing he'd lift his thigh—put a little more pressure on that hot, swollen spot between my legs.

His gaze cuts to the side, and he sneers, snatching *Gypsy and the Night King* off the edge of my bed. "You want a fairy tale?" he spits, waving it in my face. "*I'm* your fucking fairy tale. I'm nailed to your soul, Orlaith, and believe me when I tell you there is no happily ever after. Not for me, and certainly not for you."

He tosses the book on the bed and retreats a step, leaving me gasping for air and clinging to the pole.

My world has tipped on its axis. I don't recognize myself,

and I have absolutely no idea who this man is standing before me, looking at me like he despises me. *Truly* despises me.

Right now, the feeling is mutual.

I hate that he's lied to me all these years—hurt me in ways that are unforgivable. And I hate that even now, after everything he's done, my body is still hot and so fucking raw for him, my muscles throbbing with need for him to dig up into me.

I'm confused, scattered, and done.

I'm. Fucking. Done.

"Get out," I mumble, barely loud enough to hear.

The words are fragile, dented things, and I watch something in Rhordyn's eyes shatter. Even the sturdy breadth of his shoulders softens as he heaves a sigh and massages the bridge of his nose.

"Mila—"

"*Get. Out!*" I bark, and this time my words are no longer delicate. They're loud and obtuse—boulders tossed to maim.

Shields harden his eyes, and I watch him detach. It feels like a slap to the face, but I relish the sting.

He nods, stuffing hands deep into his pockets as he moves away, keeping his gaze trained to me the entire time. "As you wish."

He makes his way to the door strewn across the floor, picking it up and leaning it against the wall before pausing.

I glare at his broad silhouette, waiting for him to cross that line so I can fall apart in peace.

He peers at me over his shoulder. "The necklace. I need you to put it back on."

It's not a request, but there is a vulnerability in his stare that would burrow into my inquisitive heart if I let it.

So, I don't.

Instead, I douse it with a bucket load of bitter.

"You didn't use your *manners*."

His eyes widen, shadows slithering across them as his upper lip peels back from his teeth. "I will not *beg* you to protect yourself, Milaje. Put the fucking necklace on. Now."

His voice is thicker than I'm used to it being—more weighty, almost bestial. But I hold his gaze, refusing to blink or shift or soften, wondering how he likes the taste of his own medicine.

He wants me to hide—to *protect* myself—and I'd love to understand why. But he never tells me anything.

I, too, refuse to beg. To dash the remaining droplets of my pride at the feet of a man who left me in the dark for nineteen fucking years. And I will not put that necklace back on while he's standing there, watching me. Perhaps the old Orlaith would've done it by now, but that girl is gone.

He made damn sure of it.

"*Leave.*"

I swear I hear his knuckles pop.

He rumbles low, shaking his head in sharp, unbridled motions, before stalking out the door, leaving an encroaching emptiness that flattens my lungs.

I crumble to the floor, letting my head fall into the cradle of my trembling hands.

I've been living a lie.

No wonder it felt like my skin was too tight to fit my jutting bones—like my colors didn't sing for my soul. How could they when I've been trapped inside the shell of a woman who *isn't me?*

Rhordyn's seen me struggle, yet he kept me wrapped in my barbed-wire skin.

Hands pushing through my hair, I stare across the room to the chain and stone and shell left discarded on the floor.

No concrete explanation or a single lick of remorse.

I force myself to stand on unsteady legs and walk toward the vanity, retrieving the necklace on the way, ignoring the pillow slip lying in a crumpled heap beside it.

All this time I've been fawning over this piece of jewelry as if it were Rhordyn's heart hanging around my neck, but it was just a pretty ruse to keep me contained.

My fist tightens around the chain as I steal a glimpse of the woman in the mirror ...

She's a masterpiece; the most exquisite rose given shape and life and a fluttering heartbeat. She's the sun and the soil and light that bathes the world on a beautiful day.

She's broken, lonely, and hiding from her past.

But it's hard to keep hiding when I'm staring at the unveiled truth.

The shape of my eyes ...

The cut of my chin ...

The map of my freckles ...

I look like him. Like the little boy I've painted too many times to count—the one who lives in my nightmares.

Only in my nightmares.

Wide eyes that stare at nothing.

My lids flutter closed, twin tears darting down my cheeks as I sever the sight of my loss.

I survived. He didn't. And something deep, deep inside is bellowing through the blackness that it should have been the other way around.

How am I supposed to handle that?

I can't.

And I just know that tonight, while my consciousness is

sleeping, my *sub*conscious will end up perched on the edge of that shadow-filled chasm that exists in my dreams, trying to force my hand. That it will threaten to jump.

Again, I'll refuse because the monster you know is safer than the monster you don't.

I open my eyes, lift the necklace, and yield to the invasive gulp that suffocates my skin as I drape the chain around my neck ... watching all my luster bleed away. It only takes a few seconds before the real me is gone—painted over by a plain ruse that chafes my soul and hides the person I really am.

The beauty.

The pain.

The *coward.*

CHAPTER 40

ORLAITH

They came stomping up the stairs, boisterous voices tossed back and forth the entire way. I thought one of them would knock the other out before they made it to the top, but it seems that was just wishful thinking.

Now, they're outside my freshly rehung door, stabbing each other with vulgar expletives like a couple of mindless brutes.

I sigh and drop off my perch on the windowsill, plucking a path through my belongings still littering the floor from Rhordyn's looting. Passing the vanity, I pause ... skin prickling.

Stomach twisting.

Slowly, very slowly, I look sideways into the mirror, stealing a peek at the lie. Studying the rope of flaxen hair hanging over my shoulder for even the slightest hint of an opaline hue.

Nothing.

The ruse is flawless; a thought that makes me feel sick to my stomach. I have no idea how it works, or what Rhordyn's done to allow his filthy lie to prosper.

Ripping my gaze away, I stalk to the door and swing it

open to see Cainon trussed up against the wall by a fiery faced Baze—the former hanging in a lazy lump with a mocking smile curling his lips.

Baze's wooden dagger is poised at Cainon's throat, and a loosened bead of blood is trickling down that golden skin.

I knife my overprotective escort in the back of the head with a glare. "*Baze*."

"Orlaith." The word is pushed through clenched teeth. "Apologies for the interruption. I know how much you dislike impromptu visitors in your *personal* space. I was just escorting Cainon back down the stairs."

The Southern High Master plucks a piece of flint off Baze's lapel, like being held at daggerpoint is an everyday occurrence. "Why don't you let my *promised* decide if she'd like me in her personal space or not," he says, patting Baze on the cheek like a condescending ass.

Baze bristles, pressing more weight into Cainon's chest. "Want me to roll him down the stairs or toss him off the balcony?"

Sweet merciful—

He's going to earn himself a duel. Or a beheading if he ever ends up in the South.

"*Neither*," I bite out, hand sweeping in a wide arc, inviting Cain into my space.

Baze throws me an incredulous stare. "Are you kidding me?"

"Obviously not," Cainon offers unhelpfully, leading Baze to hiss an inch from his face.

I nearly slam the door on them both.

Baze guts me with a glare, perhaps waiting for me to change my mind and scuttle back into my shell. But I'm not the same girl I was yesterday. In fact, I have no idea who I am anymore.

All I know is I'm pissed, confused, and I have several bones to pick. Unfortunately for Baze, he's sitting almost at the top of that pile.

"Let him in."

I hear Baze's teeth grind, watch the vein in his temple pulse. He finally slides back a step, letting his dagger fall from the notch dug into the High Master's throat.

Cainon swipes the nick and wipes the smear of blood on his pants. "I should have your head for that, boy."

"Fucking try it," Baze drones, reclining against the wall.

A low, predatory laugh rumbles deep in Cainon's chest. "Careful what you wish for."

I groan, turning my back on them and making for the window, dodging books and piles of clothing before climbing onto the sill. I look up in time to see the victorious smile fall right off Cainon's face as he pauses on the threshold of my deluge of mess.

"You—ahh—redecorating?" he asks, foot suspended midair as if he's trying to find somewhere to step.

Baze plants himself near the door, mapping Cainon's back like he's picturing all the gory ways he wants to hack him open. "Just terrible housekeeping skills. But I guess that's *your* problem now, isn't it?"

I'm going to murder him.

"You can leave," Cainon states with a dismissive bat of his hand.

Baze lands his shoulder against the doorframe and cleans dirt from his nails with the pointy end of his dagger. "Not with a rake in her room, I won't."

The Southern High Master retrieves a bottle off the

ground and pops the cork, sniffing the contents and screwing up his face. "You're toeing a fragile line today, old friend."

"Emphasis on the *I don't give a fuck*."

"*Ba—*"

"At least not until you need my help, right?" Cainon jabs.

I massage my temples, wondering if Kai has any air pockets in his loot-den so he can swim me down for a vacation. "Baze, just go. I'm a big girl, and I can look after myself."

"With all due respect," he replies, returning his attention back to his nails, "your actions of late contradict every word that just came out of your mouth. And while you still live under this roof, it's *my* job to make sure you're safe. If he stays, so do I."

Cainon opens his mouth, but I cut him off with a glare that ... strangely seems to work. Eyebrow arched, he perches on the edge of my vanity and settles in for the show.

It grates me—having an almost stranger in my space—but I want to hear what he's got to say. And as for Baze; I don't want him to leave just yet.

We need to have words.

"I'm not asking you to abandon post, Baze. Just sink down a few steps and give me some privacy."

He hisses despite my placating tone that betrays none of my bubbling desire to kick the crap out of him, then finally does what I asked, mumbling something about being overpaid and underappreciated as he disappears from sight.

Cainon's features harden.

He stalks toward me, and I shiver from his razor-blade perusal. "You don't look so well."

"I'm fine," I say, toying with the end of my braid.

"You're lying to me."

I absolutely am. And I probably shouldn't start this relationship relying on my crutch of fibs, but here we are.

He puffs out a sigh and glances around the room, striding toward my painting station—the long wooden bench that curves around a third of my wall space. The windows above usually spill light across the table and potted seedlings lining the sill, but it hasn't for days because the clouds refuse to shift.

He touches the cloth covering my half-finished piece from Whispers while assessing my collection of rocks, fingers skating over a mini rendition of reaching hands emerging from a lick of gray paint.

My heart pinches, and I look away.

The owner of those arms only lives in my nightmares.

"You paint these yourself?"

"I do."

He plucks one off the table—the practice piece I did before painting Kai's stone.

An island of jagged, crystal spires pinned to an otherwise empty ocean decorates the face. There are little birds in the sky and a cherry river flowing from the peak of a cone geyser in the center.

He nods, and I can see some sort of reverence in his eyes as he weighs the stone in one hand. "This one. I know of an island that looks just like this. A place I used to visit with my father ... before he passed."

His words are heavy, creating a mournful tension that thickens the air and yanks at my heartstrings.

"I'm sorry for your loss, Cainon."

"It was a long time ago."

I nod, unraveling my braid to keep my hands busy. "Well ... you can have the rock if you like?"

I expect him to say no. It's not customary for a female to gift her promised something in return for his cupla, but this seems fitting considering our ... *odd* circumstances.

"Are you sure?" he asks, cradling the thing like it's prone to shatter.

"Of course."

The strong column of his throat works, a smile teasing the corner of his lips as he pockets the piece and advances.

I glance out the window, finger-combing my hair until he's standing right next to me. Taking the weight of my hair and splitting it off into three sections, he starts to weave a side braid with smooth, controlled motions.

My spine stiffens, heart lurching at the unfamiliar contact.

I watch Cainon's hands work, a long minute passing before he finally speaks.

"I must return to the Bahari capital. I received an urgent sprite, and my boat will be leaving on the next tide."

His tone is flat. Unyielding.

Something coils inside me, like a snake preparing to strike.

"And?"

"You will accompany me."

It's not a question.

Blood rushes from my face, and I swear my entire tower sways.

I'm not ready.

"*N-now?*" I stutter, heart hammering, mind scrambling.

What about Shay? And Kai? And who's going to water my plants? I'm not sure I can trust anyone else to keep them alive.

I steal a glance at that piece of cloth Cainon was touching.

The lump it's hiding ...

My wall in Whispers isn't finished. I haven't even ground down my commissary bluebells and made the damn paint because I've been too locked in my own head.

"*Now*, Orlaith."

The eviction notice is dropped on my lap like a boulder.

I glance out the window, waiting for words to form on my tongue.

He grips my chin, using it as a handle to turn my head. "You wear *my* cupla. You're *my* promised. I know you've been ... sheltered, but for you to continue living under another male's roof would be uncouth. Especially when that roof belongs to another High Master."

"I know all these things," I mutter, glancing down at said cupla.

A shackle or a ticket to free me from a cage I never realized I was living in? I'm not sure. I don't know anything anymore. It's hard to tell truth from lie when you've spent the majority of your life living under a veil of skin that never belonged to you.

All I know is what I have in front of me. What I've always clung to. The thing that has always kept me on track ...

The circles I spin.

I have unfinished turns, and if I leave before they are complete, I'm convinced everything will unravel. That the world will be off-center.

"I can't."

He lifts a caramel brow, the line of his jaw hardening.

Hands stilling.

Something flashes in his eyes that makes me feel utterly defenseless.

"Not *yet*," I quickly add, painting my lips with a smile. A mask atop a mask. "I have unfinished business I must finalize before I can leave. It's important."

To me.

He whips the hairband from my wrist and ties off the braid, then pushes back, stalking toward the western window that overlooks the bay. He plucks a dead leaf off one of my magnolia saplings and flicks it to the floor. "You're wilting here, Orlaith. It's obvious to an outsider looking in."

I hear Baze clear his throat, and my cheeks burn.

I wonder how much of this conversation will be relayed to Rhordyn. If he'll even care that someone else is taking such a keen interest in my well-being, or if he'll be more concerned about the fact that he's losing his blood bag.

Looking at my feet, I twiddle my thumbs ...

I *am* wilting, but only since I discovered Rhordyn has been lying to me all these years. Since he told me he only did so to maintain a pledge to a dying woman, and I realized I'm more than just a burden.

I'm a thorn in his side.

"So, you want more time?" Cainon asks, jarring me out of my reverie. He sounds open to compromise, and that's not something I'm used to handling.

I lift my chin and attempt to fortify my spine. "Yes."

His hands tighten on the windowsill, knuckles whitening, and for a moment I think he's about to deny me. But with a long sigh, he spins, a silky smile hooking one corner of his mouth and exposing that cheek dimple I'm beginning to grow fond of.

He's a very handsome man. Deeply masculine, stacked with smooth, confident sex appeal.

This forced pairing could be worse.

He grips the leash of my braid again. "Two days, Orlaith. No more."

My heart plummets.

That *barely* qualifies as a compromise ...

"I'll leave a ship and two personal guards to escort you to my territory when you've ..." he clears his throat and glances around, "finalized your affairs."

I try to ignore Baze's distant muttering.

"That's"—ridiculous—"generous of you," I say with a loose smile.

He pulls my braid until I'm leaning forward and his breath is hot on my ear. "Tug those roots out. Cut them off if you have to. This is not the right place for you." He drops my hair and spins. "Two days. Or you can expect the escort of an entire *fleet*."

My mouth pops open as he stalks through the door without a backward glance.

Why would he make such a ridiculous statement? Perhaps he's trying to impress me with all his pretty boats. Either that or he thinks the threat will help pry me from this tower.

All it really makes me want to do is punch him.

His footsteps fade and I finally relax, resting my cheek against the cool kiss of the window while I study the forest far below.

From up here, it looks like a blanket of moss; soft and inviting compared to the jagged edges of Castle Noir. Yet here I am, staring down on that forest as if it's about to crack its maw and devour me.

"Come in," I mutter, voice monotone.

Heavy footsteps advance, pausing not too far from me.

Letting my anger simmer until it's a gusty firestorm, I

peel my cheek from the glass, only to be scalded by Baze's own cinder stare.

My head snaps back. "*What?*"

"You know what," he spits, stance widening as if we have swords in our hands and he's preparing to duel. "What about your training? What about your life and all the people who care about you?" His hands bunch at his sides, knuckles milky. "The ones who would rather *die* than see you revert back to that small, silent child who never knew how to smile?"

I glare at him for a long moment before shaking my head. "I don't remember that."

"*Exactly.*"

We may not be wielding weapons, but he lands that word like a strike to the back.

He takes a step forward, jerking his chin at my painting station. "Who do you think made your first paintbrush, Orlaith?"

My heart misses a beat, but I maintain my sealed lips and stoic shield, giving his omission something to bounce off.

He points out my western window, arm outstretched. "Who do you think planted that wisteria and sowed your love for growing things? Then watched you smile for the first fucking time when you planted your very first rosebush in the grounds downstairs? The one you grew from a seed? *Who,* Orlaith?"

Him ...

The backs of my eyes sting, but I refuse to blink. Refuse to let my tears spill. His words are flaming barbs tossed to maim, and the old me would be nursing her wounds ...

But she's gone.

Right now, his fire has nothing to catch on, because I'm already ash.

I slide off the windowsill and raise my hands to the back of my neck, unclasping the necklace. It drops to the rug with a heavy thud, and that tightness peels off me inch by merciful inch, leaving raw skin that feels as if it's just taken a life-saving breath.

Baze stumbles sideways, hand darting out to steady himself against the post of my bed, all the color draining from his face as his mouth opens and shuts.

He doesn't speak. All he does is stare, and I can see bits of my brilliant reflection in his glazed eyes ...

I hate it.

I draw deep, then ask the question that sets a noose around the neck of our life-long companionship. "Did you know?"

"Orlaith—"

"Did. You. Know?"

His shoulders roll forward, and he releases a jagged sigh that fails to sever me from the blow brewing in his beseeching stare. "Yes ..."

It hits like a boot to the chest.

Harder.

It hits so hard I'm surprised I can still breathe.

Part of me wants to hack the wisteria right off the balcony and watch it fall to the ground, because that's what he just did to us.

I nod. "You're dismissed."

His eyes widen and his foot pushes forward. "*Laith—*"

I reach behind my back, crack the drawer of my console, and tug out the talon dagger—the hilt branding my palm as I unsheathe the weapon and stake it in the air between us.

His next step falters. "*Where the fuck did you get that?*"

"Does it matter?"

This talon is so much *more* than a threat, something I know he registers by the way his eyes go flat and defeated. By the way he casts his gaze to the ceiling as if my forgiveness is etched up there on the stone.

It's not.

I'd rather handle my worst nightmare than accept whatever placation he has to offer.

He's lost me. Whatever I thought we had, it's broken.

"No," he says, swallowing. "I guess not."

"I said leave."

He offers a curt nod, then turns and walks from the room, head down, shoulders hunched. I wait until I can no longer hear his footfalls before I sheathe the weapon and toss it at the wall, then fall to the floor and shatter.

CHAPTER 41

ORLAITH

Seated half-way down the jagged staircase carved into the cliff, I watch Cainon's ship cut through the choppy bay while plucking immature heads off a ridge posey bush and stuffing them in a jar.

Patience has never been my virtue, and this poor plant is bearing the weight of that.

I'm frustrated, restless ...

I need to see my best friend, but I can't do that while Cainon's distant regard is heating my face and working hands, as if he can't bring himself to look away. He's standing on the bow of the slim boat—a tall, imposing figure, spyglass pointing my way.

Can he see the agitated bounce of my knee, or how I'm tearing at this bush so violently my fingers are red and sore?

I glance at the lone ship still parked at the end of the pier, deflated sails spun around its masts.

Waiting for me.

Two days ...

"So dramatic," I mutter, ripping a few more buds, putting a little extra bite into the motion. I don't usually take the posies until they're in full bloom, but that won't happen for at least another month.

I'll be gone by then.

Once the bush is bare, I close the jar, watching the grand Bahari vessel edge toward that line I've never swum across, strung between two points of the large, rocky bay. Not a physical line, but in my mind it's so concrete that part of me expects Cainon's ship to smash against it and sink.

It doesn't, of course.

The bay spits the vessel into the open sea, blue sail bloated and boasting gold trimmings that stand out against the gloom. That regard peels away, and I draw a full breath for the first time since I started climbing down these stairs.

The bulbous, gray clouds rumble as I unravel the braid Cainon so meticulously plaited, studying his cupla.

The deep blue stone marbled with threads of gold sits snug around my wrist, held in place by a gilded chain that pinches the two ends together. Small grooves line one side of the stone, evidence of its separation from Cainon's half.

It's frowned upon to remove them—an age-old custom that casts back thousands of years. So long as you're coupled, a female is supposed to wear these things until the day she dies ...

With a shrug, I unlatch the chain, then stuff the thing in my bag and stand.

I'm not ready to tell Kai everything—to drag my topside troubles into the depths of our friendship—but I'm desperate to see him. To fall into him and to feed off his banquet of comfort.

Wind whips at my trailing hair while I leap down the stairs toward the bay below, landing ankle-deep in pitch-black sand. I close my eyes, allowing the pull of the ground to soothe my internal discord ... at least until a husky voice saws through my internal reverie.

Tug those roots out. Cut them off if you have to. This is not the right place for you.

Eyes popping open, I tip my head and sigh.

Well, Cainon. That's easier said than done.

I lump my knapsack atop a jagged rock, then jog toward the boisterous waves so reminiscent of my current circumstances—whisking in fast, unrhythmic motions that show no promise of letting up. Fully clothed, I charge through the sand into icy water that shocks my lungs still.

The ocean bed drops away instantly, and I lift my feet and swim, taking lashing after lashing of frothy whitewash that dwarfs me in both size and power. It pulls me, bullies me, shoves up my nose and makes the back of my eyes sting. It tears at my hair and fake skin and tangles me with kelp, but I keep swimming ...

These waves remind me of the psychological beatings Rhordyn dishes me, because like these waves, he *just doesn't stop.*

He's unrelenting. Unapologetic. So callous in his punishments that I barely have a chance to catch my breath. And to dish such a brutal blow when I was already struggling to float?

Asshole.

I beat the waves with my hands and feet, giving them just as much as they're giving me, while still getting tossed about as if I'm nothing more than a piece of weed.

I'm reminded of summer swims when I was small—when the crystal-clear water was warm, gently lapping at obsidian sand. The only other noises were the calling gulls and Kai's robust laughter.

Now the ocean is *roaring* at me, and I want to scream back and tell it to *stop.*

Please stop.

Just make it past the breakers ... that's all I have to do. Once I'm there, the sea will calm and I'll finally be able to pause.

Take a deep breath.

Recover a little ...

I swim and swim and *swim,* getting pushed back with every wave, feeling like I'm making no progress. But then the ocean calms, and I'm cutting through with ease.

Realizing I've made it through the breakers, I stop and spin, wiping at my stinging eyes and battling for breath, shoulders burning and body numb from the cold.

Euphoria blooms when I see I've swum further than I *ever* have on my own—almost half-way to my Safety Line.

The current begins to pull me backward, and a thundering roar flays me with a blade of fear.

I whirl.

My mouth drops open, eyes going wide ...

"Fuck."

I didn't make it past the breakers at all.

Not even close.

I'm smack in the middle, being charged by a wave taller than the ancient trees in Vateshram Forest.

I arc my neck to see the peak peeling down like a mammoth sea monster eyeing me up for a killing strike ...

I'm going to die.

I'm drawing a breath that'll likely be my last, when a powerful force of silky brawn and glinting scales surges through the face of the wave and wraps me in a firm embrace —one hand cradling my head and urging me into the crook of his neck.

My breath pushes out in the form of a whimper, and I wrap my legs around Kai's trim hips.

A split-second later, the wave crashes down on us like a rockslide, and we're ripped into by its frothing maw. Clinging to each other, we tumble over and over and over until I have no idea which way is up.

Which way is down.

We're jerked and jerked, as if we're caught in the hand of a violent fist testing how much our bones can yield without *snapping.*

My head feels like it might pop, and my ears burst in an explosion of pain.

I fight the urge to open my mouth and *scream*—resist the temptation to draw an ill-fated breath. But then we're surging forward, Kai's powerful tail propelling us through the darkness and into the light.

Thud-ump.

Thud-ump.

Thud-ump.

My lungs burn, muscles bunching ...

We break the surface and I draw a gasping breath, reviving myself with big gulps of Kai's scent. He bangs my back, forcing me to cough and splutter and heave against his chest until I'm certain I'm going to cough up a lung.

"*Treasure?* Are you okay?"

"I'll live," I rasp, and he cradles me closer, keeping us afloat with the gentle back and forth of his hips.

Glancing around, I realize we're well past the breakers, though the surface is still choppy enough to splash. The wind out this far is biting cold, and I shiver, teeth chattering, mind still whirling from the wave's twisting might.

I nuzzle Kai's neck again, letting my spent body wilt.

Partially because I want to leech off his warmth ... *mainly* because I'm worried what he'll see if he looks at me.

Will he notice my mask? Now that I know it's there, it feels so blatantly obvious. Like it's cracking in places, exposing who I am beneath.

The luster.

The *ugly.*

I just want to pretend everything's okay. Like I'm not destined for that boat moored to the brittle dock just beyond my Safety Line, taunting me with its bobbing presence. I want to pretend I don't have a blue and gold cupla hidden in my bag on the shore.

Kai threads a hand into my hair and grips tight. "You should not have come out this far by yourself, Orlaith. You know it's not safe."

I'm in too deep. It felt appropriate.

I almost say it aloud, but I don't want to drag him down, too.

"I just needed to swim ..."

"In *this* weather?"

I close my eyes and shrug.

His chest vibrates, as if some great beast is trapped within its confines, shaking the bars of his ribs.

"You're smarter than that. Who knows what could have snatched you up?"

"Perhaps that's what I wanted?" My reply is instant.

Too instant.

He tugs my hair, forcing my chin high. "Open your eyes, Orlaith."

A command laced with a powerful undertow impossible to deny.

My lashes sweep up and I peer into wild, seagrass eyes

spilling so much wrath I almost flinch. But the moment our stares tangle, all that anger melts off his face, replaced by such a tender regard it stings the back of my eyes with a thousand pins.

"What's wrong?"

The question probes my soul, making me shudder.

I love that he asks; that he cares enough to do it.

Not that it makes me want to answer.

He loosens his grip on my hair, and I tuck myself against his chest again. "Nothing. I'm fine."

His lips skim up my neck, and he plants the next words straight in the shell of my ear. "Your lies don't work on me, Treasure."

I'm warmed by his gentle approach to my fib, like he's chastising me in a loving way.

Still ... I pull deep draws of his salty scent rather than validate the statement with an answer. For not the first time, I wish I had gills so I could slip into his safety net forever. Wish there were some tonic I could take to wipe my memory, my *emotions,* and dissolve this crushing sense of obligation.

"I know."

I dig my nose closer to his neck and *breathe,* his beat pushing against every inch of me, as if I'm deep inside the throbbing heart of the ocean.

"Then what is it?" he asks into the crook of my neck. "Gift me all your problems, Treasure. I'll toss them in my trash trove."

I tug back, seeing his handsome, heavy-lidded regard. "You have a *trash trove?*"

He shrugs a shoulder, lips curling into a half smile that flashes the sharp tip of his canine. "Anything for you."

His grin is infectious, and I fold forward, wishing I could stay right here forever.

But the moment I close my eyes, those shadows rear up, and every drop of happiness falls right off my face.

"I don't want to lose you," I say past the lump in my throat.

I swear the ocean calms a little, like it's listening in.

A long pause, and then; "I'm not going anywhere, Treasure."

I bite down on a sob. Maybe he's not ...

But I am.

CHAPTER 42

RHORDYN

Every footstep is a proclamation, like I'm staking war with the stone. There are no torches blazing my path down this staircase, the darkness almost too dense to breathe through, let alone see anything. But I've walked this staircase thousands of times.

Too many times.

I'll probably walk it a thousand times more.

My grip tightens on the hooves, the stag's sodden underbelly warming the back of my neck. The ground is slippery beneath my boots, and not just from the blood running down my body, wetting the floor, casting the otherwise stale air with the stench of death.

This deep below the castle, the walls seem to weep.

Perhaps they've seen too much over the years ... I know I have. My eyes are just as weary as my soul, but unlike these walls, I'm all dried up.

I come to a landing barred by a door with a small grate inviting a peek into the room on the other side—a little less obscure than the stone stairwell I just descended.

Balancing the animal on my shoulders, I clank the deadlock aside and kick the door. It swings open, rusted hinges protesting with a squeal.

The hairs on the back of my arms lift.

She's looking, *watching ...*

I step into the holding chamber the size of Orlaith's quarters, stone walls on three sides and strong, metal bars lining the other. A round shaft of silver moonlight shoots down from the high rooftop window, offering little reprieve other than to etch out the shape of the square room and to highlight the blood on my body, casting it black.

I let the stag slip off my shoulders, landing behind me with a wet thud. My hands drop to my sides, and I crunch them into fists, chin falling to my chest ...

My wrist feels too light.

You lied to me.

Her voice may have been fragile, but everything else was the opposite. Her upper lip was curled with hate, she had fire in her eyes, and she looked at me like she saw through my skin to the monster I am beneath.

Part of me was relieved—screamed for her to look deeper. To delve until she ripped herself on all my sharp bits. Perhaps then she'd see why I'm stuck in her orbit ... unwillingly. Why drifting too close would destroy *everything.*

But instead of looking, she told me to go.

Guess I should be happy.

I shake my head and sigh, knuckles popping, wishing I could pop the bubble on my fury just as simply. It's knotted in my shoulders; my neck. It has claws dug into my back and my lungs and my fucking chest.

Stepping toward the bars, I look down at the chain bolted to the ground. It's thicker than my arm, tugged taut, traveling straight to the roof where it's threaded through a hole in the stone.

I grip it with both hands, lean all my weight back, and *yank*.

There's a shuffling sound in the distance, a soft mewl as the length of chain wrestles me. But inch by stubborn inch I lug it through the hole, until sweat is dripping down my spine and there's a mound of metal links coiled on the floor at my feet, rising to my waist.

I hook the chain on a prong protruding from the ground and let go, shaking my hands out, fighting for breath.

Always a battle. Not *once* has she made it easy on me.

The barred door has no lock. Just a deadbolt I slide across before kicking it wide. Turning, I look to my kill that has no blood left to spill.

I'm wearing it all.

I only meant to snap its neck—a swift and painless death. But then I heard the rip of flesh and muscle and sinew, and the head came away from the rest of it, forcing me to leave the remnants of my wrath in the forest for the flies to feast on.

A deep growl rattles through the room.

"All right, all right ..."

Hefting the animal onto my shoulders, I charge into the cell that smells like shit and piss and dead things. Like feral, chaotic rage that has nowhere to release.

I make for the middle and drop the stag, looking at the ravaged thing, aware that I'm being watched from a blackened corner. "Your favorite, minus the head."

Her only response is a low, animalistic rumble that riles me more than it should.

I look to the roof—to the sliver of moon I can see through the hole up there. "Don't be like that. You know I hate it when we argue."

No answer.

My attention drifts to chunks of stone scattered about the base of the far wall, and I huff. "Been having another go at that hole, I see?" Arching a brow, I look back to the pocket of shadows by the bars, straight into black eyes glazed by a lick of silver light. "Did you think I wouldn't notice?"

One blink and a slight tilt of her head. Other than that, I get nothing but silence.

Always the silence, never anything *more*.

I sigh, pinching the bridge of my nose. "Don't choke it down too fast," I mutter, storming from the cell. I slam the door closed, slide the deadlock into place, and unhook the chain—watching the entire length whip back through the hole so fast it sounds like I'm standing in the heart of a thunderstorm.

Bones pop and crack and crunch, things splat, and deep, satiated rumblings have me rolling my head from left to right before spinning toward the door.

Sometimes, I imagine that *thing* is far more perceptive than it really is, but it's all a lie I tell myself.

I exit the holding chamber and pull the door shut, ascending stairs veiled in darkness so thick it feels like a second skin.

You lied to me ...

Yes, I did.

Orlaith hates the mask I forced her to wear. Message received loud and clear. There is no honor in my decision, but I'll stand by it until I'm shoved in the ground. Would sooner tear the world apart than let *them* catch a glimpse of her luster.

If that makes me a monster in her eyes, well ...

About fucking time.

CHAPTER 43

ORLAITH

An outside picnic *seemed* like a good idea, except this thick, fluffy toast doused in butter and a smear of honey is failing to sweeten the bitter taste in my mouth. It's the first solid thing I've been able to look at in days without my insides knotting, and I can't even enjoy it.

I scowl, stuffing my mouth full, back to the wall and staring out across the courtyard veined with exposed roots that dig through the cracks in the pavement. They anchor an ancient oak to the center, almost entirely caged by three castle walls of black, the tree's branches providing a relatively sheltered sanctuary. The opening looks out on a stretch of grass that gives way to Vateshram Forest—the dense foliage bathed in a dreary, gray light.

Not a single blade of sun has broken through the clouds in *days*.

Thunder bludgeons the sky, and my gaze rolls up.

"That was a loud one," Kavan mumbles, pushing caramel hair from his pale blue eyes. He peeks between branches at the threatening clouds, face pinched in a frown.

Vanth grunts, not even bothering to look up from the spot on the ground he's been staring at for the past ten minutes.

His long, wheaten hair is pulled back in a low bun, seemingly a common look for Southern males. His appearance is sullen; striking blue eyes overridden by thin lips constantly set in a half-scowl that gives him a sour look.

Both Bahari guards are leaning against the oak's knotted trunk, garbed in dark blue tunics and battle-ready boots that rise to the knee, gold buckles polished to a high gleam. Carrying spears everywhere they go, they're ever ready to dive into war, and I'm ever ready for them to leave me the hell alone.

Thing is, they have no idea how to lighten their steps, and they trudge after me—more likely to *lure* danger rather than frighten it away.

I can no longer lurk or go privately about my business. Every move I make is *chaperoned.* They even stand outside the door, close enough to hear me pee while I'm using the latrine.

I sigh, studying my toast half wrapped in the waxy material Cook packaged it with. It came accompanied with a forced smile that never met her eyes and only poured salt in my wound.

"Is that nice?" Vanth asks, eyeing my toast.

"You'd know if you hadn't insulted Cook by telling her she undercooked the veal last night," I say, but all I get in response is a grumbling slur of words that bring me more satisfaction than they should.

I'd usually be having breakfast with Baze at this time, a thought that sits like lead in my chest. Though it's been a few days since I showed him the *real* me, I just can't bring myself to face him.

No breakfasts, lunches, dinners, training ...

Nothing.

Baze knows full well how much I struggle with my identity. I air that frustration with him every morning. Bastard had the antidote this entire time and chose not to use it.

Real friends don't do that to each other.

The guards mutter between themselves about how much they can't wait to get back to the South, and I take another bite, anticipating Vanth's question before it ruptures from his mouth.

"Weren't we supposed to set sail yesterday?"

"I still have things to take care of, Vanth. I'm a very busy person, you know."

I don't bother mentioning my deep-seated fear of stepping over my Safety Line; a leap I intend on ignoring until I'm all out of avoidance tactics. I haven't been shoved out the door yet, and I'm hopeful Cainon will send those ships ahead of my arrival—buy me a little more time to ease out of my shell.

"So far," Vanth proclaims, pinching the bridge of his thin nose, "all you've done is pick flowers, *plant* flowers, debark a tree, shed a bramble of all its thorns, collect rocks, accost a gardener for seemingly doing his job, shave moss off a boulder, pluck fungi off a pile of horse shi—"

"That reminds me," I interrupt, rummaging through my knapsack with my spare hand. "Those mushrooms need to be cured, but first I'll have to collect some thermal water from Puddles. Fingers crossed I have an empty jar in here somewhere or I might have to dart back up Stony Stem ..."

They groan in unison.

"Found one," I announce, waving it around. I shove it back in my bag along with the remainder of my breakfast, right next to the rock I finished painting in the early hours of the morning while I was struggling to sleep.

I smile to myself.

It's the perfect addition to my wall—the final piece in my current reach. With so much unfinished business storming over me, *this* is something I can control.

This rock belongs in its home, but I can't place it with those two at my back, nosing in on all my business.

I close my bag, sling it over my shoulder, and stand.

"We off again?" Kavan asks, lifting a lazy brow while Vanth stifles a yawn.

Perfect.

I've been luring them everywhere since well before sunup, darting up and down Stony Stem on several occasions to retrieve things I'd purposely forgotten. I even got them to carry a few rocks up my tower—ones I've been eyeing for a while but were too heavy for me to haul.

I've never heard two grown men grumble so much.

I should be nicer to them, but the way their eyes crawl across my skin when they think I'm not paying attention has sown a caustic seed.

"Yup. Places to be, things to do. You sure you two don't want to just ... sit this one out? I can swing by and pick you up later. Maybe bring you both some of the servant's gruel?"

They push off the tree, sighing in perfect, disgruntled symphony. "We're coming."

Damn.

"Lovely," I lie, flashing a smile. It melts right off my face the moment I turn for the wooden door pressed in the wall next to me and tug it open.

They may be good at sticking to me like a bad smell, but I have one very special advantage ...

I know this castle like I *should* know the back of my own hand.

They don't.

I stalk down a hallway that has no windows—only sporadic sconces that cut the gloom into fiery segments. It's a special hall, harboring all sorts of secrets. It's the precise reason I chose to sit where I did while I ate my unsatisfying breakfast.

Take that little door to my left, and it'll lead you in a roundabout way to Puddles. Take those stairs to the right, the ones that shoot skyward in an almost vertical manner, and you somehow end up in the kitchen a level below ground.

Take this inconspicuous hall that splits off into a shadowed elbow—the one I'm taking right now—and you're being twisted up by The Tangle before you even register you forked off in the wrong direction.

A smile cuts across my face and I break into a sprint, worming my way through the wiggly hall at a ferocious speed, only stopping once I hit a sharp bend; back pressed flat to the wall as I listen.

Footsteps thunder after me, and my smile grows.

Suckers.

Sprinting again, I take shadowed side tunnels and stairwells, backtracking several times in case their senses are sharp enough to track my scent. Finally, convinced I've thoroughly lost them, I skip down a well-lit hallway with nothing chasing me but blessed silence.

I may never see Vanth and Kavan again, and right now, I can't find a single lick of empathy in my heart to care.

I should be concerned by that slap of realization. The fact that I'm *not* only adds to the growing pile of evidence I'm trying to ignore ...

I'm losing myself.

I walk, lighting torches, casting my art in a golden sheen that lifts some elements off the wall while digging others deeper into the rock.

When I first stumbled upon this place, the compulsion to embellish it was too much to ignore. It was dark, tucked away, abandoned.

Private.

I began painting, one stone at a time; a mural of tens, then hundreds, then *thousands* of whispers all pieced together.

Sea-green eyes, a silver sword with a floral hilt, a half-eaten moon, storm clouds hanging over a wilted weed, a burning tree, pewter scales that ricochet light.

Pausing, I brush my hand over one of a white rose in half-bloom, revealing the hint of petals flecked with a familiar constellation of twinkly freckles.

The little boy always jumps out at me the most ... in one way or another.

I've painted him many times because he's such a constant in my dreams. Visiting often, gifting me with that wealth of a smile and his reaching hands.

I let my fingers drift off the stone and keep walking—keep skipping my gaze along the individual rocks.

It took three years before I realized the tiny paintings were building something much bigger. That my whispers were the seeds of something I'd buried deep in the pit of my soul; germinating, reaching for the light of day.

Despite my efforts, it's not the smaller paintings I see right now.

It's the bigger picture they make up.

The crowd of people staring out from the stone—tall as

me and just as lifelike, as if they have hearts in their chests that push real blood through their veins.

They aren't whispers at all ...

They're screams.

Some have angular marks drawn on their foreheads, some don't. Some are closer, some are standing farther away, their features less defined as if my tiny, two-year-old memory was too hazy for my subconscious to paint a clear picture.

I keep walking, drifting past haunting stare after haunting stare, looking past the ghosts I didn't intend to paint, trying to focus on the small pictures I did.

Failing.

They're watching me; ghostly perusals scalding my skin and refusing to let me ignore them.

The first time I noticed one staring out at me from the wall, lording over me with eyes that seemed to follow my movements, I fell over. Ran from here so fast I forgot my bag and had to return later when I'd managed to compose myself.

That night, I saw the same man in my nightmares ... in pieces.

Saw him get feasted on by the same three beasts that haunt me every time I close my eyes.

I spent two months painting another section only to realize the little stones were all building blocks to yet another person staring out at me. Somebody else I'd seen burned bits of while I'd slept.

Somebody else who lost their life that day.

I realized I was painting a grave. Fixing faces of the dead down here in the dark where they could exist in a different way—an abstract eulogy that hurts to look at. Especially now. Because at the very end of this mural, on the verge of that hungry darkness, is the little boy who looks like me.

The *real* me.

And this whisper weighing down my knapsack ... it's his final piece. I know it is, even though it's not what I intended to paint.

It took him years to show up in the overriding picture, as though I'd hidden him deeper than the rest.

That thought feels dangerous.

I come to the edge of the light and drop to my knees, digging through my bag. I bypass the mouse-filled jar and pull out another heavy with freshly mixed mortar. My palate knife comes next, then finally the stone wrapped in cheesecloth.

No pickaxe. I won't be decorating any more pieces.

This story ... it's over. Today, I place the final full stop.

I unwrap the layers of material and look upon my work.

On this fist-sized stone, I painted a pair of hands much the same as Rhordyn's sketch; soft and relaxed, at ease in their restful state despite the thorny vine I wrapped around them.

Bound them with.

Those vicious thorns dig deep, spilling trails of red—such a stark contrast to the blue flowers sprouting from the vine. Feeding off the blood.

I use my palette knife to clear out the old mortar, then scoop a glob of fresh stuff from the jar, my hand unsteady as I spread it around before pressing the whisper into place.

I keep it hidden behind the flat of my palm, drawing deep breaths, trying to convince my heart to stop beating me up from the inside.

Because I know ... I just *know* that although my wakeful

state has painted a pair of hands wrapped in a thorny vine, my subconscious has somehow woven it into the final piece of *him*. That it has put him back together again—no longer in bits scattered throughout my nightmares.

I may not jump into that abyss in my dreams, but this ... *I've done this*. Pulled crumbs of shadow from that chasm and dripped them from my fingertips, even if it wasn't intentional.

I've done this.

The thought gives me courage to let my hand drop, though it swiftly snaps up to shield my heart.

The little boy appears to lift off the wall, as though he might push free from the stones and bridge the gap between us.

I hold my breath, waiting ...

Waiting ...

But he just stands there with a puckered brow, peering out through wide eyes that look like crystals. Just stands there with outstretched arms and empty hands.

He doesn't step off the painting like part of me had hoped he would. He doesn't blink or breathe or smile.

He doesn't tell me why I can't let him go.

But how could he? I gave him rocks for eyes. Rocks for his ears and his mouth and his hands.

I pieced him together with mortar.

Not real.

A weight lands in my stomach, so heavy I stumble back.

My vision of him blurs and I blink at the haze, feeling a wetness slide down my cheeks. The sensation releases a plug pitted deep inside my heart, and suddenly my lungs are heaving, breath coming in hard, fast gasps.

My back collides with the wall, spine grating down stone until I'm sitting on the ground, knees caught against my ribs.

I look up into his eyes, map the freckles on his face, examine the painting like the open wound it is ... and I let myself unravel. Let my unbridled emotions dismantle me in a way that feels hopelessly insignificant. Because he's in pieces.

I'm not.

And all the while he stares ... and stares ... and stares.

Unblinking. Unseeing. Yet I've never felt so *seen*.

I sit for what feels like hours, leaking my own self-hatred while I rock back and forth, wishing someone would wrap me in their arms and cuddle me.

The back of my neck tingles.

My chest stops heaving, face smoothing, as if somebody bunged the spill of my emotions.

I sense an overwhelming presence, like there's suddenly less air for me to breathe. Less space for me to move.

So acutely aware of the blackness that seems to push against my side, I glide my gaze to the right and peer into the void ...

I'm not alone.

Someone ... some*thing* is watching from the shadows. I can feel their keen attention sliding over my skin like the sharp tip of a blade.

"Wh-who is it?" I rasp, only confirming my suspicions when rather than bounce back at me like my words usually do down here, they're *absorbed*. As if something devoured them before they had the chance to echo.

I swallow, feeling every sense sharpen as I lower my hands to the floor and roll forward, perched on all fours while I reach for my bag.

Something rumbles—the sound deep and heavy, like a mountain's growl—and I freeze, unable to breathe or speak or blink, every muscle knotting with a wild fear I've never felt before.

All I want to do is *move*. To scream and run and leave my bag and never look back.

But my instincts have other ideas.

They want me to keep my chin high, stare pinned to the dark. They want me to back away, showing as little fear as possible.

Although it makes no sense to me, for once in my life, I listen.

Slowly—so damn slowly—I begin to move again, keeping my eyes speared into the body of darkness while I grab my bag. Another sawing rumble rolls through the gloom, threatening to maul my composure into messy ribbons.

I snatch the torch and leap to my feet, lifting my chin and walking backward down the hall—every blind, unhurried step feeling like a feat in its own.

I don't dare blow out the other torches as I go, knowing that if I do, I won't be putting any space between myself and whatever it is that's hunting me.

Let them burn out. Let them become nothing but charcoal nubs unable to illuminate my loss. A sheath of black to forever keep this graveyard safe—a nicety I wish Rhordyn had given me.

Committed to his lies rather than this painful in-between.

I stumble into the comforting light of the common hallway and slam the door shut, scurrying backward in a burst of frightened energy. My back collides with stone and I drop to the ground, drop the torch, legs trapped against my chest to quell the rising tremors paying tribute to the frantic beat of my heart.

Eventually those torches will blow out, and then this place will no longer belong to me ...

Perhaps that thought should lighten my shoulders.

It doesn't.

CHAPTER 44

ORLAITH

The crisp air hits my lungs, feeding me the sweet smell of impending rain. Not the sort that lashes the seas, but the sort that wets the earth for days and always leaves me feeling empty.

Approaching my Safety Line, I find a comfortable position beneath a large tree, its leafy branches heavy with nuts. The ancient trunk offers me something to lean against while I pluck through fallen acorns, waiting for Shay to get brave enough to detach from that lump of shadow hanging off a large, mossy boulder.

Sometimes he needs a little coaxing, especially at this time of day.

But I'm patient, filling the waiting moments by shucking helmets off acorns, peeling back their hard, outer shell until all I'm left with is the creamy center. Ground down, it's one of the thirty-four ingredients required to make Exothryl, but it's also the base for my homemade glue.

A perfect guise.

I have a small pile by the time Shay starts to advance, like a sooty leaf flicking about on the handsy wind. He's tense today, not himself—jerking from one slice of shadow to the next.

The hairs on the back of my neck stand on end.

The forest is dead quiet. Even the birds seem to have lost their desire to sing ... a soundless void only severed by my uneven breaths.

Something's not right.

Shay dashes into the same pool of shade I'm sitting in, and my heart forgets how to beat as he hovers, watching me, head tilted to the side.

His essence seems to *probe.*

It's nothing forceful—just a cold pulse of incorporeal fingers pressing against my cheeks.

"Shay? ... Are you okay?"

The way his essence is uniting with my skin, it's so ... *personal.* Like he's checking me over in a manner his hands could never achieve without draining all the fluids my body needs to function.

That touch veers from my cheeks, trails across my left shoulder, down my arm. My lungs fill with stone as my gaze traces the specter of his touch until it lands around my wrist; around the cupla partially visible beneath the cuff of my shirt.

He makes a soft clicking sound that stiffens my spine before the sensation whips back, and I watch the tendrils of his form flit about—a hypnotic dance that looks anything but peaceful.

He knows I'm leaving him.

The realization is a boot to the chest.

I roll onto my knees and inch closer. "Shay—"

The shadows cloaking his face recede, revealing the starched face of his inner self—those small, beady eyes like tacks.

I pause.

Their regard pokes at me. Scrapes at me. *Digs* at me.

His milky lips peel back, exposing his maw. Again, that clicking sound spikes out of him, assaulting me in little airy bursts that chip at my bones.

He's angry with me.

Guilt pools in my belly and weighs me down, threatening to derail all my good intentions ...

"I'm sorry," I whisper, but he makes this acute hissing sound that slays my heart. "Shay, you don't understand. I have to g—"

He flattens against my Safety Line, sending me tumbling back onto my ass.

"NO!"

The word shatters out of him like it was forced through a throat that wasn't built to shape words.

My mouth pops open in silent shock as I look up at my friend, heart in my throat, eyes wider than they've ever felt before.

That sable gaze softens, a squeaking sound leaks out, and then he wilts ... folding into himself until he's no longer hanging over me. His face vanishes behind that smoky veil, and I taste his shame in the air between us.

"Shay, it's okay," I say, lifting off the ground in increments. "I understa—"

He shrieks, darting through the trees.

I spin to see Baze charging across the vast grounds with storms in his eyes, and I panic, flinging the mouse in Shay's general direction before sweeping my acorns into the empty jar and kicking the evidence of my shucking beneath a pile of leaves. I shoulder my bag and stand, muttering a long line of profanities as I stalk into the open with my stare stuck to the ground.

I know I can't avoid him, but perhaps he'll take note of my body language and let me pass without luring me into a conversation I don't want to have.

"We need to talk, Orlaith."

This day can go to hell.

"I have no interest," I mutter, barging toward the castle.

"I rescued Tweddle Dick and Tweddle Dumb from your ... *Tangle.*"

My feet stop of their own accord, mimicking the motion of my heart. I spin, hands bunched into balls as I strike him with a venomous stare. "*And?*"

His eyes widen, a muscle in his jaw pops, and it's hard to ignore the shock of his tired, disheveled appearance—like he's wearing all my internal bitter on his outside.

His shirt is crumpled, hair a mess, pants stained ...

"You're spiraling."

"I'm *fine.*"

Arms crossed, he pins me with a scrutiny that digs all the way to the bone. "You've never been very good at lying, you know."

"Unlike you."

My words are arrows, and I can tell they find their mark by the way his attention spears to the rumbling sky.

He sighs, studying the turbulent clouds, and I can sense Shay watching from a puddle of shadow between two gnarled trees.

"Hovard just left a gift in your tower," Baze drudges out, turning wary eyes on me again. "Something Cainon instructed him to make in your size."

I frown. "Well ... what is it?"

"A gown," he says, brow arching. "Fashioned from cobweb silk that's stained *Bahari blue.*"

All the fight drains out of me as my shoulders drop ...

Shit.

His head cants to the side. "You look uncomfortable. Is it the gown or the color?"

Earthen eyes glimmer with scarcely veiled amusement that nibbles at my composure, nerves, and *patience.*

"The *gown,*" I hiss, and his low chuckle fills the void between us with all the humor of a laughing rock.

He dashes through my personal space with his well-oiled gait. "*Lie,*" he growls, breath hot on my ear before he lands his shoulder into my own and sends me stumbling.

By the time I've regained my composure, he's gone.

CHAPTER 45

ORLAITH

The dress has all the modesty of a deciduous tree in the fall.

I stare at the *gift* like all those long, deep blue tendrils dusted in gold are going to peel off the mannequin and strangle me. The bands are artfully placed to emphasize the female form and flounce her ... *assets.*

I had no idea this was the fashion of the South. If I had, I may have found a different way to secure those ships. Pirated them, or ... something.

Anything.

Hindsight has a cruel sense of humor.

Brushing a hand through the skirt, I wonder how I'm expected to move in this thing if everyone can see my undergarments every time I take a step. Or perhaps I'm not *supposed* to wear any, and this dress is intended to offer glimpses of something untouchable.

Something that belongs to *another male.*

Putting space between the garment and me, I stare at it with a renewed surge of disgust. One pull on any of the strips crisscrossing the front or back and the entire thing would flutter to the ground. Though that's probably the point. For it to rip and fall in a careless heap before bodies join *and—*

"Stop," I snap, the word battling a resounding crack of thunder. "Pull yourself together, Orlaith."

I tie my hair into a heavy knot and unbutton my top. It falls to the ground, and I begin unbinding my breasts, tossing the length of stretchy material aside before pushing my pants and underwear down.

Standing in nothing but my masked skin, I unclasp the garment, a fraught sigh slipping out. The dress is featherlight, and I struggle with the concept that something representing so much weighs so very little.

I step into the waistband, fastening the clip at the small of my back, brows pinched as I try to solve the rest of it. It takes a few tries, but I finally find the right holes to slip my arms through, managing to fasten it between my shoulder blades without the help of a second pair of hands.

In a flutter of Bahari blue and gilded trimmings, I edge toward the mirror and meet my reflection.

My insides gutter, the strong line of my shoulders softening.

"Oh my ..."

Bands slice across my body like licks of navy paint, covering me yet ... *not.* You can still see the outline of my nipples, peaked from the pinch of cold, my under breasts entirely exposed.

The lines sweep and swirl, complimenting my shape, emphasizing the parts of me I've tried so hard to hide. And when I shift my leg or move about, little slivers of my bum are exposed.

Sex. This garment has painted me in sex.

I try to clear the lump in my throat, my cheeks pinched a

shade of pink from the fire sizzling my veins. I've spent most of my life hiding from my reflection, but now I want to avoid it for an entirely different reason.

Shame.

Red-hot, burning shame, because this dress has made something *abundantly* clear ...

I've sold my body.

The distant sound of a horse whinnying travels through the open window, holding a distressed cadence that has me turning from the mirror and dashing toward the door in long, ass-revealing strides. I pull it open and step onto the balcony, assaulted by a blow of icy wind.

The clouds are heavy, blocking the light, making the forest look dark and haunted. There's a charge in the air that smarts my skin in a way that has nothing to do with the cold ...

Movement snags my gaze, and I watch a spotted gray horse clamor through the front gate, lugging a cart down the packed-earth path. He's lathered in sweat, frothing at the bit, but that's not what has my eyes narrowing.

It's the female lumped on the upper seat, barely clinging to the reins, her head flopping around so much it's hard to see past the mess of her inky hair.

Perhaps she's asleep?

They get halfway across the lawn before lightning mosaics the clouds. A second later, thunder crackles loud enough to rattle my bones, and the horse rears up, squeals to the sky, then crumbles—sending the cart tipping sideways.

The woman is tossed through the air, landing in a boneless heap on the manicured grass.

She doesn't move. Doesn't even scream.

I'm back inside, yanking my door open and bounding down Stony Stem in the very next instant.

There's the sound of footfalls chasing me, Vanth and Kavan yelling for me to stop but doing nothing to penetrate my resolve.

I move like the wind, limbs churning, mind an axe. There are no hurdles for feet that defy the laws of gravity, and that's what mine do.

Barely feeling as if they touch the ground.

I reach the bottom of my tower, hair slipping free of its band as I weave down a barrage of tunnels and stairwells until grass cushions my steps. The space between myself and the cart seems to evaporate in seconds, and I fall upon the female in a flutter of blue and unbridled hair.

With hands too steady to be mine, I roll the woman onto her back, and a sharp sound splits the air.

It takes me a moment to realize it came from me.

She's petite, pretty, with big, brown eyes that are wide and wet and painfully familiar.

Mishka—the Medis from a neighboring village—but she doesn't look the same as she did a few days ago at the Tribunal ...

Her skin is gray, all the color drained from her sunken cheeks. Her pupils are so dilated the black is almost consuming the brown, and they're seeing but ... but *not.* There's an acrid stench wafting off her that sticks to the back of my throat, and I glance down her body to seek the source.

A sturdy hand grips my chin and *yanks,* forcing my gaze skyward.

Pewter eyes snatch my breath.

"*No,*" Rhordyn growls through clenched teeth, dropping

to his knees on the other side of Mishka and unhooking his jacket buttons. "Don't look."

Holding my stare, he drapes the jacket over Mishka's midsection while I study every speckle in his smoky stare. Eyes that offer a blanket of comfort while also plying me with a sense of dread.

More footsteps encroach, crunching through what sounds like broken glass, pausing.

He breaks our eye contact to look past me. "Any liquid bane?"

"Smashed."

Rhordyn swears so sharp I flinch.

"The horse, Baze."

"On it."

I look over my shoulder to see Baze step around a spilled leather satchel and walk toward the felled animal. The horse is trying to arch his head off the ground, allowing me a glimpse of shallow slash marks along his neck. Grisly wounds seeping a rank-smelling liquid that's inky and thick and—

Something tore into him.

"Go, Orlaith."

Rhordyn's voice snags me, and my head swivels, stare landing on Mishka's unseeing eyes ...

On her bleeding lips and restless chest.

"No," I mutter, maneuvering her onto my lap. "She needs elevation and water. Her lips are cracked."

I shift my attention to Kavan and Vanth, watching the scene unfold through wide eyes, spears hanging at their sides. "Make yourselves useful and go fetch a pitcher!"

Nobody moves, Mishka continues to battle for breath, and my insides twist into messier knots.

Frantic, I turn to Rhordyn. *"Why aren't you helping?"* I hiss, smoothing Mishka's hair back from her face.

She releases a sob that's half whimper, then calls out for her mom.

Again.

My heart folds.

I cradle her head and sooth her fevered brow, just like Cook used to do when I was sick. "It's okay. You're going to be okay ..."

A bolt of lightning highlights the carnage in a fierce, silver light. The first heavy droplets of icy rain begin to fall, and I lean forward, trying to shelter her from the worst of it.

Her pupils shrink, focusing. Her face crumbles, as if she's just acknowledged something awful. "Help m-me ..."

I grip her flailing hand and squeeze, staring into wide, wild eyes. "I will. You're safe now, I promise."

Rhordyn leans so close his chilly lips skim my ear. "Her wound is from a Vruk."

The words land like death blows, but I dash them off.

"Has anything vital been severed?"

"No."

There's a brief, gurgling squeal behind me, and I gasp, attention swinging to the horse now bleeding out through a slash in its throat—to Baze, crouched beside it with a bloody dagger hanging from his hand.

The animal is no longer breathing. Moving.

Making any sounds.

I blink, and a wet warmth slides down my cheeks.

"It hasn't severed anything vital," Rhordyn continues, his words a whispered assault on my ear. "But it will rot her. *Slowly,* in vicious, vile increments that will suckle her sanity and turn her rabid, until she finally drowns on her own composting lungs."

I drag a shuddered breath, attention drifting back to the woman who seems to have lost that sheen of lucidity from her stare. "But she's ... *she's ...*"

Rhordyn shifts, and another bolt of lightning draws my attention to the dagger poised in his steady hand.

Our gazes clash.

"Look away," he orders, and there's an unapologetic savagery in his stare.

It bites my chest, snatching my ability to draw a full breath.

I remember Mishka standing before Rhordyn at the Tribunal. Remember her hands resting atop her lower stomach like a shield.

My tears flow freely.

Look away, he said.

But I've been looking away my entire life.

"No."

"Look. Away."

His words rattle with steely command, but I lift my chin and squeeze that cold, trembling hand. Looking down, I give Mishka all of me, leaving nothing but scraps for the man with the blade.

Her eyes are dancing, breaths distorted.

"Tell me about him," I whisper, grabbing her other hand and resting them both atop her abdomen, trying to ignore the warm, putrid liquid now leaching through Rhordyn's jacket. "Tell me about the man who gifted you his cupla."

Rhordyn's regard is a brand on my face.

I know what's coming, but I refuse to look away. To hide behind a line that's only fortified in my imagination. He wanted me to train—to learn to wield a sword and dodge a deadly blow—but he can't shield me from everything.

He can't shield me from *this.*

"V-Vale," she rasps, cheeks swelling with the beginnings of a smile. "His eyes are like the s-sea. I knew I was his the m-moment I looked into them."

My lower lip wobbles, so I tuck it between my teeth. "I love that ..."

A soft nod.

"I d-dreamt our baby has his eyes," she whispers, each word landing a chisel to my chest.

I wonder if she knows. How much of her is painfully aware of what she's lost.

"A little girl ..." her gaze shifts, landing somewhere faraway as her chest rattles with another inhale. "But we'll see."

My next breath slices me up, poisoning me with the residue of her scarcely veiled pain.

I hope she's seeing that dream. That she's blissfully unaware of how shredded that part of her body is. That she believes she's holding her mother's comforting hands, and not those of a stranger.

A cough has her buckling in my lap, perfuming the air with more of that putrid smell.

I hold her tighter.

"You'll see," I lie, blooming a smile so hollow it hurts. "You'll see her soon."

Mishka's lips part, but then her body jerks and—

Something warm leaks onto my thighs as her eyes widen, then gutter, and I hear the stark hiss of a withdrawing blade.

My heart stumbles a beat.

I don't want to look, but my eyes drift of their own

accord, halting on the spill of blood pushing through a clean slice on the left side of her chest ...

"You—" I sever my sight of the wound that's scoring me in a way that feels permanent. "*You just—*"

Rhordyn wipes his dagger on the grass. "Stopped her suffering," he spits, as if the words were spikes in his tongue.

Our stares collide, and though he doesn't reply, his cold, detached eyes say everything.

Not the first ...

Probably not the last.

My throat clogs, every breath feeling like a step in a ladder I don't want to ascend.

This is what I've been hiding from; what Rhordyn's been facing whenever he leaves the castle grounds.

No wonder he sits on that throne wearing dead eyes.

Another fork of lightning splits apart the shrieking silence, and the sky loosens its load, dropping a curtain of water between Rhordyn and I.

Neither of us blink.

He's watching me, his scrutiny as heavy as my heart. But there's something more there—like he's reading every sharp breath, seeing past the skin he's forced me to wear.

He's checking for cracks, but I have none. All I have is blood on my hands and a honed resolve.

I have to go.

"Kavan, do you know where to find the morgue?" Rhordyn asks, voice monotone, stare unwavering.

I hear my guard step forward. "Yes, High Master. We've had a thorough tour of your castle ... more than once."

I can't help but feel that's aimed at me.

"Take Mishka's body and have her wrapped. Retrieve her

cupla. Since her promised is from the Bahari capital, it's now *your* responsibility to return it to him."

My throat clogs.

Her promised ...

"Vanth, you'll send a priority sprite so the man has prior warning."

There's a long pause, then, "And what about Orla—"

Whatever question Vanth had dies on his tongue the moment Rhordyn turns his head, glancing over his shoulder at the man.

Vanth drops his head in a servile gesture. "Of course, High Master."

I swallow as Mishka's body is lifted, leaving nothing but a bloody, putrid stamp I can smell and feel, but can't bring myself to look at.

Cainon was right. I dug my roots in—hid from a hurting world just as wounded as I am. Rhordyn may have slipped a mask over my face, but I was the one who chose to blind myself to the carnage.

Every second I spend here is another life lost. One more dream that'll never manifest ...

I have to go. *Now.*

"Baze," Rhordyn bites out, gaze narrowed on me again. "Make sure they find their way."

"Sir."

More retreating steps, until all that's left are me and Rhordyn, a felled horse, and this frigid tension I want to shatter.

"This is not your weight to bear, Orlaith."

"You've lost the right to dictate what's important to me. You're not my High Master anymore."

His eyes flash luminescent. "You have no idea how wrong

that statement is, Milaje. And fleeing Ocruth is not going to soothe the guilt you nourish simply because you *survived.*"

The allegation is slung at my soul, and I flinch—spine stiffening, fingers curling.

"Get out," I snarl.

Get out of my head.

Rhordyn's upper lip peels back. *"Never."*

The word is volleyed at me like a threat ...

By the way he's posturing himself, I get the haunting sense that stepping onto that boat bobbing by the jetty is going to be a much bigger hurdle than I initially anticipated.

I should have left yesterday ...

Shit.

Perhaps I can still get to it. As long as my feet are touching that Bahari-bourne deck, Rhordyn can't remove me without inciting some sort of war.

He's overbearing, but he's not stupid.

My pulse sounds like a war drum as I lift my chin, pushing my shoulders back. "I'll be leaving now."

"And what about your guards?" he asks, deadly calm. "You're just going to sail off and leave them here?"

"They can hitch a ride on a trade ship."

No love lost there.

"They're *your* people now, Milaje. *Your* responsibility." His gaze darts down to my cupla, back up. "You're their future High Mistress, are you not?"

Asshole.

I leap to my feet and run.

CHAPTER 46

ORLAITH

I make it about two dozen steps toward the ocean before I'm swept up and tossed over Rhordyn's shoulder, landing a blow to my stomach that knocks the air right out of me. Recovery proves difficult when every powerful stride he takes lands another assault to my gut, preventing me from drawing a sufficient breath.

We're inside the castle by the time I manage to haul my lungs full. I let out a furious scream, pummeling his back with my fists and swearing like I've heard the guards do when they think they're out of earshot.

He doesn't slow, doesn't even grunt ... as if he were cut from the walls of this castle. So I prepare to sink my teeth into a slab of solid back muscle.

"No biting," he murmurs, flipping me off his shoulder and catching me in a cradled position. "Those teeth can do far more damage than you realize."

"Put me down," I bellow, shucking against his grip. I free an arm and tear my fingers down his shirt, popping buttons and clawing his skin.

All I get in response is a throaty rumble before my arm is pinned down the side of my body. "You keep at this," he says with a deep, gravelly cadence, "and that pathetic excuse for a garment is going to fall right off you."

I stop moving. Instantly.

The glint in his otherwise stoic stare tells me he finds a sadistic sense of amusement in my sudden compliance, which only serves to rile me more.

Choosing to look at anything other than his intolerable face, I glance around, realizing *exactly* where we are ...

Headed down the corridor I've walked a thousand times with hungry, scent-starved lungs and empty hope in my chest. A corridor that leads to only one place.

The Den.

My throat clogs, nerves on fire, gaze shifting to the line of Rhordyn's jaw that looks sharp enough to split wood on.

To the caged look in his eyes.

A week ago, being carried down this corridor would have pitted me with a seed of anxious excitement, but that was before I learned about the lies. That was before he put a sword through Mishka's heart and smothered us both in blood.

"Rhordyn ... I need you to put me down."

His grip tightens, and my heart finds a berth in my throat.

We reach the door to his personal chambers, and I'm tossed over his shoulder again while he undoes the handle, storms inside, then slams it shut behind him.

I'm flung to my feet, and it takes four stumbling steps to gain balance, a task made far more difficult by the fact that I'm suddenly choking on the potent perfume of his scent. Layers upon layers upon layers of it diving down my throat and shoving my lungs full.

It snares me. *Unhinges* me.

Flicking my tangled hair back with an angry toss of my hand, I spin to face Rhordyn and freeze.

There's something about the way he's looking at me—a wildness that's hunting every breath. Every blink. The flutter of pulse in my throat.

But it's not just that.

It's the way he's standing over me, smothering my view so all I can see is *him*. So every breath I draw has come from his chest, and each release is consumed by the same.

I quickly realize I'm entirely out of my depth, and I have one of two choices: swim ... or *drown*.

"Cover yourself," he grates out, and I only have a second to shield all my important bits before his hand whips out and strikes through several strips of Cainon's gown, the movement so swift I barely feel a thing.

Scraps flutter to the ground while others cling to my wet skin, though Rhordyn's too busy digging through his drawer to pay attention to my half-naked state. A shirt is tossed at me before he begins to pace the room, back and forth in front of the massive bed.

His strides are long and violent, hands ripping through sodden, silver-kissed curls.

Figuring he wants me to put the damn top on, I peel the remaining few scraps of blue from my body before tugging his shirt over my head, but I'm snagged the moment I do, pausing with my head halfway through the hole.

Digging my nose into the soft, luxurious fabric, I draw a quiet breath through the fibers, letting my lids flutter shut ...

All I can smell is *him*.

He's worn this recently, perhaps even slept in it.

This material has been wrapped around his body. Touched him in ways I've never been able to.

The realization spikes heat through my veins that spears right between my legs. My skin tingles, and I have to clamp my lips shut to stopper a moan while forcing the rest of my head free, features smoothing in an effort to mask the utter ecstasy twisting me up.

But Rhordyn's not looking at me—at the hem that falls to mid-thigh or the sleeves hanging around my elbows. He's too busy pacing like some tortured beast.

He glances down to his own ruined top as if he just remembered I gouged his chest, and he tips his head, muttering words to the roof that make no sense at all. Gripping the hem, he tugs it over his head in a single motion, revealing powerful bricks of muscle I can't peel my eyes from.

But it's not his fierce, statuesque beauty that has me staring. It's the blood dribbling down his torso, drawing from four deep scratches that cut straight through segments of his silver-scrawled tattoo.

My tongue sweeps across my lower lip as I slide forward one staggered step—

"*No,*" he barks, and my gaze snaps up.

He's still, pointing at me, the muscles along his jaw popped and prominent.

My head kicks back. "Stop talking to me like I'm some disobedient puppy!"

"If you were simply disobedient, we wouldn't be in this mess," he states, launching into another barrage of back and forth.

I sigh. "What *mess,* Rhordyn?"

"How many days did he give you?" he asks, avoiding my question altogether.

"What the hell are you talking about?"

He nails me with a glower that makes me feel naked despite the sheath of his top and the full-time mask I'm cursed to wear. "*Days*, Orlaith. How many?"

Ah, right.

I should have figured he'd be talking about Cainon. The only splashes of color in this entire room are the shreds of material lumped at my feet and the dark blue cupla shackling my wrist.

That, and the blood we *both* wear.

"He didn't give me a time frame, you incredulous bastard."

He stalks toward me, chewing up the space between us in four powerful strides. "*Two* things," he growls, ticking off his fingers. "Baze isn't deaf, and unless you can learn to do it convincingly, stop fucking lying to me."

A test ...

I should have known.

I don't waste time pretending to be remorseful. "Well, stop asking questions you already know the answer to!" I yell, cold, pissed, barely holding myself together, and so very ready to be done with this conversation. "And Cainon was just being dramatic, so let's not jump to conclusions."

His eyes widen, that violent aura sizzles with an entirely new level of chill, and I find myself glancing around his den for anything I can use as a weapon—something to prod him with to let him know I'm not here to be pushed around.

"No, he was being *diplomatic*. He's had his eyes on Ocruth for years, and evidence suggests he's simply been waiting for the perfect opportunity to strike."

The statement has me tripping internally. Outwardly, I try to show nothing but stark confidence.

"You're wrong." I shake my head. "That's not what this is

about. He made a deal with you: use of his ships in exchange for *me*. He won't back out of the trade and risk the cost of war with his two neighboring territories all for a couple days without his promised."

Rhordyn's eyes seem to solidify, and I swear the temperature drops. "First rule of politics, Milaje. Never show your hand unless you know *exactly* what you're up against."

I open my mouth to reply, realizing my mistake, but he's already charging toward the far wall where a window resides. The glass is swung open, and he leans out, peering left and right ...

My brow pinches. "What are you looking for?"

He pulls back in, the dense coils of his hair now dripping fresh rivulets of water down his bare back, chest, and shoulders. "Support beams," he mutters, storming down the line of the wall.

My frown deepens. "You said that in a *very* accusatory tone ..."

"Did I?"

He opens another window and shoves his head outside, pulling back in a second later and lumbering toward the door wearing an expression hard as slate.

"Woah, woah, woah ... where are you going?"

"To slay a Vruk."

My stomach drops.

"And ... and what about *me?*"

He stops and gestures around the room with a sweep of his hand. "Make yourself at home. I'm going to suggest a nap. I could be awhile."

He continues toward the door, and I don't think.

I just act.

I launch after him, grabbing his arm in a feeble attempt

to keep him here. But he whirls in a riot of muscle and might, snatching my wrists and pinning them behind me before he slams me against the door like I'm just as sturdy as he is.

All the breath pushes out of my lungs as his other hand wraps around my throat, tipping my head until I'm staring into wielded eyes that hold no mercy.

One squeeze could end me. I can feel it in the strong muscles shielding my front—in his aura and his confidence and the breath so brazenly assaulting me.

He tugs at my wrists, shoving my breasts forward, arching me against his form. My body responds to his nearness like I'm a shadow hinging off his motion. The puppet on a string he accused me of being.

I hiss in his face, trying to jerk free. But he pushes closer, harder; making my heat rage and throb as if to battle his frosty strike.

He clicks his tongue. "Don't come at me with that fire, Milaje. Not unless you're ready to be torn to shreds. And I don't mean your body—I mean your fucking *soul*," he says through clenched teeth, squeezing just enough that I feel his fatal strength wrapped around my throat. He nuzzles his nose into the side of my neck and whispers, "I mean that pretty heart you think is so bruised."

"You know *nothing*."

"No ..." the word batters my ear, his hand slipping from my neck and trailing around my back, where it settles atop the ladder of bones curled around my lung and heart. "I know *too much*."

I freeze, all my fight dissipating as if one tiny movement could impale me with a deadly strike.

"These right here?" he rumbles, tapping my ribs with the

tips of his fingers. "We're *both* tucked beneath them. Stuck in this fragile cage together."

"Then break out," I plead. "Set me *free*, Rhordyn!"

His body seems to calcify around me, and for a moment I think the man might have finally turned to granite. Until his grip on my wrists becomes bone-bruising, his other hand spearing up to coil my hair around his arm and pull.

He tugs me taut like a loaded bow.

My mouth pops open, chin tipping to the ceiling, and Rhordyn's forehead connects with mine.

The world around us stills, paling in significance to the mountain of man poured over me.

We're nose to nose. Eye to eye. Lips so close, his chilled breath is spilling into me. "I'll give you anything, Orlaith. Anything but that. Don't ask again."

The words are spoken hauntingly calm, as if his heart stopped beating a very long time ago.

Another stunted response.

Another dead end.

The back of my eyes sting, a lump swells in my throat, and all I want to do is cry. But I can't afford to spend more tears on him.

Not now.

Not *ever* again.

"Why not?" I'm proud of myself when I manage to keep my voice steady. "Just answer me this one question, and don't you dare answer with a grunt. After everything, I deserve a truth and you damn well *fucking* know it."

Nothing. He says nothing. Just murders me with his silence again.

Which tells me *everything*—bleeding me in an entirely different way than the drops of blood I gift him nightly.

I close my eyes, severing myself in a way I can't physically achieve. But then his grip slips from my hair, driving up to support the back of my head. His fingers spread, lacing through my thick locks and making me gasp.

He loosens a frosty breath that steals the fire from my cheeks. "Simple, Milaje. I refuse to live in a world where you don't exist."

My eyes pop open. "Wha—"

His lips bruise mine in an assault that steals my ability to speak.

Breathe.

Exist.

He melds me to his rampant will, my fire swelling to meet his ice as I give myself to the clash of teeth and tongues and lips.

We're two oceans colliding in a battle for space. There are no winners; only chaos and desolation. Only blurred edges and the complete loss of one's self. But at this moment ... I couldn't care less.

He may be kissing me like he hates me, but I was forged by his acrimony. This is the only language I *know*.

He cleaves me apart with the spear of his tongue, spilling a heady rumble deep down into me, drugging me with his raw, hungry sounds.

I'm lost in a downward spiral of desperate, carnal need for the taste of him and the scrape of his teeth against my bottom lip, commanding me to surrender in a way that feels so basely primal.

He drops my wrists, and my fingers dive into his curls as his hands skate past the hem of my shirt, bunching it up around my hips and baring my behind.

Clawed fingers dig into the plump, prickled flesh, and he catches my bottom lip. Holds it between his teeth.

Growls.

I shiver from the base of my neck to the tips of my toes, hooked by his stare as I'm spread apart, his fingers skimming so close to that sensitive crease that's immune to his lies. That remembers only the way his fingers swirled around my entrance, teasing ... *coaxing* ...

My lids flutter closed.

He snarls and takes my weight, wrapping my legs around his hips and slamming my back against the door.

Heat spikes at the apex between my thighs. Delicious, surging heat that makes me grind and grind and—

I groan, my mind a messy, instinctual thing that's driven by one thing and one thing only ...

Him.

"You're staying right the *fuck* here, do you hear me?"

His words pour between my lips like liquid chocolate, and I gobble them down, mind focused on my bare and exposed core flooding with another wave of hot want.

I can smell it—my desire for him to sate my body and unbridled mind. To take my pain and cleave it apart with a plunge of rampant pleasure. Because this world is cold and cruel and callous, and I just want to feel good for a bit. Feel close to somebody.

Close to *him.*

He carries me to the bed, his demanding mouth eating up my hungry moans, and I'm punched into the mattress, a motion which would have felt violent if he hadn't fallen with me like a landslide.

I'm lost beneath him, entombed by his flexing might, drunk on his scent, his feel, his force ...

I jerk my hips in invitation for the steel-like bulge pressing against my inner thigh, aching for him to push at my entrance.

For him to dig into my body like he's dug into my soul.

I weave my hands between the press of our bodies ...

Desperate.

Seeking.

My fingers barely brush his laces before he nips my lip and whips off the bed.

"Be good," he states, making for the door without looking back. He's pulled it open before I've even had a chance to blink or lick at the sore on my lip, slamming it shut behind him, leaving me sprawled on his bed with my legs spread and the cloying bouquet of my arousal thick in the air.

There's the sound of a key sliding into place, and the clank that follows drops my heart into my stomach and rips me from the cloud he set me in.

No.

No, no, no ...

I scramble up, clamber toward the door on legs that barely remember how to work, then grip the handle and *twist.*

It doesn't budge.

"Rhordyn!" I slam my hand against the wood, then my foot when he doesn't answer. "*Rhordyn!* If you leave me locked in here, I'll never forgive you! *Do you hear me?*"

No answer. Just the incriminating silence of an empty hallway. I can't feel his presence near.

He's gone.

It doesn't stop me from screaming his name, over and over, until my throat is just as ruined as my pride. I punch the door until bone collides with wood and blood stains the grain.

But it's not enough.

I keep going—fingernails gouging, foot swinging, hand slapping, shoulder barging until I'm empty and spent and the sutures of my sanity split.

You're staying right the fuck here ...

Rhordyn's haunting words ring like a bell in my ears, and my knees give out, colliding with the floor in a way that would probably hurt if I could feel.

But I'm lost. Numb and broken. My entire awareness tunneled down to the failure gnawing at my insides ...

He pillaged my weakness. Offered me a drink from his well and I gulped with greedy draws until I was intoxicated and mindless. Then, he tossed me down the hole and left me there with no way out.

Now all I can do is drown.

CHAPTER 47

ORLAITH

My knees are bunched against my chest while I cradle my corrupted head ...

He locked me in his room.

I could look through all his stuff, discern my own thoughts on him from his personal space, but I won't.

I've lost the will to care.

Now that he's gone, all I can see is Mishka's flat, unseeing stare. All I can hear is that gasp of surprise as Rhordyn put a blade through her heart.

The Vruk may have gotten to her first, but *he* took her final breath, as if he wanted to bear the brunt of her death.

I wonder how much blood has wet his conscience over the years? I'll probably never know because he gives me nothing but empty riddles.

I refuse to live in a world where you don't exist ...

The skin on my neck blazes; a fiery stamp left from his firm grip that seemed to threaten me.

In that moment, my life was in his hand—one capable of crushing me with a single squeeze. It both thrilled and shocked me, because part of me *wanted* him to grip a little tighter and shackle me with the emotions he hides so well.

I wanted him to *snap* so I could prove just how resilient I really am. So I could prove that although I've hidden in his shadow all these years, I'm not some fragile flower who folds into herself after receiving a few bruised petals.

Perhaps that's what he was waiting for when he pulled that sword from Mishka's heart. For the pain to make me wither. But death plants a seed in you, and my insides are already *littered* with shoots I can't seem to hide from.

I lift my head, fingers sliding through my hair and gripping hard, staring at the opposite wall blank of anything other than a few tall windows reaching for the high roof and looking out across Vateshram Forest.

There's nothing decorating Rhordyn's room; the only softness being his lush four-poster bed and a black comforter that now reeks of the cloying scent of my arousal.

My gaze lands on the easel, on the delicate sketch no more finished than it was when I was here last.

I sigh, tipping my head against the door ... studying.

Wondering where he learned to draw like that, trying to picture him doing it. Jealous of that stretched piece of cloth for the careful attention it's received ... for the way he's left his mark upon its surface.

If he were drawing me, I would imagine him digging the coal into canvas—gouging through it in places—ripping cloth from the wooden frame, screwing the picture up, flattening it out again, forcing it to yield to his will.

It's tempting to stalk over there and destroy the art out of spite. But then I realize that it, too, is locked in this room. Stashed away like some cloistered treasure.

I look to the door that leads to his personal bathing chamber, and my heart skips a beat, eyes widening ...

Breath *catching*.

A soft laugh bubbles in the back of my throat, growing

into something manic and twisted. The seed of realization blooms into a surging wave that promises to blow apart Rhordyn's firm-handed control.

Leaping up, I jog to the door, but seize the doorframe as I pass, slamming to a halt ...

I groan and jerk back into the room, dashing to the small table parked beside the easel. A bowl is tipped, the bits of coal scattered, and I use the hem of Rhordyn's shirt to wipe the inside clean.

My gaze flicks to my wrist—to the blue lines webbed beneath the delicate, translucent skin.

I take a moment to consider the possibility that I've gone terribly mad before I snarl, picturing my arm as his own damn neck and sinking my teeth in.

Deep.

The agony is instant, but I just dig further, imagining him trying to shake out of my hold. Or perhaps yielding to *me* for a change.

Warm liquid swells against my lips, and I release my wrist with a gasp, suspending it above the bowl and watching blood fill it in dribbling increments.

Hating it. Loving it just as much.

This sadistic parting gift is as much for me as it is for him.

After a while, the flow of blood slows, but there's enough collected for him to do whatever the hell he does with it. Hopefully he knows how to ration himself to make this last for the rest of his life, because this toxic *thing* between us is over.

If he wants more, he'll have to bleed it from my slit throat.

I bind the wound with a strip of blue material, tightening the knot with my teeth.

Leaving the bowl on Rhordyn's bed where he won't miss the damn thing, I turn my attention to his dresser ...

If I can find his caspun stash, my life over the next month will be significantly less complicated.

I yank the drawers out and scatter their contents, rifling through his clothes.

"Come on ..."

I'm starting on his bedside table, tossing his personal items in the same disrespectful manner as he tossed mine, when a thought has me flattening to the ground, searching for a loose stone beneath his bed.

It doesn't take me long to find. It's in the exact same place as the one in my tower; five stones back from the wall.

"How original of you," I mutter, lifting it to reveal a cavity beneath the floor. Reaching in, I pull out a fist-sized package wrapped in calico and secured with a long piece of string. One sniff tells me I've found what I need, and I don't bother moving the stone back into place or cleaning up my mess before starting down the stairs, heading to Rhordyn's personal thermal spring.

He left my room in shambles, it's only fair I repay the favor.

The air becomes thick and warm as the tunnel opens into a domed cavern, stairs descending beneath the surface of water that's reminiscent of swirling, liquid gold in this low light.

The stalactites clinging to the roof look like the fangs of a hungry beast ready to chomp down, and the stark silence reminds me just how secluded this place is. I try not to let that thought sink too deep as I consider what it is I'm about to do.

I stop on the threshold and secure the bundle of caspun around my ankle, then step down into the spring.

Unlike *my* pool, this one allows me to keep my feet on the ground for longer. Water laps at my breasts while I walk toward the wall that separates this place from Puddles, Rhordyn's shirt swaying around me with the stirring water.

Once I'm near, my gaze plunges into the deep where that hole is punched through the rock, allowing water to flow back and forth between this thermal spring and my own.

I'm not sure I'll fit through, but it's my only option. If I wait for Rhordyn to return from his hunt, I have no doubt that boat will be forced to leave for the South without me.

Cainon would be well within his rights to assume I've been held against my will.

War would spark. A war that's better spent on the *real* enemy—not some possessive bickering between two neighboring High Masters who seem determined to engage in a pissing contest.

I draw a few big breaths, filling my lungs, fueling my blood and brain and austere resolve.

One final, shuddering breath and I dive below the surface, propelling myself into the deep where it's warm and dense, the light filtered and dim. My vision is hazy, and I feel around until I find the breach in the wall.

Puddles is *right there,* on the other side.

Weaving a hand through to test the size—the irregular shape—I realize how tight it's going to be ...

The thought is dismissed in the very next second.

There's no room for uncertainty.

I thread one arm through at a time and flatten my hands against the wall. Bulbs of anticipation burst in my belly as I *shove*—only to ricochet backward from the snag of my hips.

They're too wide.

The haunting knowledge lands a blow to my chest, knocking a bout of air from my lungs. Mind scrambling, white-hot panic boils my blood, and my movements become frantic.

I push, and push, *and push,* shoving hard, legs churning, finally letting out a squeal that's distorted by water that feels too thick.

Too hot.

My limbs grow numb and heavy, and my chest starts to jerk, running out of breath.

I need to get out.

I bend at the hips, using my knees to propel myself in the direction I came in ... but my shoulders snag, the momentum slamming the back of my head against stone, pushing another burst of bubbles up my throat.

Emptying me.

Mind spinning, I lose track of which way is up.

Which way is down.

I lose control of my limbs and lungs, trapped on the threshold between two very different forms of captivity.

The realization comes, sudden and violent, that I'm going to die. That my lungs won't pull another breath, and I'll be found here, wedged in a hole because I fought to escape a man who's put a roof over my head since I was too small and young to fend for myself.

A man who saved me from the grisly wrath of three Vruks that should have torn me to shreds.

My subconscious roars to life in those final, frantic moments when my heart slows and my body begins to spasm. In its wakefulness, it tosses little slices of memory at me in a random, disjointed manner.

There's grass beneath my feet, sun on my face, a house in the distance blowing smoke from its chimney.

I like that house. I like the vines stuck to its walls and the way the sun touches it.

Home.

I see that little boy again, except he's not so little compared to me. He's sitting on the lawn amongst a patch of pretty flowers—legs crossed, hands stretched in my direction.

Reaching.

"You can do it! Just push your arms out like you're flying and slide your foot forward ..."

I peep down at my feet, up again.

He nods. "You've got this, little one."

He's smiling at me, and I want to go to him.

I shuffle, lift a foot, step over a yellow flower ... look up again.

That smile is so much bigger now. "You're doing it, Ser! Momma's gonna be so proud of you!"

My knees wobble, and I fall, but he catches me—*always catches me.*

His laughter spills over my face as I'm tickled into a ball, and I feel true happiness burst inside my belly.

Why did I bury this memory so deep? I want to live in it forever ...

Our laughter echoes until it sputters out, and I'm no longer in the field with cheeks sore from giggling. I'm in a cozy room I recognize. One that smells like yummy things and makes me feel safe, but it looks strange from down here, where I'm huddled in the corner under the eating table.

I make a sound, feel something wet slide down my cheek,

but the little boy puts his hand over my mouth and holds me tighter.

"Shh. It's okay," he whispers in my ear. "I'll look after you. Always."

But I don't think it's okay.

There are lots of strange people in the room. I can see their dirty boots from under the tablecloth—can hear their mean voices.

They're making my heart scared.

"I don't know what you're talking about. Now please, get out of my home and leave me to finish my meal in peace!"

Mommy.

Why is her voice mad?

"There are three meals on the dining table ... *Search the room!*"

Feet move, heavy things go sliding across the floor, bits of paper land everywhere, and someone steps on the picture I was painting for the boy holding me tight.

A hand drops down and picks it up.

Paper rips, and I feel the sound somewhere in my chest.

The boy slides me against the wall, then puts a finger to his lips for me to be quiet. He's holding something sharp, and I think he might be scared like me because his hand is shaking.

I reach for him.

He turns away at the same time the table flips, making me cry out.

There are people everywhere, but the ones I know are in the corner crying.

I've only ever seen them happy.

Other people are dressed in gray, and they have strange marks on their foreheads. They're looking at me with angry eyes that make me want to hide again, but there's nowhere else to go.

No.

No more.

I've seen these people on my wall ... In pieces in my nightmares. I know what's coming, and I don't want to watch them get feasted on.

But my subconscious is strong, and I'm weak ... dying.

It holds my eyes open and forces me to look.

The scary, angry people step closer, yelling things I don't understand, pointing fingers.

One of them has my mommy. Sparkly tears are dripping down her cheeks. Maybe she needs a cuddle?

"Mommy ..."

Her face crumbles.

A big man walks toward me and the boy. His head is shiny, and there's one of those wood-cutting things hanging from his hand. I think it's called an axe.

Why is there red stuff dripping from it?

"No! Please! I beg you, they're only kids!"

I don't like the way Mommy's voice sounds. It makes my eyes sting.

The man looks at the boy. "Get out of the way, kid. Mercy is not preserved for those who stand against the stones."

The boy runs forward with the sharp thing held above his head. His scream stands out the most ... until Mommy makes a louder sound at the same time the axe is swung.

He stops.

I push to my feet, try to follow ...

Watch him fall.

Watch the light leave his eyes.

I take one, two, three whole steps, then slip on the sparkly stuff spilling from the hurt in his chest. But he doesn't catch me. The tickles never come.

Mommy keeps screaming, louder and louder.

I crawl through the wet, curl up beside him, and wait for him to blink ...

Smile ...

Laugh ...

For him to stop looking at the wall and tell me everything's going to be okay.

Big, strange hands pull me away from his warmth, and my nightgown is ripped, the top of my arm poked over and over.

I kick, wriggle, *scream*—louder than Mommy and the squealing sounds in my ears.

Put me down ...

Put me down!

But the words don't sound the same as they do in my head because I never needed to speak. *He* did it for me; somehow knew what I wanted to say.

And now he's broken on the floor in a puddle of wet.

I feel something inside me growing from the place where my heart is, and it *hurts* ...

It hurts so much I think I'm going to crack open and everyone will see my insides.

I think I'm broken, too.

The memory shifts—an ocean pulling back into itself before another wave strikes.

The roof caves, someone screams, and all I can smell is pain; *burnt* pain that makes me want to spew.

I'm watching from the outside, no longer in my child-body.

Nothing is.

It's all escaping through the splits in my skin and my eyes and my ears and my wide-open mouth—an oily blackness spilling out in vicious, torrential spears.

Burning.

Silencing.

Seeping through the ground and melding with the dirt.

The floor is gone, so are the walls. The roof is in smoldering piles, making the night glow red.

I'm in the center of it all, as if the world is rushing *away* from my body contorted in the dirt.

My clothes are burnt.

I can't see my mommy anymore.

All I can see are bits of bodies everywhere, big and small, scattered all over the ground as if they were flung like rag dolls that fell apart mid-flight. Some have upside down v's carved into their foreheads, others are the people who changed my bed sheets and cooked me yummy food.

The power did not pick and choose. It just ... *did.*

It killed.

The thought jerks me into consciousness.

I kick forward, my body now at a slight angle that allows me to slide further through the hole. A jagged piece of rock drags a line of fire from my hip to my knee as I wiggle out, freeing myself from the chewing jaws of stone.

Bubbles pour from my mouth, racing me to freedom.

I explode through the surface—choking, spluttering, heaving breath into my starved lungs. Breath that tries, and fails to temper the storm lashing my conscience.

Wading to the edge, I crawl out on hands and knees, drawing life into myself while grating layers of skin from my shins.

I barely feel the sting.

Barely notice the squealing bathers dashing from the pools, snatching their clothes, and running up the stairs as if they see the truth in my eyes.

See me for what I really am.

I make it almost to the wall before I vomit, the spill of water and bile having nothing to do with my almost drowning and *everything* to do with my sudden wave of vertigo from the fall.

Because I'm no longer standing on the edge of that chasm deep in the folds of my subconscious. I'm down in the guts of it, trying to claw my way out with desperate, bloody fingers.

Trying to escape the slew of ebony roots coiled in a sizzling slumber—the pile larger than life itself.

An oily blackness spilling out in vicious, torrential spears.

Burning.

Silencing.

I vomit again, my body repelling the septic revelation it's being forced to swallow ...

It was me.

CHAPTER 48

ORLAITH

Murder guts you, leaving nothing but an animated shell. I realize that while I sit, balled on the wet ground, rocking back and forth in a puddle of my own bile.

All these years, I've been hiding from myself. Functioning without a pulse.

The Vruks didn't slaughter everyone that day. They simply caught the scent of a sizzling meal and came running to gorge on the carnage I created.

Me. A tiny, two-year-old child.

I rock and rock and rock, ripping at my hair, clawing at my arms, my neck, my scalp ...

Me.

There is no pretty way to paint over all that ugly.

I severed my tether to humanity at the tender age of two —lost control and butchered not only the people who broke into our home and took my brother from me, but also the servants, the cooks ... my *mother.*

I murdered my mother ...

I shudder, dry heave, pray it was a swift and painless death. Pray she didn't suffer.

Her scream echoes through my mind; the sound she made when the axe was swung—

Of course she suffered. She watched her son bleed out, then saw her daughter turn into a monster.

Watched me die in a different way.

Rhordyn took me in and dressed me as a lamb, not realizing I'm actually the wolf. Except my weapons aren't fangs and claws, but an inky fire so noxious it *severs*—leaving fleshy, bubbled bits that weep their life.

My rocking becomes so violent my bare skin grates across the stone.

No wonder the people in Whispers haunt me. That their perusals *burn.* No wonder part of me tried so hard to put them back together.

I thought the unintentional paintings were my gift for the ones who lost themselves that day, but it was an overflowing well of guilt worming its way out of me in any way it could. Forcing me to *look.*

So many faces.

So many wide-eyed, condemning stares.

Murderer ...

A strangled sound claws out of me, raw and roughly hewn.

Did my subconscious create my Safety Line as a way to cage me *in?* Perhaps it considered me best kept isolated should I lose control again?

And what if that *does* happen? Do all the people who run the estate end up being torn to bits—their scorched remains scattered throughout the castle halls? Does *Baze?*

Rhordyn?

I release a low, throaty whimper.

They call me a child-survivor, when I'm actually their unbridled demise just waiting to unleash.

I need to atone for everything I've done, and I can't do that if I'm tucked high in the clouds.

No.

All I'm achieving here is to waste my life, living in a protective bubble I don't deserve—one that could burst at any moment, be it from the inside or the out.

Cainon's proposal was much more of a gift than I realized. Fate is giving me a chance to *save* lives, and I refuse to look at it any other way. It's too late to go back and change things, so I'll have to do what I can with what little I've got ...

A blue and gold cupla.

I claw up the edge of that mind-chasm, heaving and bruised, broken and bloody. There's not a single part of my insides that isn't ugly, so unlike the real me hiding beneath this skin I wear.

The irony isn't lost on me.

Landing on the ledge, I tamp that gulf full of enough shadow to smother the pile of slumbering death and spin, shutting off my mind's eye.

Refusing to look at the past again.

I lift my head, teeth chattering, body trembling.

I have to go.

Rolling forward onto skinned knees, I scoop water from the edge of the spring, using it to wash my face and legs and the bile from the ends of my hair. I remove the calico package from around my ankle and stand, wavering on unsteady feet.

My vision splits, collides. Splits, collides ...

I draw a deep breath and take one step toward the stairs, then another, until I reach the wall and can use it as a crutch.

Tentatively, I begin the climb, legs shaking beneath my weight. But I push myself, feeling my body grow a little stronger with every inhale.

It's not until I'm halfway up the chute that I realize Rhordyn's shirt is ripped, exposing my right thigh and a long, fleshy wound that's dribbling blood.

"Shit," I mutter, glancing down the stairs, seeing a peppered trail of red everywhere my foot has been.

I'll have to bind that before I can go anywhere.

I exit the stairwell and hobble down the hallway, every unsteady step bringing me closer to Rhordyn's inevitable return.

If he finds me like this, I'm screwed. He'll probably chain me to a wall somewhere and bark at me until I scream my truth.

My heart skips a beat, and I double my speed, shoving myself into a jog—teeth gritted, fists bunched.

Pushing past the zap of pain that lances up my leg every time it drives forward, I practically fly up Stony Stem, rounding on the echoes of an argument. Vanth and Kavan are at my closed door, doused in blood and rain, throwing profanities back and forth. Their disagreement comes to a silent crescendo the moment they notice me standing four steps below, and they almost leap out of their boots.

Seriously, worst guards ever.

Kavan looks me up and down, wide eyes settling on my bloody thigh. "What the hell happened to you?"

"You're bleeding," Vanth proclaims, as if it isn't obvious. "And dressed in a man's shirt."

I ignore his righteous tone and shove past. "We're leaving," I rasp, pushing the door open, tossing the month supply of caspun on my bed.

"What?" they bellow as a clap of thunder shakes the tower, followed by a flash of light that etches everything in an eerie brilliance.

Ignoring the calamity the sky is unleashing, I wrap my hair in a knot on my head, using a large pin to prod it in place before rifling through my drawers for something to bandage my bloody thigh.

"Mistress!"

Kavan's use of the title makes me bristle. In truth, I'd forgotten they were there.

"The boat," I snip, tearing a strip free of a tattered shirt. "We're sailing for the South. Now."

Vanth snort-laughs, though the sound is barren of humor.

I spin. "Something funny?"

"Yes, actually. You've been stalling for the past few days, and you choose *now* to leave? Have you even looked outside?" He points out the western window. "Only someone with a death wish would sail in that weather." His eyes narrow. "Unless you *want* our ship to sink ..."

"Why would I wan—" I shake my head, dismissing his condemning tone. "Look. We either sail now or you can return to the Bahari capital with nothing but *this,*" I say, shoving my shackled wrist in his direction. "Because once Rhordyn gets back from his hunt, I'm stuck here. For good."

My attention darts between the two, and I wait.

To be fair, these guys haven't exactly been pushing to get me on that boat. If they take the cupla and go, Rhordyn's theory will be proven correct—that Cainon was only in this to stir the political pot.

I'll never live it down, but sailing off into an encroaching storm with a boat full of people I don't know or trust would be the height of stupidity if I haven't at least tested Rhordyn's theory.

The two share a look, neither of them taking a single step inside my quarters.

"Fine," Vanth grumbles, pointing at a basket in the corner of the room. "You have five minutes to fill that with stuff, wrap that wound, and change into more ... *appropriate* attire. If we're doing this, we have to be out of that bay before we lose the remaining light and your *naïvete* damns us all to a watery grave."

He pulls the door closed before I can say another word.

My button-down is rolled to my elbows, my tight, waist-high pants offering an extra layer of pressure for my bandaged thigh. Sporadic gusts of icy wind whistle down the callous steps behind me, assaulting my ears, threatening to toss me down the cliff and no doubt take out my spear-wielding guards on the way.

Every few steps, I steal a peek over my shoulder, half expecting to see Rhordyn charging after me.

"Can you guys move any faster?"

Vanth grumbles something and they both quicken their pace. Hard to be sure, but I think they might be getting sick of me.

The basket I'm carrying is light, only full of essentials. The fact that it's all jammed inside a pillow slip that smells of Rhordyn should be entirely discounted.

I know I was supposed to burn the thing, but I kept thinking of reasons not to.

I'm not okay.

These wet, slippery stairs feel like increments toward the gallows. Like I'm being led to an execution block and not a boat destined for a foreign territory where I'll be sworn in as a High Mistress, surrounded by people who aren't *my* people.

Tanith, Cook, Shay, *Kai* ... I'll even miss the grumbling gardeners. I'll miss the trees and the flowers and the bushes I've grown from seeds. I'll miss the view from my spot where I've always felt safe despite my haunting past ...

My stomach churns.

The rain has abated. If I were the sign-seeking type, I'd believe this is right, even though my heart is screaming for me to turn back and *run.* For me to hide in my tower, lock the door, and never come out.

My boots finally hit the sand—boots I wore to prevent from sinking my toes deep and grounding myself. I can't afford to dig new roots when I'm nursing the nubs from the ones I've recently severed.

Our hurried footsteps dent the sand as we sweep around the bay. We're almost at the jetty when Baze steps out from behind a jagged line of rocks that have always reminded me of shark teeth.

My heart slams to a halt. My feet do the same.

He's dressed in black leather pants and a loose cotton shirt only half tucked in. Three buttons hang open at the neck, as if he got dressed so fast he had no time to put everything in place.

He pushes back the disheveled flop of his hair with a dash of his hand, revealing eyes that appear almost black, reflecting the dark smudges stamped beneath them.

My brow pleats, gaze falling to the wooden sword hanging from his fist ...

I mutter a curse.

"Take this to the boat." I shove my basket toward my closest escort while holding Baze's stare. "I'll be right there."

"He's *armed,*" Vanth hisses, refusing to accept my belongings.

I glance sideways to see him white-knuckling his wooden spear, blue eyes narrowed on Baze.

"You'll be fine." I push my basket at his chest again. "Just take this."

He snatches my things and thrusts them at Kavan. "No, I'm worried about *you.*"

Oh.

"Well ... that's sweet." I sweep my hand around and weave it under my shirt, retrieving the Ebonwood sword I'd stashed there.

Baze's eyes narrow, and he begins to stalk forward.

My grip tightens.

"But with all due respect," I say, low and steady, "you'll both just get in the wa—"

Vanth charges, spear at the ready, kicking up sand with his booted feet. I snarl and dart forward, dropping low and sweeping my leg out, knocking Vanth's feet out from under him.

He drops like a boulder, flat on his back, mouth working like a fish out of water. His wide eyes draw wounded gulps of me looming over him, as though he can't quite work out how he ended up down there, in the sand, with my sword kissing his carotid.

"What the fu—"

"You don't touch him," I hiss through clenched teeth, digging the sword a little deeper. "And if you insist on getting between us, that spear has to work its way through *me* first. And then you'll have to explain to your High

Master why you impaled his promised. Do I make myself clear?"

He squirms a little. "Crystal."

The word itches so much my upper lip peels back.

I release him from the nip of my blade, leaving a bead of blood dribbling down his neck. He leaps to his feet, wipes at the wound, and studies the red smear on his palm with an insulting amount of shock in his eyes.

"Go," I tell a round-eyed Kavan who's regarding me as if this is the first time he's laid eyes on me. "Prompt the captain to prepare the ship. I won't be long."

He looks me up and down. "Cainon's getting much more than he bargained for."

It's far from a compliment.

He stalks off toward the jetty with a narrow-eyed Vanth in tow, tossing cursory looks over his shoulder every few steps.

"I hope you're ready to watch that ship sail away without you," Baze volleys, snagging my full attention.

So this is how it's going to go, then.

"I'm leaving of my own free will," I counter, moving the majority of weight onto my strong leg and widening my stance, sharpening my focus. Assessing his every breath, every blink for signs of what to expect next.

If Baze is going to try and stop me from leaving this stretch of sand, I'll have no choice but to fight.

"Only because you haven't been fully informed," he snaps back, mimicking my motions, readying himself for a battle I doubt either of us wants. His shoulders flex as he passes his sword from one hand to the other, the gems on his ring glinting in the low light, catching my gaze.

Catching my interest ...

I slide my foot back half an inch, anchoring to the sand. "I'm afraid it's *you* who is uninformed, Baze."

His lips curl up in a half sneer. "I doubt that."

We leap forward at the same time, black swords crossing with a sharp, wooden clang that seems to echo down the beach and almost makes me gag.

Fucking Ebonwood.

We hold—stares as locked as our swords. Our muscles. Our warring resolve. Though where I'm sure and steady, I swear his hold is a little less stable than it usually is.

Than it *always* is.

"Don't do this," he grates out, his hot breath fogging the air.

I can see the torment in the depths of his eyes. Can see that he hates this just as much as I do—what this turn of events has done to everything we've built.

"It's already *done,*" I snip, referring to the cupla cinched around my wrist.

My life began to unravel the moment I accepted it, but I can't bring myself to regret it. Not when so much is hinging on this union.

There's suddenly a well of sentiment in his stare. "You don't know what it's like out there, Orlaith. You have *no* idea what you're up against."

"And whose fault is that? Who kept me in the dark for nineteen fucking *years?*"

I shove away, then stab forward.

His blade sweeps in and knocks my strike to the side with another jarring clang, taking a large bite from my composure. I snarl, letting that discomforting sound fuel me as I whirl, coming down at him from another angle.

He dodges.

This may be a wooden sword but when it whips through the flutter of his shirt, it's just as merciless as steel—leaving a gaping hole that exposes smooth slabs of muscle contained in a flawless wrap of porcelain skin.

For a moment, I think he let me get so close to gutting him. But when my gaze flicks to his face, I see twin seeds of shock in his tawny eyes ...

Seems this new sword isn't so bad after all.

Tossing it from one hand to the other, I root my feet in the sand, keeping as much weight off my right foot as possible.

His attention darts to my wrist, and a darkness falls over his face. "Did they hurt you?"

I roll my eyes. "You mustn't have very much confidence in your training abiliti—"

His sword whips out, the flat side landing a blow to my right thigh, sending a lick of pain shooting down my injured leg.

I yowl as it buckles beneath my weight, and he whirls around, taking my armed hand with him, pinning it behind my back between the press of our bodies.

"I thought I taught you to always shield your weakness," he seethes, immobilizing my other arm and shredding the bandage with a smooth flick of his blade.

The dark blue tourniquet flutters to the sand.

A laugh bubbles out as he studies the deep, crescent wound punched through my wrist. "What did you do, leave him a doggy dish full of blood?"

The fact that he worked that out so fast is a little concerning.

"Yes ... actually, I did." I stomp his bare foot with my solid boot—something he's not used to me wearing.

He howls, pulling away just enough for me to slip my arm free. I twist out of his hold and dip low, the hilt of my sword clouting the back of his knees.

He drops like a rock, a dense *oomph* pushing from parted lips as my knee collides with his chest. All my weight is pressed into the one point of contact, the sharp tip of my sword poised atop his heart.

There's a war in my chest, and I take a moment to check our surroundings—to ensure we're hidden behind the shark-teeth stones and that my two guards are well and truly out of sight.

It's just us on the beach; nobody bearing witness to my victory aside from Baze's wounded pride.

I zero in on his hand that's holding my knee, as if he's considering an attempt to shove me off. Gripping his ring, I watch his eyes widen while all the blood drains from his cheeks. "Always shield your weakness, huh?"

"*Orlai—*"

I pull.

The shift is instantaneous, the utter vision of him so shocking I whip away from the safety of the rocks, leaving him in the maw of their protection while I marinate in the open air.

I can barely bring myself to draw breath, because I don't recognize that man.

Not one bit.

His hair is so white it appears to harbor its own light source, his ears pointed at the tips, the outer shell lined with the same crystalline thorns that decorate my own. And his *eyes* ... they're big and round.

They remind me of *his.*

But it's like they've been dipped in dirty water, dulling

their shine. And those black smudges beneath his eyes are now darkened dents in his face.

My gaze roves down, breath catching.

Heart stilling.

Every visible inch of Baze's pearly skin—aside from his unfamiliar, statuesque face—is *scarred.* Riddled with bite marks big and small. Some are perfectly mirrored crescents, as though teeth were simply stamped upon his flesh. The rest are so messy, I can't imagine how long they would've taken to heal.

But his *neck* ...

The skin there is puckered and bunched in places, gouged in others, as though it was wrapped in a barbed wire collar years ago. Like he fought against it, shredding himself beyond repair.

My insides gutter, stare shifting from the man I thought I knew to the castle casting us in its big, boastful shadow.

Did Rhordyn have anything to do with this ... this *torture* Baze has sustained over the years?

I blink, feeling a warm wetness dart down my cheeks. "And you had the nerve to call *me* a liar," I rasp, and the voice is not my own.

It's fragile.

It's the voice of a girl who just realized how lonely she's been for the past nineteen years.

I regard the dazzling pits of his eyes. "How very hypocritical, when you know *exactly* how it feels to be living in a skin that doesn't belong to you."

He's crestfallen, trying to cover his torso with the scraps of his shirt.

Part of me feels guilty for stripping his mask without his

consent, but the feeling swiftly disintegrates the moment he opens his mouth.

"He won't let you go, Orlaith."

I retreat another step, eyes hardening. Trying, and failing, to picture this beautiful, broken man as the Baze I've come to know and love.

The Baze I thought was *unbreakable.*

"He's already lost me," I respond in a voice too soft and vulnerable. I lift my chin to counter the weakness. "At least this way I'm securing those ships for the people who really matter."

"So *naïve,"* he spits, shaking his head, top lip peeling back —blue from the cold. "You get on that ship, and he will hunt you. You have *no* idea what he's capable of."

An oily blackness spilling out in vicious, torrential spears.

Burning.

Silencing.

"Yeah, well, I think that sentiment works both ways," I rasp past a smear of bile, pushing the probing image deep into that chasm of death and destruction and heart-impaling regret.

I look at the ring sitting in my palm; the perfect mask to hide his pain. Just like my necklace, it feels too light to be heavy with so many secrets.

Right now, it's my only guarantee he won't chase me to the boat.

I swallow, waving the piece of jewelry at him. "I'll leave this on the jetty, and if you want to keep your ... your *secret,"* I push out past the lump in my throat, "I suggest waiting until we're gone to collect it."

His lip twitches, and he stabs his gaze at the sand beside him, as if he can't bear to look at me.

Taking that as my cue, I spin, stalking toward the quay. "And someone needs to water my plants," I throw over my shoulder, rolling my sleeve and concealing my torn-up wrist.

Feeling like a boulder has landed atop my chest, I climb the stone stairs that rise from the sand and merge with the elevated wharf, keeping my shoulders back, walking with the ruse of a certainty I don't possess.

I scale aged, weather-beaten planks slippery from the rain, chin notched high, ignoring the odd flick of silver frills through the waves to my side.

I hope Kai doesn't try to accost me ... If he does, I'll fall apart. Scatter on this dock and refuse to pull myself together again.

He'd probably still wrap me in his ocean arms and tell me everything's going to be okay. But it's not. And it shouldn't be.

Not for me.

I count each of the five hundred and twenty-two steps it takes to reach the boat with the big blue sail, its deck busy with the bustling energies of numerous seafaring men.

Baze's ring scalds my palm, and I dare a peek back down the jetty that's hazy from a spray of sea mist.

He's nowhere to be seen, and I wonder which he's more ashamed of: his scars or his heritage.

Me? I'm not hiding from anyone but myself. My fake shell might be tight and uncomfortable, but what's below the surface is much worse ...

A beautiful, malignant disaster.

Kneeling, gaze still pinned to the dim scoop of the bay and those shark-tooth stones that decorate its gloomy smile, I set the ring down. When I rise, I somehow feel heavier.

My attention swings to the long, sleek boat that's built specifically for cutting through the harsh terrain of an unforgiving ocean ... not that it alleviates my chest-cinching anxiety.

Toes barely kissing the ramp, my feet anchor to the pier. The strong, sturdy, familiar pier I've looked down on every day for the past nineteen years, never imagining I'd be in this position.

It feels more like a plank because once I step onto that vessel, that's it. I'm across my Safety Line.

Those final steps seem insurmountable.

My pulse *whooshes* in my ears, louder than the crashing waves.

Strong, resilient, composed ...

I glance up into a mix of unfamiliar faces. The captain is staring down his nose at me from the deck—gray hair tied back, blue blazer pinched with golden buttons that hug a strong physique.

He scans my face as if he's seeing all the cracks there. "The tide's dropping. If we don't leave now, we'll smash our keel on our way out the bay."

"Shit," I mutter without moving my lips.

Always shield your weakness.

I draw on the sea air, then step onto the ramp—every muscle in my body braced to pounce. The sword hanging from my hand becomes the victim of my crushing fist, each footfall taking me deeper into unsafe territory.

But that drop to the deck comes too swiftly, and I swallow again, trying to force my sledging heart down my throat as I look at my feet ...

I feel like I'm standing on the edge of that chasm in my mind, peering into the gloom, afraid of what might be down there. Knowing it's likely something hideous that will rock me to the core.

But I can't afford to hide anymore.

You can do it! Just push your arms out like you're flying and slide your foot forward ...

His voice sings to my tortured soul, shooting steel into my spine. I nod to myself—to *him*—stare stabbing out across the bay.

I picture his hands outstretched and waiting. Picture his big, half-moon smile. Pretend I'm moving toward that bolt of happiness that struck me as I fell into his arms and was tickled into a ball.

Breath held captive, I step onto the sturdy, hard-wood deck ...

I expect to feel some immediate shift in the air. Expect my entire body to fold over in unimaginable pain, or for a Vruk to spring forth and slash at me with talons that squeal with every swipe. I expect many things, and though none of them happen, I feel no relief.

I just took the most important step of my life, and those tickles never came.

My fault.

All my fault.

I release a fractured breath, trying not to blink—worried that if I do, my emotions will spill down my cheeks and everyone will bear witness to my fragile state.

My *weakness.*

Captain studies me through pale eyes, many years etched in the wrinkled skin around them. He makes a gruff sound, then mutters something below his breath before relaying a bunch of orders to his crew.

Kavan shoves my basket at me and stalks toward the

stairs that disappear below deck. Vanth stays a moment longer, watching me with a guarded expression that makes me want to fidget.

"You're on a Bahari vessel now, *Mistress.*"

The last word is tossed at me like a threat.

"Thank you, Vanth. I'm well aware."

"Good."

He scores me with scrutiny for a moment longer, gaze flicking to my cupla before he follows the same path Kavan just took.

The moment he disappears from sight, I loosen a tight breath ...

Perhaps he didn't take too well to being knocked on his arse.

Everyone begins to buzz around, preparing to break away from port. Desperate to tuck into a quiet corner, I make for the bow of the boat where I can look down on the wake it will soon be carving through the merciless, gray ocean.

I remove my hairpin, letting my heavy locks fall around me like a shield, as if it could protect me from the stares drilling holes in my back.

Gripping my baby conch, I search for another sign of those silver frills stirring up the water, but Kai is nowhere to be seen.

A painful pang of regret twists my insides ...

I should have been honest with him, but Kai would want nothing more than to rescue me, and he can't save me from myself.

I close my eyes and lift the shell to my lips. *"I'm so sorry ..."*

The words are whispered, and I swear the shell speaks back to me, though when I lift it to my ear, all I get is the breathing sound of the ocean.

Glancing out across the bay, I'm unable to stop the tear that slips free, using my shoulder to wipe it away.

Strong, composed, resilient.

I shouldn't look to Castle Noir—know that if I do, it could plant yet another seed of regret.

Not that it stops me.

My eyes flick up, stare landing on the dense, black smudge protruding from the cliff like a grisly diadem. Salty air whips at my hair, seasons my lips, and chills my cheeks as I explore everything I hold so dear ...

It's hard to breathe looking up at my whole life from afar, so I dip my nose into the basket, letting *him* fill my lungs and soothe my chaotic mind.

"Outward bound!" one of the sailors shouts, and the boat peels away from the dock. The main sail is lowered and wind fills its belly, lurching us forward with such force I'm compelled to drop my basket in exchange for gripping the rail.

A deep rumble rattles the air, as though a mountain just shifted from its ancient perch. The hairs on the back of my neck lift, and my gaze lashes to the tip of Stony Stem perched high in the sky like the pinched bud of an immature bloom ...

To the robust shadow of a man standing on my balcony, watching us leave.

Rhordyn.

He looks so out of place, his severity contradicting the pretty, delicate blooms of my wisteria vine twisting around the balustrade.

An icy trail of perusal carves across my face, to my wrist, before whipping down my leg as if tasting my blood from afar.

My breath becomes prisoner to lungs that have forgotten how to function ...

He won't let you go, Orlaith. He will hunt you.

The echo of Baze's parting words rattle me to the core, though a stronger, more dominant part of me rears up, almost *welcoming* the challenge.

He can try.

I square my shoulders and pretend Rhordyn's arctic scrutiny isn't flaying me from afar as the wind pushes me toward the arms of another man.

THANK YOU

Thank you for reading To Bleed a Crystal Bloom! I hope you've enjoyed Orlaith's journey so far. This story first came to me in a dream, and it hasn't let me go since. I'd planned the entire series before I wrote a single word—it just *spoke* to me.

The characters.

The world.

The relationships.

There is so much story left to tell. In many ways, I've barely chipped the surface with the first installment, but I really wanted to give Orlaith's origin the justice it deserved.

These characters have a long way to go before we reach that final full stop, and I can't wait to take you on this journey with me.

Again, thank you for reading!

—Sarah

ACKNOWLEDGMENTS

This story took an entire year to create, and I couldn't have done it without the help of my friends and family.

My babies—thank you for being so patient while Mummy wrote her book. Thank you for the endless supply of jokes and loves and hugs.

Josh—my love. Thank you for supporting me, for loving me, and for always believing in me. Thank you for being two whole parents in the last few months leading up to my release. You're amazing, and I'm so lucky to be doing life with you.

Raven—honestly … words evade me. What would I do without you?

Thank you for being my rock, for bringing a brightness to every day, and for the endless deep belly laughs.

Thank you for talking me out of a ditch a thousand times over, for standing up for this story when I was at my weakest, and for giving me the courage to make it across that finish line. Your friendship means the absolute world to me, and I can't wait to be back in the sprint room together, quoting Pride and Prejudice, and drinking all the coffee we were meant to give up six months ago.

Mum—thank you for your unending support. For knowing when to empathise, and when to tell me to pick myself up and keep going. Thank you for all the heartbeats you poured into helping me polish this story. I love you.

The Editor & The Quill—Chinah, thank you for everything you poured into this story. Thank you for your friendship, your mastery, your attention to detail. Thank you for digging so deep and for the late nights and early mornings. You go above and beyond, and I'm so lucky to have you in my life.

Brittani—thank you for your friendship, your laughs, your listening ear, your attention to detail. Thank you for listening to hours and hours of voice messages when I first came up with the idea for this story and had to blurt it all out. You're amazing, you really are!

A.T. Cover Designs—Aubrey, thank you for the stunning cover. For pouring so much heart and soul into every single one of my graphics, and for bringing my story to life visually. You are incredibly talented, and I'm constantly blown away by everything you do!

Affinity Author Services—thank you for going out of your way to make things as easy as possible for me when I had to push my release date back! And for the words of wisdom that were priceless and so very needed.

Philippa—thank you for your eternal support, and for giving our babies a change of scenery when you knew I needed to knuckle down and reach that finish line!

Sarah. Xo

ABOUT THE AUTHOR

Born in New Zealand, Sarah now lives on the Gold Coast with her husband and three young children. When she's not reading or tapping away at her keyboard, she's spending time with her friends and family, her plants, and enjoying trips away in the snow.

Sarah has been writing since she was small, but has only recently begun sharing her stories with the world. She can be found on all the major social media platforms if you want to keep up to date with her releases.

Made in United States
Orlando, FL
31 October 2024